Praise for Brenda Nov

Trust Me "genera
—*Publis*

"A clever, impeccably plotted thriller." (Top Pick)
—*Romantic Times BOOKreviews* on *Trust Me*

"In *Trust Me*...Brenda Novak expertly blends realistically gritty danger, excellent characterization and a generous dash of romance into a chilling, thrilling novel."
—*Chicago Tribune*

"Novak has outdone herself with this series. She is a great storyteller."
—*Once Upon a Romance*

"*Trust Me* is a page-turner.... Sure to become a much-loved keeper-shelf read.... I highly recommend *Trust Me* and suggest Brenda Novak be added to your 'to buy' list today. You won't be disappointed, trust me."
—*Romance Reader's Connection*

"No one can send chills down my spine as Brenda Novak can."
—*Huntress Reviews*

"When I open a Brenda Novak story, I...delve headfirst into a scene so vividly portrayed that I am with the characters each step of the way."
—*Romance Junkies*

"The third book in Novak's trilogy is creepy and absorbing, and the characterizations are excellent. Plan to stay up very late to finish this one!"
—*Romantic Times BOOKreviews* on *Watch Me*

"Whenever I see a new Brenda Novak book, I buy it and read it, pronto. I can always count on her for a solid, exciting story, full of adventure and romance."
—*New York Times* bestselling author Linda Lael Miller

Also by BRENDA NOVAK

WATCH ME
STOP ME
TRUST ME
DEAD RIGHT
DEAD GIVEAWAY
DEAD SILENCE
COLD FEET
TAKING THE HEAT
EVERY WAKING MOMENT

BRENDA NOVAK

THE PERFECT COUPLE

Recycling programs for this product may not exist in your area.

ISBN-13: 978-0-7783-2667-0

THE PERFECT COUPLE

www.MIRABooks.com

Printed in U.S.A.

To Channie...

For believing in me from the start.
Thanks for the early investment.

Dear Reader,

The Last Stand is a fictional victims' charity located in Sacramento, California, the brainchild of three women, victims themselves, who decided to fight back. In the first three books of this series (*Trust Me, Stop Me* and *Watch Me*), you met Skye, Sheridan and Jasmine. But they didn't work entirely alone. They had the help of Jonathan Stivers, a crack P.I. who's sacrificed a great deal of his time to lend a hand. This is Jonathan's story. When he's presented with the most puzzling case of his career, he can't help but get involved. Little does he realize he's just met the one person who can make him come to terms with his own demons.

I think Jonathan's a great character. So is the woman he falls for. But it was Colin, the villain, and Tiffany, his wife, who intrigued me most while I was writing this novel. When I set out to tell their story, I had to ask myself, "What would make a woman go along with a husband who could do such terrible things? How do couples who kill come into being?" The answer sort of surprised me—because I found it all too believable. Colin's wife is a tragic figure. Maybe she's not a victim of Colin's, but she's definitely a victim of her own insecurities. When I realized that, I knew I had the answer.

If you'd like to read more about this book and others I've written, please visit brendanovak.com. There you can take a virtual tour of the offices of The Last Stand, read a prequel to the whole series that isn't published anywhere else, download your choice of two very cool 3-D screensavers, view a regular book trailer as well as a unique 3-D trailer for *The Perfect Couple,* sign up for my mailing list (which gets you invited to my annual cyber-Christmas party) and enter my monthly contests, where I give away all kinds of fun things. You can also learn more about my annual online auction for diabetes research, an event I sponsor at my Web site every May (my youngest son suffers from this disease). Together with my fans, friends, fellow authors and publishing associates, I've managed to raise over $700,000 to date. Don't miss the auction in 2010. It's going to be amazing!

For your own pair of 3-D glasses, send an S.A.S.E. to Brenda Novak at P.O. Box 3781, Citrus Heights, CA 95611.

I hope you enjoy *The Perfect Couple!*

Brenda Novak

"Love is a devil.
There is no evil angel but Love."
—William Shakespeare
Love's Labour's Lost

1

Sacramento, California

The bump that came from the trunk of her car surprised Tiffany so much it nearly sent her careering off the road and into one of the houses along the right side. What was going on? The fourteen-year-old boy she and her husband had called "Rover" was supposed to be dead. She couldn't dump his body if he wasn't!

What should she do? She gripped the steering wheel so hard her knuckles showed beneath her skin. She needed to stop and see what was going on. How had someone who'd been *killed* come back to life? And was Rover merely in a panic because he'd regained consciousness in a dark, confined space? Or was he trying to knock out a taillight in hopes of gaining the attention of the car following behind?

She couldn't believe he was still breathing, let alone coherent enough to execute such a plan. He was too young to be that smart, too scared to defy them. But—if he was alive—Rover had to know this was the end. He'd never see his parents again if he didn't do *something*. Wouldn't that make him willing to take *any* risk?

Tiffany wasn't sure. It always astonished her how

cowed and controllable the teenagers her husband brought home really were. Colin had a way with them, knew just the type of individual to pick.

Another *thunk* caused her palms to grow slick with sweat. Damn it! This wasn't supposed to happen. It'd certainly never happened before.

Could anyone else hear the racket Rover was making?

She glanced in her rearview mirror. The black SUV that'd been following her for the past few miles was still there. The driver, a middle-aged woman wearing sunglasses, had lowered her window to take advantage of the warm spring weather. The wind blew her dark hair back, revealing an oval face with full lips, the kind of face Colin would probably find attractive, despite the obvious age difference. But the woman didn't look any more interested in Tiffany than she had before.

Or maybe she was. She seemed closer now....

More movement, sounds of distress, drew Tiffany's nerves taut. *I've got to pull over.*

But if the driver of the SUV had seen or heard anything unusual, she might stop, too. And how would Tiffany explain having a boy in her trunk? Especially one in Rover's condition?

Think! It was better to keep driving. She'd turn at the next light and hope the SUV went straight. There were several ways to get to Highway 50. Once out of the city, beyond Placerville, she could pull down a dirt road in the mountains where she'd be hidden by pine trees.

But then what? It was one thing to dump a body, another to be the reason that person was no longer living.

The noise coming from her trunk became louder, more insistent. If the lady behind her didn't hear it, a pedestrian at the next crosswalk could.

Tiffany drew in a deep breath. She had to get this right

or Colin would be upset. And if she screwed up, they'd both go to prison.

Heart hammering, she reached into her purse and fumbled around until she located her cell and managed to push the speed-dial button that would ring her husband's cell.

"Hello?"

"Colin, he's alive!" she blurted into the pause that followed, but then his recorded voice cut in and she realized she'd gotten his voice mail.

"I'm afraid I'm not able to take your call right now..."

Frustrated, she punched the End button. Colin thought it was funny to bait people into believing they had him on the phone. She usually laughed when he caught her on it. But she wasn't laughing today. She needed him. *Now.*

"H-e-l-p! Mo-om? Da-ad? Someone *help* me!"

That was Rover screaming!

Taking the next right, Tiffany gave her car too much gas. When the tires squealed, two men leaving Lamps Plus looked up, and she regretted her lead foot. She didn't want to draw attention to herself.

At least the black SUV continued down Madison. That was a small relief.

Her hand shook as she dialed Colin's work number. "Come on, hurry. I need to talk to my husband," she muttered through the subsequent ringing.

Finally, Misty, the receptionist with the frizzy red hair, picked up. "Scovil, Potter & Clay Law Offices."

"M-Misty? This is Tiffany Bell. Is my husband there?"

"Let me see." There was a long pause. Then she came back on the line. "He's in a meeting."

"Will you get him for me?"

"He's with the boss."

As a new hire only a year out of law school, Colin had

to be careful to keep the other lawyers happy, especially Walter Scovil, the most senior of the senior partners. But nothing was more important than this.

"I'm sorry, it's an emergency."

"Oh! Is everything okay?"

Hoping to stanch the tears burning behind her eyes, Tiffany blinked repeatedly. "His, um, his mother fell and…and she's hurt."

Colin hated his mother, wouldn't have walked across the street to see her even if she was on her deathbed, but most people didn't know that. It wasn't something he typically shared. They both knew what other people would think if they heard him calling his mother the names he used.

"I feel terrible," the receptionist said. "I'll get him for you."

The stoplight ahead turned red, and traffic in front of Tiffany began to slow. She studied the intersection, wondering if she could switch into the right-hand-turn lane, or catch a green arrow on the left. Anything to avoid coming to a complete stop. But too many vehicles blocked the way. She had no choice but to wait for the light.

Biting her lip, she eased her foot onto the brake…and let her breath go only when she didn't hear a peep from Rover. Did that mean he'd died?

"Tiffany, why are you calling?"

At the sound of her husband's voice, she lost the battle she'd been fighting with her emotions. As she wiped the tears rolling down her cheeks, she saw the man in the truck next to her staring and averted her eyes. "It's Rover," she whispered into the phone.

"What's wrong?"

"He's *alive.*"

"What?"

"He's alive!"

"He can't be."

"He *is.* He's in the trunk banging around and crying for help."

"Then pull over and take care of it!"

"Here? In the middle of Fair Oaks?"

"Shit! No, of course not." He was silent for a few seconds. "What street are you on?"

"I'm heading south on Hazel, trying to reach Highway 50."

"Wait until you get out of town, then pull over and deal with the problem."

She'd figured out that much. It was what came next that made her uneasy. "What do you mean, 'deal with the problem'?"

He kept his response low. "Just what I said. Finish the job."

Kill Rover? Herself? Her stomach flip-flopped at the thought. The boy had been Colin's toy; the cleanup should be Colin's job. "But…I don't have a weapon."

"Use a piece of wood or…or a rock if you have to. It's not hard."

Tiffany's jaw went slack. How had what'd started as a little fun grown into this? Sometimes, lying awake at night, she couldn't believe how badly their lives were spinning out of control. And yet she didn't know how to stop it. Colin didn't even want to try. He was too addicted to the adrenaline rush, to the sexual excitement, to the power, and he'd sucked her in with him by repeating the same old promise, "Just one more time. I'll quit after this."

Now she wasn't only participating in a peripheral way; she was tying up his loose ends. "You're kidding, right? You know I don't have the nerve for…for *that.*"

"You don't have a choice!"

The light turned green. The guy in the truck next to her gave her an appreciative smile as they both accelerated, but she wasn't worried that he'd suspect her of any wrongdoing. Rover hadn't made a sound for several minutes. "But—"

"Do it, or I swear to God, Tiffany…"

He didn't finish. He didn't have to. She knew what he'd be like if she didn't fix this. He'd punish *her* now that he no longer had his "pet."

"Okay. I got it. I—he's not moving anymore."

"So you called me for nothing?" He sighed into the phone. "You're pathetic."

"How can you say that after everything I've done for you?"

"Don't start. You wouldn't be anything without me. You were a fat slob when I met you." He lowered his voice further, but she figured he had to be in his office with the door closed or he wouldn't have spoken as freely as he had. "There wasn't a guy in high school who'd even *look* at you, with your greasy hair and filthy clothes. And now all my friends drool when you walk by. *I've* turned you into a pinup. *I've* taught you how to take care of yourself."

Unfortunately, taking care of herself proved to be an ongoing effort. He demanded she work out two hours a day. He weighed her regularly and monitored every morsel she put in her mouth. He wanted her at a steady hundred and twenty pounds, with breasts the size of watermelons, he said. But she wasn't quite that large. Fortunately, Colin was more concerned with keeping up appearances than fulfilling his porn-star fantasy, which tempered what he'd had the plastic surgeon do to her body. In the end, he'd settled for an augmentation that made her a full D cup, and he had her nose fixed and her cheekbones enhanced. They still owed over nine thousand dollars to Visa for those improvements, but he didn't seem to care about the expense. He loved that they were the most admired couple in the firm and in the neighborhood.

"What other men think doesn't concern me," she said, and it was true. He was the only person who mattered in the world, the only one who'd ever loved her. She didn't want to lose that.

"If I mean so damn much to you, do what you have to do!"

Without any recent noise from the vicinity of the trunk, Tiffany was feeling more confident. She rolled down her window to let some cool air into the car and pulled her sweat-soaked blouse away from her body. "Yes. Of course. I've got it."

"That's better."

The entrance to Highway 50 came up on her right, and she accelerated onto the on-ramp. It would be hard for anyone to hear Rover once she was on the freeway. "It just scared me for a minute, that's all."

"I know, babe. But you're stronger than you realize. You belong to me, don't you? Every thought you think, every move you make, all comes from me, and I've trained you well."

She knew he was too possessive, but she considered herself lucky. It made her feel attractive, desired, secure in his love. He took her to the tattoo parlor every once in a while to have his name tattooed on a different part of her body. So far, both breasts, her ass and the inside of her thighs said, "Colin's." But she didn't mind. He wouldn't bother with the time and expense involved if she wasn't an important part of his life. Only people who tried to contest his will ran into problems.

Shivering, she remembered the incident that had

finally brought their relationship with Rover to an end. It was the boy's own fault, she told herself. He knew Colin, knew what he demanded. If Rover had obeyed, as usual, it might've hurt for a while but he would've recovered. There wouldn't have been any reason to kill him.

Instead, she was driving to a remote location to dump his corpse.

"What should we have for dinner tonight?" she asked, hoping a change in topic would make Colin respond favorably.

"I don't know. I have to get back to that meeting."

"Okay." She was still on her own with this terrible assignment. But at least she'd been able to connect with Colin, to get instruction. "Good luck."

"Thanks for watching my back, Tiff. I'm gonna show you how much I love you tonight," he said and hung up.

She smiled as she dropped her phone in her purse. With Rover gone, they'd be alone at last, the way Tiffany liked it best. She knew she was stupid to get jealous of her husband's toys—or pets, as he called them—but she didn't like how much he seemed to enjoy some of the stuff he made them do. Especially the boys. They satisfied him more than she could, even with the fake boobs and the tattoos and the dangerous domination games they'd begun to play. Sometimes she got the impression she was just for looks, part of his image, a trophy for his lawyer friends to envy.

But that couldn't be true. Colin shared everything with her, including his pets. Rover had been doing the housework for weeks.

Drying her tears, she turned up the volume on the radio and began to sing along. This wouldn't be difficult. She'd head past the rented cabin where they'd once spent Thanksgiving before Colin's dad had bought his own place. Then she'd pull deep into the woods and roll the body out onto the ground. When that was done, she'd drive to the grocery store and get the ingredients to make her husband a romantic dinner. She'd let Colin chain her up and whip her afterward, really get into it. If she was lucky, he'd forget all about Rover and forgive her for bothering him at the office.

She was almost herself by the time she found what appeared to be a safe location. She hadn't heard Rover since he'd cried out for his parents. He had to be dead. She'd seen what her husband had done to him.

But he wasn't. When she opened the trunk, he jumped out at her. With his left eye swollen shut, his lip busted and ugly cuts and black bruises darkening his bare white skin, the boy resembled some kind of monster gone wild. He knocked her to the ground, but he didn't attack her. He ran faster than she'd ever dreamed possible, sobbing for help as he went.

He was so loud, she dared not follow. After scrambling to get back in the car, she tore off, ignoring the groaning of the BMW's struts when she raced over one bump or another. The car didn't matter. She had to get out of sight before Rover attracted someone's attention.

And then she had to think of a way to break the news to Colin.

2

Samantha Duncan had never been so bored in her life. She'd thought it would be neat to skip school. But any "fun" had ended the first week. With her mother working all day, Sam found it too quiet and lonely at home. Especially *this* home. Although it was by far the best house they'd ever lived in, she no longer cared about the "amenities," as her mother called them. She felt like excess baggage—an inconvenience Anton Lucassi tolerated for the privilege of sleeping in her mother's bed.

But she didn't want to think about that. It gave her a stomachache on top of the fatigue. She needed to "occupy her mind with something constructive"—another saying her mother had picked up after hanging around with Lucassi. What exactly that should be, they never explained. But she needed to figure out *some* form of entertainment. It was only Monday. She wasn't sure how she'd get through another four days until the weekend, rambling around the place on her own. The fact that there'd be a third week and then a fourth of the same misery nearly brought her to tears. The kids slaving away at school were the lucky ones.

The telephone rang. Lifting her head from the chaise, she shaded her eyes against the glare coming off the pool and groaned—it was her mother's fiancé. *Again.* Anton was such an uptight freak. What did he want *this* time?

She almost didn't answer, but she knew he'd call back if she didn't.

"Why'd my mother have to get with you?" she grumbled and pressed the Talk button. "Hello?" She used a sleepy voice, hoping to convince him he'd awakened her from a nap, but he didn't seem to care.

"Sam?"

Did he expect someone else to be answering his phone? "Yes?"

"You're not leaving the TV projector on all day, are you?"

That was why he'd called? "No."

"Good. The bulb doesn't last very long, and they cost over three hundred dollars to replace."

"I didn't know that," she said. But it was just her way of being a smartass without getting in trouble for it. He'd told her about the bulb at least a hundred times. He had her mother so nervous she'd break his stupid projector that Zoe had bought Sam her own DVD player and asked her not to even use his TV. Fortunately, Sam liked movies. She liked to read, too. But it'd be nice to watch a TV show to break up the monotony. It wasn't as if she had an unlimited source of movies and books.

"It's not a toy," he was saying.

Did she treat it like a toy? "Got it."

"So, what are you doing?"

"Not destroying anything."

"What?"

She'd mumbled the words because she knew it wouldn't be smart to let him hear. "I said I was sleeping."

Again, he ignored the opportunity to apologize for disturbing her. "You're not out by the pool, are you?"

Was there something wrong with that, too? "Actually, I am. I thought I might as well tan while I slept."

"Don't get any oil on the cushions of those lounge chairs."

"They were expensive," she mouthed as he said the words, and rolled over in disgust. "I'm not using any oil."

"You're not upset, are you? Just because I'm trying to teach you to take care of personal property?"

He'd noticed her tone. Squeezing her eyes shut, she focused her energy on hiding the irritation that made her want to scream, "Go away and never talk to me again!" She would've done it if not for her mom. Zoe was so excited to finally *have* something and *be* someone. Samantha didn't want to ruin it for her; she'd already ruined enough just by being born. "I'm not upset."

"Good girl. Have you heard from your mother?"

Not half as often as she heard from him, although Zoe's calls were far more welcome. "She checks on me when she can. If the people at her work weren't such jerks, we'd be able to talk more." Her mother had tried to stop by for lunch last week and nearly been fired because the length of the drive had made her late.

"They're not jerks. That's the real world, Sam. She has to be responsible to her employers, just as you'll have to be responsible to your employers someday."

Thanks for the lecture. How did her mother put up with this guy?

"Sam?" he said when she didn't answer.

"I'm here. But…I'm really tired."

"Okay, I'll let you go back to sleep."

"Thanks. By the way, I turned off all the lights in the house." She was making fun of him again, but he didn't get it.

"Glad to know you're listening. I'll see you later." Not

later enough for her, but she forced herself to end the conversation on a positive note, mostly because she thought it was funny to be overly polite.

"Thanks for calling." She smiled. He had no clue how she really felt about him, or that she understood exactly how he really felt about her, despite what he pretended to her mom.

As she hung up, she was distracted by the sound of a door opening and closing in the neighbors' backyard. Tiffany and Colin Bell weren't normally home during the day.

Drawn by signs of life beyond her own lonely existence, Samantha got up and crossed the freshly mowed grass. Still weak from mono, she walked slowly, but she could tell she was getting stronger. The doctor said she'd be back to her old self soon. She was almost two weeks into what he called a "four-week cycle," whatever that meant. As long as she could return to school, she didn't care.

She managed to reach the fence. She could already hear Anton scolding her for stepping into the flower bed the gardeners had planted a month ago, but purposely ignored the fact that it would make him mad. It was because of this stupid flower bed, and all the others in the yard, that she'd had to give up her dog to that family Anton had found. She still couldn't believe her mom had gone along with *that.*

Hoping whoever had come outside hadn't gone back in, she peered through a knothole. The wife of the attractive couple she occasionally spoke to out front was there. But Tiffany Bell wasn't dressed for work as she'd expected. An employee at some nursing home, she usually wore a uniform—a cheery floral smock with blue scrubs and squishy white nurse's shoes. Today, she had on a holey pair of jeans, some grubby tennis shoes and a T-shirt tight enough to make her boobs look even bigger than they did beneath her nursing smock.

"I bet those are fake," Sam muttered, glancing down at her own flat chest. At thirteen, there was no reason to give up hope, but she didn't seem to be developing very fast. While her best friend, Marti Seacrest, was already a B-cup, Sam didn't even need a bra. Her mother called her a "late bloomer," as if it wasn't a big deal. But the boys at school ignored late bloomers. Any guys who bothered to notice her called her Brainiac, but they didn't stare at her the way they did Marti.

"What am I gonna do?" Tiffany moaned.

Samantha looked around the yard. She didn't see anyone else. Could Tiffany be talking to her?

"Excuse me?" she said.

Tiffany's head jerked toward her so fast Samantha could almost hear the bones in her neck crack. "Who is it? Who's there?"

Sam immediately realized her error, but it was too late. Palms against the rough wood of the fence, she leaned closer. She could see Tiffany's body but not much of her face. Her neighbor was standing in the shade of the patio cover. "It's me. Sam. I'm home from school today. Actually, I've been staying home for a while."

"Why?"

"I've been sick."

"You seem okay to me."

"I'm getting better."

"So what are you doing, staring through the fence?"

"I'm bored." She missed her friends. She missed her mother even more.

Tiffany didn't answer. She remained on the porch, clicking her nails. Sam couldn't hear it, but she could see the motion of her fingers.

"What's wrong?" Sam asked.

"What makes you think something's wrong?"

Not only was Tiffany acting strange, she was dressed like a bum. She never grubbed out. She always wore stylish, name-brand jeans, heels, nice sweaters or pretty summer blouses.

"You seem…nervous. And you're not usually home this time of day."

Her neighbor raised her voice. "You know my schedule?"

"Not really. I—"

"You just said I'm not usually home this time of day."

"Because…don't you work?"

"You tell me, since you seem to be keeping track."

"I'm not keeping track of anything," Sam said.

"Then what makes you think I'm nervous?"

Sam could *feel* it. But she could also tell that she was somehow saying all the wrong things. "Sorry, I didn't mean to bother you."

"Wait!"

She wasn't interested in talking anymore, but Tiffany's voice caught her before she could step away.

"How long have you been staying home from school?"

The suspicion in those words made Sam uneasy. She'd heard that tone from adults before, generally from Anton since he'd come into their lives. But Sam hadn't "misbehaved." She closed one eye to see through the knothole more clearly. "For the past ten days or so."

Her neighbor moved outside the shadow of the patio cover. In the sunlight, Samantha could see that Tiffany had been crying. Mascara ran from her eyes, which were red and puffy.

At least now she understood why her usually very nice neighbor was acting so weird. No one liked to be seen crying. "Can I help?" she asked.

Tiffany crossed the lawn. The Bells didn't own a pool or even a barbecue. "How often do you do this?"

"Do what?"

She motioned toward her house. "Watch us."

Her alarm increased. "I don't...*watch* you."

"You were just staring at me through the fence, weren't you?"

"No. Not really. I mean, I heard you come outside and I was bored, so..." She cleared her throat. "I thought I'd say hi."

Tiffany was close now, close enough that Samantha could see a dark-red substance smeared on her shirt. It looked like...*blood.* Had she cut herself? Maybe that was why she'd been crying.

"Are you hurt?"

Tiffany's eyes narrowed. "No."

Sam nibbled at her bottom lip. "That's not blood?"

Her neighbor glanced down, staggered to the side and rubbed her forehead. "Shit! Shit, shit, shit! I—I didn't realize!"

"Do you need help?"

"I can't...I don't know what to do. It's been a bad day. A *very* bad day."

"I could call the paramedics."

"No, don't call anyone!" Fresh tears made new tracks in her mascara. "Just tell my husband I...he needs to come home."

"Where is he? At work?"

She stripped off her shirt and threw it away from her as if she couldn't bear the feel of it, and didn't answer.

Surprised that her neighbor would stand outside in her bra, which was skimpier than most and definitely too small, Samantha tried again. "What's his number?"

"His...what? I can't...I can't remember it right now."

Suddenly, she doubled over, struggling to catch her breath and vomited on the grass.

What was going on? Samantha had no idea, but it was obviously serious. She had to get Colin. He'd know what to do. "Is your husband listed in the directory of your cell phone?"

"Yes, that's it." She was breathing hard, but she wiped her mouth and tilted her head back as if she was done being sick for the moment. "My cell."

"Okay. Stay right where you are." Sam ran toward the gate that would let her in the front yard but stopped when Tiffany started crying.

"I'm sorry," she moaned to no one in particular. "I'm so sorry."

The torment in Tiffany's wail drew her back to the fence. "For what? Tiffany, it'll be okay."

Falling silent, Tiffany rocked into a sitting position. "Yes, it'll be okay. It wasn't my fault. He won't blame me."

"What're you talking about?"

With a sniff, Tiffany wiped her eyes, spreading mascara even farther. "Nothing. I'm not feeling well. Not...thinking straight."

"Don't worry, I'm on my way," Sam said and hurried over to do what she could to help.

3

Zoe frowned as she hung up the phone. She'd been trying to reach her daughter for the past two hours, but she couldn't get Sammie to pick up. Was it because she couldn't hear the phone? Maybe she'd fallen asleep with the radio on—

"*Excuse* me?"

Jan Buppa, the office manager, stood over her desk. Preoccupied with worry, Zoe hadn't heard even a rustle or a footstep, which wasn't surprising since she sat out in the open with the other clerical support staff and had learned to ignore most of the noise and movement so she could get her work done.

Generally, ignoring the chaos was a good thing—but it was always better to see Jan coming.

"I hate to interrupt a daydream that looks as absorbing as that one," her boss said, "but you *do* plan to finish those leases before you go home, don't you?" She waved toward the stack of folders Zoe had been working on since she came in. It was enough to keep her busy for three days, but Jan expected her to finish before five.

Zoe remembered Anton telling her how lucky she was that he'd been able to get her on at Tate Commercial and forced a smile. The owner was one of his tax clients. She had to be careful so her behavior never reflected poorly on him. "Of course. You promised the agents they'd have these by tomorrow morning, and they will."

"Glad to hear it. Just wanted to be sure you hadn't forgotten that we're under a deadline."

Zoe gritted her teeth as Jan turned on her heel and marched to her own desk, wishing once again that she didn't need this job quite so badly. If she stayed to finish the leases, she'd get home even later than usual. She hated that Sammie was on her own so much as it was.

She imagined telling Jan to go to hell. That distracted her for a few seconds but, as usual, the temptation was soon countered by Anton's voice in her mind: *Jan's just mad that you got the position instead of her daughter-in-law. Anyway, the first year might be tough, but you have to do* something *while you get your license. Where else will you be able to learn more about the kind of real estate you hope to be involved in someday? Being successful requires sacrifice.*

He said that as if he had a corner on sacrifice. It annoyed her that he could be so patronizing when he'd always had a nice place to live, a hot meal. But, in some ways, he was right. If she meant to significantly improve her situation, she had to make concessions. Except for Jan, she would've been happy working at Tate Commercial. It was a great opportunity, the perfect start to her career. Zoe wanted to make good, to prove to herself more than anyone that she could be everything her father was not. But she was so worried about Samantha….

Despite Jan's lingering gaze, she called her fiancé.

"Hello?"

"Anton? Have you spoken with Sammie today?"

"I checked in at noon. Why?"

"I can't get her to answer the phone."

"She's sleeping. I woke her when I called."

Zoe glanced at the clock on the wall. Noon was three hours ago. "She's got mono, Anton."

"Which is why she's napping. It's not unusual."

The tone of his voice told her he thought she was overreacting. Maybe that was true, but Zoe didn't want to take any chances. "What time will you be home tonight?"

"Six or seven."

"Why so late? Tax season's over."

"And now I'm taking care of all the clients who filed extensions."

"Come on, can't you spare twenty minutes to drop by the house and let me know she's okay?"

"You want me to drive over there?"

Zoe had been battling a headache all day. Absently, she rubbed her left temple in an effort to ease the pounding. "Yes."

"That's ridiculous. What could possibly have happened to her?"

"I don't know. That's why I want you to check. Maybe…maybe she decided to go swimming and hit her head."

"She's not allowed in the pool. The water's too cold, anyway."

Sunlight, coming from the closest floor-to-ceiling window, spilled across her desk. "The weather's been unseasonably warm the past few weeks."

"Not warm enough for swimming. And she's thirteen years old. She knows better than to get in the pool alone."

"Anton, I'd do it myself if I could, but I'm stuck here until—" she bowed her head so Jan couldn't see that she was getting upset "—who knows what time it'll be when I finish."

This statement was met with a lengthy pause. Finally, he blew out a sigh. "Okay. I'll go over there. But I'll only call you if something's wrong. Just last week they told you to reserve personal calls for your lunch break."

She didn't care half as much about her job, or even Anton's reputation, as she did Sammie. "Call me in any case. As long as I finish the work on my desk before I go home, I should be okay."

"Fine. I'll talk to you in ten minutes."

After he'd severed the connection, Zoe dragged her attention back to her computer, where she'd been inserting special clauses in a seven-year lease for some retail space in the South Natomas area. She finished that document and sent it to the printer, then started on another, but Anton didn't call. Had he gotten busy and forgotten he'd promised to check on Sam?

The clock indicated that it'd been twenty-five minutes since they'd hung up.

He'll get to it, she told herself, and decided to wait ten more minutes. If she hadn't heard from him by then, she'd call him again whether it risked an argument or not.

The seconds ticked by. Slow. Ponderous. Filled with anxiety.

Eight minutes later, her cell vibrated and she snatched it off her desk. Caller ID showed the house number. *There you are.*

"Anton, is she okay?"

A strained silence followed.

"Anton?"

"I can't find her," he said.

Zoe might've thought he was teasing her for worrying, but he was far too serious for that. His words hit her like a punch to the gut, so hard it was several seconds before she could speak. "What do you mean you can't find her?"

"I've looked everywhere. The back door is unlocked, and there's a book by the pool, but she's gone."

Zoe's heartbeat grew so loud it drowned out the *clack, clack, clack* of typing from the desks of the other administrative staff, the conversation of two agents standing at the edge of the bullpen near the copier, the hum of the printer. "Did she leave a note?"

"Not that I can see."

"But…that doesn't make sense. Where would she go? She knows she's not supposed to leave the house. The doctor said she's probably still contagious."

"I'm guessing she walked down to the Quick Stop for a candy bar. I'm heading over there right now."

"You checked the pool?"

"I checked the pool."

Thank God her daughter wasn't floating in the water. "Did you notice any sign of a struggle?"

"None. Don't even let your mind go there, Zoe. You know we live in a safe neighborhood."

Rocklin was one of the most desirable suburbs in the Sacramento metropolitan area, and the crime rate was among the lowest in California. It was a completely different experience from the seedy L.A. trailer park she'd grown up in. Maybe kidnapping, theft and murder happened regularly in her old neighborhood, but not here.

"It's possible one of her friends came by on the way home from school," Anton was saying. "There's no reason to jump to conclusions yet."

"I'll call Marti's parents."

"Don't do it from work."

"For something like this? Why not?"

"I'll take care of it. If you're not careful, you'll lose your job. Then how will you feel when you learn this was just some typical teenage stunt?"

Samantha didn't pull stunts like this. But Zoe knew as soon as she launched that argument, Anton would bring up the time Sam had said she was going to band recital but went to a boy's house with her best friend instead. *Teenagers are teenagers, Zoe. You have a lot more of this kind of stuff to look forward to,* he'd said then.

Was she being too protective? "I wouldn't be so worried if she was well. But she's not supposed to exert herself."

It was a reasonable argument, one Anton would understand. But Zoe knew she'd be worried regardless. She'd had some pretty terrible experiences in her day, experiences she'd been working to protect Sam against. The rape that had resulted in her becoming pregnant at fifteen was one of them. Just imagining her daughter in the hands of a man like the one who'd forced her onto the floor of her own father's trailer made her body go clammy with sweat. Had someone spotted Sam when she sneaked out to the store, thought she was pretty, followed her home?

Zoe didn't realize she had her eyes shut until she heard Jan's voice again. "What's it going to take to keep you working today, Ms. Duncan?"

"I—" Swallowing hard, she looked up. "I'm having some personal problems."

"We don't have time for personal problems."

"I'm afraid this can't be helped. I know these…leases are important." How? Why? They were nothing compared to what Zoe feared, but she didn't want to overreact. Maybe Anton was right and Sam was merely acting out. "But could I…could I go home for an hour or so and come back tonight to finish up?"

"You want to leave in the middle of the afternoon, when you have a stack of work on your desk two feet high?"

"Yes." *Desperately.* Sam was all she could think about.

Jan shook her head. "Women like you are all alike."

"Women like me?" Zoe echoed.

"You come to the interview batting your eyelashes

and showing that curvy figure off to best advantage in some short skirt—" she wiggled her flat-as-a-pancake behind as if imitating the way Zoe walked "—and then once you're hired you want to spend all your time on the phone or painting your fingernails."

"Meanwhile, more deserving but less attractive options languish at home, is that it, Jan? Options like your obese daughter-in-law?"

Zoe wasn't sure who was more surprised—Jan or the secretaries sitting close by. All three stopped typing, and their mouths formed perfect Os.

Jan's face went red and her eyes bulged. "*What* did you say?"

"You heard me," Zoe snapped. "And for your information, I didn't bat my eyelashes or interview in a short skirt. And I've never painted my nails at work."

"Neither have you done the job you were hired for!"

"That's not true! If it was, you would've fired me long ago. You've been looking for any excuse since the day I started," she said. Then she got her purse out of her desk, slammed the drawer and headed for the exit.

"Don't you walk out of here," Jan called after her. "If you do, you won't be allowed back."

Zoe turned at the door. "I won't be coming back."

She tried to appear calm and in control as she presented her back to the sprinkling of agents in the bullpen and the secretaries in the reception area. But inside she was quaking. Quitting her job would cause a major argument between her and Anton. If they broke up, she and Samantha would have to move out. Zoe couldn't afford a place in this area, not on her own, especially now that she was out of a job. That meant Samantha would have to transfer to a different school, and the cycle would start all over—the same cycle Zoe had been trying to break. She'd just climbed a little higher on the ladder of success before falling on her ass again.

"Why did I let that bitch get the best of me?" she asked herself over and over as she stalked to her car. It kept her from focusing on the real problem, the fact that she still hadn't heard from Anton. Why hadn't he called?

She tried him four times in as many minutes, but kept getting the beep that told her he was on another line.

Who was he talking to?

He probably had Sam with him but was caught up on a business call. Otherwise, he would've switched over.

But when she got home, she discovered that wasn't the case at all. She found her fiancé sitting on the front steps, his head bowed. As she drew closer, she could tell he was deep in conversation.

He was talking to someone at the police department, making a report.

Her hand went to her throat. "God, no!"

Concern etched deep grooves in his forehead as he looked up and covered the mouthpiece. "I can't find her, Zoe," he said. "She isn't anywhere."

Zoe fell to her knees on the rough cobblestone walk.

"But I'm getting help." His eyes pleaded with her to understand how badly he felt about taking the situation too lightly. "That's why I haven't tried to reach you. I wanted to…to have something positive to tell you. I wanted to get a detective on this as soon as possible."

"A detective?" she whispered, scarcely able to grasp that her daughter was missing.

"Don't panic." He asked whoever was on the phone to hold and set the cell on the ground. Then he hurried over and pulled her to her feet, supporting her until they were inside the house. "It'll be okay," he said, easing her onto the couch.

He returned to his call as if he could take care of it all. But if he couldn't take care of it, nothing would ever be okay again.

4

Samantha tried to peer through the keyhole of the door, but it was useless. She couldn't see anything. She couldn't hear anything, either. Had Tiffany left?

She hoped not. She needed to pee. She'd had to go for a while, but she couldn't get Tiffany to respond. After helping her neighbor in from outside, she'd asked for a way to reach Colin, and Tiffany had said her cell phone was upstairs. Sam had gone up to look for it and Tiffany had followed, telling her it was in this room, the room over the garage. But there wasn't anything in here except a bare mattress. When Sam had turned to question Tiffany about it, Tiffany had shoved her in and locked the door.

Why, Sam couldn't imagine. Tiffany was obviously having some sort of mental breakdown. Maybe she'd actually gone *crazy*....

It was a chilling thought, perfect for the movies. Picturing herself at school, telling all her friends the dramatic story of how she'd been forced into a room by her neighbor who afterward had to be carted off to an asylum, had kept Sam intrigued for a while. At least the drama of the afternoon had broken up the monotony. But she'd been in here so long she was getting creeped out. Why wouldn't Tiffany let her go home? And where was Colin? Shouldn't he be back from work by now?

She was sure he'd be embarrassed once he knew, but she was afraid she'd wet her pants before he found her.

Groaning in frustration, she turned away from the door and paced another circle around the room. With their neat yard, preppy clothes and matching BMWs, she'd believed her neighbors had good taste. But this part of the house certainly didn't show it. There was nothing wrong with the floor. It was the same hardwood her mother's boyfriend had in his place. And the ceiling fan overhead was nice. But there was a questionable stain on the mattress, and the windows were covered by murals that looked like they'd been painted by a first grader.

Pausing in front of a scene showing several hay piles, more lemon colored than wheat colored, a blue sky and puffy cotton-candy clouds, she tried to wedge her hand behind the art. There had to be glass underneath; from the front driveway these windows looked like they had blinds. If she could reach the panes, there might be some way to break one and call for help. Then Tiffany would be in real trouble.

But the mural had been painted on thick pieces of wood hammered tightly to the wall. Sam had no chance of prying any of the boards loose and broke a fingernail trying.

"Ow!" She smacked the wood with her fist, then jammed her wounded finger in her mouth. Why would anyone want to block the windows? Anton had a bonus room over his garage, too, but he used it for a pool table, card table and minibar. "That's what you do with a room like this," she grumbled, shaking the sting away. "Only you allow people to *use* it," she added.

Music, coming from downstairs, filtered up to her. Someone was home. Was it Colin?

Forgetting about her injury, she hurried to the door.

"Colin?" She banged three times. "Hello? Hey, I have to go to the bathroom! Let me out!"

She had no idea how long she'd been locked up, but she knew it must be late. If she didn't get home soon, her mother would return from work to an empty house.

"My mom will be home any minute. I have to go!"

Nothing.

"Tiffany?"

Approaching footsteps made Sam's heart race. "Hello? Please, I need to use the restroom."

"Sam?"

It was Tiffany, all right. "What?"

"I'm trying to cook a nice dinner and you're really getting on my nerves. Will you shut up?"

A nice dinner? Tiffany seemed strangely calm. What'd happened to the panicked, crying woman Sam had seen in the backyard?

"Just let me out and I won't bother you anymore. My mother's going to freak if she finds me gone."

"I'm afraid I can't do that."

"Why not? You don't know how she is. She's very protective. I can't even watch HBO."

"She sounds like a good mom."

Zoe was a good mom. Suddenly it felt like an eternity since Sam had seen her. Heck, after the past few hours, Sam wouldn't have minded *Anton's* company. "Can you let me out?"

There was a slight pause. "I don't think so."

"But I'm about to wet my pants."

"Oh…*fine!* Give me a minute, will ya?"

At last! While waiting for Tiffany, Sam shifted from foot to foot and breathed a huge sigh of relief when, once again, she heard movement in the hall. "Hurry, I can't hold it any longer."

"I'm coming, I'm coming."

The lock clicked, but the door opened so hard and fast it hit Samantha in the shoulder. Then Tiffany tossed a metal bowl at her, which struck her in the head. She fell as Tiffany slammed the door and slid the bolt home.

Tears sprang to Sam's eyes as she rubbed the painful bump on her temple. "Tiffany?" She sounded like a panicked baby, but she couldn't help it. "I don't understand. Why'd you do that? Aren't you going to let me out?"

"I told you, I'm cooking dinner," she called back. "We'll go over the rules later. Just pee in what I gave you."

Rules? Sam's gaze shifted to the metal mixing bowl still rolling on its side. She couldn't use it. It was too late. She'd already gone in her bikini bottom.

Tiffany felt better by the time she heard her husband's car in the driveway. She'd showered and changed, and then burned the shirt with Rover's blood on it in the fireplace. Now she was wearing nothing but a black lacy bra that barely contained her large breasts and a thong with a pair of six-inch heels. The scent of expensive perfume, Colin's favorite, mingled with the warm garlic bread she'd pulled from the oven and the candles she'd lit on the mantel.

With a final glance at her preparations, she smiled. Everything was just right. She'd even managed to clean up most of the pots and pans so Colin wouldn't have to look at a stack of dirty dishes.

He'd be so pleased.

"Tiff?"

As he came through the front door, she posed at the opening to the kitchen.

"Yes?" she said in her sultriest tone.

His eyebrows shot up. "Wow, what a greeting." A lascivious grin curved his lips as he gave her the once-over. "To what do I owe this pleasure?"

"I thought you might want to make another movie." He enjoyed pretending he was a porn star. She suspected he shared the videos they made with some old friends of his, which bothered her, but she rarely permitted herself to think about it. If she questioned him or complained, she'd only start an argument. And what did it really matter? He was doing it to show off. She supposed she could allow him that. At the end of each session, he had her point to the tattoos that branded her his.

Anyway, tonight she'd do whatever Colin wanted. She needed to keep him happy, to soften his heart before telling him about Rover.

"Do I get to eat dessert first?" he asked.

She ran her hands over her breasts, then lifted them out of her bra. "Before *and* after if you want."

"It must be my birthday." As eager as he sounded, he took time to put his briefcase in the office off the main entrance.

She went back to stirring the pasta sauce so it wouldn't scorch. "Hungry?" she called.

"For you." She hadn't realized he was so close. Coming up from behind, he hefted her breasts with his palms. "You smell so—"

When he fell silent, Tiffany's stomach muscles tensed. Had she missed some detail? Forgotten and used that hairspray he'd told her he hated? What?

"You didn't shave?" he said.

"Sh-shave?" She'd been in too much of a hurry. "I did this morning. You were in the shower with me, remember?"

"How many times have we gone over this? You have to do it morning *and* night."

"I usually do, but it takes so long. And I couldn't feel any regrowth. None." She rubbed her arms and still didn't feel the stubble that must've set him off. How had he noticed when she couldn't? He was so much more sensitive to appearances, smells, tastes, *every nuance.*

"I wouldn't ask you to do it if it wasn't important."

"Of course not. I know that. I just…I was worried about getting dinner ready before you got home." She wouldn't have had time to run to the grocery store *and* cook if she'd shaved. He made her remove *all* her body hair.

"Don't give me excuses. Completely bald. We've talked about this."

"I am bald where it really counts." She tried to compensate by rubbing her hand over the zipper of his pants, but he stepped out of reach.

"You don't want me very badly if you didn't shave. Do you think I have any desire for a woman who feels like a porcupine?"

Did that mean he was going to make her sleep on the floor again? "I—" She searched for a way to distract him. She was sure the news that Samantha Duncan was upstairs would make him happy, but she had to save that surprise for later. She'd need something good, something *better* than good, to make up for letting Rover escape. "I made your favorite dinner." She offered him her prettiest pout. "You're glad about that, aren't you?"

"I would've been if you'd shaved." With that, he walked out of the kitchen and turned on the television.

Tiffany peeked out at him. "Can I—can I get you a glass of wine?"

"Sure," he said, but when she brought it to him, he grimaced. "Put your damn tits away. I'm not interested in touching you if you can't take care of yourself."

This was their first night alone, and she'd ruined it. Why did she always have to screw up? He tried to teach her what he expected, but she never seemed to learn. "I'm sorry. If—if you want, you can spank me later."

"And have you sulk for two days? No thanks."

"I won't sulk. I promise."

He held up his glass, swirled the wine and took a sip. "Okay. But only if you let me film it."

"Fine."

"And show it to the guys with you present when they come over tomorrow night."

Her eyes flew to his face. He'd never asked her to watch with them before. He'd hinted at it, let her know Tommy Tuttle from high school would probably get a kick out of a group evening. And his other buddy, James Pearson, would love to join the fun. Tommy had a bum leg and felt too self-conscious to approach women; James used to be married, but his marriage had lasted only a few months.

Tiffany didn't like the idea, was afraid of where it might lead. But if she agreed, maybe Colin would go easier on her when she told him about Rover. "If that's what you want."

He waved for a coaster, and she nearly twisted an ankle trying to get him one. "That's what I want. Now get dinner on before you put me in a bad mood again."

Proud that it was almost ready, Tiffany returned to the kitchen to serve their meal while he watched the news.

"Come and get it," she called five minutes later.

He sat at the dining table while she filled his plate. She did so very carefully, making sure no two foods touched. She hadn't forgotten that lesson, not since he'd thrown his glass at her and broken her cheekbone.

Finished, she took her seat across the table and waited for him to sample his food. She didn't have permission to eat until he gave the okay. Sometimes he was on dessert before he let her touch a single morsel, just to see if she'd eat a cold dinner rather than disobey him.

Tonight, she didn't mind if he never gave the signal. She was too nervous to eat, anyway. And, as appetizing as the bread smelled, she couldn't have garlic. She was afraid it would make her breath stink.

"How'd it go today?" he asked while he ate.

She swallowed hard. She wanted to tell him what had happened with Rover, get it over with. But she couldn't do that now. He'd blame her for ruining his meal on top of everything else. "Fine."

"Fine?" His fork stilled. "Last I heard you were in a panic."

"I calmed down." She motioned to his pasta. "How is it?"

"Delicious. You hungry?"

She didn't want to ruin the enjoyment he received from denying her, from proving to himself how much she loved him, so she nodded.

"How hungry?"

"Starving."

"Stand up."

Surprised, she jumped to her feet.

"Come over here where I can see you."

She held her breath as he pulled her close, made her turn around and examined every inch of her. "Is something wrong?" she finally asked.

"You're getting fat."

In his vocabulary, *fat* was worse than *ugly.* She couldn't help wincing. "But I—I weigh the same as I did yesterday."

"Don't argue with me! Nobody knows your body better than I do." He eyed the Caesar salad, garlic bread and fettuccine primavera she'd prepared. "This shit has too many calories for you. Get a frozen dinner and nuke it."

She'd eaten frozen diet dinners so often over the past few years they all tasted like cardboard to her, but he generally praised her if she left food on her plate. At least that would be easy tonight.

By the time she returned, he'd finished his meal. Stretching out, he nursed another glass of wine while watching her eat, and she picked cautiously at her food.

"Very good," he said. "I like that. Delicate. Feminine. So many women eat like pigs these days."

When she smiled, he leaned forward. "Take your tits out again."

She hesitated. "Don't you want me to shave first?"

"No. I need that stubble or I won't be able to punish you like I've got planned."

See? He cared about her. She had to make him angry before he could hit her. "I understand, Master." She took out her breasts, even stroked herself to get him excited. Then she abandoned the rest of her meal so she could do the dishes and satisfy him that much sooner.

He stopped her when she was halfway to the kitchen. "Put that down. I'm ready *now.*"

But he hated it when she left dirty dishes out. "What about cleaning up?"

"You can do it later."

So he *was* eager. That was hopeful. It gave her the courage to say what had to be said. She had to do it before he punished her, so it would all be over at once.

She put the plate she was holding back on the table as he came around to meet her. "I—I have to tell you something first."

"What is it?"

Her acrylic fingernails curled into her palms. "Um...you know how I said everything went okay today?"

His eyes narrowed with suspicion. "Yes?"

"It didn't go so well." She could barely force herself to look at him.

"What do you mean it didn't go so well?"

She dropped to her knees and held up her hands in supplication. "It—it wasn't my fault, Colin. Please understand. He was *alive!*"

He grabbed her by the wrist. "You *knew* he was alive. You called to tell me that."

"But I didn't expect…I mean, he'd quit moving. And…and then I opened the trunk and…"

He used his free hand to pinch her nipple, twisting so hard she cried out before she could stop herself.

"And what, Tiffany? *What did you do?*" he asked, his voice as rough as gravel. "You didn't let him get away. Tell me you didn't. I could forgive you anything but that."

He still had her nipple in a viselike grip. Tears welled up, but she didn't struggle or cry out again. Experience had taught her that would only make matters worse. "There was nothing that I could do," she whispered. "He…he sprang out at me and—" She swallowed a yelp as he yanked her forward and bit her on the shoulder.

"And what, you stupid bitch! And *what?*"

Panting from pain and fear, she struggled to think. "And ran away. He—knocked me down. He was yelling. He—"

"Why didn't you go after him? You were in the woods, for crying out loud! And there's no way he could've run very far. You saw what I did to him. You *helped* me."

Because he'd made her. She'd hated every minute of it. "I couldn't go after him b-because—" Colin clenched his other hand in her hair and used it to yank her head back, but she kept trying to explain, talking so fast her words ran together. "He was screaming bloody murder. I panicked, Colin. Please, please don't be angry. I'll do anything you want. *Anything.* I said you could have your friends over tomorrow night, didn't I? If you want, we'll put on a show for them, do it live."

He pinched even harder. "You should've been prepared. But you weren't."

She blinked, trying to see through the blur of tears. "Yes."

"Yet you just told me everything went fine! I was sitting right across the table from you."

"I didn't want to ruin your dinner." Dizzy from the pain, she closed her eyes. "I knew it would upset you."

"And lying doesn't upset me?" Because she expected the blow, she flinched, which infuriated him. "Turn over," he said and removed his belt.

She knew what was coming, but at least he'd let go of her nipple. Covering her breast in a fleeting moment of relief, she rolled over before he could kick her. She could survive this, she told herself. He spanked her even when he wasn't angry. He enjoyed it. And she didn't mind. Except tonight the beating was far more vicious, and he wouldn't stop. The more he hit her, the more he wanted to hit her.

Bile welled up in her throat, but she choked it back. If she vomited on the carpet, he'd make her lick it up, like he did with Rover.

"You—" *whack* "—idiot!" He didn't raise his voice. He knew how to avoid unwanted attention from the neighbors. He was an expert at blending in, appearing calm and normal, no matter what. "Do you—" *whack* "—want to see me—" *whack* "—in prison?" *Whack, whack.* "Is that what you're after?"

He kept hitting the same place on her back. She wasn't sure how many blows she could withstand. In desperation, she rolled over, lifting an arm to stop him, but she realized that was a mistake when he threw down the belt and slipped his hands around her neck. "I should kill you! You know that? You don't deserve me. Look at this place. Look at everything I've given you!" He began to squeeze. "You aren't worthy of it."

Black spots danced before her eyes, just like the time he'd used Rover's choke chain on her a few weeks ago. She was about to lose consciousness. She had to tell him about Samantha Duncan. That was the only way to stop this. But she couldn't breathe.

Although her survival instinct urged her to fight, she forced herself to remain pliant. He wouldn't really kill her. Once his anger was spent he'd cry and apologize and be as sweet as ever. Tomorrow, he'd be putting salve on her wounds.

At last, he dropped his hands from her neck. But he wasn't finished. He still had that *look* on his face. He drew back his fist, but she raised a hand to stop him while gulping for the air to speak. "Wait...don't hurt me again." She sucked another breath into her burning lungs. "I—I have a present for you."

Curiosity made him hesitate, but his eyes were still razor-sharp with cruelty. "What is it? If it's the promise of your lousy body, I'm tired of it."

"D-don't say that. I—I love you."

"You love me, but you can't follow simple directions?"

"Rover doesn't know *anything*." Now that she could breathe, she was thinking more clearly. "You—you brought him home in your trunk. He was blindfolded. He doesn't know who we are or where we live."

He slugged her anyway, which he was usually careful never to do. She'd have to call in sick tomorrow.

"What do you have for me?" he demanded. "It better be good."

Dazed from his latest blow, she scrambled to organize her scattered thoughts. What had she been trying to tell him? It *was* something good, something that would stop all this....

She had Sam. Samantha Duncan. That was it!

"You—you know the girl who lives next door?" She dashed a hand across her wet cheeks. "The one you've been admiring?"

She had his attention now. She could feel the alertness in his body. He'd always been intrigued by Sam's mother, probably because Zoe Duncan hardly seemed to notice him. "Yes?"

"I have her locked in Rover's old room upstairs."

Releasing her, he staggered to his feet. "You're kidding."

"No. And—" she swallowed hard, hoping it would be enough "—she's all yours, your new pet. I won't...I won't complain or...or try to stop you...no matter what you want to do with her."

"*You* snatched her?"

She tasted blood at the corner of her mouth. Dabbing at it with her tongue, she nodded.

"What, are you crazy? Our *neighbor's* kid?"

Fear paralyzed her. Had she misread his many references to Zoe and how pretty she was, how pretty her daughter, Samantha, would be when she grew up? Would this only make him angrier? "It—it doesn't matter where she's from if no one knows she's here," she whispered.

Rubbing his chin, he paced to the couch and back. "But now we can't let her go. Ever."

"Do you *want* to let her go?" Tiffany's whole body hurt—her shoulder, head, back and legs—but she was so afraid of what the next few minutes might bring she could scarcely feel it. "You said it was too much risk. Isn't that why you're upset about Rover?"

He didn't answer. "Did anyone see you?" he asked, his tone tempered with caution.

"No one," she said. "I swear it."

Stepping over her, he hurried to the stairs and took them two at a time.

5

Heavy footsteps pounded down the hall. Sam heard them, knew instinctively they weren't Tiffany's. Tiffany wasn't much bigger than she was.

It had to be Colin. He was finally home.

She tried to feel some relief, some of the hope and confidence that had sustained her all afternoon. He'd get her out of here and have his crazy wife committed. That was what she'd told herself. But the longer she sat in her urine-soaked bikini on the wooden floor of a room that had no windows, the more she began to doubt that the help she'd been counting on would arrive. Why was there a mattress in here? And what was that stain in the middle of it?

Sam hadn't ventured close; she didn't really want to know. But avoiding it meant sitting on a hard floor without so much as a blanket or a pillow. And although it had been warm during the day, it was cool in the evenings. Being wet made it worse. She was chilled to the bone.

The bolt slid on the door.

Braced for whatever might happen, she watched Colin open the door and block the empty space with his body.

Taller than Anton, who said he was six feet, Colin had brown eyes and thick, curly dark hair. He had it slicked back and was dressed in a suit. Samantha had often admired him as he came home from work. *My neighbor is* so *hot,* she'd once told Marti on the phone. *You should see him. I hope I have a husband like him someday…*

Are you talking about the guy whose wife has the big boobs?…

That's the one. They're like…the perfect couple.

Colin didn't look so good to her right now, however. He wasn't smiling, as he usually did when they met out on the street. He remained in the doorway, sizing her up in a manner that made her cringe.

"Can I *please* go home?" she asked.

"We'll talk about that later. Get up."

He spoke softly, but his words were nonetheless a command. Aware of the fear causing her to shake, and the embarrassing stench of urine, Sam rose to her feet.

His gaze immediately shifted to the wet spot she'd left on the floor. "You're not potty trained?"

He was being mean. Hugging herself, she rubbed the gooseflesh on her arms. "It—it was an accident. I d-didn't have anywhere to go."

He pointed to the bowl Tiffany had hit her with earlier. "What do you think that's for?"

She didn't answer. It wouldn't matter what she said. He wanted her to feel bad.

"Can you remember to use it next time?" he asked.

She fought to push words past the lump in her throat. "I don't want to pee in that. I just want to go home."

"Sorry, that won't be possible."

Sniffing in an attempt to avoid a complete breakdown, she licked her lips and tasted the salt of her own tears even as she struggled to stifle them. "Why not?"

He surprised her with a bright smile. "We need a new pet."

"P-pet?"

"That's right."

"But…" Her tears fell faster. "I'm not an animal."

"No, you're better in some ways. You can do more than fetch a stick, play dead and roll over, can't you?" He grimaced at the wet mark on the floor. "But we do need to get you trained. And just so you can't say I didn't warn you, I won't tolerate this kind of accident in the future. I'll let it go this time because it's your first day, but if you do it again, you'll go without food or water until I decide otherwise."

Was he serious? Sam gaped at him, wondering if she was having a nightmare. "You can't keep me here."

"That's what they all say."

"Who?"

"You think you're my first? You think I don't know what I'm doing?"

That terrified her more than anything so far. "You don't understand! I'm sick."

"You look fine to me. I mean, you're a little knobby-kneed and flat-chested but you're what, thirteen?"

She nodded.

"That's the perfect age."

"For…"

"Coping. It's amazing what the human psyche can endure. I find the study of it absolutely enthralling. In a few weeks, you'll adjust. You'll probably even start to like it here, to love me as a good pet should."

That would *never* happen. "But I have mono. I'm contagious. That's why I've been home from school."

The glee fled his face. "What did you say?"

"I have no energy, no strength. It's terrible. If you got it, you wouldn't be able to work or—or mow your lawn or—"

"I *have* to work. I belong to a very prestigious law firm. And you don't think a house like this pays for itself, do you?"

"See? You don't want to get mono. It lasts a *long* time."

"The stupid bitch can't even get this right," he muttered.

Sam stepped closer. "You'd better let me go."

"It's too late for that," he snapped and slammed the door as if he feared breathing the same air would be enough to contaminate him.

"Wait!" Sam called after him. She wanted to ask if she could wash up, but she dared not remind him that she was to blame for the mess. "I'm cold. And hungry!"

"You'll live!" His response drifted back to her, and then he was gone.

Sam couldn't prevent the sobs that racked her body. She wanted her mom.

No longer concerned about the stain, she threw herself on the mattress. There were worse things than a stain of questionable origin, worse things that mono, worse things than living with a potential stepdad she didn't like. At least she and Zoe had always had each other, no matter how many times they'd had to relocate, or bail Grandpa out of jail, or go down to the soup kitchen just to stop their stomachs from growling.

Now, even though her mother lived right next door, Samantha had the terrible feeling she'd never see her again.

Colin was expecting the knock when it came. He knew the neighbor girl couldn't go missing without a search. The police would canvas the whole area.

"They're here," he murmured when Tiffany emerged from the kitchen to stand behind him.

Putting the TV remote on the coffee table, he got up and turned to survey the room. Everything was in order. He'd made his wife get dressed and repair her makeup. Then he'd gone back upstairs to drug his new pet. He'd hired a contractor to do some soundproofing in "the pen," as he called it. He'd claimed he was planning to buy a drum set and didn't want the neighbors to be bothered by the noise. But it wasn't as soundproof as he'd hoped. Fortunately, the sleeping pills he'd given Samantha in a glass of juice must've worked because she'd stopped yelling. He hadn't heard from her in more than thirty minutes.

One day soon, she wouldn't dare yell at all….

"What if they want to see me?" Tiffany asked as he started for the door.

Her lip was swollen. But accidents happened. It wasn't as if she'd ever been seen with bumps or bruises, not since he broke her cheekbone with that mug. And she'd had her elective surgeries right after that, so they'd had a good excuse for all the bandages. "Tell them our heads collided."

The knock came again, and her eyes flicked to the door.

"Now go into the kitchen and finish the dishes," he said. "Don't come out unless I call you."

He waited until the water went on in the sink, then he answered the door. But it wasn't the police. It was Sam's mother and the guy she was living with. Which meant the police would be by later. *Great…* The next few days wouldn't be easy, but Colin could be patient when he needed to be. All he had to do was lie low.

"Hi, there." He arranged his expression in a sympathetic frown, feigning surprise at the tear streaks on Zoe Duncan's lovely face. The physical opposite of Tiffany, she was tall and slender with breasts that were barely a C cup. But they were real; he could tell. He could also tell Zoe had been beautiful her whole life because she was so stuck on herself. He'd tried flirting with her once, but she kept talking about his wife as if he might forget he had one, and he resented it. It wasn't up to her to remind him of his wedding vows.

"What's wrong?" he asked. "You seem…upset."

Most of the makeup had been wiped from her eyes. "Have you seen my daughter, Samantha?"

He scratched his head. "No. Why?"

"She—" Her voice broke, and the man beside her—Anton Lucassi, if Colin remembered correctly—touched her elbow. Years older than Zoe, than all of them, he pretended to have a lot more class than he really did. Lucassi was basically a pretentious bastard. Colin didn't like him, either.

"She was gone when we got home from work," he explained. "We can't find her."

"Have you called the police?"

Zoe spoke again. "Yes, we've been on the phone with them for over an hour."

"But it's not time to panic yet. She's only been gone since this afternoon," Anton chimed in. "They figure maybe she ran away."

"She didn't run away," Zoe said.

"Sam recently told her grandfather she was thinking about running away, so we can't rule it out," Anton insisted.

Despite a visible effort to avoid an argument, Zoe succumbed. "Where would she go?"

Anton scowled. "Runaways usually don't have a plan. That's how they end up on the streets."

Lifting her chin, Zoe addressed Colin. "The police are on their way. They plan to look into it. But…we thought we'd ask around ourselves, see if we can develop…some idea as to where she might be."

"I see." Colin rubbed his neck, drawing out his response to make it more believable. "Wow. I'm terribly sorry. I wish I had better news for you. Is it possible she's just at the movies or off with friends?"

Zoe shook her head. "She's not the type to leave home without notifying me—"

"That's not always true," Anton cut in.

She remained resolute. "She would've called me."

"Whatever's going on, she sounds like a great kid," Colin said before they could argue some more.

"She *is* a great kid. And—" Zoe's voice cracked again but she held up a hand to let Lucassi know she'd finish her own sentence "—and she has mono. She's not supposed to exert herself, which only adds to my worry."

"Of course it would. What parent *wouldn't* be rattled?" Colin clucked his tongue in commiseration.

"What about your wife?" Zoe glanced behind him. "Do you think—"

"Tiff?" he broke in. "I doubt she saw anything. She's been inside all day, a little under the weather herself. But I'll definitely check and get back to you if she has."

"Thanks." Anton handed him a card. "Call us anytime, day or night."

"Definitely. Now you've got *me* scared."

Anton tried to lead Zoe away, but she wouldn't budge. "I'm sorry," she said, her eyes brimming with fresh tears. "But would you mind if *I* asked your wife? I—I have to hear her response with my own ears. Otherwise…" She let her words fall off.

Her persistence irritated Colin but he smiled as if he understood. "Right. No stone unturned. I get it. I should've thought of that." He called over his shoulder, "Tiffany, babe, can you come here for a minute?"

"Yes?" She poked her head around the corner.

To him, her busted lip looked obvious, but she was keeping her distance, and he was fairly certain the shifting light from the candles on the mantel made it difficult to see her clearly. In any case, Zoe and her partner didn't react to the injury. "Have you seen the neighbor girl? What's her name…"

Zoe filled in his pause. "Samantha."

"I know Sam," she said. "But…I haven't seen her today. Why? Is something wrong?"

"We hope not," Anton said.

In her eagerness to press her point, Sam's mother stepped forward. "If you run across anything that might help us find her—"

"We'll call, of course," Tiffany said.

Colin rewarded his wife with a smile, but then Tiffany surprised him by continuing the conversation. "What's going on?" she asked.

Any concerned citizen would've asked the same. But Colin didn't want the neighbors conversing with Tiffany. "Don't worry, I'll explain," he said as if he was doing it to save them the grief of having to repeat their story.

"Thanks," they murmured and started to walk away, but Colin called them back.

"If it comes to organizing a search party, please let us know. We'd be happy to participate."

When they thanked him again, he smiled kindly into their grateful faces and shut the door.

"Do you think they bought it?" Tiffany whispered in the ensuing silence.

He grinned. "Hook, line and sinker."

"She won't be contagious forever," Tiffany said, obviously hoping to placate him.

At first he'd been frustrated and disappointed to hear of Sam's illness. He didn't want to risk catching it. But the girl wasn't going anywhere; they had plenty of time. "She's part of the family now," he said. "I can wait."

6

"Hey, I've been trying to reach you. Where the heck have you been?"

Jonathan Stivers immediately recognized the voice of the person he most wanted to avoid. Stifling a curse, he turned from riffling through his messages at the empty receptionist's desk to see Sheridan Cole—Sheridan Granger as of three weeks ago—in her office doorway. With her dark hair pulled into a ponytail and a happy blush to her smooth skin, she looked even prettier than normal. But now that she was married, he didn't want to feel that hitch in his gut anymore.

Unfortunately, there wasn't any way to stop it. That was the reason he'd made himself scarce since she'd returned from her honeymoon. He ran his own business and worked out of his house, so it was possible to keep a safe distance—most of the time. He only helped at The Last Stand when they needed him. He was occasionally based out of their offices, of course, especially because they had volunteers who could take care of any clerical stuff related to The Last Stand's cases. But today he'd waited until five to come in, assuming Sheridan would be gone.

"Sorry, been busy," he said.

"Not with our cases. I've hardly seen you since I got back from Hawaii."

"My real job's getting in the way." Although he didn't mind his pro bono work, he had to take enough paying clients to cover his mortgage and expenses. She knew that. Occasionally, they paid him for his work, but only if the charity could afford it and only when he was putting in as many hours as they did.

But he realized it wasn't what she'd meant.

She folded her arms. "You working on anything interesting?"

He forced his eyes down to his stack of messages so he wouldn't stare at her—or wonder about the nights she spent in her new husband's arms. "A sister searching for her little brother, who was adopted out at birth. A creditor looking to be paid by some loser who's trying to disappear. A bail bondsman who wants my help tracking someone who skipped." He shrugged. "The usual."

"Sounds like you're making the big bucks. And getting popular. Pretty soon you won't have time for us."

Part of him wished that was true. Not that he cared much about money. Beyond having a sufficient amount for his needs, he didn't see the point of chasing the almighty dollar. He'd spend any extra on his pro bono efforts, anyway. He just knew it'd be easier on him if he didn't have to confront Sheridan quite so often, or worry that Skye Willis or Ava Bixby, Sheridan's two partners at The Last Stand, would guess how he felt. They'd know already if they weren't so absorbed in their cases. He'd never met three women more driven by a cause. Of course, they had reason to be driven. But it was their passion for what they were doing that made it impossible for Jonathan to walk out on them. They were making a difference to victims of violent crime every day.

"Yeah, I'm stockpiling a ton of money right now." He eyed a note from Skye that seemed urgent. She'd left three messages on his voice mail, too, which he'd ignored. That was why he'd finally dragged his ass in, hoping to avoid Sheridan, but hoping to see her, too. "I'm not ready to buy a Ferrari just yet, though."

"You'll never buy a fancy car. Even if you had the money, you'd give every last dime to some bum on the street before you ever got to a dealership."

He thumped his forehead. "So *that's* why I'm always broke."

"Exactly," she said with a chuckle. "Too many bums in your life."

"I don't seek them out," he grumbled.

"No, but you *see* them when most people turn a blind eye."

When she said flattering stuff like that, it made him think she cared about him. But four years of working with her had taught him that the way he cared and the way she cared fell into two different categories. "You said you've been trying to reach me?"

"The number of messages I've left on your voice mail should've told you that."

What's going on? Why haven't you responded? That was what she really wanted to know, but he ignored the unspoken question, feigning preoccupation. "So… what's up?"

Her eyes widened at his lack of an apology or even an explanation. "I've just been…missing you. It feels strange to go so long without talking to my best friend."

Friend. It'd be easier if they were enemies. At least then he wouldn't feel guilty about wanting another man's wife. "Yeah, well, you've been busy, too. Catching the man who shot you sixteen years ago. Finding the love of your life. *Marrying* him."

"Do I detect a bit of jealousy?" she asked.

His breath caught in his throat—until her next words revealed what she really meant.

"You'll find the love of your life someday. It always happens when you least expect it."

It had happened to her. She'd gone to Tennessee to uncover the identity of the man who'd shot her when she was in high school and come home engaged to Cain Granger, the brother of the boy who'd been killed in the same incident.

"I'm not in the market for marriage," he said.

She smiled dreamily. "You would be if you knew how great it was."

God, was he going to have to sit through a recital of what she'd found with another man?

"I'll take your word for it. Anyway, I've gotta go. Skye needs me." He crossed to Skye's office, one of four that branched off the reception area. He could hear her on the phone behind the closed door and was relieved that he'd soon have a distraction. But Sheridan spoke before he could escape.

"We've found a log cabin just outside Auburn we're thinking of buying. It'll be perfect for Cain. Plenty of room for his dogs. Lots of space. Mountains."

"That's good." Jonathan wished she'd go back in her office and leave him alone.

"Cain and I are driving up there tonight. Would you like to come along so you can see it? We could have dinner afterward."

He almost laughed out loud. "As much as I'd *love* to see Cain, I'm afraid I have to pass."

Ignoring the confusion on her face, he knocked at Skye's door. She called for him to come in, but he didn't budge when Sheridan said, "You don't like him, do you? That's why you haven't been returning my calls. Cain and I are a package now, but you won't accept him."

Jonathan grimaced. "You don't need me to accept him, Sher. You don't need me at all anymore." Stepping into Skye's office, he shut the door behind him. "What's with the cryptic messages?" he demanded as soon as she looked up.

She cocked an eyebrow. "Hello to you, too."

Pinching the bridge of his nose, he took a deep breath. "Sorry, I'm in a rush."

"Is it something you can cancel?"

"Cancel?" he repeated in surprise. Skye was usually more respectful of his time, especially since he donated so many pro bono hours.

"I need the best. It has to be you," she explained, and he realized that what he'd interpreted as being high-handed actually stemmed from panic.

He held out her message and read it again: *Something's come up. Please, please get in touch with me today—Skye.* "I guess my other commitments aren't so pressing that I have to leave right this minute," he conceded and dropped into one of two bright pink, yellow and orange chairs across from her desk. "What's wrong?"

She pushed whatever she'd been working on aside and rocked back. "A friend of mine called earlier, someone I met at a victims' support group after Burke attacked me the first time."

That was also where she'd met Sheridan and Jasmine, another partner who'd since left Sacramento. "A woman?"

"Yes."

"Who is she? Do I know her?"

"I don't see how you could. Her name's Zoe Duncan. She's never been involved with the charity. I'd actually lost touch with her until this morning. She saw the ad in the *PennySaver* a few weeks ago, recognized my name. She said she'd planned to call for social reasons, but that soon changed."

Skye raked her fingers through her shoulder-length, choppy hair—the result of a recent cut. "Her daughter's missing."

He considered that for a moment. "What happened?"

"She disappeared."

"When?"

"Yesterday afternoon."

"How old is the girl?"

"Thirteen."

"Was she troubled, likely to be a runaway?"

"The age might make you wonder, but she's a straight-A student."

"Smart kids run away, too, Skye."

"Not smart kids who are at home recovering from mono. If she wanted out, she would've waited until she felt better. Besides, there were no serious problems at home."

He ran a finger over his bottom lip. "She was living with her mother, then?"

"Yes."

"What about her father?"

"He was released from prison about three months ago."

Jonathan rested his elbows on his knees. "That's an interesting coincidence. What was he in for?"

"Rape. One count. The woman he attacked was a fifteen-year-old girl. He served thirteen years of a twenty-year sentence."

An ugly suspicion stole over him. "Don't tell me…"

"Yes, Zoe was his victim. That's how she got pregnant with Sam."

His jaw dropped. *"She had the kid?"*

"Yep."

The shock inherent in this information finally enabled him to push his encounter with Sheridan to a corner of his mind. "Holy shit!"

"Exactly."

"I'm guessing she testified against him."

"You guessed right."

"Makes you wonder if this asshole got out, did a little research and swiped the kid for revenge."

Skye picked up the photograph of her husband and two children prominently displayed on her desk and gazed down at it. "Yes, it does."

"Does Zoe know he's loose?" he asked.

"She didn't mention it to me, so…I doubt it. Like most victims, she'd rather not look back."

"It's got to be him."

"It might be. But if so, I'm hoping he just wants to see his daughter, be part of her life. He'd have to know Zoe wouldn't be friendly to the idea. Maybe the desire was so strong it forced him to take drastic action."

"Either way, sounds like a good place to start looking." He rose to his feet. "I'm assuming the police have already been notified?"

"They have and they're taking this seriously because of her age, but they're not completely convinced we're dealing with an abduction."

"We just came up with at least two reasons she's more likely to be a kidnap victim than a runaway."

"Yeah, well, I didn't tell you that her grandfather isn't much of a role model, either. He's been in and out of jail most of Zoe's life for petty crime and drug charges, but he was all she had so she more or less hung on to him. While he was going through Sam's belongings this morning, the detective assigned by Rocklin PD came across a letter she'd written to her grandpa last week but hadn't mailed."

"And…"

"In it, she talks about how much she hates Anton Lucassi."

"Who is…"

Skye drew a deep breath. "The man they're living with. Zoe's fiancé."

"Has anyone spoken to the grandfather to see if he has the girl?"

"Zoe hasn't been able to get hold of him. She's left several messages, but he's living in L.A., so it's not as if she can easily drive over and check."

Jonathan moved to the window and stared out at the parking lot. "What does Zoe have to say about the letter?"

"She claims Sam might not have been enthralled with Lucassi, but they didn't have a *bad* relationship."

"Meaning no abuse."

"I spelled that out with her. Yes."

"Have you met him?"

"No. But according to Zoe he's very nice. He owns a tax-preparation company and treats her better than any of the other jerks she's hooked up with over the years."

That didn't necessarily mean anything. "Does he have a record?"

"Not even a speeding ticket." She cleared her throat. "So…are you interested in helping out? I'll pay you as much as you need on this one, Jon."

He refused the promise of money. He knew it was always in short supply at TLS. Sometimes he helped with the fund-raising that kept their doors open. "I'm fine for now. I'll let you know when they're about to repossess my car."

She smiled for the first time since he'd walked into her office. "That old hunk of junk? No one would bother with it."

"Hey, it runs," he said. "My clients might think I'm overcharging if I had a fancy ride."

"Who would ever believe you overcharge? You hardly even remember to bill."

"Because I don't have any clerical support."

"Because you're not concerned about money." She sobered quickly. "So…are you on board for this?"

He adjusted the blinds. "Why not?"

"Thanks, Jonny." Coming to her feet, she circled the desk to hand him a sticky note. "Here's the name and last-known whereabouts of the ex-con."

"Franky Bates," he read. "Wasn't the killer in *Psycho* named Bates?"

She was too preoccupied to respond to his trivia question. "I called Lancaster, where Franky served his time, just to get a feel for what he was like as an inmate."

"And…"

"He found God while he was in prison."

Jonathan rolled his eyes. "Most of them do. But the devil's still their best friend the minute they get out."

Skye shifted some files so she could sit on the corner of her desk. "Zoe's beside herself. I really hope we can help before…"

She didn't need to finish her sentence. *Before it's too late.* That was what they always hoped. "I'll have to talk to her."

"Of course." Twisting around to grab her message pad, Skye held it out to him. "I've got her address and phone number right here. Why don't you put it in your database?"

He stored practically every piece of information he came across in the BlackBerry he pulled from the front pocket of his jeans. It was the only possession he prized because it facilitated almost everything he did. He figured he didn't need a secretary as long as he had his personal digital assistant and a good computer at home.

After recording Zoe's phone numbers and address, he gave the pad back to Skye. "Okay, I'll do what I can."

She followed him to the door. "What will you tell Zoe about the likelihood of finding Sam alive?"

"I hope I don't have to tell her anything."

"I avoided a direct answer, but I know she'll ask you the same question."

He hesitated with his hand on the knob. "It's been more than twenty-four hours, Skye. If Samantha was abducted by a stranger—and in this case, I think her rapist father qualifies, despite your optimistic father-daughter–bonding scenario—you and I both know it looks grim. It's probably over already. But I can promise to go after whoever took her."

Skye gripped his forearm. "Zoe's been through so much. I can't stand the thought of her hearing that."

"Then I'll tell her the sooner I get the information I need, the better Sam's chances will be."

"Thank you."

Keeping his head down to avoid another encounter with Sheridan, he walked out of the office. But once he reached his car, he sat behind the wheel, wondering whether he should go back in and apologize. If he couldn't have Sheridan in a romantic sense, he wished their relationship could be the way it was before she'd gone to Tennessee.

"Yeah, her husband would like that," he muttered and put the sticky note Skye had given him on his rearview mirror. A young girl's life could be in danger. It was time to forget his own stupid problems.

7

A tall, thin woman much younger than he'd expected, and prettier too, answered Jonathan's knock almost as soon as he'd lifted his hand. Wearing a brown-and-blue sweat suit and fleece-lined slippers but no makeup, she swayed in the opening as if she'd dashed for the door at first sign of a visitor without taking time to find her balance. Obviously she'd hoped to see someone else on her doorstep, presumably someone with her daughter in tow.

"Ms. Duncan?"

"Yes?"

"I'm Jonathan Stivers." He provided his business card. "Skye Willis from The Last Stand sent me over to talk to you about Sam."

Before she could speak, a man came up behind her. "Zoe, damn it, what are you doing? You know I would've gotten it. You're supposed to be lying down."

The dark smudges beneath her eyes—amber-colored eyes that matched the golden brown of her long hair and would've been downright stunning if they weren't so flat and hollow with pain—testified to the fact that she needed rest. But Jonathan knew there wasn't any point in trying to force her. She *couldn't* sleep. She was in the numb aftermath of tragedy—a place where people moved and breathed but had stopped *living*.

Resisting his efforts to guide her back to wherever she'd been "resting," she tucked her hair behind her ears and opened the door wider. "Thank God you're here. Please, come in."

"Let me handle it," the man said.

Jonathan wanted to believe this was Zoe Duncan's father or brother. The age difference should've suggested such a relationship. But body language identified Mr. "I'll Take Over" as the live-in lover Samantha Duncan hadn't liked: Anton Lucassi.

"Zoe?" Lucassi pressed.

A spark of emotion lit her pale face. "No, Anton! *I'll take care of it.*"

Clearly unhappy with this response, Anton shook his head. "You're going to wind up in the hospital. And then what good will you be to Sam?"

As far as Jonathan was concerned, they could argue later. "You're…"

"Zoe's fiancé," the man said.

Just as he'd suspected. "Great. Mr. Lucassi." He smiled. "Let's not worry about a nap right now, okay? We need to focus on the problem at hand. Could you both take a few minutes to sit down with me?"

A muscle twitched in Lucassi's cheek. He didn't like being overridden but eventually gave a curt nod and led them into a living room decorated in white and black with several art deco sculptures. It reminded Jonathan more of a high-rent office than a living room.

"Can I get you a drink?" Zoe asked. Her offer was polite, automatic, an attempt at normalcy. But Jonathan could sense how fragile she was. He had the impression her composure might shatter at any moment. And Lucassi wasn't helping. Although he was clearly doing his best, the friction between them was as apparent as her desperation.

"No, thanks." Jonathan seated himself on an expensive-looking leather couch. Taking a small recorder from his pocket, he situated it on the glass coffee table in front of him. "Do you mind if I record our conversation?"

"I'd rather you didn't," Anton said.

Jonathan felt his eyebrows slide up. "Is there a reason?"

Lucassi selected a chair opposite the leather couch. "I'm worried about Sam and what this is doing to Zoe. But everyone knows that in a situation like this, those closest to the girl are always the first to be investigated. I was the last person to talk to her, and found her gone. I'm guessing that I'm going to become a suspect at some point. And that makes me nervous."

"*Did* you harm Sam?" Jonathan asked point-blank.

Lucassi rocked back. "Absolutely not!"

"Then relax and let me do my job. I was a cop here in Sacramento for six years before I hung out my own shingle. I've been through this a few times, and I've learned it's best to record conversations that could reveal important information so I don't lose any of it. It also helps to be able to watch the expressions of the people who are speaking, which is difficult to do while I'm writing."

Anton shifted uncomfortably. "In case they're lying."

"Yes. But if you're not lying, you don't have to worry."

"There's been more than one innocent man sent to prison."

"I'm not trying to pin this on anyone." Jonathan held his gaze. "All I care about is finding Samantha."

Lucassi blinked, then nodded, and Jonathan scooted forward. "I'm here to help you, okay?"

Zoe Duncan perched on the edge of her seat, her back straight, hands folded in her lap. "Don't listen to Anton. He's just…we're both so…frightened and confused."

"I understand." What was this beautiful young woman doing with a man like Lucassi? *He treats her better than any of the other jerks she's hooked up with over the years,* Skye had said. Considering Lucassi's condescending manner, those previous relationships must've been bad indeed. Jonathan couldn't have tolerated someone like Lucassi for five minutes. "For the record, could you both state your full names and birthdates?"

"Zoe Elizabeth Duncan. September 13, 1980."

Nineteen-eighty. That meant she was Jonathan's age. Briefly, he tried to imagine a girl in his sophomore class as a rape victim, having a baby at fifteen or sixteen—and keeping it. They'd been mere kids at sixteen. To top it all off, Zoe hadn't had the support system he'd enjoyed. Knowing what he did about her father, he wondered how she'd gotten by in those early years.

But now wasn't the time to ask. He turned his attention to Lucassi. "And you, sir?"

"Anton Kenneth Lucassi. November 1, 1965."

Fifteen years between them. Jonathan would've guessed at least that much. "Mr. Lucassi, you mentioned you were the last to talk to Zoe's daughter, and the first one home. Could you tell me what happened yesterday?"

"I called Sam over lunch to see how she was. She said she was fine and—"

"Wait a second." Jonathan held up a hand. "Over *lunch?* Yesterday was Monday. Why wasn't she in school?"

"She has mono," Zoe explained. "She's been out of school for over a week."

"I see."

"So both of us have been checking on her quite often," Anton continued. "But about three hours after I talked to her, Zoe called me at the office, worried because she couldn't reach her."

"Where were you?" he asked Zoe.

"Work."

"This was about three o'clock?"

"That's right," Lucassi said. "She asked me to come home and check on her."

"Which you did."

"Reluctantly," he admitted. "I couldn't imagine that anything bad had happened to her. This is a nice neighborhood, you know? But when I got here—" he shook his head helplessly "—she was gone."

Jonathan crossed his ankles and leaned back, hoping to encourage Zoe and Lucassi to relax by appearing relaxed himself. "And you, Ms. Duncan? When was the last time you saw your daughter?"

"Before work yesterday. I went in to her bedroom to say goodbye, as I always do."

"Where do you work?"

She began digging at her thumb cuticle. "I used to work at Tate Commercial, but I don't anymore. I quit yesterday."

"When you found out your daughter was missing?"

"No. Before. Sort of," she corrected. "I couldn't reach her. I was distraught. My temper got out of hand."

"I see." So she was feistier than she seemed in this zombielike state. "Has your daughter ever taken off on her own?"

"No."

Lucassi made a noise of disagreement. "Zoe, tell him everything."

She covered her face as if trying to compose herself. But it didn't make any difference. Tears spilled over her lashes when she dropped her hands. "She got angry when I decided to move in with Anton because it meant we had to give up her dog."

"She took off running down the street, and we had to chase her in the car," Lucassi added.

"Where was she going?" Jonathan asked.

"Nowhere." It was Zoe who answered. "She was…running because she was upset. Any child would be upset over losing her dog."

"She said she'd rather live on the street than let Peanut go." Lucassi again.

Zoe wiped her tears. "But once I explained to her what this move meant to us, she eventually calmed down."

"But she talked about running away again, in a note to her best friend," Lucassi said.

Skye had mentioned only the letter to the grandfather. "Where did you find this?"

"In her backpack."

"But you don't think she was serious."

Lucassi shrugged. "Who can say? It's possible. I wasn't aware of how she felt about me."

Had he cared enough to notice? "And how did she feel about you?"

"We had Marti Seacrest over last night. That's her best friend, her only close friend. Sam hasn't been at this school very long, and at first, she was pouting over the dog so she refused to acclimate. Anyway, when we showed Marti the note, she finally admitted that Samantha was always complaining about how…uptight I am."

"Do you consider yourself uptight?" Jonathan asked.

"Of course not." He nudged Zoe's knee. "Would you say I'm uptight?"

When she stared at him without answering, he frowned. "I'm not uptight. Sam just wasn't used to having any rules." He turned to Jonathan and lowered his voice as if confiding a great secret. "They've always lived in dumps, so they've never had to worry about taking care of personal property."

"At least she could keep her dog in those *dumps*," Zoe said.

"You're blaming me for the dog? You're the one who wanted to move in here. You liked the schools, the neighborhood."

Anger flared in her eyes. "You forced me to choose."

"And you made the right choice. Her education is more important than keeping a dog in the house, with all that hair and the *smell*." He wrinkled his nose. "The dog's fine, by the way," he added. "I made sure it went to a good home."

"I still don't understand why Peanut couldn't have lived in the backyard," she said.

"Because we have landscaping back there. And the damn thing wouldn't quit barking."

Jonathan coughed discreetly. "Can we move on?" They fell silent, and he continued. "In what condition did you find the house when you arrived home yesterday, Mr. Lucassi?"

The two exchanged sulky glances but stopped bickering. "No different than it is now," he said.

As far as Jonathan could tell, there wasn't so much as an out-of-place magazine or a gum wrapper to disturb the pristine cleanliness. He couldn't imagine a child living in such a mausoleum; it wasn't any surprise to him that a dog would be out of the question. But that was none of his business. "Were any of the doors open? Was the shower running, the TV on? Did you notice anything at all? Describe the scene for me."

Growing more agitated, Lucassi rubbed his hands back and forth on the arms of his chair as he spoke. "The doors were all closed and locked, except the one leading to the pool. She'd been tanning when I called, so I walked outside, expecting her to be asleep on the chaise. Instead I found the iPod we gave her for Christmas, a towel and a book."

"Any food?"

"Food?"

"A brand of soda you might not have purchased? A Starbucks coffee cup even though Sam hates coffee? Anything like that to indicate she might've had a guest?"

"Nothing."

Nothing wasn't helpful. Stifling a sigh, Jonathan stood. "Would the two of you walk me through the house?"

Lucassi jumped to his feet, but Zoe said, "*I'll* do it."

Her fiancé might've argued with her about that, too, but the phone rang. Glancing at a set of double doors that probably led to a den of some sort, he nodded and went to answer while Zoe took Jonathan out to the pool through the kitchen.

"You have a nice place," he said as they stepped onto the patio.

"That's what I thought," she said. "I saw what Sam never had, what I wanted to give her—the success, the better schools, the safe environment." She laughed bitterly. "The safe environment," she repeated on a little sob.

He touched her arm to gain her full attention. "This isn't your fault. It could've happened anywhere."

Her throat worked as she swallowed. "But it wasn't *supposed* to happen here. That's why I went along with giving up Peanut."

"I know," he said.

She took a deep breath. "Will you level with me?"

A warning prickle traveled down his spine. He knew what she was going to ask and didn't want to answer that particular question. "I'll be as honest as I can," he hedged.

"It's been over twenty-four hours. What're our chances? Will we ever find my daughter alive?"

Squinting into the setting sun, he studied the pool area. He needed some detail, some clue. Soon. If Sam had been abducted, her chances dwindled with every passing minute. "That depends on a lot of factors."

"Like…"

It was his turn to draw a deep breath. "Do you think it's possible the man who raped you might've taken her for revenge?"

What little color she had in her face drained away. "No! He's in prison."

Far from eager to dispel that assumption, Jonathan cleared his throat. "Not anymore."

She gaped at him for several seconds. "He's out? *Already?*"

"It's been almost thirteen years. That's actually better than the average."

She shook her head. "He doesn't even know about her."

"Could he have found out? From a friend of your father's perhaps?"

"No."

"What about your mother?"

"She's never been part of my life."

"How did Franky know you in the first place?"

"He didn't. Not really. Anyway, I don't want to go into it. He's not aware Sam exists, okay? Please don't mention it again." She glanced over her shoulder, then lowered her voice. "Anton doesn't know. No one does, except my father, and only because I was fifteen and living with him at the time. Sam thinks her dad died in a car accident before she was born. I—I wouldn't want her ever to learn the truth. She might assume that—" she broke down, the sentiment she was trying to express too painful "—that maybe I didn't want her." Bringing a hand to her chest, she continued to force words through tears. "It might make her doubt…my love…or think she's…not as good as—" she sniffed, struggling to go on "—other girls…or some craziness like that… you know?"

Jonathan had no idea what made him do it. Probably the rawness of her need. But the next thing he knew, he had her in his arms and couldn't let go because she was clinging to him and sobbing quietly into his shoulder.

"We'll find her," he whispered. "You've gotta hang on for her sake."

It didn't matter that they'd just met. Empathy made the physical contact seem completely natural—until Lucassi stepped outside.

"Do you comfort all your clients with such tenderness?" he asked.

Jonathan felt Zoe go stiff. When she pulled away, she seemed to stagger, and he wished he could've consoled her for a few minutes more. At the same time, he could understand why Lucassi might not like what he'd seen. "Only those who aren't getting it elsewhere," he said and strode to the side of the pool.

"Ask for anything you need and stay as long as you'd like," Zoe said. Then she must've gone inside, because when he turned back, Lucassi was standing on the patio alone.

8

Colin hovered at the window, peeking through the blinds, just as he'd done for much of the previous night. Watching the activity at the Lucassi household proved fascinating, better than anything he could've anticipated. Loath to miss a single thing, he'd had trouble making himself go to work today and had hurried home as soon as possible. He'd never been this close before, never been able to witness firsthand the chaos caused by his actions.

Technically, in this instance, they were *Tiffany's* actions. But she'd taken Samantha for *him,* and he wasn't unhappy about it. He wasn't even worried about Rover anymore. If Rover had been capable of revealing any damaging details, the cops would've knocked on his door already. The only police officer Colin had seen was the investigator who'd stopped by earlier this evening to ask if he'd seen Samantha Duncan.

"What's going on?" Tiffany asked.

The television blared behind him. Colin spoke over the actors' voices. "Someone's over there."

"Another cop?"

"No."

"Probably a friend or family member. People have been coming and going all day, bringing food and being supportive." She smiled as if she shared his enthusiasm for the drama playing out next door, but he knew she didn't. Fortunately, he didn't care. She did what he needed her to do. What did it matter whether she liked it or not?

"Any of the neighbors stop over?" he asked.

"A few, why?"

He leaned against the wall, hoping to catch a glimpse of the people inside the Lucassi house. "Zoe moved in a couple months after we did. I didn't think she knew anyone well enough to have them gather round her. She's certainly never been very warm with us."

"She hasn't been unfriendly."

"She's been a cold, aloof bitch, and don't try to tell me differently. I've barely been able to get her to say two words to me the entire time she's lived there."

Tiffany seemed torn as to how to respond but ultimately backed off from whatever she'd been tempted to say. "I'm sure the neighbors are sympathetic because of the situation. And Anton's been living here a lot longer."

"Who else came by?"

"His pastor, his parents, his secretary."

He'd expected her to say something like, "A man in a white SUV, a lady in a red Audi." "How would you know his pastor from his tailor?"

"I could hear Anton talking as he walked people to their cars."

Straightening, Colin folded his arms. "You were close enough to hear *that?*"

"I was out front, weeding. I figured since I was home I might as well do some yard work."

Appearances mattered. The neighbors were less likely to pay attention to them if they kept the place up. But he'd made Tiffany call in sick for a reason. "If I didn't want the nosy busybodies at that nursing home making a big deal about your lip, what makes you think I want the neighbors to see it?"

Uncertainty flickered in her eyes. She was so powerless against him. It turned him on, made him want to take what she'd offered last night. But ever since he'd learned about Samantha, he'd been too preoccupied to even touch Tiffany.

Later, he promised himself. There was always later. That was the great thing about marrying someone like her, someone overlooked by others, someone whose gratitude for his love made her more loyal than a dog. She'd never leave him, no matter what he did.

"No one saw my face," she said. "I kept my head down the whole time, didn't speak to anyone." She gave a little laugh. "I don't think they realized I was there. They were too concerned about Samantha."

Irritation combined with arousal to make his muscles tense. But the activity next door was more exciting than the prospect of a bondage session with his wife, so he let it go. For now. "Who do you think is driving that old Mercedes sitting out front? That piece of shit's got five hundred thousand miles on it if it's got ten."

She went to the window on the other side of the fireplace and peered through the blind. "I've never seen that car before. It wasn't there earlier."

"The driver's maybe six-two, around two hundred pounds. Athletic build. Definitely needs a haircut."

She raised both palms. "Doesn't ring a bell."

The man he'd just described suddenly walked through the gate, coming from the backyard of Lucassi's house. "There he is!" Colin whispered, and Tiffany, who'd started to turn away, changed direction.

"Could he be a detective?" she asked, squinting out at him.

Colin made a noise of disgust. "You were here when the investigator showed up last night, Tiff. You know what he looks like."

"But…there could be others, couldn't there? Maybe the police put together a task force."

"Not this fast—especially when they still think she might be a runaway."

"Shows what they know."

"What's that supposed to mean?"

"She wouldn't run away from a mother who loves her that much."

He didn't react to the wistful note in her voice. Tiffany had never been loved by anyone. Her mother, shot to death five years ago by Tiffany's brother, had been an even worse bitch than his own mother. His mother used to beat him on a regular basis, but Tiffany's had ignored her. After seeing that neglect take its toll through all the years they'd gone to school together in Modesto, he'd decided extreme indifference was worse than abuse, at least abuse that stopped short of permanent physical damage. "They don't know Zoe. And neither do you. My mother made sure no one ever saw my bruises. Maybe Zoe's the same way. Maybe she's not nearly as nice as you want to believe."

"She's nice," Tiffany insisted.

The phone rang, but he didn't move. Tiffany would answer it. She did anything she could to make his life more comfortable. That was the price she paid for being wanted.

"Hello?"

He listened with half an ear while watching the man outside search the ground. Then Lucassi's guest looked in his direction, and he jumped away from the window. Colin doubted he could be seen; regardless, he wasn't about to take the chance.

"Colin?" Tiffany said.

He didn't want to be bothered. "What?"

"Tommy needs to talk to you. He said you never called to tell him what time to come over tonight."

Torn by his fascination with his neighbor's guest and the obligation to respond to his friend, he hesitated. Realizing he wouldn't be able to figure out the identity of the guy next door simply by spying, he walked over to accept the handset. "'Lo?"

"Hey, man, what's up?"

"Nothin'."

"We playin' poker tonight?"

Colin had never revealed any of his pets to his buddies and he wasn't about to start now. But he was willing to have some fun with Tiffany, maybe even let *them* have some fun with her. They talked about her hot body, what she'd become since he'd married her, as if they dreamed about her all the time. But if they came over, he'd have to account for her busted lip. And if the drugs they'd given Samantha wore off and she started screaming again, the noise could be difficult to explain.

With all the activity next door, it was too risky. "No, I'm swamped. I had to bring home a shitload of work."

"You sure you can't carve out an hour? I rented the best porno you've ever seen, man. I know James will get off on it big-time."

"Not tonight."

Disappointment filled a short pause, but Tommy tried to cover it. "Okay, no problem."

"You can come over on Friday," Colin said. By then things should be safe enough to party. "And I'll have better entertainment than a damn movie."

"What's better than a skin flick?" Tommy said with a laugh.

"Actual *skin,*" he replied. "You bring pizza and beer, have James bring the rest of that baggie he's been saving and I'll provide the fun."

Tiffany was staring at him when he hung up. He could sense her misgivings, but he didn't care. She'd enjoy herself. He'd make his friends beg for her, do anything she asked, let her be in charge. By the time it was all over, she'd probably ask if they could do it again.

"What?" he said, challenging her stare.

She ducked her head. "Nothing."

He went back to the window. He could no longer see the man poking around next door, but the old Mercedes was still at the curb.

Who the hell was this guy? Something about him put Colin on edge. He was younger than the detective Colin had met, and he seemed so…intense. Determined. "There's *no* way anyone can trace Sam to our place, is there?" He'd asked before, but he wanted to make sure Tiffany was telling him everything.

"*None,*" she said. "She came over on her own."

"Did anyone see her?"

"I don't think so. But even if someone did, all we have to do is say she left a few minutes after she stopped by. Just because she was here doesn't mean we did anything to her. We don't have criminal records or any motivation that they know of. You're an up-and-coming real estate attorney. I have a respectable job. We have excellent credit. We keep our place clean. They'd need more than a brief sighting of her going in our house to get a search warrant, wouldn't they?"

She was only repeating what he'd told her in the past, but she was right. They'd need a damn good reason to search his home.

But that guy next door *bothered* Colin.

"When's the last time you checked on Sam?" he asked.

"I fed her before you got home."

He twisted around to arch an eyebrow at her. "What'd you give her?"

She answered so low Colin couldn't make out the words.

"*What* did you feed her?" he asked again, letting her know by his tone that she'd better speak more clearly.

Her sheepish expression made her seem almost child-like, especially with that busted lip. "The leftovers from last night."

He propped his hands on his hips. "*My* food?"

"You don't like to eat the same meal two days in a row."

"But that's not what she's supposed to get. This isn't some damn luxury hotel."

"I—I didn't know if I should feed her the same stuff I did Rover or…or if she was going to be a different kind of pet."

"I like dogs best," he said.

"So…you want me to feed her the rest of what we have in the garage?"

"Of course. Why waste it?" He went back to the window. It was getting dark. Once the light went on in Lucassi's kitchen, Colin could see Mr. Lucassi speaking to his guest. Where was the pretty Zoe? "When it's gone, let me know and I'll buy another bag," he added.

Tiffany perched on the edge of the couch. "Okay."

"She feeling any better?"

"I couldn't tell. She didn't say much. When I brought the food, she asked if she could go home. That's all she ever asks. When I told her no, she rolled over and went to sleep."

"She didn't eat?"

"Not a bite."

"She'll be sorry for that." Colin could no longer see anyone in Lucassi's kitchen. They'd moved to another room, out of range.

Giving up his vigil, he decided to go upstairs and look in on his new pet. Now that his friends weren't coming over, he'd have some time to train her.

Samantha's room was spotless. Her clothes hung in color-coded groups in the closet, with her shoes neatly paired below. The bed was made, her drawers were neat, her jewelry rested inside a wooden jewelry box on the dresser. The only juvenile aspect in this room was the bulletin board that leaned against the dresser mirror. Jonathan guessed Lucassi had refused to let her hang it on the wall. A man so concerned with objects wouldn't want to hammer an extra hole in the Sheetrock simply to display what he would consider "junk."

Pausing in front of the bulletin board, Jonathan examined the items he found there: photographs of Samantha with another young girl, Samantha at Disneyland with an older man who had a Sam Elliott mustache, Samantha with her mother. There were pictures of Sam and Zoe with Lucassi, too, but they were positioned so that Lucassi didn't show. It could've been inadvertent, but Jonathan thought it probably wasn't. Hiding Lucassi's image revealed Sam's desire to erase him from her life.

"See? There's nothing in here." Lucassi spoke from where he'd taken a seat at the girl's desk, which held one schoolbook and a sheet of paper with yesterday's date written above answers to several algebra problems. There were undoubtedly more personal items in the drawers—she had to put her stuff *somewhere*—but this book was the only item out of place in the whole house. Obviously,

Samantha had spent some time studying before going out to the pool.

"Who's this?" He held up the picture of Sam with the older man.

"That's her grandpa, Ely Duncan. And if you haven't figured out from that ridiculous mustache and all those tattoos, he's not like most grandparents."

"How's he different?" Jonathan had heard a little already, but he wanted to see what Lucassi had to say on the subject.

"He's an old biker, has a record, can't seem to keep himself out of jail."

"Does he care about Sam?"

"I don't think he cares about anyone but himself, or he would've given Zoe a better childhood."

"He cares."

Zoe stood in the doorway, her face freshly washed, her hair in a ponytail. She was trying to rally. "He's just—" she searched for words "—too dysfunctional to live life any differently."

Jonathan brought the picture closer, studying the hard-bitten man who was Zoe's father. "Where is he now?"

"L.A."

"If he's not in jail somewhere else. She hasn't heard from him since she moved in with me," Lucassi added.

"He's not in jail," Zoe said. "Detective Thomas, who's been assigned to Sam's case, has already checked into it. He's even had someone from the Los Angeles police go by the trailer, but…so far, nothing. No one knows where he's at."

Jonathan spoke to Zoe. "How many months has it been since you've had contact?"

"About nine."

"Is that normal?"

She motioned as if to say it was as normal as not. "Communication between us has been spotty for years. But this is longer than usual." She paused. "We got into an argument last summer."

"Over…"

"He wanted Sam to stay with him for a week so he could take her to Disneyland."

"He's taken her there before, I see."

She inclined her head. "Once. Two years ago. I was there, too."

"You refused to let her go again?"

"I refused to let her travel to southern California alone. I didn't trust him to provide a safe environment. And—" she paused again "—I was starting a new job, so I couldn't go with her."

Considering what'd happened to Zoe while she was in the care of this biker dude, keeping Sam home made sense. "Have you notified him about this?"

"I've left messages. Several, in fact. I…haven't received a response."

"He's probably lying in an alley, on a drunken binge."

Jonathan ignored Lucassi. "And this is Sam's best friend, Marti?" He pointed to another photograph.

"That's right."

"Can you give me her parents' contact information? I'd like to talk to her, with their consent."

"Of course." She knew the girl's address and telephone number by heart. She dictated it to him, and he recorded it in his BlackBerry.

"If it helps, the police have already questioned her," she said. "She claims Samantha wasn't acting any differently and that she hadn't met anyone new, that she would never run away."

"Have the police canvased the neighborhood?"

She nodded. “This afternoon.”

“No one saw anything,” Lucassi said. “It’s as if she just…disappeared.”

“The gate was standing open when you found her gone.” Jonathan had asked about that when they were out back.

“That’s right.”

“She didn’t disappear,” he said. “Either she walked away, or she knew her abductor and welcomed him in.”

“What makes you so sure?”

“She wasn’t dragged out of here.”

“She wouldn’t walk away,” Zoe said.

Jonathan agreed. That was what scared him. Sam’s actions weren’t consistent with those of a runaway. There’d been no inciting event. She hadn’t confided in her best friend or packed a single item of clothing. Beyond that, she’d been ill, and had been doing her homework. If she was planning to take off, why would she bother completing her school assignments?

But if she knew and trusted her abductor, the culprit was more likely her derelict grandfather or her mother’s self-righteous boyfriend.

Jonathan pinned his hopes on Ely Duncan. If it was Anton Lucassi, a man who could sit in her room and pretend such concern without a flicker of regret, Sam was already dead.

9

"So what do you think?" Skye's voice sounded tinny as it came through the phone.

Jonathan stood in the kitchen of the two-bedroom, two-bath fixer-upper he'd bought off Broadway. The house had potential, but it'd been thirteen months since he'd taken ownership, and he still hadn't found time to make a single improvement. Because he usually worked while he ate, his kitchen had become more of an office than the spare bedroom, where he had an old desk and all his files. "I don't think it's the rapist father."

"Why not?"

Jonathan's dog, an Akita named Kino, nudged his hand, demanding attention. The woman next door dog-sat while he worked; Akitas required a lot of social interaction and wasn't a good breed to leave home alone for long periods of time. But Ronnie, short for Veronica, had to go to San Francisco today, so Kino had been cooped up and was eager to go out.

Jonathan planned to take him for a walk, even though it was nearly eleven. But first he wanted something to eat. "Chill out for a second," he told the dog before returning to his conversation. "Sam *knew* whoever it was."

"So there was no sign of a struggle," Skye was saying.

"None." He rummaged through his refrigerator. "And since she believes her father was killed in a car accident, I don't think she'd welcome some stranger who claimed to be dear old dad."

"I wondered how Zoe had handled the story of Sam's conception, but I didn't want to pry."

Jonathan tossed two of three to-go containers in the trash because the food had gone bad, found the leftovers from last night and put them in the microwave. He wasn't in the mood for lasagna, but he didn't dare trust anything else in his fridge—except maybe the ketchup, mustard and pickles. "She's kept a very tight lid on it. Only her father knows."

"Anton doesn't?"

If Skye had met him, she wouldn't be surprised. "No. And Zoe didn't act as if she wanted him to learn."

"The more people who know, the greater the chance Sam will find out."

He bent to watch the food turning on the carousel. "But if you can't trust the man you love, what does that say for your relationship?"

"Maybe they're not that close."

"They're *engaged.*"

"Engaged doesn't seem to mean as much as it used to."

Crossing his arms, he leaned against the counter. "I doubt she'd tell him even if she married him. I think she's afraid he'd look down on her. Or hold it over her head. She doesn't want to give him that much power." He took his food out, but it was still cold so he put it in for another two minutes. "Or maybe it's just that he already has no respect for her father. Knowing what happened on Ely Duncan's watch would only make that worse."

"Sam could've opened the door to Franky," Skye argued. "Some kids will open the door to anyone. They don't realize how dangerous it is. They've been taught to be polite, so they respond to any knock with a smile."

"The front door was locked when Lucassi came home. It was the back gate that stood open."

"So what's your point?"

Feeling the effects of another fifteen-hour day, Jonathan glanced at the coffeemaker. He'd never sleep if he succumbed to the temptation, but...until then he could use the caffeine boost. "I think it's more likely to be Lucassi than Franky."

"But he has no criminal record."

"That doesn't mean he didn't do it. If it was a stranger, she would've screamed for help. It's reasonable to expect that *someone* would've heard her. The next-door neighbor was home all day." Purposely ignoring the blinking light on his answering machine—probably calls on his other cases that he no longer had time to worry about—he picked up the photo of Sam that Zoe had given him.

"He certainly would've had the opportunity," she agreed.

"If someone was taking her by force, if she tried to get away, there should've been a chair or table knocked askew." He held the picture closer, studying the missing girl. "Her drink wasn't even spilled. And whoever took her wasn't interested in her iPod. It was right on the table, in plain sight."

"Okay, so maybe you have to take a closer look at Lucassi. But you can't eliminate Franky Bates as a possible suspect."

"If I spend the next few days tracking down this ex-con and it's a false lead, we've lost a lot of valuable time. You know what they say about the first forty-eight." He thought of Zoe, how beautiful and fragile she was and, oddly, how good she'd felt in his arms. It'd been years since he'd noticed a woman in that way, a woman besides Sheridan, and it made him feel hopeful and creepy at the same time. Zoe was already committed. What was it with him?

"Ignoring Franky is a big risk," Skye said.

He set the picture on a stack of files that represented some of his other cases. "I know. But this business is about risk. I have to follow my gut—and move fast."

"So you think it's Lucassi?"

"Or the grandfather. Sam was on friendly terms with Ely, even though he and Zoe are somewhat estranged."

"Don't tell me Zoe finally wrote off her old man."

"No. Nothing that permanent. She wouldn't allow Sam to visit him alone last summer, for obvious reasons, and it made him mad. That's all." The microwave beeped. He opened the door to remove his dinner—and nearly dropped it when it burned him. "Shit!"

"What's wrong?" Skye asked.

Kino tilted his head, watching him as if to say, "How stupid can you be?"

"What're you looking at?" he grumbled.

"Excuse me?" Skye said with a laugh.

He opened the cardboard lid of the container and waved away the steam. "I'm talking to Kino."

"Jon, you really gotta find a woman."

His mind instantly conjured up an image of Sheridan cuddling with her husband. "I'm too busy."

She lowered her voice, giving it a meaningful inflection. "Now that Sher's married, maybe you can move on."

Jonathan stifled a groan. Apparently, Skye hadn't missed as much as he'd hoped. "I don't know what you're talking about."

"Oh, really? Then what's going on between the two of you?"

He scowled at Kino, who tilted his head in the other direction. "Nothing."

"Jonathan, she's heartbroken."

Did he want to hear this? No. Sheridan couldn't feel any worse than he did.

Getting a fork from the drawer, he poked at his lasagna, but he'd apparently turned it into a substance tougher than rubber.

So much for dinner, he thought, and tossed it in the garbage. "She's happily married. She'll get over it."

"And you?"

He grabbed a piece of bread and motioned his dog toward the door. "I'll get over it, too."

The sound of the lock turning sent Sam scrambling to get under the mattress. If she didn't want Colin to see her in her swimsuit, it was her only option.

She'd heard about men who wanted to touch little girls in inappropriate places. It was all she'd been able to think about since Colin had come into the room last time. Anton called them pedophiles. Her mother called them scum, the lowest of the low. Colin seemed like scum to her. But Sam wasn't sure he was a pedophile. Could pedophiles be handsome young lawyers? Did they have beautiful wives like Tiffany?

Sam had seen part of a news show about older men who got in trouble for trying to hook up with girls her age over the Internet. Some of those men weren't *completely* ugly. She wished she could remember more about it, but she'd instantly put the whole idea out of her mind because she'd been so positive it could never happen to her. Sex was too gross to think about, even with a boy her age. And she hadn't been worried about Internet stalkers. Her mother wouldn't even let her have a MySpace page or go on Facebook.

The door opened and Sam caught a glimpse of a

large dark shape before Colin blinded her by snapping on the light.

"What are you doing trying to hide?" he demanded.

Squinting against the brightness, she watched him come in and lock the door behind him. He had something in his hand....

Her heart dropped. It was a whip!

"Wh-what's that for?" she asked and felt tears immediately fill her eyes.

He caressed the leather handle. "This? Just for fun. Does it look like fun to you?"

"N-no. Not if—if you're going to hit me w-with it."

"That's the good news. Whether or not I use it is entirely up to you."

She pressed her palms into her eyes, trying to stop the tears. She couldn't sit there and blubber like a big baby. She had to convince him to let her go. "How is it—how is it up to me?"

"If you do as I say, I won't be forced to use it."

Oh, no. The lump in her throat grew to the size of a grapefruit. He *was* a pedophile. She could tell by the way he was looking at her, the way he was smiling.

"Please," she murmured. "Just leave me alone. I've never done anything to you. If you let me go, I swear, I-I'll never tell them it was you and Tiffany who...who locked me up. I'll say it was someone else, someone who...who was wearing a mask."

"Right. You'll blab it all as soon as you feel safe."

"I won't!" she said.

"Quit with the bullshit. You're not going anywhere. Now get out from under that mattress and let me take a look at you."

She didn't move. Her skin crawled at the thought of what he might do if he liked what he saw. "Why—why do you want to k-keep me here when you have such a—such a pretty wife?"

"That's a good question. I've asked myself that many times. But…I don't know. I guess it's for the same reason I own a whip. Because it's fun. Now get up!"

"I can't. I'm s-sick. And if—if you come too close—"

"You've already warned me. So let me warn you." He kicked the mattress off her, and she instinctively curled up and tried to disappear into the seam between floor and wall. "If you refuse to respond to a direct command ever again, you won't have to worry about being sick because you'll be dead." He cracked the whip against the wall beside her, and the sound made her cry out.

"Shh," he snapped. "That's the first rule I'm going to teach you. No matter what, you have to be quiet."

Was there a chance anyone would hear her, even if she screamed?

He cracked the whip again. The tail of it flicked so close she could feel the air stir above her head. This time, she was too frightened to voice more than a terrified whimper. But even that was too much.

"I said be quiet!" His voice was a threatening growl.

The whip arced through the air again. Sam was sure it would hit her. She saw it coming and braced for it by covering her head. *Don't make a sound. Don't make a sound….*

She heard it snap and waited for the pain to follow. She didn't see how he could've missed. But he had. Even he seemed surprised by that.

"You're lucky," he said. "My aim's not so good tonight." The leather slipped through his hands as he coiled it back up.

One tear after another streaked down her face. She

couldn't stop them so she didn't try. "Why do you want to hurt me?" she whispered.

"You can't guess the answer to that?"

"No." She shook her head, helpless.

"And here I thought you were smart." His mouth twisted in a mean sort of grin. "I'll give you a hint. It's the same reason I own a whip."

"B-because it's *fun?*" she said, her voice trembling.

"There you go!" He put the whip under one arm so he could clap. "Excellent. You and I will get along fine. I can already tell."

"Colin?" Tiffany interrupted by knocking at the door.

"What do you want?" he hollered back.

"Your father's on the phone."

"Tell him I'll call later."

There was a slight pause. "Are you sure? I was thinking it might be better if he believes you're available, that tonight is like any other night. You know, until the flap dies down. It is late…"

He folded his arms and just stood there for a few seconds, staring at Sam. "Every once in a while she shocks me by proving she has a brain," he said.

Sam didn't respond.

"I shouldn't be in here, anyway. All it does is make me crave what I can't have—not yet."

"Colin?" Tiffany said again.

"I'm coming."

At that point, Tiffany must've left because she didn't speak again. Colin rattled off a list of rules, said Sam would be tested and that she'd better not forget a single one. Then he added a promise that *really* frightened her, more than the whip.

"You've got two weeks to get over…whatever illness it is you have," he said.

"Mono."

"Yes."

"Or what?" she whispered.

He laughed softly. "Do you really want to know?"

"No."

"That's what I thought."

When he was gone, Sam memorized what she'd been told. She didn't want to give Colin any reason to use the whip he thought was so much fun. But, to her relief, the minutes dragged into hours and he didn't come back.

It was late, after midnight, but Zoe couldn't sleep. She sat on the front porch, cradling the cordless phone in her lap and watching the dark street, listening for the sound of her daughter's feet hurrying down the sidewalk or Sam's voice calling out a relieved "Mom!"

But nothing happened. Just like the night before.

At least Anton had gone to bed. Zoe wasn't sure how much more of his companionship she could take. No matter what he said or did, it hit her wrong. Or maybe her irritation came from the odd little resentments that had suddenly sprung up, resentments she hadn't even known she was harboring. Over Sam's dog. Over the way Anton protected himself and his belongings. The house had never felt less like *her* house. Even the way he represented Sam's grandfather bothered Zoe, despite the fact that it was true. *She* could list Ely's faults, but Anton couldn't, not without making her mad.

Zoe wasn't sure if she was fed up, or simply stressed, but it felt a lot like fed up and that complicated *everything*. "Fed up" meant she'd have to leave Anton as she'd left every man who'd come before him….

Where would she go this time? She'd sold her furniture when she moved in. He'd expected her to contribute to the household expenses, which were higher than she'd ever faced in the past, so she turned her entire paycheck over to him every two weeks and had absolutely no savings. She hadn't planned for the worst because he was supposed to be her knight in shining armor, the one man who could be the father she'd always wanted for Sam.

Instead of realizing that dream, she'd stripped herself of her ability to make it on her own. She'd even quit her job.

But she couldn't leave this place, anyway. Not now. Not without her daughter. Just the thought of Sam returning to find her gone sent pain lancing through Zoe's already aching heart.

Tears rolled down her cheeks, but she didn't wipe them away. She was too tired to fight the emotion that welled up. This helplessness was almost as bad as the fear. Zoe felt as if she was sinking in quicksand. She couldn't rush around and search as she would've imagined herself doing—if she'd ever imagined herself in such a situation—because she might miss the knock or call that would bring her daughter home. The moment she left her post, she worried that she should've stayed on guard. Yet, sitting here, she wished she could be out looking, taking aggressive action.

So she remained in limbo, caught between the fear of leaving and the fear of staying—and felt the quicksand rising ever higher.

She stood abruptly and went inside for her keys. If she didn't fight the crippling shock and panic, she was afraid she'd soon be incapable of *anything*. But the ticking of the pendulum clock, the only sound to break the silence in Anton's otherwise still house, reminded her of what her fiancé would think of her driving around at this hour—that she was acting rash, that she was being impetuous not to stick to their original plan. He'd promised her they'd get up at first light, create flyers with Sam's photograph and organize a search party. He'd insisted the police were doing all they could and she should trust Detective Thomas to do his job. The media had already picked up the story and had run a short piece on the news asking anyone who might've seen Samantha to get in touch with the Rocklin Police Department.

But even with all of that, their actions seemed puny against the potential horror. They had to do more. The most random detail might be the one to unravel the mystery.

Praying for added strength, she returned to the rocking chair on the porch without her keys. But in her current state she had no idea how she'd survive until the sun came up.

The smell of a cigarette drew her attention to the house next door. Someone had come out in the few seconds she'd been gone.

Straining to see, she searched for the source of the smoke drifting toward her and spotted her neighbor, Colin, sitting on his front step.

"I didn't know you smoked," she said.

She didn't need to raise her voice. Sound carried easily on the cool night air.

Colin got up and crossed to the split-rail fence that separated their two yards. Dressed in a pair of faded jeans, a sweatshirt that was on wrong side out and fur-lined slippers, he looked more casual than she'd ever seen him, nothing like the dapper attorney of daylight hours. "I don't, normally." He flicked his ashes off to one side. "Just when I'm restless." He took a long drag. "Tiff and I have been hoping to start a family. I would never have believed it's not safe here."

Sam's disappearance was making everyone feel vulnerable. "It's…" So many words crowded Zoe's tongue, but they were equally inadequate. "Shocking," she finished.

"Of course it is. If *I'm* this upset, you must be… beyond miserable. I saw it on the news tonight."

The sympathy felt good. She needed it, but, for some reason, she couldn't accept it from Anton. She couldn't even let her fiancé touch her right now. "I'm completely…" Again, she struggled for the right word, but this time she found the perfect one to describe how she felt. "Lost."

He walked around the fence and approached the porch. "I'm so sorry."

His commiseration made it even harder not to cry. "Thank you. I appreciate that."

The end of his cigarette glowed eerily in the dark, lighting the lower portion of his face as he brought it to his mouth. "What can I do to help?"

"We'll be having flyers printed in the morning. Could you circulate some?"

She must've been staring at his cigarette because he offered it to her, and she surprised herself by taking it.

The smoke burned her lungs, but she inhaled deeply, remembering the calming effect she used to get from nicotine. It'd been so long since she'd had a cigarette… She'd been nineteen and living with Johnny Ruzzo, a chain-smoker who grew so abusive she'd had to leave him for Samantha's sake.

"Of course," he said. "I'll call in sick if necessary." He glanced behind her at the house, where Anton was sleeping, and the resentment Zoe had been battling reared its ugly head again, only with a new face. How was it that Anton could sleep when this neighbor, who was virtually a stranger, was too rattled by Sam's disappearance to shut down for the night? Had Anton *ever* been there for her emotionally? Or had she been overlooking the characteristics she didn't like in order to maintain the idyllic life she'd been trying to achieve?

Her actions, his actions—it was all so confusing.

Colin shoved a hand through his curly hair. "Why wait till tomorrow?"

Zoe stiffened with his cigarette halfway to her mouth. "What'd you say?"

"You obviously can't sleep." He tapped his chest. "I can't, either. Let's go over to the copy place on Douglas and create the flyer. It's open twenty-four-hours."

"But—"

"That way, we'll be ready when everyone wakes up."

His words made sense to Zoe, provided her with an alternative to the agonizing wait. "You want to go with me?" she clarified.

"Of course."

"But it's so late. I can't expect you to—"

"Stop it." He dismissed her words. "I don't mind at all."

With a nod, Zoe returned his cigarette. She appreciated his take-charge, do it now attitude. Waiting endlessly while Anton slept was only making her crazy. "Okay," she said. "Let me grab my keys."

"No need." He took a final drag, dropped the cigarette on the concrete walkway and ground it out. Then he pulled his car keys from his jeans pocket and dangled them in front of her. "I'll drive."

Zoe tried not to imagine Anton's irritation at seeing a cigarette butt outside his door. "But I'll need Sam's picture and my purse—"

"Of course. You get what you need. I'll start the car."

As Zoe dashed into the house, gratitude for Colin's willingness to befriend her at her lowest moment evoked a sob of relief. "Thank God for neighbors," she muttered.

* * *

Colin sat next to Zoe at the bank of computers in the far corner of the copy shop. "Should we put anything else on it?" he asked.

Zoe stared at the flyer they'd created. *Never* would she have expected to find herself in the position of needing something like this. The experience of the past two days was surreal. And the camaraderie that'd sprung up between her and her lawyer neighbor enhanced the dreamlike effect. Prior to the past twenty minutes, she hadn't known Colin Bell beyond a passing wave and a few polite comments on the weather. Now she felt closer to him than to Anton.

"That's it." They'd included Sam's picture, her date of birth, her height and weight, a description of the swimsuit she'd been wearing, the date she'd gone missing and the place where she was last known to be, as well as contact information for the police and Zoe's cell-phone number. "Unless you think I should give my address, too," she said.

"No, that wouldn't be safe."

"I'm willing to do anything if it'll help."

"But you don't know what some mentally unstable person might do. I've heard of a mother who received phone calls saying her daughter was still alive, only to find out later that the guy who took the girl murdered her almost instantly."

She winced. "You mean someone connected to the *killer?*" She could hardly say the word. She didn't want to think about what happened to most girls taken by a stranger.

"No, I mean unrelated parties."

"Who would harass a grieving mother?"

"You got me. But it happens, so be prepared. Giving out your cell-phone number is bad enough. You definitely don't want to reveal your address."

Feeling a release of tension for the first time since she'd realized her daughter had disappeared, Zoe leaned back. She should've come to the copy house earlier, before Anton went to bed. "Getting this finished…helps," she said with some satisfaction.

He grinned at her. "Too bad it takes a tragedy like this one for two neighbors to get acquainted, huh?"

She touched his forearm. "I can't thank you enough, Colin."

"You don't need to thank me." He covered her hand. "It's the least I can do."

Smiling, she pulled away and glanced at the clock cover on the wall. There'd been one guy working on a project when they arrived, but he was gone. They were the only people in the place, besides the employee who'd been steadily feeding the commercial-size printers. "It's almost dawn," she said.

Colin got to his feet. "Then we'd better get these printed if we want to circulate them before everyone leaves for the day."

"What about your job?"

He hid a yawn. "I'd call in sick like I said, but I forgot that I have an important meeting. I'll pass out flyers, then go in to the office for a few hours."

"Taking a short day won't cause problems for you at the firm?"

He shrugged. "Are you kidding? They don't want to lose me."

"Too bad you have to go in at all. You'll be exhausted."

"I'll get by."

Sleep deprivation made Zoe swoon as she came to her feet, but Colin steadied her, an expression of concern on his face. "You okay?"

With a sigh, she nodded. She'd already survived being

raped by a twenty-one-year-old when she was fifteen. That had been so traumatic she couldn't think of it without feeling ill. But she had Samantha because of it, so she couldn't entirely regret what she'd suffered.

"I'll be fine."

"You'll find her," he said.

She stopped him before he could walk away. "Do you really think so?"

"Of course." He gave her a quick hug. "And I'll do everything I can."

There'd been times in the past when she hadn't liked the way Colin looked at her. He seemed a little *too* appreciative, *too* aware of her as a woman, which made her uncomfortable. He had a wife. But she must've misjudged him, because he was the one who'd helped her through the most harrowing night of her life. Even last night hadn't been as bad. Last night she'd been able to convince herself that Sam's disappearance was a terrible mistake that would soon be made right. Now too much time had passed to believe that.

"Thanks again," she said.

He was already walking over to the counter. "No problem. You want these printed in color or black and white?"

"Color." Zoe didn't really have the money, but she was afraid people wouldn't recognize Sam if she didn't provide as close a likeness as possible.

He whistled. "Color's a buck a copy."

"I don't care," she said. "I'd give *anything* to have her back."

"She's a lucky girl…"

Zoe hesitated. *Lucky?*

"…to have a mother who loves her so much."

"Thanks," she whispered.

She was tempted to tell him how Sam had been conceived. She needed to talk—about how she'd felt when it happened, about her struggle trying to decide whether to keep the baby, about the day she'd gone to the abortion clinic and then bailed out because she was too frightened to go through with it. Her father had felt too guilty about what she'd already endured to force her. And that had led to a child, *her* child, the one thing she treasured most in life. It was hard to believe how close she'd come to ending the pregnancy. Maybe that was why she wanted to talk. It felt as if she could trust this young lawyer with anything. He'd have no reason to tell anyone. But the clerk interrupted before she could make up her mind.

"What can I do for you?" she asked Colin.

"Give me a thousand copies of this." He pushed the flyer toward her.

The clerk jotted down the information as Zoe joined them at the cash register.

"How would you like to pay for your order?"

Zoe reached into her purse. "By credit card." She had no idea how she'd settle the bill when it came due. Anton wouldn't be happy that she'd gone the more expensive route and would probably refuse to help her. His first wife had robbed him blind when she'd left him for another man and that had made him cautious about spending money. He'd say she was being foolish, as he'd said in the past when she'd splurged on items for Sam she couldn't really afford.

But she'd worry about that in thirty days.

If Sam was back, she'd figure out some way to meet the obligation. If Sam wasn't back…salvaging her credit would be the least of her problems.

10

Anton was standing on the porch, holding a cup of coffee when Colin and Zoe returned. Zoe waved as Colin parked, but her fiancé didn't respond.

"Uh-oh." Colin clicked his tongue. "I think you're in trouble."

"He's definitely not happy," she agreed. But he looked well-rested, which rankled almost as much as the anger apparent in his expression.

Colin touched her on the leg. "I'll explain where we were, if you want."

"No. You've done enough for me. Thank you."

The weight of his hand remained. "Will you stop thanking me? You act like you've never had a friend."

With the transient nature of the people she'd known in her childhood, and the number of times she'd moved as an adult, her life had been too unstable for long-lasting relationships. It hurt too much to separate after bonding with someone, so she didn't let herself care too deeply. Not for anyone but Sam. Sam had been her best friend as well as her daughter.

But thinking of their closeness made her chest ache just when she'd finally been feeling a bit better.

As she got out of Colin's BMW, she collected a box of flyers from the backseat; Colin insisted on carrying the other. He walked with her and gave his to Anton when they'd climbed onto the porch.

Anton's mouth formed a hard, straight line. "What's this?"

"Flyers." He rubbed his hands as if he'd been hard at work, which was true. "We bumped into each other in the middle of the night, both suffering from insomnia, so we figured we'd make use of the time."

Anton's eyes cut to the cigarette butt on the walkway, then lifted to Zoe. "You couldn't have told me? You didn't assume I'd wonder where you'd gone, especially with your car still in the driveway?"

The realization that he'd been genuinely worried made her resentment dissipate. Was she merely searching for a target, taking her fear and stress out on Anton? It was possible. "I'm sorry," she said. "I was so caught up…I—I didn't even consider what you'd think if you woke to find me gone."

His forehead rumpled as if he was struggling to suppress some emotion. He reached out to her, then hugged her as best he could while they were each holding a box of flyers. "Don't do that again."

"I won't," she murmured.

Colin cleared his throat, probably to remind them that he was still around. "I should get going. I have a lot to do today." He started to move away but stopped before clearing the grass. "Hey, I almost forgot my part of the flyers. I'll take surface streets to work and drop one off at every store between here and downtown."

"Would you?" Encouraged that they were already disseminating information, Zoe smiled. She felt bad about frightening Anton, but Colin had really helped.

"Of course. Give me…half," he said.

"That many?"

"I'll leave some with Tiff, have her hit the stores I can't."

Zoe handed over her box. "You've been great, Colin."

"Don't mention it." He winked. "I'll report in later."

Standing next to Anton, Zoe watched him walk to his house. When he was gone, Anton bent to pick up the cigarette butt. "He smokes?"

She knew how Anton felt about that, and chafed at the memory of sharing Colin's cigarette. "Apparently only when he can't sleep."

He went over to the side yard to toss the butt in the garbage.

"Are you ready to start passing out flyers?" she asked when he returned.

"I am."

"Good. Let's go."

She hiked up her purse, but he shook his head. "I'll do it. You've got to get some sleep. You've been up for almost forty-eight hours, and you've hardly eaten a bite. I don't know how you're still on your feet."

The pain was easier to tolerate if she was actively working. It was the doubt that set in when she stopped that hurt the most. And the way Anton kept trying to hold her back, to get her to slow down, made it worse. "I can't, Anton. I don't care about pacing myself. I don't care about being exhausted. I'm *frantic,* and I have to do whatever I can. I don't care what it costs me. Can't you understand that?" She gripped his arm. *"I have to find Sam. She's the only thing that matters to me!"*

The color drained from his cheeks, which had been red a moment before. "*I* don't matter?"

She forced herself to ease the tightness of her grip. Had that really come out of her mouth? "I-I'm sorry. I didn't mean it," she said. But deep down, she was afraid she did.

* * *

Tiffany was sitting at the kitchen table in a bathrobe and slippers when Colin strode in. Every line of her body drooped, but he didn't care. He'd finally gotten his attractive neighbor to notice him, had spent hours alone with her and was in a great mood.

"Where were you?" she asked.

He could hear the distress in her voice. She was so afraid of losing him—and no amount of reassurance made any difference. The belief that she wasn't worthy of his love, of anybody's love, came from someplace so deep she'd never overcome it. She had Nancy, her lousy mother, to thank for that. And the brother who'd shot Nancy. By getting himself locked up, Seth had reinforced Tiffany's fear of abandonment.

Colin supposed the way he treated her didn't help. But she was lucky to be with him. He could've had someone much more confident—although the effort involved in keeping a woman who was his equal wasn't worth it to him.

"I've been out." He dropped the box of flyers on the counter with a solid thud. "Where's breakfast?"

"I didn't make any. I didn't know when you'd be back."

He propped his hands on his hips and scowled at her sleep-tousled appearance. "Are you *trying* to convince me you're ugly?"

She wouldn't meet his eyes. "No."

"Then why haven't you showered?"

It was rare that he saw her out of bed with her hair mussed and her face devoid of makeup. He'd let her know from the very beginning that he expected her to be her most attractive at all times. That meant she had to shower twice a day—once in the morning and once after visiting the gym before he arrived home each evening. Maybe other men could tolerate their women walking around looking like hags, but he wanted Tiffany to be the bombshell he'd created.

"It's only 6:00 a.m.," she said, growing sullen.

"So? You're wasting time. Go!"

She got up, only to hesitate at the entrance to the dining room. "Why won't you tell me where you've been?"

He got a box of cold cereal from the cupboard and poured himself a bowl. "Why do you think? Because I was with another woman." She gasped, but he couldn't resist torturing her a little longer by conjuring up a lascivious smile as he opened the fridge. "And it was *awesome.*"

Her chin quivered. "Is—is it the receptionist at your office?" she whispered, scarcely able to say the words.

"Misty?" Tiffany was so gullible. He chuckled to himself. "That fat bitch? Give me *some* credit, please."

"Then who?" She began to pant—obviously hyperventilating. If he let the joke go on, she'd probably pass out and hit her head.

"*Stop it,* Tiff," he said. "I'm *joking,* okay? You know you're the only one for me. I was with Zoe! The woman next door?"

She hiccuped as she fought to rein in her emotions.

"We were making flyers." He thumped the box he'd brought in. "Didn't you see this? Didn't you wonder what it was?"

"I don't understand." Her eyes, still glazed with hurt, searched his face.

He set his cereal and a gallon of milk on the table, then put his arms around her. "Calm down, okay? I'm here. I'm never gonna leave you. We were at Kinko's making flyers with Sam's picture on them. Isn't that hilarious?"

Tiffany managed a weak laugh. "Oh!"

"Good thing I love you. Because your insecurities drive

me nuts. Jeez!" He patted her bottom. "Go get showered before I change my mind about hanging on to you."

"Okay," she said, but didn't move.

"What is it now?" he snapped.

"How did you hook up with Zoe? You were in bed with me when I fell asleep."

"I got up to check on Samantha and went out for a smoke. Zoe was in her front yard."

"So you offered to help her?"

He allowed himself a self-indulgent smile. "Brilliant, huh?"

She touched the box of flyers. "Why'd you bring them home?"

"I only brought *some* home, stupid. I told her we'd distribute them."

She blinked uncertainly. "And...will we?"

He poured the milk. "You bet. Why not? What could be more convincing than two sympathetic neighbors doing all they can to help?"

Tiffany smiled, but he knew it wasn't because she liked the idea. She wasn't the type to enjoy deception, even deception as masterful as this. She was relieved to learn she'd been worried for nothing. That was all. "You're so clever."

"Damn straight."

"Colin?"

He'd already taken his first bite. "Hmm?"

"It's been a while since..." She unfastened her robe and let it fall open. "Aren't you starting to miss me?"

Finding her seductive expression lacking after the time he'd spent with Zoe, he scowled. "I'm eating. Can't you see that?"

She ducked her head as if he'd slapped her. "But...you've never gone a whole day, let alone two."

She was feeling neglected. "I'm saving up," he said.

"For what?"

"I've got the boys coming over Friday night."

"You're going to—to prostitute me to your friends?" she asked, belting her robe.

"It's just sex, Tiff. It doesn't mean anything. I want to show you off. Because I'm so proud of you."

"But I don't have any desire to—to be with them."

"I'm not talking about an affair. I'm talking about a gang-bang party. You'll be so high you won't even care."

She didn't respond.

"Come on, don't be a downer. I've already promised the guys a treat."

A pitiful expression claimed her face. "Do I *have* to do it, Colin?"

With a curse, he knocked the cereal box off the counter, flinging Wheaties all over the floor. "Why are you doing this? Why do you have to ruin it for me?"

She'd covered her head at the outburst. "I only want to make love with *you*," she said as she peeked out from between her arms.

"If you won't show my friends a good time, you'll never be with me again," he said. "Now clean up this mess. I gotta shower or I'll be late for work."

"I brought you something."

Samantha huddled in the corner, watching as Tiffany came into the room, locked the door behind her and slowly advanced. She was holding a tattered blue blanket, the kind someone would throw away or allow a dog to maul and chew. But even an old rag appealed to Sam. She had no idea what the weather was like outside. There was no way to tell without windows. But she was freezing. Tiffany had left her in the urine-stained bikini bottoms, probably as punishment for wetting herself.

She'd asked for clothes, but they hadn't provided anything else for her to wear.

"What day is it?" She was beginning to lose track of time. She spent almost every minute curled up, trying to deal with the cold, her constant hunger and the terrible fear that Anton had already convinced her mother they were better off without her.

"It's Wednesday. Colin just went to work."

Sam hated Colin. She didn't want to hear about him. But it was good to know he was gone. Last night had been so freaky.

"Aren't you excited?" Tiffany frowned, obviously disappointed by Sam's response. "Colin told me I could reward you with this if you'll recite the rules to me."

Reward her? More pet stuff. If Tiffany was crazy, Colin was even crazier.

Sam hugged her knees to her chest, for warmth as much as cover. "Why aren't you at work?"

"Colin thought I should give my lip another day to heal," Tiffany explained with a shrug. "It's practically healed, don't you think?"

"I think you should leave him."

The smile disappeared from Tiffany's face. "Don't say that. He's my husband."

"I don't care. He's not nice to you. He's not nice to anyone."

"You don't know what you're talking about. He loves me—he'd walk through fire for me."

Samantha jutted out her chin. "What about your lip?"

"We bumped heads, that's all."

"He told me he'd smash my face like he did yours if I didn't quit crying."

Tiffany arranged an errant curl. Her hair was nearly perfect. She had makeup on, too. "You're a smartass, you know that? Here I am, being good to you, and look how you're acting." She tossed the blanket toward the door. "Colin would never allow me to give this to you now."

Instantly regretting her behavior, Sam tightened the grip she had on her legs. "Wait, I know the rules." She hated to cave in so quickly. Maybe she wouldn't have if she'd been fully dressed. But she longed to cover herself almost more than she longed for human food.

Tiffany tilted her head in consideration. "Are you asking me for another chance?"

Samantha remembered how hard it was to get underneath the bulky mattress. What would happen when she got well and Colin was no longer afraid to touch her? "Yes."

Tiffany's eyebrows rose in challenge. "Yes, *Mistress.*"

"Yes, Mistress," she repeated, but inside she was chanting, *I hate you, I hate you, I hate you.*

"Fine." Tiffany was smiling again. "Tell them to me."

Samantha hadn't eaten any of the pellets Tiffany had poured into the bowl by the door, but she felt like throwing up anyway. "I'm to address him as Master and you as Mistress."

Tiffany laughed. "I guess I gave that one away. What else?"

Sam stared at the litter box in the corner. "I'm to use that—" she pointed "—for a toilet and clean it myself every other day."

"And?"

"If I behave, I'll be rewarded."

"With what?"

"Regular food. Treats. Better clothes. A chance to see the sun."

Wrinkling her nose, Tiffany used the toe of her shoe to push the kitty-litter box farther into the corner. "Did he say that? About the sun?"

"He said I'd get to do chores." But to work she'd have to leave this room, and the other rooms had windows. That was what she focused on—the chance to see the world outside: her street, her house, her mother.

"And if you try to escape?"

"He'll kill me," Samantha replied. "If I make any noise, he'll kill me. If I don't do exactly what he says, he'll kill me. If I don't do what *you* say, he'll kill me."

"Perfect." With a sigh, Tiffany dragged the blanket over to Samantha, and Samantha scrambled to cover herself with it.

Tiffany studied the food in the dog dish. "You're not eating."

Samantha glared up at her. "Would you?"

"You have to eat. At least *some* of it."

The feel of the blanket brought such relief Sam wanted to cry, even though she'd already cried so much she didn't see how there could be any more tears inside her.

"Samantha? I'm talking to you. Do you want me to take that blanket away?"

No! She'd do anything to keep the blanket, anything to stop the cold and provide a barrier against the fear. "N-no, Mistress."

She was trembling all of a sudden, and she had no idea why.

"Look at you," Tiffany said, as if the sight sickened her. "You're going to wet yourself again if you don't settle down."

Fresh tears dripped from Sam's chin. "I c-can't st-stop."

A hint of kindness entered Tiffany's eyes. "I'll tell you what. If you eat some kibble, just to make yourself start getting used to it, I'll bring you a sandwich later."

Was this a trick? Samantha thought it might be but changed her mind when Tiffany spoke again. "If you ever tell Colin I gave you anything but that dog food, you'll never get another morsel out of me, do you understand?"

Hope flared in Samantha's chest and the shaking began to subside. Was it possible that Tiffany might become a friend in this hellish place? "I w-won't tell him," she said. "I swear."

"Okay, then. Make me one more promise."

"What's that?"

Drawing close, Tiffany lowered her voice. "You won't resist Colin no matter what he does."

Samantha twisted her fingers into the torn blanket. "Why not?"

Tiffany's stare drilled into her. "He'll *kill* you," she said without blinking. "He wasn't lying about that."

11

Jonathan woke with a start. He hadn't realized he'd nodded off.

Blinking, he scraped a hand over his stubble-covered chin and checked his watch. It was after nine, and he was still at the kitchen table with his laptop, where he'd been sitting since he'd walked Kino late last night.

"Shit," he muttered through his fingers.

Kino, who'd been napping at Jonathan's feet, whined in response and got up, eager for another walk, but Ronnie would have to take him. Jonathan had to find *something* that might lead him to Zoe Duncan's father. And he had to do it fast. Time was slipping away….

He'd already spent hours searching various databases, including LexisNexis, for information on Ely Duncan. But everything that came up was so dated he didn't believe it'd be relevant.

He decided to switch to the phone, to develop a chain of people to follow—someone who'd heard some gossip and was willing to share it or who could point him in the direction of a friend or relative who might tell him more.

Using a crisscross directory, he got the telephone numbers of Ely's neighbors, but the ones he was able to reach wouldn't talk to him. They didn't trust him, even though he told them he was working for Ely's daughter.

He figured he could continue to call, but he didn't feel optimistic. These weren't the kind of people who'd be forthcoming with details about anyone, and it probably didn't help that the police had already come by. He suspected that Ely's neighbors had spent a good portion of their lives avoiding school counselors and teachers, then cops and probation officers, possibly even bounty hunters.

He would've thought Ely himself had jumped bail. That would certainly explain why his neighbors were so tight-lipped. But Jonathan had checked for an open court case and hadn't found one.

Yawning, he leaned back in his chair and dialed Zoe's cell phone.

She answered on the first ring. "Hello?"

He winced at the eagerness in her voice, knew what she was hoping to hear. "It's me. Jonathan."

"Do you have anything?"

Nothing on Ely, but in the wee hours of the morning, he'd gone to the trouble of searching for a few details on Franky Bates. He had Franky's mother's address in San Diego. Chances were always good a mother could locate her son. He also had proof that Franky had applied for a job at a restaurant in the same city—a job he hadn't got—and even tried to get a credit card at the local Macy's. "I'm afraid not."

He waited a moment, giving her time to deal with the disappointment, then continued. "I pulled up the addresses directly surrounding the one you gave me for your father. I've called at least ten of his neighbors. Most don't answer."

"Anything before noon is too early."

They didn't have the luxury of waiting. "I managed to rouse an R. Butler."

"R?"

"He told me his first name was Rhett, but he was chuckling when he said it."

"Rhett Butler. Funny guy."

"He thought so." Frustrated by his lack of progress, Jonathan got up and began to pace.

"I take it he wasn't cooperative."

She sounded so despondent he hated to tell her any more, but he needed her help. "Not that you'd notice. He told me he's never met your father. I also spoke to a Tilly Smith and a Heather Hatfield. Any chance you know either of these folks?"

"No. What'd they say?"

"Pretty much the same thing."

"The people who live at Mount Vernon Mobile Home Park don't like strangers snooping around. They have too many of their own secrets to guard."

He paused to gaze out the window over his kitchen sink—and saw a yard that'd gone mostly to weeds. When had that happened? How long had it been since he'd taken time to mow?

With a grimace, he turned away. His neighbors were probably getting impatient, but the lawn would have to wait another few days. "I definitely got that impression."

"So you can't find my father."

Let alone Sam. "I haven't found him *yet.* But I won't give up. I'm going to L.A."

"You think that'll make a difference?"

"I do if you're with me."

There was a moment of surprised silence. "But I've been away from that area for so long. I doubt I know anyone."

"You'll have a better chance of getting through to the neighbors than I will, or the police."

"But the people you spoke to might tell me the same thing. It's entirely possible they really *don't* know my father. The population rises and falls depending on when the cops come through on a drug bust."

He couldn't imagine her as a little girl, growing up in all of that. The person she'd become didn't even hint at such a beginning. Unless you were talking about the distrust that lingered in her eyes, and a tendency to hold the world at arm's length. How long had she been running from the trailer park? Probably since well before she'd actually left it. Now, here she was, living at the opposite end of the spectrum in a respectable, upper-middle-class neighborhood, a perfect example of minivan, soccer-mom suburbia. "I understand, but I think it's worth the chance. It's only an hour's flight. Let's hop on a plane, pound a few doors, get folks talking."

"I can't leave Sacramento. What if Sam…I mean, she could come home and—"

"You have a cell. Anton can head up the search efforts in your absence. You trust him, don't you?"

She didn't answer.

"He's your fiancé."

"But we're talking about *my* daughter. No one cares about her as much as I do."

"We're working against the clock, Zoe. We've got to trust him and the police on this end. Meet me at the airport, and we'll get on the next available flight. This is too important to leave to anyone else."

"Okay," she said at length.

"Is there someone, a friend or relative who can help Anton?"

"There's Colin, I guess."

"Colin?"

"My neighbor. He's doing what he can."

"If they find her, someone will call you."

"I know. It's just…it's so hard for me not to be here."

"Don't worry. We'll turn around immediately if there's a reason to do so, even if it means I have to rent a car and drive you back. I think we have to visit L.A." And maybe San Diego. As long as Franky was close and accessible, Jonathan figured he might as well look under that rock and, if possible, determine whether or not Sam's biological father was involved. He had no plans to take Zoe with him on that little side trip, however, so he saw no need to make the situation any worse for her by mentioning it. "Can you reach the airport in forty-five minutes?"

"I'll try. Should I pack anything?"

"Bring some clothes. Depending on what we find, and the availability of flights, we may have to stay over."

"Stay over?"

"Depending on what we find," he reiterated.

"Hopefully, that won't be necessary," she said.

Someone in the background—probably Anton—said, "What's going on?"

She covered the phone to respond. But Jonathan could still hear. "I'm going to Los Angeles with Skye's investigator."

The other voice grew louder and, at that point, Jonathan knew for sure it was Anton. *"The man who was hugging you in my backyard?"*

By the time Zoe arrived at the airport, Jonathan had purchased her ticket. He'd called while she was en route to tell her they'd be leaving from the new terminal. He was waiting by the skycaps in front when they pulled to the curb in Anton's Escalade.

Anton wasn't pleased that she was going. He'd scarcely said a word the entire ride over and grew even more morose when he saw the man who'd be escorting her. As she got out of the SUV, he came around to hand her the small carry-on bag he'd retrieved from the backseat, his jaw clenched.

She hated that he was making this harder on her than it already was. She wasn't even sure she was doing the right thing. Sam could be close, and in trouble. But it'd been two days since her daughter disappeared. Maybe Sam wasn't in Sacramento anymore; she could be anywhere.

Holding a stack of flyers, Zoe scanned the crowd, searching, just in case. She wasn't thinking coherently anymore; she'd been without sleep for too long.

Jonathan studied her for a moment, wearing a frown. "You look tired," he said.

She had her hair pulled back and was wearing some makeup, but she hadn't been able to conceal the dark circles under her eyes.

"Thanks," she muttered.

He didn't apologize. "Have you gotten any sleep since Sam went missing?"

Her smile felt so brittle she wondered why she bothered. "I can sleep once we find her."

Anton gave her a quick hug. "We'll get through this," he said tersely, but she got the impression he was trying to convince himself more than her.

His embrace didn't make her feel any better. It was too mechanical, too strained. And there were so many people. She had to check every face—the businessmen, the tourists, the families and all the children. Especially the children.

"Zoe?" Anton prompted.

She blinked, shifting her attention. "I'll call you later." She was acting almost robotic, but a more genuine response required thought and feeling, and she didn't want to break down. She had to carry on at all costs. For Sam.

He squeezed her arm and left without even speaking to Jonathan. Embarrassed by the all-too-obvious slight,

Zoe avoided the private investigator's gaze by turning to see the people behind her.

"Let's go," he said and started off.

She hurried to catch up and, when she did, almost slipped her hand in his. He'd seen devastation before. She'd gathered that from the world-weary mantle he always wore. He wouldn't rebuff her—because he understood. But it was a strange impulse for an engaged woman to have, especially with a man she'd barely met.

"I hope we'll be able to locate my dad." Feeling like a completely different person without Samantha, she moved through the crowd, wheeling her bag behind her. He looked down the line of people waiting to clear security. "We'll give it our best shot."

"How did you get my ticket?" Belatedly, she realized that this wasn't the way air travel worked in the age of terrorism. "Didn't you need my ID?"

"I talked to a skycap."

"So?"

"I told him you forgot your ID and had him print your boarding pass along with mine."

"They'll do that?"

"Depends on their level of motivation."

Which he'd obviously enhanced, much to her chagrin. She'd spent a thousand dollars on the flyers. Who knew what other expenses she'd incur? This trip wouldn't be cheap. And she and Anton fought about money more than anything else.

She swallowed hard. "How much do I owe you?"

He glanced back at her. "Nothing."

Pride warred with relief. "The Last Stand is paying for it?"

His lack of a response suggested it was. They were paying his bill and travel expenses, after all. That was what the charity was supposed to do for people like her, she told herself in order to feel better about accepting their help. But it rankled. She wanted to be self-sufficient. She'd had her fill of secondhand clothing and government handouts when she was a child, and again as a teenage mother.

"Be grateful you met Skye Willis and forget it," she muttered under her breath. Although she'd heard from Detective Thomas several times this morning and knew the police were assigning extra officers to look for Sam, Skye made it possible for her to be more involved in the search.

They reached the top of the escalator and joined a line snaking almost to the skywalk that straddled the street below. But Zoe was still puzzled about how Jonathan had managed to get her a boarding pass. "That guy who gave you my ticket—isn't that a breach of security?" she asked.

"Not really." He stepped out of line to gauge their progress. "They'll check your boarding pass against your ID here."

"You seem nervous."

"I don't want to miss this flight."

"What're the chances?"

"We're cutting it close."

Did they really need to take this trip? It was a logical move, but if her father could help it'd be the greatest irony ever. Ely had never been there for her when she needed him. And the prospect of seeing Ely didn't appeal to her in her current state. They'd had such a terrible argument the last time they'd talked on the phone. She wished she was stronger, better prepared for the inevitable confrontation.

You have no right to demand any kind of a relationship with Sam.

She's my granddaughter.

How can you say that to me? You didn't even want me to keep her!

I was trying to protect you.

It was a little late to protect *me, don't you think? That should've happened before you left me alone with Franky Bates.*

That barb had hit its target. She could remember her father's voice growing hoarse with emotion. *You were too young to be saddled with the responsibility of a child.*

Tell the truth, Dad. It wasn't about me. Nothing was ever about me. You knew you'd continue to spend our grocery money on your next fix and didn't want the added guilt of taking food from a baby.

She'd been in her car alone, talking on her cell. Since that day, she'd often wished the conversation had taken place somewhere she wouldn't have been able to speak so freely. But the stress of starting a new job, regret for denying her daughter a trip Sam would love and anger that she couldn't trust her own father enough to allow it had all combined to put her on edge.

Jonathan's voice cut into her thoughts. "Do you have your ID ready?"

She fumbled through her purse, searching for her wallet, and showed her driver's license to a uniformed security officer. Then she put her bag on the conveyer belt along with her shoes, purse and sweater—but when her belongings went through the X-ray, she didn't move. She stood there, rooted to the spot, clutching the flyers to her chest while watching the people around her act as if nothing in the world was wrong.

Although she hated to draw attention to herself, she couldn't remain silent. What if someone here had spotted Sam?

Jonathan had already reclaimed his shoes when he glanced back and saw that she hadn't come through. Then his eyes lowered to her hands, gripping the flyers like a lifeline to Sam. "We'll miss the plane," he cautioned.

"I just want to put up her picture."

It was so important to Zoe she could hardly breathe, and he must've realized she wouldn't budge without doing at least that much, because he didn't fight her. Pulling a member of security aside, he bent his head and murmured a few words.

Five minutes later, copies of the flyer were taped up in several places and everyone in line was staring at her. Some were even whispering, "Is that *her* child?"

"Yes!" she shouted to the group at large. "She's my only child. I have to find her. Will you help me? *Please!*"

Her plea met with shock and sympathy and open curiosity, but no one stepped forward.

A moment later, Jonathan had taken her hand and was dragging her down the terminal at a trot, her bag bumping behind her. They caught the plane just as the flight attendant was closing the door.

12

Colin didn't interrupt his work when Misty, the firm's receptionist, knocked at his office door.

Concentrating on a purchase agreement for a land-development company, he barked out, "What is it?"

Misty poked her head in. "Got a message for you."

He held out his hand without looking at her, and she came in far enough to drop a piece of paper in his palm.

Slapping it down on his desk, he kept working. He'd get to it later. He had to make up for the preoccupation that'd been damaging his productivity since last weekend, when Rover had started acting up. He hated the prospect of bringing work home with him tonight. He wanted to be available to console Zoe.

"What's this?"

At the sound of Misty's voice, Colin swiveled away from his computer to see that she hadn't left. Instead of hurrying on, as she usually did, she was pointing at the stack of flyers on the edge of his desk.

"That's my neighbor's little girl," he said.

"She's *missing?*"

"Says so, doesn't it?"

She didn't take offense. Focused on what that flyer meant, she frowned, causing unattractive dimples to appear on her pudgy face. "How sad!"

The whine in her voice grated on his nerves. The flyer elicited the same reaction from almost everyone, especially women. But Misty's instant concern bothered him. She was so damn sentimental. Single at thirty-five and more than a little overweight, she was always cooing about some stray dog or cat she'd taken in. She got behind a new cause every week and pressured others to join her. One day she was pushing cookies for the Girl Scouts, the next it was coupon books for Little Leaguers or magazines to benefit the local elementary school.

The only fund-raiser he'd ever supported her in was a Walk for Diabetes. Not because he gave a damn about saving anyone. He didn't know many people in the world worth saving. He just thought it'd be funny to offer a large sum as incentive to make Misty finish the whole walk, then watch her have a heart attack.

Unfortunately, she came through it unscathed. He'd thought he'd at least enjoy the fact that he'd made her go to such effort to collect a hundred dollars she wouldn't get to keep. But the organizers gave her a stupid "I'm making a difference" pin that brought her so much satisfaction he swore he'd never help her again.

If it were up to him, he'd fire her on the basis of being fat and annoying. But the other attorneys loved her and her "big heart," as they said. If her heart was big, it was because *she* was big, but that didn't stop the rest of the lawyers from bringing her little treats and gifts for Administrative Professional Day or Christmas. She had a number of stuffed animals hiding in various cubbyholes around the office and constantly purchased plaques and statues with sickeningly sweet quotes. Her current favorite was, "Three grand essentials to happiness in this life are: something to do, something to love and something to hope for."

If she only knew what he was hoping for her…

"So…you're helping them?" she asked.

He smiled at the respect in her voice. That was new. He and Misty didn't get along well, but one act of perceived kindness had her second-guessing her assessment of him. God, she was a sap. "That's right."

"Oh." She fingered the corner of the stack. "Maybe you're not that bad…"

He cocked his head. "Don't tell me you've been judging me. You're a good Christian woman."

Her teeth sank into her bottom lip. "But when I put up that notice in the break room about the homeless kitten, someone wrote, 'Die, kitty, die,' and Marnie said she thought it was you."

Gasp—could he really be so terrible? He barely refrained from laughing in her face. "It was me. But I was joking, of course. Who could be so cruel about a cute 'puddy tat'?"

She seemed cheered by his childish response. She thought they'd established some common ground at last and felt relieved to see him acting in a manner she could relate to. She lived in such a small, protected world…. "That's what I figured."

Eager to get back to business now that he'd taken a moment to impress the firm's own Mother Teresa, Colin cleared his throat. "You found a good home for the kitty, didn't you?"

"Yes."

"There you go." He smiled blandly. "Was there… anything else?"

"I'm just worried about your neighbor's little girl. I'd be happy to help if you need it."

Colin almost told her to get lost. He was enjoying his involvement, didn't want any competition for Zoe's attention. But after the way Misty had reversed her opinion of him, he saw this as an opportunity to improve his image with the whole firm. With the neighborhood. With the cops. No one would suspect a neighbor who was working so hard to bring little Sammie home.

"I'm putting together a search party for this weekend, if you have a few hours," he said, but he knew before he asked that she'd agree. People like her didn't have lives of their own. She had nothing to do but earn herself another meaningless "I'm making a difference" pin.

"Where will you search?"

"Around the neighborhood and in the raw land adjacent to our development." He'd be sure to send Misty right through the thorny blackberry bushes that clogged the creek.

"You think she might be dead?"

"I hope not." He lowered his voice. "This is…just in case."

"Of course I'll help you," she said.

Surprise, surprise. "Great."

"Maybe some of the other attorneys and secretaries will want to pitch in. Do you mind if I ask them?"

"Not at all. Tell them I'm planning to spend the whole day, if necessary, since I know the family and all. I don't expect that much from them, of course, but I'd be grateful for any time they could spare." Gee, he was sounding like a regular hero. Maybe the media would pick up on his efforts to pitch in.

He imagined himself tearing up on TV. He loved Tiffany all the more because she'd made it possible for him to enjoy this added dimension to an already exciting game.

"Do you want the people who are interested to call you?" she asked.

Why be bothered by twelve separate interruptions when he could make his grand impression all at once?

"No, we'll meet in the parking lot at Sierra College, eight o'clock Saturday morning."

Her eyebrows knitted. "But that's two days away. What if she's found before then?"

Samantha would never be found. Not alive, anyway. But he'd tripped on his own confidence. He had to be more careful.

He pushed a notebook toward her. "Have everyone who's coming sign up with their name and phone number. I'll contact them in the event the search is called off."

"I hope she's returned to her family long before then."

Knowing how much Zoe would love him for arriving with the calavry made him smile. She'd been so grateful last night. He'd never forget the charge that went through him when they made physical contact.

"Me, too," he said.

Overcome by sheer exhaustion, Zoe fell asleep almost before they could taxi down the runway, and she didn't move during the flight. But it was only an hour later that they landed in Los Angeles, and an hour wasn't nearly long enough to give her the rest she needed. Jonathan regretted having to wake her, but he couldn't very well carry her off the plane.

"Zoe?" He nudged her. "We're here."

Her eyes opened to reveal irises that were dark-brown in the center and light-brown at the edges with varying shades of amber in between. He'd halfway expected her to be confused after coming out of such a deep sleep, but she wasn't. She winced as if she didn't want to face the burden that awaited her. But once the aisle was free, she stood and marched off the plane.

They had their luggage, so Jonathan led her directly to a counter where he could rent a car.

"Why don't we take a cab?" she asked.

"It's not the best way to travel when you need to be mobile."

"Are we going somewhere besides the trailer park?"

"If we have to. We're down here to do whatever we can. I have no idea how hard or easy that'll be, but we need to plan for the worst."

He took out his Visa and rented a Prius, and soon they were heading for Mount Vernon Mobile Home Park. They had to fight through congested traffic, but the clear blue skies and sunny, eighty-degree weather made Jonathan wonder why he hadn't settled farther south.

According to the GPS he'd rented with the car, they'd have a thirty-minute drive, but Zoe was already digging at her cuticles as if dreading the moment they'd arrive.

"You okay?" he asked, drawing her attention from the window.

"As okay as I can be."

"What's wrong? Besides everything," he added.

She managed a chuckle. "It's been so long and yet—" she stared up at the palm trees that lined the road "—the memories are as vivid as though I never left."

Those memories were painful for her. She didn't want to come back. She was only doing it for Sam. He regretted being the one to ask for yet another sacrifice, but he had to do his job or they might never recover her daughter.

"Where's your mother from?" he asked, hoping to distract her from her nerves.

"Alabama."

He checked the GPS as they came to a large freeway interchange. "Where'd your parents meet?"

"Here, at a club."

"How old was she?"

"Eighteen."

"What brought her all the way from Alabama? College?"

She laughed. "No. The same thing that brings a lot of young girls to L.A.—the dream of becoming a movie star."

He sensed a measure of disgust in her voice, but if her mother had Zoe's looks, Jonathan could understand why she'd believe she might have a shot…. "Did she get any parts?"

"She once had two lines in a *Dukes of Hazard* episode. And she was an extra in *Little House on the Prairie*."

Not an impressive résumé. "I can't imagine that paid very much."

"No."

Half wishing he'd rented a convertible, he adjusted the air-conditioning vents. It was that kind of day. "How'd she get by?"

"From what my father told me, she worked at various low-paying jobs and lived with whatever man would take her in."

What a history. Jonathan was almost sorry he'd asked. "Is that how she came to know your father?"

"He was making good money back then."

A definite attraction for a struggling actress. "What was he doing?"

She arched an eyebrow. "He says he was operating a perfectly legal transmission-repair business."

"But…"

"I'm pretty sure it was a chop shop. In any case, he served two years for grand larceny, my entire fifth- and sixth-grade years, so…draw your own conclusions."

"Nice," Jonathan said with a whistle. "Who'd you stay with while he was incarcerated? Your mother?" She'd already told him her mother had never been part of her life, but maybe that wasn't as unconditional as it sounded.

Shifting in the seat, she pulled her seat belt away from

her body as if it was too constricting. “No, she was long gone by then. I stayed with his girlfriend.”

The GPS said they had ten minutes before they reached their destination. “Was she nice to you?”

“Nice enough. But she was the one who got my father into drugs, so I don’t feel too friendly toward her.”

“She was an addict?”

“One of the worst. I’d be surprised if she hasn’t overdosed by now.”

“The relationship didn’t last, I take it.”

“No. They broke up shortly after my father got out of prison.”

Jonathan drove in silence. After several minutes, he asked, “How long were your parents together?”

“I doubt they were ever officially a couple. He provided a place for her to sleep and she provided…” Her voice dropped. “Well, I’m sure you can guess what she provided. That’s how he ended up stuck with me.”

Stuck with her? “When did she leave?”

“Before I was born. But she came back, long enough to dump me on his doorstep with a note saying she wasn’t about to let an unexpected pregnancy ruin her career.”

Apparently, Zoe’s mother was even more irresponsible than her father. “What happened to her from there?”

“I have no idea. We never heard from her again.”

“Are you ever tempted to track her down? See what’s become of her?” That was the type of thing he did for people all the time. He could help her, if she wanted, but she didn’t hesitate before responding.

“No.”

Her life had been the exact opposite of his, he realized. He had supportive parents and the best big sister a guy could ask for. “What about extended family?”

Propping her elbow on the window ledge, she anchored her fingers in her hair to keep it from blowing into her face. "My father has a couple of brothers with kids, but we didn't socialize with them. I don't think they wanted to feel any responsibility for me. They were tired of cleaning up his messes well before I came along."

"You don't know them?"

She squinted into the distance. "I met them once or twice, but they both left California not long after Grandma died. One settled in Idaho and the other in Kentucky."

"Your dad's from L.A., then?"

"Bakersfield, which isn't too far away."

"Do these uncles and cousins know Sam?"

"No. I mean, they might know she *exists.* But they don't know *her.*"

"What happened to your father's parents?"

She reached for her purse, found a pair of sunglasses and slid them on. He got the impression she felt better after that, as if they gave her a shield of some sort, a way to hide the emotions coursing through her. "His dad died in a hunting accident when he was small. His mother worked at the library and did her best to raise him and his brothers alone. She died fairly young, too, from a blood clot after gallbladder surgery. I was eight."

"Were you close to her?"

The tenseness around Zoe's mouth softened. "Very. She didn't have a lot to offer us financially. But she loved me, and took me in whenever my dad got in trouble. It broke her heart to see what had become of her oldest son."

They were less than a mile from the mobile home park. Zoe clasped her hands over her purse and Jonathan stopped questioning her about her background.

"It hasn't changed much," she said as they spotted the Mount Vernon sign, which was broken on one side and had fallen against the pole.

He pulled off the busy road, onto the rutted driveway. "How long's the sign been like that?"

"Since I was here last."

He eyed the dilapidated, rust-stained metal-sided homes and shook his head.

"What?" she prompted.

"I can't imagine any child being raised here."

"I wasn't a child for long," she murmured.

13

"He obviously hasn't been around for quite a while." Zoe stood on the rickety landing of the mobile home where she'd grown up and gazed out at the untended land between the trailers—ground no one really claimed but folks in other places might call a yard. She'd already knocked but there'd been no answer, and the door was locked.

Jonathan had also donned a pair of sunglasses, which he'd retrieved from his luggage when they'd stepped into the bright sunshine. He looked exceptionally good in those glasses; his face, so lean and rugged, would've been right at home on a recruitment poster for the marines. How old was he, anyway? Her age? Younger?

Probably younger. She felt ancient.

"How do you know?" he asked.

"The weeds." She waved at the spot where her father always parked his truck. "If my father had been here recently, they would've been smashed by his tires."

"That's one way to deal with weeding." Jonathan removed his glasses and lifted a hand to block the glare as he peered through a window.

"Around here, it's the *only* way."

"I wonder if that would work for my yard."

She checked under the mat for the key her father used

to leave for her, but it was gone. "We'll have to break in," she said.

He lowered his voice. "You arrived at that conclusion pretty fast."

"I didn't come all the way down here for nothing."

He grinned. "I like the way you think. Give me a second."

He went around back and, a moment later, she heard a popping sound. There was some noise from inside the trailer, then the front door swung open. "Your wish is my command."

The chain rattled above them as he waved her in. She glanced over her shoulder to see if anyone had noticed their actions. "Quick work."

"I've seen bathroom stalls with stronger doors."

The place was filled with the same secondhand furniture and threadbare carpet she remembered all too well, but it was tidier and actually *cleaner.* That came as a surprise. When she'd lived here, she'd been cook, housekeeper and maid. "He couldn't have picked up after himself *before?*" she grumbled. Even when she'd come to stay for their Disneyland trip it'd been a mess.

Jonathan walked up behind her. "What'd you say?"

"Nothing." Nothing important. Sarcasm was just her way of dealing with the nostalgia rushing over her like a giant tidal wave, carrying her into the past. And now that she was home, she was faced with a new fear, one she hadn't allowed herself to feel so far. What if the father she pretended to hate wasn't even alive anymore? What if he'd overdosed or run his truck off a cliff?

The last words they'd said to each other would be the last words she'd ever get to say to him….

She should've called him back and done what she could to mend the rift. But she'd been trying so hard to gain Anton's approval, to be like him. Normal. Successful. A regular suburban parent. She could keep up that facade only by remaining as disdainful of her father's weaknesses as Anton was.

But now she felt as if she didn't know the person she'd become. Did she really want to be a carbon copy of Anton, or any of his family or friends? Most of them had no sympathy for the struggles people like the ones in this trailer park dealt with on a daily basis. Wasn't *she* one of *them?*

"Hey."

Blinking, Zoe shifted her attention to Jonathan. "Hmm?"

"If your father was hurt, or worse, you would've been notified."

She smiled at his understanding. He was so vital, and supportive in a nonjudgmental way. Nothing like her fiancé. Somehow, Jonathan didn't have to resort to absolutes and a regimented routine to compensate for—

Stop it! Why was she thinking such unkind thoughts about Anton? Because she blamed him for Sam's being gone?

That wasn't fair.

Somehow she'd always been able to cope. But she couldn't cope with this....

Suddenly the obvious occurred to her. Although Ely had long since paid off the trailer, he didn't own the piece of ground beneath it. He had to pay a monthly fee for the space; everyone in the park did. "Someone's keeping up with the rent or there would've been notices on the door," she said.

Jonathan flipped a switch and the light came on. "The utilities haven't been turned off, either. Where does he get his mail? If we can find out the last time he picked it up, that might give us some answers."

"It used to come through the slot next to the front

door. But a few years ago, the post office put a bank of boxes out by the street. I saw them when I visited nearly two years ago." With Sam. When they'd gone to Disneyland and had such a great time—until Ely went out afterward and came home stinking drunk, hollering about how he never got to see them anymore. She'd dragged Samantha out of bed and they'd left before dawn.

"We'll have to check with the neighbors, see if someone's collecting it for him," he said.

Clinging to the hope that her fears, at least about her father, were unfounded, Zoe moved through the trailer. She saw what she'd seen on her last visit. Her room hadn't changed since she'd left home, with her own baby, at seventeen. The white dresser with the missing knobs still hugged the closest wall and even had some of her old jewelry draped over the mirror. The poster of David Hasselhoff she'd tacked up at thirteen still covered the opposite wall. The stickers she'd affixed to the closet doors hadn't been removed.

Now that she was an adult, it was difficult to believe she'd gotten pregnant a mere two years after her father bought her the pink "princess" bedspread. Two years older than Sam was now.

"You did some fine decorating in here," Jonathan said, his sunglasses now clipped to the neck of his T-shirt.

A faint smile curved her lips. "Thanks."

He touched her elbow. "Are you coping with this?"

"Yeah, I'm fine," she said, but *fine* was a relative term. She'd definitely been better.

"What are you thinking?" he asked.

She was remembering the day her father had bought her that bedspread. She'd wanted it so badly he'd spent the money even though it meant they'd probably go hungry the next week.

Maybe she'd been too hard on him…. "Nothing that will change the world."

"No one's all good or all bad, Zoe."

"That's unfortunate, isn't it?" She took a deep breath. "It'd make life so much simpler if we could classify everyone into neat categories."

"It'd certainly make police work easier." He crossed the hall to peek into her father's room, and this time she trailed after him. "Anything strike you as odd?" he asked.

"The beds are made."

"That's all?"

"It doesn't smell like pot."

"Your father's drug of choice?"

"It's cheaper than the rest, so…out of necessity, I suppose."

"Makes sense." He walked around the bed and stopped to pluck a photograph from the mirror. "This is you?"

Sure enough, it was her second-grade picture, the one in which she was missing her two front teeth. The edges of that photograph were tattered and torn—like almost everything else in the trailer. "Yes."

"Maybe your father's cleaned up his life," Jonathan said.

Ely swore he had. When they'd been arguing about whether or not Sam could stay with him, he promised Zoe he'd been clean for months and would remain that way. *Come on, Zoe. Trust me, just this once. Your old room's ready. I bought those Pop-Tarts she likes. And I've got money. I been workin'.*

She'd wanted to say yes, but she couldn't. Sobriety was one promise he'd never been able to keep.

When Jonathan went back to the living room, she stayed put. She needed a moment alone. Especially when he pressed the button on her father's answering machine and she heard her own voice echoing through the thin walls. "Dad? Dad, where are you? I need to talk to you. Please call me." *Beep.* "Something's happened, Dad. To Sam. Don't be angry anymore. Pick up." *Beep.* "Damn it, if you ever want to see me again, pick up the phone!" In the next message the anger was gone and there were tears in her voice. "Dad? Please. I need you."

Zoe rubbed her temples to relieve the tension building into another headache. For the past few days she'd struggled to hold in the tears. Now she wanted to cry and couldn't. "Where are you?" she muttered to her father's room at large. "Why can't you ever be around when I need you?"

A knock at the front door made her breath catch in her throat. Pivoting, she hurried to see who it was.

Jonathan held up a hand to forestall her as she emerged from the hall, and crossed the living room to answer it himself.

"Who're *you?*" a female voice demanded. "Are you the one who called me early this morning?"

Zoe stepped into view and felt her jaw drop. *"Sharon?"*

"Zoe!" The fifty-something-year-old woman wore a bathrobe despite the midafternoon hour. "You're lovelier than ever, missy. No wonder your dad's so damn proud of you. But…what're you doing here?"

"I could ask you the same thing. Last I heard, you'd moved to Mississippi to live with your oldest son."

Sharon Thornton wasn't dyeing her hair the same harsh black as before. Today, it was silvery gray. And while the lines in her face had deepened into harsh grooves, she seemed happier somehow. "I was there for eight long years. But the weather sucked—God, it's humid in Mississippi. And it was too crowded in that house, if you ask me. The woman Danny married—" she shook her head "—she straightened me out, but I'm tellin' ya, she was a real bitch."

Zoe silently qualified Sharon's statement with a

"...straightened me out *for now,*" but couldn't help laughing at the image of tough love her words created. "So you're living in the park again?"

"Right next door." She motioned to the beat-up red-and-white trailer a stone's throw away, the one that had belonged to old man Montgomery.

"Sharon used to live in unit 10," Zoe explained to Jon. "She babysat me every now and then."

"When I was less stoned than her daddy was," Sharon added in a rueful voice. "You poor kid. It's a miracle you survived the two of us."

Although she wasn't the woman who'd gotten her father started on drugs, she hadn't helped the problem. She'd used right along with him. But Zoe had always liked her.

"What brought you back to the old neighborhood?" she asked.

Her eyes flicked toward Jonathan and she pulled her robe tighter. "Your father didn't tell you?"

"Tell me what?"

"He asked me to come."

"Are you two...*seeing* each other?"

Sharon blushed furiously. "I think he'd like that. But I won't marry him until he pulls his life together. Now that I've climbed out of that black hole, I can't let him or anyone else drag me back down."

"Then you should've stayed away." Zoe spoke before she could stop herself.

"I didn't really have a choice. He totaled his truck a few months ago so he couldn't work. He was hitting rock bottom when he called, and I couldn't refuse him. At our age, it's now or never, you know? Where would I be if my son's bitch of a wife hadn't slapped me into shape?"

Zoe had never heard *bitch* said with so much respect. "How long have you been sober?"

"A year and three months."

At least she had a track record. "That's great, Sharon."

Her eyes sparkled with excitement as she angled her head toward Jonathan. "Is this Anton? Your dad told me you have a new man. Someone who has his own business, no less. Someone *respectable.*"

"No, not Anton."

Her grin widened. "You've traded up already?"

Zoe felt herself flush. "This isn't my boyfriend."

"But I do have my own business. Does that count?" Jonathan put in.

She gave him the once-over. "Not as much as what you've got beneath those clothes."

"Oh, God, don't provoke her," Zoe said.

"What do you mean?" Sharon retorted. "I'm just stating the obvious. What healthy young woman wouldn't want a man like him in her bed?"

Zoe's cheeks grew even hotter. "He's a private investigator." Who was also one of the handsomest men Zoe had ever seen, so she could understand why Sharon might be impressed, but she preferred to keep that opinion to herself.

Sharon's flirtatious smile disappeared and her level of enthusiasm dropped by several chilly degrees. "So you *are* the one who called me."

"Yes," he said.

"What are you doing with a P.I.?" she asked, scowling at Zoe.

"Right now we're looking for my dad. Can you tell us where he is?"

She didn't respond.

"Sharon, this isn't about him. Sam's gone missing. That's why I'm here."

The ruddy color drained from her aging face. "Gone *missing?* What do you mean?"

"She was home sick from school, lying on a chaise in the backyard, and she just…disappeared."

Sharon pressed a hand to her heart. "When?"

"On Monday." Zoe was growing light-headed; she needed to eat. "You don't think… I mean, I know my father's been asking to see her—"

"No! He'd *never* take Sam without your permission, never scare you like that," Sharon said.

"Have they been in communication?"

"No."

"No calls? No letters?"

"No, he's been in rehab, Zoe."

She froze. "Since when?"

"Almost a month ago."

"Then who's paying the bills around here?"

Sharon didn't answer immediately, which told Zoe it was exactly as she'd guessed. "You are, aren't you?"

"For the time being…."

Zoe shook her head. "Oh, Sharon."

"He's not using me."

"He's been in rehab before. What makes you think this is going to be any different?"

"Because it is. He was having a tough time of it—I'll be honest with you. Even after I got back, he kept relapsing and relapsing. But then I threatened to call you and report that he was back at it again, and that was all it took."

"Why didn't he try to tell me he was going into rehab?" she asked, using the wall to steady herself.

A flash of concern entered Jonathan's eyes as he watched her try to shake off the dizziness, but she ignored it in favor of focusing on Sharon's response.

"He was afraid you wouldn't believe him. He said he needs to prove it to you. Says he owes you that much." Tentative hope crept into her manner. "And, with summer on the way, I think he was hoping you'd relent and let Sam stay with him for a few days. He talks about both of you constantly." She waved toward the kitchen. "He has a jug of cash that he's been saving and he won't touch it. Not for anything. 'It's for Sam's trip to Disneyland,' he tells me."

Zoe couldn't listen to any more. How many times had she been through this? "How do you know he's still there?"

"I check up on him practically every day. And we write. He hasn't broken *one* rule. Not one." She smiled proudly. "More importantly, he hasn't given up. I know that because they have visiting hours on Tuesdays. I went to visit him yesterday."

"We have to call, just to be sure," Zoe said.

Jonathan pulled his BlackBerry from his pocket, but Sharon stopped him. "They won't give you any information, not unless they know who you are. Let me do it."

She punched in the numbers—and they waited, hardly breathing at all. "It's gonna kill him to hear about Sam," she muttered.

Zoe snapped her fingers to get Sharon's full attention. "If he's there, don't tell him."

Sharon's eyes latched onto hers. "How can you not tell him that his only grandchild is missing?"

"Like you said, at his age it's now or never. He's where he needs to be." The dizziness intensified as she struggled to bear up under the confusing onslaught of emotions she felt about her father—gratitude for keeping her when her mother hadn't, disappointment in his other choices, worry, disgust, love. It seemed that her relationship with Ely was filled with extremes. "If we tell him about Sam…"

Zoe didn't finish. Someone had answered at the rehab place, and Sharon was nodding to let her know she understood. "Who's this?" she said into the mouthpiece.

There was a pause. “Hi, Doug. It’s Sharon Thornton.... Good, you?... How’s Ely doing today?”

“Great.” She stared down at her slippers while she talked. “Glad to hear it.... No, no need to tell him I called. I’ll write.... Thanks, we all do what we can.... You bet.... I know, not much longer.”

She said goodbye and hit the End button.

“Well?” Zoe asked.

She handed Jonathan his phone. “He’s still there. And he doesn’t know a thing about Sam or he would’ve raised a fuss.”

Zoe clutched Jonathan’s arm, but when her fingers met with the contours of firm muscle and warm skin, she dropped her hand as if he’d burned her. “Sam’s not with him. We’ve got to get back to Sacramento.”

He didn’t seem as relieved as she did. “Tomorrow morning,” he said.

“Why tomorrow? If we head straight to the airport, we might be able to catch a flight this evening.”

“We have to go to a hardware store so I can fix the door.”

“I can have a friend take care of that,” Sharon said, shooing them out. “He’s a retired carpenter, so a broken door’s nothing. You go find Sam.”

Zoe gave her a hug. “Thanks, Sharon.”

“I’ll keep an eye on your dad, let you know what happens. I hope—I hope you find Sam.”

“I know.” Zoe followed Jonathan out, catching his arm again as they reached the car. “So are we going home?”

“You are. I’ll drive you to the airport.”

“You’re not coming with me?”

“I have one more stop.”

What more could he do? Go to the rehab place? What point was there in that? “Where?”

He wouldn’t meet her eyes. “San Diego.”

A chill crept up Zoe's spine. She knew that the man who'd raped her was originally from San Diego. "What's in San Diego?"

Jonathan didn't answer right away.

"Not Franky Bates," she said.

His voice was regretful. "Now that Ely's in the clear, we have to make sure Franky doesn't have Sam."

It made sense. But the mere possibility of *anything* bringing Franky back into her life was enough to make Zoe's knees give out. Then the ground rushed up to meet her.

Tiffany had kept her promise. She'd brought a peanut butter-and-jelly sandwich after Sam had forced herself to swallow a few dry pellets of dog food. But that had been hours and hours ago, and Sam was hungry again, so hungry her stomach cramped constantly.

Where was Tiffany? And Colin? Surely, after so long, he'd returned from work. Sam hated being unable to see out of the room and she hated her lack of clothes. But nothing hurt as much as the way she missed her mom.

She eyed the dog food by the door. If she ever wanted to see Zoe again, she needed to eat. She wouldn't be able to move if she didn't regain her strength. Merely holding on, praying, wasn't enough. Help didn't seem to be coming….

"I'm on my own," she whispered.

Finally relinquishing her hold on the ragged blanket, she crawled to the dog food. Could she choke down more of it? Would it make her sick if she did?

It wouldn't leave her any worse off than she was already. But having to lick up her own vomit if her stomach revolted made her afraid to even try. She'd been warned, and she believed Colin would enjoy following through on the threat.

Pressing her ear against the door, she strained to hear the slightest sound. Were Tiffany and Colin at home? The house seemed empty. But it was hard to tell. She didn't know why, but she couldn't hear much in this room. It might be that the Bells were downstairs having dinner—and if she made any noise Colin would come up to punish her.

He'll kill you. He wasn't lying about that....

Sam's tears dripped into the dog bowl. Barely strong enough to lift her head, she slumped over and watched them fall. Then she squeezed her eyes closed, scooped the pellets into both hands and shoved them in her mouth.

After chewing as fast as she could, she washed the food down with water from the second bowl. For all she knew, that water had been taken out of a toilet. It would be like her "master" to do something so gross. But she had no choice. She had to be strong enough to escape if the opportunity arose....

Dog food tasted so terrible she couldn't believe even *dogs* liked it, but at least those pellets filled her belly, momentarily easing the aching and growling. Soon, she was feeling a bit better—until she spotted something that sent her fear spiraling to new heights.

There, along the baseboard, she found a series of little marks, made with a sharp object or maybe just a fingernail. They weren't random; they were grouped in fives. Four straight lines, then one slanting through the four; it was how her mother kept track of the flyers she bundled for the real estate agents at her office. The "pet" who'd been trapped in this room before her, the one who'd probably left that stain on the mattress, had been keeping track of something. And Sam was pretty sure she knew what because she was tempted to do the same.

These marks represented days. Days spent inside this

room, locked up and treated the way she was being treated—like a dog.

Lying on her stomach, she swept her gaze along the row of groupings, counting and recounting—and staring at that final mark, which was all by itself.

Sixty-six in all. Sixty-five and then one.

What happened on day sixty-six?

14

"What's wrong?" Tiffany asked.

Eager to tell Zoe about the posse he'd formed to search for Sam on Saturday morning, Colin had gone next door as soon as he arrived home from work. But Anton Lucassi had told him Zoe was "out of town."

"She's not out of town," he said, stalking around the living room. "That's stupid. Where would she go?"

Tiffany finally mumbled a sentence he couldn't quite hear.

"What?" Grabbing her by the blouse, he hauled her up from the couch, lifting her off the ground until their noses touched. "If you've got something to say to me, speak up."

"I said you seem to care more about Zoe than you do about Sam."

With a scowl, he let her go. "The girl's sick. What can I do with her when she's infectious? You think I wanna get mono?"

"No," she muttered.

"That's right."

"But you could train her. You spent hours and hours training Rover. You loved it."

"Yeah, well, she's smarter than Rover. It won't be as much fun." Besides, the excitement going on next door wouldn't last forever. He wanted to be with Zoe, wanted to share every emotion-filled minute.

He remembered her accepting his cigarette, bringing it to her lips…. "I bet he's lying," he said as he adjusted himself.

Tiffany's eyes flicked to the proof of his arousal. "Who?"

"Anton."

"But he doesn't have any reason to lie about Zoe."

"He sure as hell does! He wants to get rid of me. He sees me as a threat."

"Why would he see you as a threat?"

"Because I'm a hell of a lot younger than he is, that's why. I can give Zoe pleasure he can only dream about. I bet he can't even get it up half the time."

Dread shadowed Tiffany's features. "Why are you talking like that, Colin? Are you teasing me again?"

He wasn't teasing. But there was nothing to be gained by letting Tiffany know how much he was coming to admire Zoe. He'd originally considered Zoe stuck up, had only been tempted by the challenge she provided, but after spending time with her he realized that she was just…cautious.

He wondered what had made her that way….

"Colin?" Tiffany prompted.

"Of course I'm joking," he snapped. "What do you think? You're such an easy mark."

She raised her chin. "Then why are you mad at Anton?"

"Because I'm trying to help him, and he's turning me away."

"Trying to help him?" she echoed. "You're the reason he's miserable!"

"No, *you're* the reason," he said with a smirk. "And he doesn't know we had anything to do with Samantha's disappearance."

"He's probably not shutting you out on purpose. He's just…mourning the loss of his stepdaughter."

"She's *not* his stepdaughter."

"She will be when they get married."

Colin shook his head. "No way. Zoe's not stupid—she won't go through with marrying him. He's not nearly good enough for her."

A strange gleam came into Tiffany's eyes, a gleam that reminded him of her brother, who was currently sitting on death row. "Why are you so interested in the woman next door?" she asked. "What's gotten into you all of a sudden? You're making me regret taking Sam."

He wanted to use his fists to vent the burst of irritation that flashed through him at this small act of defiance. Already imagining the satisfaction of feeling his knuckles crush her face, he curled his fingers into his palm—but at that moment a familiar face appeared on the television behind her, making him freeze. "Turn that up!"

Motivated by the look that had, no doubt, come over him before he'd almost hit her and the sharpness of his voice, she scrambled to obey. Then she stepped aside so he could see the anchorman give a thirty-second preview of the news.

"…A boy, from Antelope, found naked and badly beaten, tells a harrowing tale. His story? He claims to have been lured into a car by a man, who tortured him for weeks. More at eleven."

Zoe stood next to Jonathan at the front desk of a moderately priced hotel on Hotel Circle in San Diego. She hated the thought of renting a room for the night, but after her collapse, Jonathan wouldn't let her head home on her own, and they'd gotten into such terrible traffic it was too late to go and see Franky's mother. Zoe figured there wasn't much point in rushing back, anyway. Detective

Thomas had called to give her an update and assured her that he and several other officers were searching, but hadn't found anything.

"Would you like a queen-size bed or a king-size bed for each room?" The hotel clerk smiled graciously.

Jonathan turned to Zoe.

"I'm getting my own room?" she asked.

He seemed surprised. "Isn't that what you want?"

Definitely not. She couldn't be alone. The worry and fear she'd been holding at bay would eat her alive. "No."

She halfway expected him to suggest the obvious—that it might not look good should Anton hear of it. But she didn't plan on crossing any lines, so she didn't see why Anton would have to know. She just had to get through another night, and being with Jonathan was easier than facing an interminable number of hours alone.

Fortunately, he didn't question her decision. He didn't even comment on it. He simply took charge as if it was perfectly normal to share a room. And she knew he hadn't misunderstood her motivation when he asked for two beds in one room.

The hotel clerk frowned as he consulted the computer. "It's our busy season. I doubt we have a double," he said, but his eyes continued to scan the screen. Half a minute later, his smile was back. "You're in luck. We've had a cancellation."

Zoe had insisted on coming in rather than waiting in the car so she could pay the bill. She knew Skye's charity had more people to help than just her, that it had to be difficult for The Last Stand to stay afloat. She didn't want to be a drain on its assets. Not when she was so grateful for what Skye was already providing. But Jonathan pushed the credit card she placed on the counter out of the clerk's reach. "I've got it."

"Jon, I can't keep…"

He cocked an eyebrow at her. "What?"

"Taking."

"Why not?"

"Because it makes me feel guilty. Like a—a slouch or—"

"I'd have to rent a room if you weren't here," he interrupted. "Give yourself a break for a change." The smile that curved his lips somehow evoked a return smile, probably the first one that had come naturally to her since Samantha's disappearance.

"You are so—" She caught herself. She'd been about to say, "Handsome." It had nearly rolled right off her tongue, probably because it would've been an honest statement. She'd thought it several times during the day, but she knew better than to say it, especially now. It was the exhaustion. She was too tired to be careful.

He studied her openly, rubbing the beard growth on his chin. "What?"

Zoe felt herself flush. "Nice." She averted her eyes, but she suspected they'd already said what she hadn't.

He didn't follow up with a comment. He signed the slip the clerk handed him and took a map of the complex.

"Stay here. I'll grab the luggage," he said and left.

When he came walking through the lobby doors with the bags, Zoe felt a renewed sense of chagrin at the admiration that must've been apparent on her face. What had she been thinking? She was attracted to this man!

And now she was pretty sure he knew it.

"How'd it go today?" Skye asked.

"Fine." Jonathan could hear the shower running and tried not to think about Zoe standing naked beneath the spray. Considering the situation, he was an asshole to even imagine it, but hormones were hormones, and he couldn't seem to curb the erotic images flowing through his brain.

That moment in the lobby when she'd started to say something and then stopped had created a sexual undercurrent that was hard to ignore. Although they'd probably been aware of each other all along, that awareness had definitely been very much in the background. Since arriving at the hotel, however, he'd felt a marked change.

"Fine?" Skye echoed, obviously surprised that he didn't launch into an accounting of the day's events. "Does Ely have Samantha or not?"

"No, Ely's blissfully unaware of regular life. He's been in rehab for the past month."

"Blissfully? I doubt it. But at least he's not in jail. Rehab's a good alternative."

"Except I was hoping he had Sam. Our other options aren't nearly as attractive."

"He can't tell you anything? He hasn't heard from her?"

"According to the woman who's been getting his mail, he hasn't received a letter from Sam in weeks."

"So you didn't meet with him?"

He adjusted the time on the room's clock radio, which was wrong by more than four hours. "No. Zoe was afraid he'd drop out and go on a bender."

"Well, she is the one who knows him."

"I'm guessing her decision has more to do with her than him. She's too fragile to deal with the issues between her and her father in addition to the current crisis."

"You have to start looking at Sam's biological father, Jon," Skye said.

"I know." He put the clock back. "I'm on it."

"Have you found him?"

Resting his elbows on his knees, he stared at the gold-colored carpet. "Not yet. But I've done some checking. I think he's in San Diego."

The shower went off and he pictured Zoe getting out and toweling herself dry. Then he rolled his eyes at his own response. What was wrong with him? He was in love with Sheridan, had been for years.

But he was tired of waiting for a woman he wasn't going to get. And Zoe's beauty and vulnerability drew him like a magnet.

He pinched the bridge of his nose in an effort to block out his growing attraction. "As soon as we get up in the morning, I'll—"

"Who's *we?*" she cut in.

"I've got Zoe here with me."

The volume of Skye's voice instantly switched to *loud.* "You're not taking her to find Franky Bates!"

"Of course not."

"Good." There was a short pause. "So what *are* you doing?"

Trying not to think of her in a sexual way. Trying to remind myself that she only wanted to share my hotel room because I seem like her safe, trustworthy helper. Trying to keep in mind that her saying I'm nice can't be construed as an invitation...

Because even if it *was* an invitation, she wasn't in any condition to be making that decision.

"I'm doing what I can while I'm here."

Zoe came out of the bathroom and steam billowed out with her. Jonathan allowed himself a quick peek and saw a strip of golden skin above a pair of pink pajama bottoms that rode low on her hips, bare arms and shoulders and a hint of cleavage showing above a spaghetti-strap top. Her long hair was wrapped in a towel.

Sucking in a deep breath, he quickly shored up his restraint with one word that was pretty much a shortcut to all the rest: *engaged.* "I'd arrange a flight for her in the morning, but that would take more time than simply having her wait at the hotel while I pay a visit to Franky's mother. We don't have the luxury of wasting *any* time."

He'd been talking to Skye, but Zoe turned to face him. "You're not leaving me anywhere."

He couldn't answer without giving away her proximity. Fortunately, Skye was talking and hadn't heard her. "You think Franky's mother will tell you where to find him?"

"Stranger things have happened."

"She might be too protective."

"I gotta start somewhere."

Frowning at him, Zoe toweled off her hair, and the scent of shampoo reached his nostrils.

Eager to get off the phone before Zoe spoke up again, he said, "I've gotta go. I'm beat."

But Skye wasn't quite done. "Wait a sec. Where's Zoe now? I'd like to talk to her."

He debated his response—and settled on the first lie he'd ever told her. Well, besides the one about his feelings for Sheridan. "She's in another room," he said. "You'll have to try her cell."

Fortunately, Skye didn't question it. "Will do. 'Night."

With a sigh, he punched the End button, tossed the phone aside and headed for the bathroom. He told himself to ignore Zoe, to stay focused on his destination. But he didn't. He looked up as he passed her, and their eyes locked in the mirror.

"Why'd you just say I have my own room?" she asked.

Lying about being together made it far less innocuous than it'd seemed in the lobby. He understood that. But did she really want others to know?

He leaned one shoulder against the wall and let his

eyes range over her. She lowered her lashes so he couldn't read her reaction, but her lips parted and the rise and fall of her chest quickened. She was feeling the same excitement that sizzled through his veins.

To prove it, he stepped up behind her, rested one hand on the curve of her waist and lightly brushed his mouth against the side of her neck.

She didn't turn and fall into his arms, but neither did she stop him.

"Feel that?" he murmured when she shivered.

Swallowing, she watched him with more desire than trust, but she nodded.

"That's why," he said. Then he forced himself to go into the bathroom and close the door.

"What will we do?" Tiffany asked. She'd been agitated all evening, ever since they'd heard that Rover had been flapping his big mouth. But now that the eleven o'clock news was over and they'd seen the whole segment, complete with shots of a now-comatose Rover in the hospital, surrounded by his concerned family, she was almost frantic. "Colin, *I* don't want to go to prison like my brother!"

"You're not going to prison, so shut up," he said. "Rover's in a freaking coma!"

"He could wake up."

"He's not going to wake up. You heard what the doctor said. He has brain damage, maybe a twenty percent chance of survival." Stretching out his legs, Colin propped them on the coffee table. He had work to do, research for a litigation case he hadn't been able to finish at the office, but he didn't feel like tackling it.

"What if he tells the police what kind of car we drive? His school's right down the street from your father's place."

"Get me a beer," he said.

She didn't move, but when he narrowed his eyes, she got up and hurried to the kitchen. He heard her open the fridge, then a cupboard. Seconds later, she was back with a cold one, which he accepted, but only after knocking her hand away when she tried to run her fingers through his hair. "Leave me alone."

"I'm your wife," she said. "You don't want me to touch you?"

"I'm not in the mood."

"So you *are* worried."

Not really. If Rover did wake up, he probably wouldn't be able to give a decent description or even remember his own name. Colin was more angry than frightened. He'd wanted to see Zoe tonight. He'd had it all planned out, everything he was going to tell her. He'd imagined them sharing another secret cigarette, a sympathetic hug, an innocent kiss, a less-than-innocent grope—

"Colin? We're not going to do anything about it?"

"What can we do? This isn't some TV show where we can sneak into his hospital room and smother him. Besides, there's no need. He won't come out of it. I hit him with a bat. His brain is mush."

"You have to at least consider the possibility."

"Why? What good will that do? Live for today, right? It's all part of the risk, the price we pay for fun."

"But I don't want to go to prison," she repeated.

Tiffany was getting on his nerves. He wasn't interested in Rover anymore. Rover was old news. He had Samantha now. And that brought Zoe to her knees—metaphorically speaking, of course, but he longed for the day when that might actually happen.

"Colin?"

"*What?*" he snapped.

"Don't you care if we get caught?"

"Will you drop it already? We won't get caught, not that easily."

"He knows our names. Our first names, anyway. Maybe we made him call us Master and Mistress, but I'm sure he overheard us talking to each other once in a while."

"He was stoned most of the time we were with him. He can try to describe us, but you've seen as many cop shows as I have. They can't find jackshit unless there's an accident or coincidence that makes some piece of evidence too obvious to miss. They work their shift and go home. They don't really care about the Rovers of the world. They only care about their next paycheck."

"Not all cops are like that."

"I'm telling you, they're idiots. How often have we heard the narrator on A&E say that if it wasn't for some piece of information—which happened to get overlooked but was in the file the whole damn time—such and such a killer would've gotten away?" He sucked the foam off his beer. "It's a miracle they catch *anybody,* Tiff. Even if they know you're guilty, they have to prove it beyond a reasonable doubt, and there's no proof to back up Rover's story." He scowled. "We wouldn't have hurt him if he hadn't refused to take off his pants. You know what happens to me when I get angry. Sometimes I can't help myself."

She sank down on the couch beside him. "He spent a lot of time with us. Who knows how much we revealed? We weren't expecting him to get away."

"But even if he says something to make the police focus on us, they'll have to *prove* we're guilty."

"They could come here and search—and then they'd find Sam. I say we get rid of her."

"We will. But there's no hurry."

"How will you know when we should do it?"

"Because I'll be paying attention."

She nibbled on her swollen lip. "I wonder if he can give them the make and model of our car."

"Quit worrying."

"Maybe we should trade it in."

"And replace it how?" Their budget was too tight. He made a decent salary, but not nearly as much as the senior partners. And Tiffany earned a mere pittance. "Maybe if you had an education and were worth more than ten dollars an hour, that'd be an option, but you're practically worthless." He grabbed her chin so he could examine her injury. "Speaking of money, you're going to work tomorrow."

"But my lip hasn't quite healed."

"I don't care. It doesn't look so bad now, and you're out of sick days."

She didn't say anything. He knew she hated changing bedpans, but why should he be the only one to slave away day after day?

"Are your friends coming over on Friday?" she asked.

"Of course." The question annoyed him at first, but it also reminded him that there were better ways to spend an evening than sulking on the couch.

"Take this off," he said, tugging on her blouse.

Obediently, she lifted it over her head, revealing one of the lacy bras he'd picked out at the mall the last time they went. He always bought her bras one size too small so they forced her breasts up and over the top.

"Nice." He ran a finger along the swell of her cleavage, over the tattoos of his name. Maybe tonight didn't have to be miserable after all. He could tie Tiffany to the bed—facedown—and pretend she was Zoe.

15

Zoe was still shaking when she got into bed. What had just happened? One minute she'd been thinking about Franky Bates, which never failed to leave a heavy, unyielding lump in her stomach; the next, Franky couldn't have been further from her mind. When Jonathan touched her so tenderly, she'd been consumed by a passion unlike anything she'd ever experienced before.

Was it simply the famous lure of "forbidden fruit"? What would she have done if he'd continued? If that hand that'd rested so lightly on her hip had slipped up to curve around her breast?

Stifling a groan, she pulled the covers over her head. She would've shoved him away, of course. And if there was any chance she wouldn't have done that, she didn't want to know about it. She felt bad enough that she'd enjoyed the sample.

Stop it. Her reaction didn't really mean anything. It was minor amidst a plethora of more critical concerns, like getting Sam home safely. Zoe wasn't herself, would never be herself again, until her daughter was safe.

"Forget it," she whispered, but try as she might, she couldn't forget. She kept imagining the smooth muscle she'd felt when she touched his arm earlier, the warmth of his breath stirring the tendrils of hair at the napc of her neck, the tingling sensation that'd ripped through her when his lips moved across her skin—

Throwing back the covers, she sat up and grabbed her cell. She had to call Anton. She'd checked in with him periodically throughout the day, knew he would've called her if anything had changed, but she needed to talk to him again, if only to remind herself of their relationship. Since Sam's disappearance, she didn't feel connected to anyone. But that was no excuse. She had to say no to more regret, no to another breakup, no to another move.

Stability. That was the goal. What her father had never been able to provide. Anton was a decent man, a steady man. She'd made the decision when she moved in with him that this was forever. She needed to remain committed.

The call-waiting feature on her cell phone beeped. She knew without glancing at caller ID that it was Skye. But she didn't switch over. She could call her in the morning. Right now, she needed to talk to Anton.

When her fiancé finally answered, he sounded as tired as she felt. "Sorry, I was on the other line with Detective Thomas," he said of his delay.

"Do you want to call me back?"

"No, it's okay. He's gone."

Zoe leaned against the headboard. "What'd he have to say?"

"Not much." He sighed loudly. "He's as baffled as we are. There've been a few leads trickling in, but none of them have panned out."

Far colder than she'd been a moment before, she burrowed beneath the blankets. "I can't go on like this," she said.

"Unfortunately, you don't have any choice, Zoe. No one ever *asks* for this kind of trouble. Sometimes it just…happens."

He sounded like her father, not her lover. Couldn't he be more intimate in his support? Couldn't he tell her he was there for her? That he'd always be there for her? That they'd get through this together?

Suddenly wishing she hadn't called, she hurried to get off the phone. "I'm exhausted. I'll talk to you tomorrow."

"Where are you right now?"

"L.A." She winced at the lie but definitely didn't want to mention San Diego.

"I know *that,*" he said. "Where are you staying?"

Afraid he'd somehow sense the guilt that'd made her contact him, she curled into a ball. "In a hotel."

Since he hadn't wanted her to go to Southern California with Jonathan in the first place, she expected his next question to be about their sleeping arrangements. But it wasn't. "How are you paying for the room?" he asked.

She nearly laughed aloud. She was worried that she might wind up sleeping with Skye's private investigator. And he was worried about a hundred and twenty-nine bucks.

"The Last Stand is taking care of it," she said. At least, she *thought* the charity was paying the bill—although the credit card Jonathan had used looked like his own.

"That's a relief. The longer this goes on, the more expensive it'll be."

"Are you angry I chose colored flyers?"

"I can see why you did it, but it wasn't the best use of our resources, especially since the police investigator told me we should offer a reward."

Of course! Why hadn't she thought of that?

Probably because she didn't have any money.

"How much?" She wished for the millionth time that she had the sort of background he did, that she could be the one with reserves in the bank and the ability to help herself.

"Ten thousand."

That was *nothing* compared to what she'd give for her daughter. But she didn't have it. And she knew how much ten thousand dollars would be to a saver like Anton. "What do you think?" she asked.

"We might have to do it."

She clutched the blankets even tighter. He was going to offer a reward, and she was going to let him—even though less than ten minutes earlier she'd been craving another man. What kind of woman did that make her?

"Thank you, Anton." She swallowed around the lump in her throat. If his money brought Sam home, she'd be anything he wanted her to be, for as long as he asked. "I—I won't let you down."

"What?"

The shower went off, and her heart pounded. "Nothing."

"Get some sleep. You're mumbling."

"Good night."

"I love you," he said.

"I—"

She started to repeat the sentiment. Then the bathroom door opened and Jonathan walked out wearing only a towel—and the words wouldn't come.

"'Night," she said again and hung up.

Zoe was positive she wouldn't be able to sleep. She was beyond exhausted, but like last night, the constant worry and agitation wouldn't allow her to shut down.

Although he hadn't spoken since getting out of the shower, she could tell from his movements that Jonathan was awake, too. He was in the opposite bed, wearing his jeans because he probably hadn't brought an alternative.

She felt slightly guilty if wearing pants to bed meant he'd be less comfortable, but she still preferred not to be alone. The muffled sounds of the hotel, the darkness, the strange furniture and shadows would've made it impossible to get through the next few hours alone—and nothing, not even getting her own room, would change the fact that Skye's P.I. held some allure for her. There'd been a spark the very first time she met him, when he'd pulled her into his arms rather than keep a polite distance as most strangers would've done. She'd just been too frantic to see that. But she would've noticed tomorrow, or the next day, if not tonight.

After rearranging the blankets, she yanked down her pajama top, which had crept up above her waist, and rolled over to face the wall. Anton was posting a reward for Sam. She needed to concentrate on how kind and generous that was instead of dwelling on the instinctive way Jonathan acted to fulfill her needs. Anton was the one who'd promised to marry her and adopt Sam, to be the kind of father she'd never had, the kind of father she wanted for her daughter.

She adjusted her pillows. Sam… Would she ever see her child again? Could Franky Bates somehow have learned of her existence?

The man who'd raped her seemed capable of anything, but—

Jon's voice broke into her thoughts. "Should I go to the drugstore?"

Her mind immediately conjured up a box of condoms. *Oh, God…* "What for?" she asked tentatively.

"A sedative."

She released the breath she'd been holding. It was okay. *She* was okay. Except she was so cold. By most people's standards it wasn't even chilly in the room, yet she couldn't get warm no matter what she did. "For me? No, I won't take one." She rolled over again. "I have to be alert in case I'm needed."

"You've *got* to sleep, Zoe. For a while."

She didn't respond. But after tossing and turning for a few more minutes, she finally admitted the truth. "Jon?"

"What?"

"I *can't* sleep. I can't even get warm."

She heard him get up and assumed he was on his way to the drugstore. But he didn't leave. He peeled back the covers and climbed into bed with her. She was about to protest, to tell him in no uncertain terms that she wouldn't let him touch her. Now that she knew she had to be on her guard, she wouldn't be disloyal to Anton.

But Jonathan didn't attempt any sexual advances. He simply wrapped his strong arms around her and gathered her close.

Pretty soon, his slow, even breathing began to sound like a metronome in her ear. For the first time since quitting her job on Monday, she felt somewhat secure. She was anchored to one spot; she wasn't going anywhere and neither was he. As a matter of fact, he'd already dozed off.

Timing her breathing with his, she eventually grew warm enough to sleep.

When the alarm went off the following morning, Tiffany woke with a raging headache and aching breasts. Colin had kept her up most of the night. He'd taken Viagra and wanted to make love again and again—only he hadn't been able to finish. Whenever she thought he was getting close, she moaned and writhed, did everything she could to help him. But it hadn't worked. At last, he'd dropped exhausted on the bed beside her, leaving her tied to the bedposts in case he woke up and wanted to go at it again. But after sleeping an hour, he had to get ready for work.

"Colin?"

His head popped up amid the mess they'd made of their blankets. "What?"

"It's time for work."

"Shit!" Shoving to his feet, he stumbled to the bathroom without even looking at her.

"Aren't you going to untie me?"

He used the toilet, flushed. "Why should I? You were a waste of effort last night."

She told herself to ignore him. He was in a bad mood. She'd known he would be.

But he wanted a response. He came back to loom over her, his eyes bloodshot and his mouth twisted in a spiteful grimace. "Did you hear me?"

"It wasn't my fault," she said. "I let you use whatever you wanted." The clamps on her breasts were proof. They were still on—he'd left them on for ninety minutes, so long she was growing nauseous from the pain.

"Whatever I wanted," he muttered as if it wasn't true. "Tomorrow night is when I'm going to do whatever I want." He finally removed the clamps. She hoped he'd kiss her breasts or caress them to ease the pain he'd caused. But he simply tossed the clamps onto the nightstand and untied her wrists. "I think you should get another boob job," he said.

Now that her hands were free, she rubbed her own breasts. "I'm not big enough?"

"Not by a long shot." His nose wrinkled in apparent disgust as his eyes swept over the rest of her. "Or maybe it's the weight you've gained. It's a turnoff."

She hadn't gained any weight. She checked every day. "You want me to weigh less than a hundred and twenty?"

"I want you to make me come just by looking at you."

Instead of untying her ankles, he shrugged and left it up to her. "You'd better hurry and get to the gym. I want an extra thirty minutes of cardio today."

She let go of her aching breasts, but her hands trembled so badly she had difficulty untying her ankles.

When she was free, she could barely walk because the bonds had cut off the flow of blood. She wouldn't have minded these minor injuries if the evening had gone the way it normally did. When Colin was happy, no one could be more charming. She loved it when she was able to please him. There'd been times he'd wept on her bare stomach while telling her how much he appreciated her love and patience.

"Are you dressed yet?" he called from the shower.

"Almost."

"When you're out today, get a choke chain for Sam, like the one we used for Rover."

Tiffany instantly forgot about her aches and pains. She'd hoped Colin wouldn't notice that their old one had gone missing. "Where's Rover's?" she asked.

"I can't find it. That's what I was looking for last night when I decided to do the wax instead."

She had burn marks on her belly and between her thighs where he'd dripped the hot wax, but she preferred the wax to the collar. Last time he made her wear it, she'd passed out. It had scared her enough that she'd hidden it during the chaos surrounding Rover. Sometimes Colin got so excited, he didn't know what he was doing.

"You're planning to have some fun with her?" she asked, relieved to think they might be back on familiar ground despite his request for another collar.

"Yeah. I'm taking the two of you up to my dad's cabin Saturday night. We'll spend Mother's Day there. It'll help us forget Rover."

"How will we get Sam out of the house?"

"The same way we did Rover. We'll drug her, put her in a box and carry her out as if she's part of our supplies."

"And what will we do with her once we get up there? We can't touch her 'cause of the mono, remember?"

"We can get her high. Remember how funny Rover was when we made him smoke crack?"

Rover had provided some of their biggest laughs. "That sounds like fun." She finished tying her tennis shoes. "I'm off to the gym."

"Tiffany?"

She paused at the door. "Yeah?"

"Sorry about last night. I think I was more upset about Rover than I wanted to admit."

"I understand."

"You love me?"

Suddenly her breasts didn't hurt quite so much. "Of course."

"If you'd rather not have the guys over tomorrow night, that's okay."

She didn't like competing with Colin's friends for his attention. But she was the one who'd let Rover escape, and after last night she wanted to prove to her husband that she could still excite him. Maybe after *that* big a sacrifice, he'd forget about Zoe. "It's okay. I'll show them such a good time they'll be thanking you for months afterward."

"Really?" The eagerness in his voice eliminated the last of her reservations. She could get through one night. Like Colin said, she'd probably have fun, too. She always had a good time when her husband was at his best.

"Really," she replied and discovered a dozen roses waiting for her on the doorstep when she returned from the gym.

The card read:

I could never find anyone else like you. You're perfect.
Love, Colin

16

"I'm going with you."

Holding the keys to the rental car, Jonathan studied the stubborn expression on Zoe's face. She'd just hung up with Skye, but Skye hadn't been able to talk her out of it, either. "What if we find him?"

The sleep had done her some good. Dressed in a sundress with a little white sweater over it, she looked slightly recovered—and prettier than ever. Jonathan wished he hadn't become so acutely aware of her attractiveness, but after last night he knew that wasn't likely to change. He could still smell her scent, still feel the silky texture of her skin against his lips….

Next to Sheridan, Zoe was the most beautiful woman he'd ever seen.

And equally off limits.

"That's the whole point, isn't it?" she said. "We *want* to find him."

"A confrontation with him wouldn't be easy for you."

"None of this is easy for me." She finished packing her cosmetics case and zipped her bag. "Ready?"

Blocking her path to the door, he touched her arm—which he might've done to get any woman's attention. But the energy that passed between them made him very much aware that he couldn't go back to believing she was just another client. She meant something to him, something *more.* And he didn't want to see her hurt or frightened. "Zoe, trust me to handle this."

"I trust you. But you and I both know my decision has nothing to do with that."

He dropped his hand because he was afraid he'd let it slide up her arm. "You *want* to confront him?"

"I have to speak to him myself, evaluate his response and draw my own conclusions in order to feel comfortable that we've done everything we can where he's concerned. I can't rely on you or anyone else to do that for me. This need...it's instinctual...a—a mother's prerogative. You understand, don't you?"

Unfortunately, he did. He even saw some value in having her along. She knew Franky, or at least she had at one time.

She smiled, but it was obviously forced because the expression in her eyes remained wary. "Besides, maybe it'll do me good to see him from an adult's perspective. To finally meet him on an equal footing. Maybe he won't seem so all-powerful and threatening."

"When was the last time you saw him?"

"When I testified in court."

"Maybe seeing him again will only bring back the nightmare."

She managed a laugh as she shook her head. "I had a baby from that experience, Jon. The knowledge, the memory, is etched on my brain forever. There's no bringing back something that's always present."

She had a point. With a sigh, Jonathan waved her through the door, hoping he wouldn't regret his decision. She'd suffered so much already. He preferred to shield her, if she'd let him, but he wasn't patronizing enough to think he knew better than she did. "Have it your way."

They walked to the car in silence. Jonathan put their bags

in the trunk, then slipped on his sunglasses and got behind the wheel. "Ready?" he said once he'd started the car.

She'd put on her own sunglasses and, once again, he got the impression they helped create a barrier between her and the rest of the world. "Ready."

He hesitated before shifting into Reverse. "There's one other risk."

"What's that?"

"If he's not the one, if he doesn't already know about her, he will after today."

He wished he could see what was going on behind those glasses, but he couldn't.

"I know."

Somehow Zoe had always intuitively understood that the day would come when she'd have to face Franky again—if only because she'd developed such a fear of him. His actions suggested that what he'd done hadn't been premeditated. He'd raped her because she was home alone and he was on drugs. The crime was opportunistic. At least that was the argument his attorney had claimed at his trial. Franky hadn't stalked her, and he hadn't tried to contact her afterward.

The D.A. who'd prosecuted him had even admitted that he seemed contrite once he came to his senses. But *contrite* held no meaning for Zoe. She'd only been fifteen when he'd forced her into her room and pulled up her skirt. She supposed it was natural to think he'd do it again if given the chance, to fear he might start harassing her if she reminded him of her existence.

They stopped at the curb in front of his mother's house and the radio fell silent as Jonathan cut the engine. Zoe wiped her sweaty palms on her dress and reached for the door latch.

Jonathan stopped her. "Why don't I go up first?"

"No," she said and got out.

The house wasn't really a house. It was one-half of a duplex in a run-down part of town. The yard had no plants, just patches of crabgrass where foot traffic hadn't worn it into the dirt. An old couch sat on the front porch. It sagged in the middle and had an ashtray on one arm.

"How long has his mother lived here?" she murmured as Jonathan came up behind her.

"Deed I pulled up said she bought it in '64, so…a while. Why was Franky at your father's?"

"His girlfriend lived in the park, in unit 5."

"And he busted into your father's trailer because he knew you were there?"

"No. Initially, I don't think it had anything to do with me. He was stoned and looking for more drugs."

"Your father was selling at that time?"

"He certainly wasn't working a regular job."

"Gotcha."

When he lifted his hand to ring the doorbell, she nearly stopped him. She needed another minute to prepare herself. But Sam was out there somewhere. She didn't have the luxury of extra time, so she made no move.

A shrunken woman, no more than five feet tall and maybe eighty years old, came to the door wearing a pair of bifocals, a purple polyester shirt with matching pants and orthopedic shoes.

"Mrs. Bates?"

Jonathan did the talking. Zoe's mouth had gone too dry to speak.

The woman at the door glanced from one to the other. "I'm Eva Norris, Sandra Bates's mother."

"We're looking for Franky."

Her eyes, the color of melted chocolate, grew darker with worry. "What do you want with him?"

"A young girl's gone missing. We'd like to see if he knows anything about it."

"He couldn't," she said. "He wouldn't jeopardize his freedom. He's straightened out."

"We just want to talk to him," Jonathan said. "Can you tell us where to find him?"

She didn't answer.

"A child's life is in danger," he emphasized.

Her gaze shifted to some point behind them, far away on the horizon. Then she yelled into the house. "Franky!"

The answer was immediate. "What, Gran?"

"Get out here."

This was the moment. Zoe was about to come face-to-face with Sam's father. The man who'd raped her.

Filled with sudden panic, she longed to grab Jonathan's hand but didn't. She had Anton to think of. She had to do this on her own.

He glanced at her, no doubt checking to see how she was holding up. But there was no time to speak. A second later, Franky Bates stood behind his shriveled "gran" and Zoe couldn't breathe. He looked completely different than she remembered—taller, broader, better groomed. And the shape of his mouth and chin! It was so much like Sam's!

"What's up?" He questioned Jonathan first, even accepted a business card but didn't look at it. His gaze traveled to her, then his eyes widened and his mouth dropped open in disbelief.

"What are *you* doing here?" he breathed, his cheeks mottled.

Jonathan spoke before Zoe could respond. "I'm a private investigator from Sacramento. I'm here to—"

"Did you take her?" Zoe cut in, too impatient to wait through the explanation.

He raised his eyebrows. "Take who?"

"My daughter." She wasn't remotely tempted to say *our* daughter, despite the marked resemblance….

He lifted both hands as if she held a gun. "I don't know what you're talking about. I did you wrong thirteen years ago. I—I've often hoped I'd have the opportunity to apologize for that, to tell you I'm sorry. *Really* sorry."

She was finally able to draw enough breath to respond, but he pressed on before she could summon the words.

"I don't expect you to forgive me, but…there wasn't a day in prison that I didn't regret it. I was messed up or I never would've done it." No doubt his grandmother heard the contrition in his voice because she put her arm around him, and he acknowledged the gesture with a sad smile. "I'm not saying that as an excuse, but I served my time, and—and I'm hoping for a second chance."

"Have you been to northern California since you got out?" Jonathan asked.

"No." He shook his head, adamant. "I haven't been anywhere but here. Ask Gran. My grandpa passed away ten days ago. The funeral was last week. Since then I've been looking for work." He pointed at a relatively new Ford F-150 parked in the driveway. "Gramps left me his truck so I could continue applying for jobs—you know, get a start. That's all I been doin.'"

Visibly relieved by Franky's apparent sincerity, Gran nodded. "It's true."

Franky was still nervous, but not the kind of nervous that made Zoe disbelieve him. He felt awkward, remorseful. Licking his lips, he talked faster, trying to convince her. "I wouldn't target you or—or hurt you again. I didn't even know you had a daughter—"

Suddenly it seemed to occur to him why they might be contacting him, and he staggered back. "Wait…she's not *mine,* is she? I mean, that's not why you're here."

Pivoting, Zoe walked away before the tears welling up could spill over her lashes. He didn't have Sam; he hadn't even known Sam existed, just as she'd thought. This trip was a complete waste. Her chest constricted and she had difficulty breathing. It'd been three days since she'd seen her daughter. Where could Sam be?

"Ms.… I don't know what you call yourself these days. And I don't want to disrespect you by using your first name, but I'm sorry."

Zoe didn't respond. Jonathan exchanged a few words with him. It sounded as if he was taking down Franky's number. Then he followed her down the walk.

"Is she mine?" Franky called out as they reached the car.

"Of course not," she said, but she refused to turn around. She didn't want to see him, didn't want to give him any more information.

"She is, isn't she!"

"No." She opened her door.

"If I don't have a kid, what's all this about?"

"Nothing that concerns you anymore." Jonathan went around to the driver's side.

Franky squeezed past his grandmother and came halfway down the walk. "What happened to her? Is she okay?"

If only Zoe knew…. "Good luck finding a job."

"Tell me what's going on! What can I do to help?"

"Nothing. There's absolutely nothing you can do," Zoe said and closed the car door.

Shoulders slumped, he shoved his hands in his pockets. "You can't drop a bomb like that on me and then just drive away!"

His words filtered through Jonathan's open door. "If

you're truly sorry for what you did, that's exactly what you'll let us do," Jonathan said and got in.

"Call me," Franky yelled after them, his voice fainter now that the door was shut. "I'll help if I can. Just…one of you call me."

The radio came back on as Jonathan started the engine. Now it sounded far too loud, but he drove off before lowering the volume. "You okay?"

"We've got to get back to Sacramento," she said.

"We're going to the airport right now."

She cleared her throat. "He gave you his number?"

"He did. Do you want it?"

"No." She had nothing more to fear from Franky Bates. She could close that chapter in her life. But what would have once been a tremendous relief brought little consolation. She wasn't any closer to finding Sam. She shouldn't have come here, shouldn't have wasted the time.

Jonathan took her hand. She knew better than to allow him to comfort her. There was too much going on between them under the surface—too much that confused and tempted her. But somehow the connection felt absolutely vital, and she couldn't make herself let go, especially when she glanced up and saw him watching her with such an intense expression.

"We can be friends," he said as if holding her hand was no big deal, as if justifying the contact somehow made it right.

"We can be friends," she repeated, but that changed nothing. The way he threaded his fingers through hers felt possessive, deeply personal…even sexual. And, at that point, she knew it was a *very* good thing that they were heading home. She couldn't fight the attraction between her and Jonathan, not while she was so frightened, so worried about Sam. Without her daughter, she didn't care enough about her own self-preservation to hang on to anything else. Including her dignity.

17

Getting home was worse than being gone. The house where she'd lived for ten months looked even more foreign to Zoe than it had yesterday, as foreign as the rest of the houses on the street, most of which were dark because it was nearly midnight on a Thursday. She'd once felt so proud to be part of this neighborhood, this community. She'd studied style magazines, changed her appearance and thought she'd finally "made it."

Smiling bitterly at the shattered illusion, she collected her purse as Jonathan put the transmission in Park. Because he'd left his car in long-term parking at the airport, he'd offered her a ride. She'd accepted with the excuse that it would save Anton from having to leave the house so late. But the ride wasn't about convenience. She wasn't ready to say goodbye to Jonathan. Or maybe she wasn't ready to see Anton. She couldn't decide which.

A light gleamed through the living-room window. Her fiancé was waiting up for her. She supposed it was nice of him, but she wished he hadn't bothered. Maybe by morning she'd be able to figure out why she was so drawn to Jonathan instead of the man she'd agreed to marry.

Was it hero worship? Admiration because he seemed to be so much more capable of helping her find Samantha? Raw physical attraction?

Whatever the reason, she wanted him in a way she hadn't wanted a man in a long time. And that only compounded her problems.

How was this unexpected attraction seeping through the haze of shock and pain when nothing else could? That confused her most of all.

"Good night," she said as she got out.

He didn't attempt to touch her. He hadn't touched her since he'd taken her hand for those few minutes after leaving Franky's place. "Don't give up hope," he said with an encouraging smile.

"No," she murmured. But if her daughter was still alive, why hadn't they found some trace of her? Received a ransom note? "Thanks for everything."

"I'll be around tomorrow. I've got an early appointment on another case, but then I'll be talking to your neighbors, Sam's teachers at school, the kids whose parents will allow me to meet with them, anyone who might have an inkling of where she might be."

If he did track her down, would she be dead? Would they discover her body tossed in a field or a Dumpster?

Despite the macabre image that thought raised in her mind, Zoe managed a fleeting smile before closing the door. Then she stood and watched as he drove off. It wasn't until his taillights disappeared around the corner that she started toward the front door.

"Who was *that?*"

The voice came from the dark stoop of her neighbor's house. "Colin?" She squinted, waiting for her eyes to adjust to the moonlight.

"Yeah, it's me. Sorry if I scared you. I heard the car and thought maybe you'd found her." The slurring of his words indicated he'd been drinking.

"No."

"No new leads?"

"No old ones, either. At least none Detective Thomas hasn't ruled out." Her small suitcase had wheels, but she was reluctant to set it down. She didn't want a conversation with Colin right now. Especially if he was drunk. She had to go in and face Anton.

He clicked his tongue. "That's too bad."

"I'm sorry to be unsociable, but I'm exhausted. I hope you'll forgive me if…" She made a move for the house, but he stopped her.

"Hey, not so fast. I've been waiting all night."

"For…?"

He didn't clarify. "Who's that guy you were with?"

He'd *definitely* had too much to drink. He and his wife threw an occasional party. Zoe and Anton had heard the loud music that sometimes pounded late into the night, but it didn't happen often, and Colin and Tiffany seldom invited more than a friend or two, so it hadn't been a problem. Maybe they'd had one of their parties tonight….

"Jonathan's a private investigator," she explained. "He's helping with the search."

"His name is Jonathan?"

She hesitated, unsure of Colin's suspicious tone. "Yes. Jonathan Stivers. Have you heard of him?"

"Not until now. But…he's a nice-looking man, I'll give him that."

How was she supposed to respond? "How'd you see more than a glimpse of him?"

"He was here the other night."

"Oh, right." She transferred her suitcase to her other hand as Colin came toward her. Once he stepped out of the shadows, she could tell that he wasn't wearing a shirt or shoes, just a pair of sweatpants. And his hair was mussed as if he'd shoved his fingers through it a few too many times.

"Don't you trust the police to handle the investigation?" he asked.

"They're doing what they can, but more help is always better."

"Actually, they're useless." He scratched his bare chest. "But this Jonathan…he's good?"

"I think so. He's smart, thorough."

"You just said he hasn't dredged up a single lead." He fingered one of his nipples, which made Zoe squirm to get farther away. She'd never seen him without his shirt and it felt odd that he'd come outside to talk to her half-dressed. She supposed he'd been in a hurry, trying to catch her. But did he have to touch himself?

"It's a difficult case," she said.

"You sound defensive."

She *was* defensive of Jonathan, which served as further proof of her infatuation with him. "I'm trying to be fair."

He dropped his hand and she staunchly ignored the puckering of his nipples. "I doubt it's as tough as everyone's claiming," he scoffed. "It's probably some registered sex offender living in our own neighborhood. I swear they should paint a big red X on each of their doors."

Could Sam be that close? It made sense, especially now that they'd eliminated Franky as a suspect and her father as a potential refuge.

She gazed down the dark street. "The police mentioned there are a few in the area." These days they were in *every* area.

"What are the police—or Jonathan—doing about it?"

"They're interviewing each one and checking on their whereabouts."

"As if walking around and passing out cards will solve any crime."

Colin was concerned about Sam, too. She felt grateful for that. But she was too much on edge to tolerate his suggestion that the forces on her side were too inept or powerless to make a difference. *Don't give up hope….*

As supportive as Colin was trying to be, he wasn't helping tonight; she had to escape him before she fell to new depths of despair. "Good night."

"Where'd he take you, Zoe?" he asked as if she hadn't just ended the conversation. Her name had come out more softly than the rest, so it sounded…intimate.

That's the alcohol. It was making him act strange. She wanted to pretend she hadn't heard him. But she couldn't repay his kindness of the other night by being rude to him now, even if he was drunk.

Extending the handle on her suitcase, she finally put it on the ground. "To L.A."

"What's in L.A.?"

Zoe glanced over her shoulder. Where was Anton? Surely he'd heard Jonathan's car pull up if Colin had. Why didn't her fiancé come to the door, take her luggage and welcome her home?

Maybe he'd tried to wait up but had fallen asleep…. "My father lives there. We were hoping Sam might've been in touch with him."

"Seems reasonable." Colin shoved his hands into the deep pockets of his sweats, causing them to dip low enough to suggest he wasn't wearing underwear.

Zoe could barely stop herself from blanching. "Yes, well—"

"We certainly missed you around here."

Missed her? She'd only been gone one night.

"That's...nice." She inched toward the walkway, but he stepped over the fence and followed her.

"I have a question."

Scrabbling for patience, Zoe waited. "Yes?"

"Did you think about me while you were gone?"

The hair suddenly stood up on the back of her neck. "Excuse me?"

He gave her a calculated-to-charm smile. "You heard me."

"But I'm not sure what you mean."

His bark of laughter made her hope he was joking, but what he said next was even more confusing. "Oh, so we're going to play *that* game."

"I don't know what you're talking about."

The porch light at Colin's house snapped on and Tiffany poked her head out. "Honey?"

Zoe breathed a sigh of relief, but he didn't even turn. "Your wife's standing on your stoop," she said.

He scowled. "So?"

"She wants a word with you."

"And I want—"

"Colin?" Tiffany interrupted.

Her second call seemed to get through to him. "What is it?" he hollered, his voice impatient and overloud.

"You've had a little too much to drink tonight. Maybe you should come in."

He rolled his eyes. "She can't get enough of me, if you know what I mean."

Zoe was afraid he might spell it out for her, but he didn't. "She's right. You'd better go inside."

"Yeah, okay," he said. Then he shrugged and walked back to his own yard. "Yeah, yeah, I'm coming," he grumbled and threw Zoe a parting "See ya tomorrow."

"I hope not," she muttered as the Bells' door closed and the porch light winked off.

Free at last, Zoe went inside her own house, rolling her suitcase behind her. But Anton wasn't sleeping as she'd expected. He sat at the kitchen table, a drink at his elbow.

"Hey, if you're up, why didn't you come out?" she asked. "Couldn't you hear Colin? He was acting so weird, almost coming on to me. I think he was drunk."

He took a swallow of his drink but continued to stare at the clock on the wall.

"Anton?" She left her bag in the entryway as his red-rimmed eyes cut to her.

"Is it true?" he asked.

Somehow she knew he wasn't talking about their neighbor. Her mind immediately reverted to those few seconds with Jonathan standing behind her at the bathroom mirror—and then later, when she'd slept in his arms. But they'd been fully dressed and hadn't even faced each other. The desire was there, which constituted enough of a betrayal, but she couldn't believe it translated into any real threat. Her current crisis made her feel instantly close to the person who best understood her pain; that was all. This wasn't regular life, the kind that goes on after tragedy.

How could Anton know about Jonathan, anyway? Jonathan had barely left.

"Is what true?" she asked.

"About Sam's dad?"

The rape. Her stomach knotted with fresh tension as she sank into a chair. "Who told you?"

"You didn't think the police would check your background?" Launching unsteadily to his feet, he shocked her by throwing his glass at the wall. The sound of it shattering made Zoe flinch. "They're searching to see if there might be someone who'd have a reason to take Sam, for crying out loud!"

"Anton—"

"Do you have any idea how embarrassing it was for me to sit here and tell Detective Thomas that Sam's father was killed in a car accident? I'm your fiancé, for God's sake! I'm supposed to know you!"

Zoe's heart pounded a jagged rhythm. "Anton, please. That must've been awkward and upsetting. But I need you to try and understand, to be on my side until…until I can get through this. Just…have some patience and give me a chance to explain."

He rounded on her. "Explain what? Why you've been lying to me *ever since I met you?* How can I be on your side, Zoe? How can I love you and support you if I don't even know you! Here I am, taking time off work, meeting with police, putting up a *reward* for God's sake—and you've known all along who probably took her."

"That's not true." She stood because she could no longer let him rail at her from above. "The last I knew, her father was in prison."

"Well, he's out now."

"Yes…"

"Did Jonathan unearth that information? The handsome young investigator who's been interested in you from the second he laid eyes on you?"

Zoe couldn't remember Anton ever being so angry. When he got upset, he tended to sulk. But this confrontation was the culmination of a lot of problems. Their relationship had been suffering, particularly because of financial disagreements, long before Sam went missing. "Anton, calm down."

"Calm down?" he yelled.

"I talked to Franky today. He doesn't have her!"

"So you didn't even tell me the truth about where you were going," he said with a mirthless laugh.

"I had no idea we'd see Franky."

"Bullshit!"

"It's true. Jonathan didn't tell me until we got down there."

"But you told him you were raped, right? You trusted *him* with the truth."

"That's not fair! He knows because of Skye. She was part of a victims' support group I attended several years ago." Had Zoe thought about it, she would've realized that the police would be privy to, or could easily come by, the same information, but she'd been too distracted to consider all the implications. She certainly hadn't expected anyone to tell Anton.

"I think you told him. I think that's what you were whispering about while you were making out in my backyard."

A bead of sweat rolled between Zoe's breasts. "We weren't making out, and you know it. I was falling apart, Anton. And he…"

"He acted in a completely inappropriate manner!"

Zoe shook her head. How could she explain what had happened in that moment? Her encounter with Jonathan at the hotel had been inappropriate, but not that hug. Jonathan hadn't expected to get anything out of the comfort he offered, and she'd taken nothing but the comfort she needed. "It wasn't the way you're choosing to interpret it. None of it."

"How can you say that, when I was the only one left in the dark?"

The gray at his temples suddenly made him seem less distinguished and merely…old. When had he changed? She'd always been conscious of the age difference, but it'd never bothered her. And why were the attributes that had drawn her to him—the fact that he was established, organized, neat, successful, stable—no longer so appealing?

Was it because of her recent preoccupation with a younger man? Or was Sam's disappearance acting like a wake-up call—an event shocking enough to make her reevaluate her whole life?

"I didn't tell you because…"

"Why?" he demanded when her words trailed off.

She struggled to explain what could only be called instinct. "Because I don't want *anyone* to know. It was a horrible experience. I'd rather forget, pretend it never happened. Can't you understand that? Think what it would do to Sam if she ever found out."

Watching her sadly, he shook his head. "Again, it's you and Sam. I'm not even a consideration."

"I— We… Please, Anton, I didn't tell you because we weren't married yet. And…and you know I've been through a lot of dysfunctional relationships. I just…it was in the past. I didn't see why you or anyone else needed to know."

"You were holding out on me, Zoe. Only telling me what you wanted me to hear. That's not being open or honest."

"There's nothing wrong with trying to protect Sam," she countered.

"Except that it's not just Sam, is it? You weren't serious about our relationship."

"I was serious enough to accept your proposal."

"You said yes with your mouth, and maybe with your mind, but not with your heart. You never fully embraced me."

Was it true? Zoe squeezed her eyes shut. Her entire world was collapsing, and there didn't seem to be a damn thing she could do to stop it. "It was in the past," she said for the third time, but there was no conviction in her voice. And deep down, she knew he was right. She'd been in love with the idea of becoming the wife of someone *like* him, of finally breaking away from the hand-to-mouth existence she'd always known and commanding a little respect. She'd never been fully in love with *him.*

God, what a time to realize it.

"How about after Sam went missing? Didn't you think it was important to mention Franky then?" he mocked.

Zoe toyed with the decorative place mats on the table. How silly, she thought, to leave these out when they were never used.

"Zoe?"

She met his gaze. "Like I said, we checked with Franky. He didn't take her."

"He's a rapist! You think he'd admit to kidnapping?"

She wished she could go back in time—a week, two weeks, a year. If only she'd never met Anton. If only she'd refused when he'd asked her out. It would've been better to keep struggling on her own. Chances were, she'd still have Sam. And she longed for her daughter infinitely more than she'd ever longed for Anton or even the dream of living comfortably and productively. "Sam's very existence came as a total shock to him. And he had his grandmother right there, vouching for him."

"His grandmother."

"Yes."

"What, grandmothers can't lie to protect their loved ones? Surely she and Franky can cover their asses at least as well as you do. After all, they're from the gutter, too."

A chill swept through Zoe. Maybe she'd kept a few secrets, but he'd been aware of her background. She'd never pretended to be more than she was. "How can you be so unkind at a time like this?"

He briefly covered his face. "You're right. I'm sorry. I'm hurt, but you're going through enough already, so I can't even have the satisfaction of venting."

She gaped at him. "My daughter is missing, and you're disappointed that you can't rant and rave about *your* unhappiness?"

"I shouldn't have let myself love you, Zoe. You're too young and beautiful for me. It's not realistic to believe a guy my age can hang on to a woman like you. Besides the age gap, we're too different. My parents warned me from the beginning. But—" he threw up his hands "—here I am."

Zoe felt as cold as a marble statue. She couldn't move, could hardly breathe. "So now I'm a mistake?"

"Continuing to pursue a relationship with you would be the mistake. Whether I want to accept it or not, this was never what I wanted it to be."

Hyperaware of the suitcase sitting behind her, Zoe's mind raced through possibilities. Her makeup and her clothing—that was all she really owned. They'd sold her car a few months ago and used what little they got for it as a down payment on her Lexus IS. They'd decided she needed a reliable and somewhat impressive vehicle if she was going to become a commercial real estate agent.

But she wasn't even working anymore. She'd never be able to make the payments by herself. "Are you kicking me out?"

"No, of course not. You can stay a week or two until…until the situation with Sam is resolved…one way or another."

"One way or another," she said, then laughed. "How generous of you."

"I didn't ask for this to happen, Zoe."

But she suspected he was relieved to be calling it quits.

He'd been as smitten with obtaining the ideal as she was—had been eager to marry a young, attractive woman. But he wasn't flexible enough to share his belongings, let alone his *life.* And now, being with her would mean seeing her through the worst nightmare imaginable to a mother. He'd already received a taste of it and wasn't interested in more. He preferred to go back to his safe, methodical existence without worry about whether or not she was bringing in enough money to pay her portion of the bills. "Is it the ten thousand dollars, Anton? Is that the real problem?" she asked. "When it comes right down to it, you just can't part with it, can you?" It wasn't an entirely fair accusation. He was more worried about money than she would've liked, but she knew it wasn't the reward that was breaking them up. She was just so…hurt and angry. And he retaliated in kind.

"Is that what you're staying with me for? So I'll supply the money and anything else you need?"

"You think I've been using you all along?"

When he wouldn't answer, she knew. He wasn't happy about being excluded from her confidence, but he could've forgiven that if she was truly in love with him. Knowing she wasn't made him feel used—and he wasn't willing to be played for a fool. His pride wouldn't allow it. Neither would he risk so much on a relationship that couldn't possibly last. She'd become a poor investment, a liability.

So what did that mean? She'd be left without her daughter, without her fiancé, without a home. And without a reward to offer for Samantha's return.

Grabbing the bottle of gin from the table, she downed the last swallow with a grimace at the after-kick. Then she went to the bedroom.

"What are you doing?" he asked, following her.

"I'm leaving."

"It's the middle of the night," he said, but there was more relief than conviction in his voice. If it was over between them, he preferred she leave now.

"I know."

"Where will you go?"

"I have no idea."

He watched her pack. "You'll land on your feet, Zoe. Eventually. You're a survivor."

She didn't bother turning to look at him. She was afraid she'd start laughing and never stop. "I appreciate the encouragement, Anton."

Ignoring her sarcasm, he remained as serious as ever. "And I really hope you get Sam back. If…if you want, you can borrow the reward money. Pay me back later."

Now he was trying to placate his conscience for letting her down. "No, thanks. I'll figure out some other way."

Suddenly eager to escape his presence, his house, his meaningless platitudes, she moved faster. Until now, she hadn't realized how claustrophobic he made her feel. He drained all the color from life.

"I'm taking the Lexus," she said.

"Of course. If it'll help, I'll make the next payment. You know, give you some breathing room until you find work."

At last, she turned to face him. "That's like telling someone who's just lost a leg that you'll provide a Band-Aid," she said, and laughter got the better of her, after all.

18

"I have a treat for you." Tiffany smiled so brightly Sam somehow found the energy to sit up. Tiffany didn't have to tell her what the treat was; she could see the piece of toast with jelly, could *smell* it.

"Why are you bringing me this?" she asked.

Tiffany lifted it high. "That sounded a bit sulky to me, miss."

"I just… I don't know why you'd bring me a treat."

"Because I'm a nice person," she said. "Why else would I do it? You know Colin wouldn't like it. He'd probably make me go without dinner tonight if he knew. But I'm taking the risk. For you."

This small kindness nearly brought tears to Samantha's eyes. "Thank you."

"You're welcome. Doesn't it smell delicious?" She waved it in front of Sam's nose.

Sam's mouth began to water. "Mmm hmm."

"Did you eat some of your food today? So I can tell Colin you're being a good doggie?"

"A little." The pellets she'd choked down seemed to sit in her stomach. Weeks, days, hours ago—Samantha didn't even know when—Tiffany had brought her a toothbrush and some toothpaste. But Sam had to use her water bowl in order to brush, which meant she either had to swallow the toothpaste or ruin her water. She'd chosen to swallow it to rid her mouth of the taste of dog food. Now the combination churned together in her stomach, making her queasy.

"Way to go! Then give me a smile. I won't allow anyone to be sad around me today."

Sam felt a slight burst of hope. "Is today…different?"

Tiffany shrugged and brought the bread within easy reach, but her smile widened almost wickedly as Sam's eyes latched onto it. "You want this, don't you," she said with a laugh.

Sam wasn't sure she could trust this new, playful side of Tiffany. Was she only pretending she'd give her the bread?

"Is that a yes?" Tiffany prompted when Sam hesitated.

She nodded.

"Prove it."

"How?"

"Show me a trick."

Sam clenched her hands in the blanket. "What kind of trick?"

"Go to the bathroom in front of me. Like a dog."

Sam's eyes went to the kitty-litter box in the corner. She'd had diarrhea earlier, so it stank, even though she'd changed it during Tiffany's last visit. "That's gross," she said.

"Why? You pee in front of your girlfriends, don't you?"

"They don't *watch* me."

"Come on. We're both girls."

Sam's heart sank. Tiffany didn't want to see her go to the bathroom. She just wanted to make Sam do something that would leave her feeling worse. She wasn't very different from Colin.

"No." She spoke so low she could barely hear herself.

"What'd you say?"

She didn't respond.

"Damn, you're stubborn," Tiffany said in disbelief. "Rover peed in front of me. He didn't care at all as long as I gave him a piece of toast."

Sam thought of those marks on the wall. She'd been following Rover's example by making her own marks, too. "What happened to Rover?"

"None of your business." She considered the toast, momentarily gloomy again. "Oh, what the hell. Eat it," she said and tossed it at Sam. "It's not like *I* can afford the calories. But if you ever refuse to pee in front of Colin, you'll regret it. I can tell you that."

Sam scrambled off the mattress to collect her prize. She was afraid Tiffany would change her mind and take it back, but Tiffany didn't seem interested in the food anymore. She slid down the opposite wall and started yakking about Colin as if Sam was her best friend. At least Sam *thought* she was yakking about Colin. She definitely heard his name, but she wasn't paying attention; she was too focused on wiping every last bit of jelly from the floor.

"It's going to be fine," Tiffany was saying. "I've been worried for nothing. Colin loves me, he just has some anger issues, you know?"

"Uh-huh," Sam said. But she had no idea what Tiffany's words meant. She was only responding to the lift in her voice, keeping Tiffany preoccupied so she could enjoy the first normal food she'd had in what seemed like forever. The butter was oh, *so* sweet....

"A lot of people have anger issues," Tiffany rambled on. "He'll work through them. He'd never let his anger come between *us*. You should see the roses he left me."

Roses or no, Samantha knew Colin had more "issues" than anger—he was screwed up in a major way, like that creepy guy in *Suburbia*.

"He's handsome, don't you think?" Tiffany asked.

Sam had just swallowed the last bite of her toast. Closing her eyes, she chewed slowly, savoring it as long as possible—

"I asked you a question." Tiffany's voice was suddenly filled with irritation. "Jeez, how much can someone worship a piece of bread? I don't get any more food than you do."

"What'd you say?" Sam asked.

"I said Colin's handsome, don't you think?"

Sam clamped her mouth shut and glared over at her.

Tiffany stood. "What? Don't tell me you want to say no."

"He's not handsome," she said. "He's the ugliest man I've ever seen."

"That's not nice!"

Sam wasn't sure where the hateful words came from. Even as they spewed out of her mouth she knew she'd regret it, and yet she couldn't stop. "He's evil and twisted and I hope he gets in a car accident on his way home from work and dies a bloody death! I'd dance on his grave because the world would be a much better place without him! *And* you! If you knew anything at all about… *anything*…you wouldn't help him. That makes you as evil as he is. You're both going to hell with all the other monsters who hurt people!"

Tiffany blinked as if she was too stunned to respond. "You little—" she started, but Sam wasn't finished yet.

"Maybe you'll kill mc. But they'll catch you, Tiffany. They'll catch you and they'll lock you up, and then *you'll* be the animal. You'll rot in a cage until the day you die, and then the demons will come for you, just like those creatures in *Ghost*. They'll drag you away to writhe in torment!"

"Vile little bitch!" she screamed when Sam had finally run out of the strength to continue. "You're going on the leash. And I'm never bringing you another treat as long as you live!" When she flounced to the door, Sam followed. She had to make a break for it. This was her only chance. But Tiffany easily shoved her back.

There was silence for several seconds. Then the door opened again and Tiffany stomped in, carrying a leash. "How dare you talk to me that way! Rover was sweet compared to you. And I'm glad you don't care about dying because Colin's probably going to kill you as soon as he gets home! You think you and Rover are the only pets we've had? Heck no! The body of the last girl is rotting in the bottom of an outhouse!"

Suddenly terrified by what she might have caused, Sam cowered in the corner. "What're you doing?" she whimpered.

"You'll see. You'll quit being such a spoiled brat after a few days of wearing *this*."

Sam wrestled with her. But in her current state, she was no match for Tiffany, who wouldn't back off even when Sam started shouting about germs and mono. After forcing a chainlike collar over her head, Tiffany yanked it so tight Sam couldn't breathe. She rolled on the ground gasping for air while Tiffany stood above her, nostrils flaring with anger as much as exertion. "How do you like that?" she taunted, yanking it still tighter.

Sam couldn't answer. Spots danced before her eyes, and in the next instant, she saw nothing at all.

It wasn't the first time Zoe had slept in her car. When she'd left home at seventeen in the old VW bug her father had bought her, she and Samantha had spent more nights in the backseat huddled up for warmth than they had in a hotel or apartment. Without a high-school diploma, Zoe couldn't get much of a job, and she hadn't had anyone to take care of Sam even if she could've found work. So they'd bounced around the state, living out of her car or in shelters—when she wasn't with a boyfriend who could help her provide a more stable existence. If that boyfriend was trustworthy and willing to watch Sam, Zoe worked in fast-food places at night. But her relationships never lasted long enough for her to get ahead. She'd always been attracted to rebels, or artist types with big dreams but little sense of responsibility—the exact opposite of Anton Lucassi, which was why she'd expected that relationship to work. He was what every mother told her daughter to look for.

Maybe she and Anton would've been more compatible had there been less of an age gap, had her background been different, had he not been jaded by the residual damage left by his first wife. He was too cautious to really love again, and she was too distrustful to love at all.

So here she was, in the middle of another breakup. She was sort of relieved she wouldn't have to listen to Anton's constant, and sometimes nagging, advice. He could be such a know-it-all. But it was discouraging to think she couldn't seem to make *any* relationship succeed.

Sitting straight, she stretched a painful kink out of her neck, then took inventory of what she had in her purse. She had to rally, stave off the pain of her current situation by being practical. This wasn't the first time she'd been down and out. She'd overcome it, regroup. But how? What assets did she possess that she might use to find her daughter and build a new life?

Her wallet contained a couple of hundred bucks, and she had a Visa card with three thousand in available credit—provided Anton didn't shut it down. His name was on the card, too, as the primary; chances were, he'd close the account as soon as his conscience would allow it. She could've rented a cheap motel room, but if he didn't close the account, every dollar spent on herself was a dollar less to put toward the search for Sam.

With a sigh, she twisted around to gaze at the garbage bags stuffed in her backseat. Together with the suitcases in the trunk, they held everything she and Sam owned. But even if she sold it all, together with her engagement ring, she'd never make enough to offer a sizable reward. Pawned engagement rings and used clothing didn't go for a premium.

She'd thought of going to Jonathan. But they'd barely met. She didn't want to jump from one relationship to another, not when she was in *this* state. It wasn't fair to expect him to help her. So…

"What now?" she muttered, staring dejectedly out the window. After leaving the house, she'd driven to the airport, where she'd gotten through the rest of the night by pretending she'd found Sam and they were about to take off on a vacation to Mexico. It was light now, but she refused to let go of that dream. She stared at the planes, imagining it all….

Mesmerized by the sound and movement, she continued to watch; she wasn't sure how long. The sun was quite a bit higher in the sky when she finally dragged herself out of her lethargy. She couldn't sit here and do nothing, she told herself, couldn't collapse beneath the despair. Sam was counting on her.

Silently promising her daughter that she'd hold tough, Zoe retrieved her cell phone from where it had gotten wedged between her seat and the console, and called Detective Thomas.

He wasn't in. It was after eight o'clock, but just barely, and that was obviously too early. Other people still had regular lives.

She pictured him sitting at breakfast with his wife,

enjoying a second cup of coffee before heading in to the office, and couldn't help resenting him for not being available. She had no right to expect more than he was doing. He'd been responsive, was checking out every lead, keeping an eye on the shelters, talking to the neighbors. But it was just a *job* to him. Sam's case wasn't very different from all the others that needed to be solved.

Curling her fingernails into the palm of her free hand, Zoe called Skye. She hated to ask her friend for more help. The Last Stand was already paying for Jonathan and had funded their trip to Los Angeles. But she knew she'd do anything, even beg in the street, if it meant finding her child. She needed to get more media coverage. Someone *had* to have seen her daughter. Maybe Skye had contacts who could help them distribute a new press release, get Sam's picture on TV again.

The phone rang three times, but at that point a beep signaled an incoming call. Expecting it to be the detective she'd just tried to reach, she switched over.

"Hello?"

"Hey, how's it goin'?"

It wasn't Thomas; it was her former neighbor, Colin Bell.

The sound of his voice immediately evoked the memory of his drunken behavior last night.

"I'm fine," she lied. Because she no longer trusted his motives, she no longer wanted his help or support. She'd do this herself, which was what life always came down to for her, anyway. "How're you?"

"Embarrassed and worried."

She didn't want to hear why. Despite that one bright spot when he'd gone with her to create the flyers, she preferred to avoid him. But he charged ahead before she could respond.

"I'm sorry about my behavior last night, Zoe. Tiffany told me I was acting like a lecher, and it probably frightened you. I don't know what got into me."

"I'd say it was one drink too many."

"It was several drinks too many," he said. "Sometimes I let the pressure at work bother me and I drink too much. But that's no excuse for making what you're going through worse."

If he'd acted cavalier about his behavior, she would've remained perturbed, but he seemed so earnest. "Apology accepted."

"Really?" he said. "You're not just saying that? I feel like such an ass."

She smiled. Her neighbor's overfriendly behavior wasn't one of her bigger concerns. At least he acknowledged that he'd crossed the line. Considering his contrition and the fact that it was unlikely to happen again now that she wouldn't be living next door, there was no point in harboring a grudge. And knowing his wife was aware of his behavior was comforting. "Forget it. You weren't yourself."

He gave a low whistle. "You're as generous as you are beautiful, you know that? But I don't mean anything inappropriate by it, so don't go all silent on me."

"Then I'll simply say thank-you," she said with a laugh.

"And now for the 'worried' part. I ran into Anton when I got in my car to come to work and he said you'd moved out."

"I have."

"I hope it didn't have anything to do with me."

Echoes of last night made her ill at ease. "Why would it have to do with you?"

"It happened so fast. I was afraid he might've made more of our being together at Kinko's than he should have."

At this she let her breath go in relief. "No, it wasn't

that. It was…a combination of a lot of things." Blind hope. Stupidity. Grasping for a personality type that didn't fit her own. Fortunately, there was no need to go into detail, so she blamed the catalyst. "I guess our relationship couldn't withstand the strain of having Samantha go missing."

"He wasn't good enough for you, anyway, Zoe. An old guy like that…I never could understand what you saw in him."

She saw safety, security. But she doubted someone as young and successful as Colin could relate. He'd never had to fight for survival.

In any case, what she'd believed Anton could provide had been an illusion. He'd let her down as much as the men who'd come before him. Maybe more.

But she couldn't blame it all on him. They probably would've broken up months ago if she'd allowed herself to see him for what he really was. He'd given her a nice home to live in, went to work each day, and avoided drugs and alcohol, but he didn't *fulfill* her.

She thought of Jonathan and the desire she'd experienced when he'd brushed his lips against her neck. That had brought about a reawakening, had shown her that she'd closed off her sexual self too soon. "I guess we weren't as well-suited as I thought."

"He didn't leave you high and dry, did he? You've got money? Because if you don't, I can lend you some."

Any trace of the bad feelings she'd had toward her neighbor disappeared. She didn't want to borrow from him any more than she wanted to borrow from Anton. They didn't know each other well enough, and she couldn't imagine Tiffany would be happy about it.

Still, it was very nice of him to offer. "I'm okay for now. Thanks for checking."

"Where are you staying?"

"At a motel." *The Lexus Motel.*

"Which one?"

She smoothed the wrinkles from her clothes. "Just a little twelve-room motel downtown." She'd seen a couple of those last night, and even before that, back in the days when she'd had a meal or two at Loaves and Fishes.

"You mean that one off Sixteenth Street?"

"I didn't pay attention. I just pulled in."

"Oh." There was a pause. "What's the latest on Sam?"

"No change."

"Really? The police can't tell you *anything?*"

She started the car and cringed when the gas gauge stopped at half a tank. "Just that they're doing all they can."

"It's not enough."

"I feel the same way." But maybe there was nothing more they could do. Even Jonathan couldn't figure out what'd happened, what'd gone wrong.

"I've put together a small search party with some of the attorneys and secretaries here in the office. I thought we'd visit the neighborhoods surrounding ours tomorrow morning and pass out Sam's picture, then comb the vacant land next to our development."

Just when she'd decided she didn't like Colin, he made another grand gesture. What was the matter with her? She needed friends. And she couldn't afford to be too selective. Especially with people who were willing to help. "The police are supposed to be out there looking today, but…it can't hurt to go over the same ground."

"My thoughts exactly."

"I really appreciate the help."

"No gratitude necessary. But can you come over for dinner tonight so we can create the routes?" he asked. "I'll pick up some maps over lunch."

If he was taking the time to do this, how could she refuse? "Sure. When would you like me there?"

"We're seeing some old friends at nine, so…why don't we do it at six?"

It was an early appointment, and he wasn't planning on making a night of it. That meant the meeting couldn't be construed as anything but business, which wiped out the last of her misgivings. "Six works for me."

"Great. See you then," he said and hung up.

Zoe sighed as she pressed the End button. Anton was history; the neighbor she hadn't liked very much, except for a few unexpected moments, was friendlier than ever. Her daughter was still missing. She had little money, no home and no job. And she couldn't forget her hotel stay with Skye's investigator. She was so lost, and he seemed like the only person she could cling to.

How could so much have changed in a few short days?

Instead of calling Skye again, Zoe decided to drive over to The Last Stand. She put the car in gear and bounced along as her tires encountered the deep ruts she'd traversed last night. But her phone rang before she reached the highway, so she stopped to answer it. "Hello?"

"Zoe? It's Jonathan."

"I know." She'd recognized his voice instantly. "How are you?"

"Hopeful," he said. "It's a long shot, but I think we might have a lead."

19

"What do you mean you invited Zoe over for dinner?"

Tiffany was supposed to be starting her ten o'clock rounds, doing a room check to make sure none of the old folks had wandered off. But Colin's call had caught her staring longingly at the candy bars inside the vending machine. Occasionally, she broke down and bought one. She'd sneak it into a bathroom stall, eat it fast, then flush the evidence because she didn't need any of her coworkers teasing her about cheating on her diet or, worse, mentioning the breach to Colin.

"Exactly what I said," he replied. "Have it ready by six."

She lowered her voice so that anyone who might come upon her wouldn't hear. "We can't have Zoe over."

"Why not?"

She rattled the keys in the pocket of her smock, which went to the door that locked the Alzheimer's wing. Although she wasn't assigned to that section, she had to keep the keys with her at all times to accommodate guests. Most days it seemed pointless to tote them around. The Alzheimer's residents received few visitors. But everyone who worked at the home had access—to make it appear less prisonlike to those who did happen to come. "What if she goes upstairs, Colin?"

"She's too polite for that. And we'll be with her the whole time. She won't go anywhere."

"This is unnecessary." In her mind, inviting Zoe into their home went beyond reckless to foolhardy. But Colin seemed to be getting more and more foolhardy. These days he had a constant thirst for stimulation and seemed to feel invincible. That combination was going to get them both in trouble.

"Are you kidding? Tiff—" He swore in frustration. "Hang on a sec. I need to close my door."

As she waited anxiously, she imagined him rounding his desk and quietly closing the expensive, heavy door to his swanky office. She'd been the fat girl others made fun of in school, yet she'd married a lawyer—one with a prestigious firm. She was so proud of Colin, of their home and what she'd become. She loved bumping into people who knew her way back when, enjoyed their reaction when they realized who she was and how much she'd changed. That actually had more to do with the reason she didn't want Zoe in her house. This was the first time her husband had been so taken with another woman. Tiffany couldn't let the infatuation continue; it could get out of hand.

He came back on the line, but his voice was so low she had trouble making out the words.

"What?" she said.

"I know what I'm doing."

"I understand it makes us look good to help, but…why can't you plan the search routes on your own?"

"Because I want her to see how hard we're working. If we can win her loyalty, she'll be the first to defend us if accusations ever arise."

"Then do it at her place, with Anton. His loyalties are important, too."

"She doesn't live there anymore. She left that old tight-ass last night. I told you they'd never get married."

This wasn't encouraging news. The thought of Zoe being available spooked Tiffany. "We could still meet her off-site. How's it smart to invite her into our house when…when you know why we shouldn't?"

"It's a preemptive strike. I've been thinking about Rover. If he does wake up and starts running his mouth, he might come up with a few key details. If any of those details match us, Zoe could get suspicious. We live right next door to where Sam went missing, after all. So we open our home, make her feel she can move around freely in it. By the time she leaves tonight, she'll be so convinced we have nothing to hide she'll immediately discount any similarities as coincidence."

"But why tonight?" Tiffany complained. This was her one chance to recapture her husband's full attention, to convince him she hadn't lost her ability to satisfy him. "I don't get off until five. And then I have to go to the gym."

A voice, cracking with age, interrupted. "Tiffany? Tiffany Bell, is that you?"

It was Mrs. Floyd in 32-D, just around the corner.

Tiffany covered the receiver to respond to her. "Yes, it's me. What do you need?"

"I can't reach my blanket."

Mrs. Floyd made up any excuse to draw Tiffany to her bedside. Usually Tiffany didn't mind. She understood the loneliness suffered by so many of their residents. But it wasn't sympathy that motivated her to duck into Mrs. Floyd's room today. She wanted to avoid the searching eye of her boss, who constantly roved around the home and could come upon her at any moment.

"Here you go." She spread the blanket over the old lady's feet.

"Tiffany?" Colin said.

"What?"

"Forget the gym for today and stop at the grocery store to buy whatever you need. Grab some tri-tip that's already been grilled. Then you'll only have to make a couple of sides. And don't forget to get some munchies for the guys."

"Who're you talking to?" the old lady demanded.

"My husband." Tiffany put a finger to her lips to indicate quiet. "So they're still coming?" she said into the phone. "Tommy and James?"

"You told me you wanted them to. Are you changing your mind now that you have me all excited?"

"No, of course not."

A shadow darkened the doorway and yet another voice interrupted her conversation. "Tiffany?"

Tiffany looked up to see her boss. "Yes?"

"Focus on your work."

"I'm sorry," she said. "I'll get off right away."

"Make it now." Folding her arms, Amanda Hargraves waited to see that Tiffany followed through.

"I have to go," she told Colin.

"Just have the house ready, and make sure you've taken precautions with our new pet," he hurried to add.

She glanced nervously at Amanda. "The usual?"

"Two pills this time. I don't want any surprises. This is going to be a big night."

It promised to be quite a party, all right. But as Tiffany ended the call, she couldn't say she was looking forward to it. Her only hope was that Colin would be pleased, that it would put him in a great mood for a weekend at the cabin.

Mrs. Hargraves gave the inside wall a thump to show her approval of Tiffany's obedience and moved on, but the bedridden Mrs. Floyd continued to watch Tiffany with interest. "There's nothing like being happily married," she said.

Tiffany shoved her cell phone in her pocket and smiled. “No.”

“You’re madly in love?”

“I’d rather die than live without Colin.”

A faroff look entered the old lady’s rheumy eyes. “I felt the same way about my Richard, God rest his soul.”

The difference was that Tiffany meant it literally. And, because of Zoe, she was facing the worst threat of her life. She should never have taken Sam. Colin wouldn’t have gotten so swept away by their neighbor if she hadn’t tried to cover up for one mistake with another.

Despite Mrs. Floyd’s complaint that it had been over a week since they’d played pinochle, Tiffany excused herself and returned to the vending machine, where she bought two candy bars and ate them both.

When she arrived to meet him at the hospital, Zoe wore an attractive sleeveless blouse with a pair of jeans that accentuated her long limbs and slender figure. But she wasn’t wearing her engagement ring. That wasn’t a detail Jonathan *wanted* to notice, but the tan lines on her finger as she opened her car door told him its removal was as rare as it was recent. Why was it gone today?

As he finished his call putting off yet another client, he noticed several plastic garbage bags, all stuffed to capacity and stacked to the ceiling in her backseat. If they contained trash, it was an odd thing to put in a Lexus. And if they didn’t… “Everything okay?” he asked as she got out.

“Fine.” With a nervous smile, she closed the door. “What’s going on?” She eyed the entrance under the covered drop-off area as if eager to draw his attention away from her vehicle. “Please tell me no one’s seriously hurt. Especially Sam.”

She knew he would’ve told her if Sam was here, so he

wasn't in a hurry to explain. Not when her clothing and personal possessions were piled in her car as if she'd hauled them out of Lucassi's house in a hurry. "Someone's definitely hurt," he said. "But it's not Sam."

"Then why are we here?" Assuming an air of total absorption, she moved past him as though she expected him to follow, but he didn't budge. Maybe he hadn't been able to find the leads he needed to figure out where Sam was. But it wasn't hard to guess what was going on with Zoe. In her passenger seat, he could see the sundress she'd worn yesterday draped over the bag he'd hefted around on their trip to L.A. There was also a blanket and pillow shoved down in the foot space.

"You moved out last night?"

When she turned, a pained expression rumpled her brow, but she shrugged. "As luck would have it, Anton and I aren't perfect for each other, after all."

He hoped to hell he hadn't caused the breakup with that little stunt he'd pulled in the hotel. "I could've told you that. But I'm still surprised by the sudden reversal."

"You could've told me that we weren't right for each other?"

It was his turn to shrug. "I don't like him."

"Apparently everyone could see we were a mismatch but me," she grumbled.

Just yesterday, he'd wanted to kiss her, touch her. And he'd made it a point to show her that, whether she'd initially realized it or not, she wanted him, too. Now she was toting her belongings around as if she had nowhere to go.

Shit... "What happened?" he asked.

She studied him for a second, then apparently decided to be honest with him. "It had nothing to do with you, so don't stand there looking so guilty."

Nothing to do with him? That was hopeful. He was

supposed to be helping her, not making her life more complicated. "Thanks for letting me off the hook, but I could use an explanation."

"There's not a lot to say. People change. Needs change. This came in a…moment of clarity."

His phone rang again, but he ignored it. It had been ringing all morning. His clients were going nuts, but none of them had more pressing business than finding Zoe's child. "Are you sure it's the type of decision you should be making now?"

"It was mutual, so not my decision alone. And I don't think there's any question as to whether it's the right one." Her gaze followed an SUV that turned in at the entrance and crept down a row of cars, searching for an open space. "The timing could've been better, of course," she added ruefully. "But the situation with Sam… It's brought out the worst in both of us, made us recognize that we're not very happy together."

"And the fact that we shared a hotel room didn't set him off—"

"It didn't even come up." She rubbed her palms on her jeans. "Please, don't worry about San Diego. I owe you an apology for putting you in such an awkward situation to begin with. I should've gotten my own room."

She was establishing some emotional distance, and he told himself he should be relieved. He had no business getting involved with her. But logic rarely curbed desire, and it didn't now. "I didn't mind sharing."

"I know." She cleared her throat. "Shall we go in?"

Not yet. He had more to say. "Nothing happened when we were together, Zoe. You said I didn't have anything to do with it, but if this breakup is your own guilty reaction to wanting me, you didn't act on—"

"It's not guilt. I have a history of picking the wrong

guys, okay?" She motioned in a careless manner. "And this is yet another example. Breakups don't hurt that much anymore."

This was the first woman he'd wanted to make love with since Sheridan, and she'd just told him she was too jaded to care. It was a warning sign—one he planned to take seriously. "Skye told me Anton's different from your usual, uh, love interests."

"He is. Which is why I forced it. But I found that a loveless relationship isn't much of an improvement over the kind I've had in the past. Without love, there isn't enough depth to survive a major challenge."

"So you're okay with leaving him."

She hiked her purse up. "I won't find any peace until I have my daughter back, but...I'll survive the breakup. I've had plenty of practice in that area."

He lowered his voice. "Why didn't you call me?"

"Because you would've offered to put me up."

"Didn't you need a place to stay?" he asked with a glance at her car.

"That's too much to ask of you."

He gave her a skeptical frown.

"And...I would've agreed," she finished.

"What's wrong with one friend helping another?"

"You're not my *friend.* You're my private investigator." Her attention shifted to the person who'd just parked the SUV, but he wasn't close enough to overhear. "And we would've wound up sleeping together."

He wished he could deny that he'd take advantage of her presence in his house, but if she looked at him the way she'd looked at him in that hotel lobby, he wasn't sure he'd be able to resist. She'd been with Anton for months, yet she was as lonely as any woman he'd ever met, and she didn't even know it. He wanted to satisfy her hunger—along with his own—but his track record wasn't any better than hers.

He started toward the entrance, and she fell in step with him. "No comment?" she prompted.

"Who knows what we would've done," he said.

The man in the SUV was obviously in a hurry. Wearing a silly grin and carrying a bouquet of flowers, he cut in front of them as if he hadn't even seen them. They stopped abruptly to avoid a collision. "New father," Zoe murmured.

Too intent to be distracted, Jonathan ignored the stranger. "So where'd you stay last night?"

"Near the airport."

His phone rang again. He glanced at the number on the caller ID, saw it was Robbie Babcock, the bail bondsman he'd been assisting in tracking down a skip, and silenced it. He'd return the call later.

"You're not going to take that?" she said.

He didn't answer her question. "Do you have a room for tonight?"

"Not yet. But I'll get one."

He decided to let her do exactly that. She had too many scars. And so did he.

They stepped on the sensor that made the automatic doors whoosh open. "Now tell me why we're here," she said.

"I read an article in the paper this morning that made the hair stand up on the back of my neck."

She faltered, then took two quick steps to catch up with him. "What was the story?"

He was a little concerned about how she'd react to this news, but he couldn't shield her. And by marching to Franky Bates's door, she'd already proven that she was tougher than he might have thought. "There was a fourteen-year-old boy found wandering in the woods near Placerville. He was abducted more than two months ago."

She stopped. "He's alive? I bet his parents are so relieved!"

He nodded. "But he was naked and badly beaten."

Her eyes were riveted on his. "What makes you think he has any connection to Sam?"

"There's not a lot," he admitted. "He turned up the day she went missing. That could easily be a coincidence, but it stood out to me. And because he's a similar age, and this type of thing is so unusual here in Sac, I called Skye's husband."

"He's a detective with the Sacramento police, right?"

"Right. He was nice enough to place a few calls to the sheriff's department and get us some more information."

"You don't think the same man took Sam."

"Not necessarily. Like I said, it's a long shot but…worth investigating." And they didn't have anything else.

"So what did you learn?"

He nearly cursed when his phone went off again. Robbie Babcock wasn't giving up easily. He wanted to get paid for hauling in a man who'd jumped bail for armed robbery. But this time Jonathan turned off his phone. He couldn't leave it that way for long—it was his conduit to the world—but he needed a few uninterrupted minutes. "The poor kid was in shock and babbling incoherently when they found him," he told her. "They couldn't get him to focus long enough to answer a single question, but every word he spoke seemed to revolve around the same theme."

She brought a hand to her chest. "What?"

"Someone he called 'Master' treating him like a dog and making him wear a collar that choked him."

The color drained from her face. "Where's he from?"

"His family lives in Antelope, only he wasn't taken from the house. He went missing while on his way home from school."

She shook her head. "Antelope's not far from where I live, but I don't see the connection to Sam. As you said, the fact that he was found the day she went missing might mean nothing. And—"

Jonathan raised a hand. "I'm not done. The deputy who rode in the ambulance with him kept asking for a name. 'Who did this to you?' He was afraid the boy would die and the case would go unsolved. And knowing there was a cruel son of a bitch out there who needed to be caught, he kept pushing."

"Did he get a name?"

"No. Just more babble—until he asked where he could find this 'Master.'"

Zoe's eyes grew round. "And then?"

"The boy assumed a deep voice and spoke his only complete sentence: 'Not just any bastard can live in this part of Rocklin.'"

Toby Simpson, the boy Jonathan had told Zoe about, was lying unconscious in intensive care with his parents by his side. After Jonathan had explained why they'd come and received permission, Zoe stepped in for a brief moment, took one look at his bruised and battered body, and all the tubes hooking him up to various machines, and felt her heart break.

Live, she prayed. *Fight back. Help us beat the monster who put you here.*

Tears slipped down her cheeks, but only a few. She was becoming accustomed to the nightmare. The hurt was quickly being replaced by a white-hot anger that transformed itself into raw determination. She would *never* give up, she promised herself. If the man who'd done this had also taken Sam, she'd spend every dime she could scrape together, every moment of the rest of her life. She'd search until she finally found him—and made him pay.

Mr. and Mrs. Lyle Simpson, the boys' parents, stood silent while Zoe gazed down at their son, then they followed her into the hall.

Zoe felt guilty for disturbing them in their grief. They'd been through so much. The last thing they needed was to have strangers show up at the hospital and bombard them with questions. But she also believed they all had to pull together to put an end to the suffering, to reclaim their children and protect others. She had no idea if her daughter had been taken by the same man, but the fact that both children were connected to an affluent part of Rocklin made it likely. This kind of crime wasn't common, and Rocklin wasn't that big.

"Was he conscious when you got to the hospital?" Jonathan asked the boy's parents.

"For a few minutes." It was a pasty, tired and shell-shocked Mrs. Simpson who answered. The weariness even showed in her voice.

Jonathan slid his hands into his pockets. "Did he say *anything* that might help determine who did this to him? A name, a characteristic?"

"No." This time Mr. Simpson, a stocky, balding man who was several inches shorter than his wife, provided the answer. "We tried to ask him, but he clung to my hand and—" He choked up and couldn't finish, so Mrs. Simpson filled in.

"Started to cry." She blinked repeatedly, fighting her own tears. "And then he slipped into a coma."

A muscle flexed in Jonathan's cheek, and Zoe knew he was having the same reaction she was. He wanted to put a stop to the man, whoever he was, responsible for inflicting such senseless pain.

"What do the doctors say?" Zoe asked.

Mrs. Simpson exchanged a worried glance with her husband. "They're not making any promises."

Jonathan had given Mrs. Simpson his business card when they first arrived. "If something changes, will you contact us? Please?" he asked.

The woman wiped her eyes and nodded. "I've got your number in my purse."

"I'm sorry we had to intrude at a time like this," Zoe whispered and began to move away, but Mrs. Simpson caught her arm.

"Don't be sorry," she said. "We'll do whatever we can to help you. Someone needs to stop 'Master'—in case…in case he hurts another child."

Zoe nodded. That child could be hers.

20

"We now know two things we didn't know before," Jonathan said as they walked out of the hospital.

The anger pounding through Zoe was so strong she couldn't keep her voice level. "What's that?" She swung open her car door with more force than necessary. "That whoever did this is a sadistic bastard?"

He seemed to consider her response. "Okay, I guess we know three things. But two of them are good."

She dug through her purse, searching for her keys. She wanted to get away from the hospital. Away from the broken boy. Away from the grieving parents who'd made such a deep impression on her. Because watching them wait and hope was too hard. In two or three months, maybe sooner, she could be them. If she was lucky enough to find her daughter alive.

"*Good?*" she echoed. "I guess I missed that part."

"Think about it." Resting one hand on her door, he stood in the opening. Had he been any other acquaintance, it would've seemed casual and nonthreatening, but his body penned her in and he was close enough that she immediately got behind the wheel to put some space between them. She didn't want to feel what she was feeling for Jonathan. Not in the midst of so many other turbulent emotions. As bad as she was at relationships, why ask for more trouble?

"I don't want to think about it."

"We've limited our efforts to the Rocklin area," he said.

"If we're looking for the same man."

"We could be."

"Even so, it's not as if the police will start searching houses."

"They can't stop us from knocking on doors. It's a small geographic area. And whoever took Toby has some privacy because he keeps his victims for a long time, which rules out Anton, Franky and your father, even if other information hadn't already done so."

"We know three people it's *not.* That's supposed to make me happy?"

"Happy is a relative term. I'm telling you we're better off today than we were yesterday. The fact that he hangs on to his victims, that he likes to play with them, tells us something about the type of person he is."

Frustrated because she couldn't immediately locate her keys in the jumble of things she'd dumped in her purse, she dropped it in her lap and stared up at him. "That's not enough. Did you *see* that boy?"

His eyes met hers. "He's alive, Zoe."

"Barely. You might not be able to say that tomorrow. I'm willing to bet there were a lot of times over the past few weeks that he wished he was dead."

"My point is this abductor had him for more than two months. That's an extraordinarily long time to keep a victim. Most stranger abductions end in death within the first few hours. I'll have to check with Jasmine—"

"Jasmine?"

"Skye's former partner. She's one of the founders of The Last Stand and has become an excellent profiler. She got married not too long ago and moved to Louisiana, but she still does freelance work and consulting. I think she might be able to help us figure out what kind of individual we're dealing with."

"'Master' suggests a man."

"A sadistic man, as you said. But we need more information."

Zoe shrugged despairingly. "We're not dealing with a man at all. We're dealing with a *devil.*"

"But the particular type of devil he is means there's hope that Sam's still alive."

Zoe wasn't feeling much hope at the moment, just a powerful thirst for vengeance. It was the only way to compensate for everything she'd lost, the only way to remain strong and keep fighting.

Grabbing her purse, she rummaged for her keys again. "I want Sam back. But even if I don't get her back—" she looked up at him "—I won't rest until this bastard's in prison."

"We'll catch him," he said.

Her fingers finally encountered her car keys. "The sooner the better."

"What are you planning to do today?"

She put the key in the ignition so she could roll down her window, and he stepped back and closed the door. "I'm going to the media." She'd been planning to solicit Skye's help. Now she knew she didn't need it. The Simpsons' story provided more fodder for her own. "Then later I'm having dinner at the Bells'. What about you?" she asked.

"Your former neighbors?"

"Colin is putting together a search party for Saturday. We'll be creating the routes."

Jonathan turned on his phone and winced at the number of calls he'd missed. He didn't really have time to take on this case and yet, except for a brief meeting this morning, he'd wiped his schedule clean. Now he was further behind than ever. "I'm heading back to your old neighborhood to ask around some more. Because Sam was home by herself for so many days before she went missing, and wasn't seen out and about, I think the kidnapper was someone close."

"But the police have approached everyone. You've already spoken to a lot of my neighbors, too. What good does talking do? Whoever it was won't simply admit it."

"I know it seems like a long shot. But everything is. I'll explain what happened to the Simpson boy, which will convince anyone who doubted the danger. Maybe they'll remember some detail they didn't consider significant before. You have to keep working the mine, Zoe."

"The first night I met you, you said Sam probably knew her abductor."

"I still believe that."

She shivered. "Then he *has* to be close...."

Leaning on her window ledge, he bent down to peer into her backseat. "So are you coming over later?"

She started the engine. "No. I don't even know where you live."

He took out his card, wrote on the back and handed it to her. "There's a key under the mat if I'm not around."

"I'm not coming over," she said, but when she put his card in her purse, he offered her a knowing grin.

"The dog's friendly."

"Jonathan, I don't even know who I am anymore. I can't get involved with anyone."

He straightened and stepped away so she could leave. "I have a spare bed."

The question was whether or not she'd use it....

Something was up. Samantha knew it instantly.

She'd expected Tiffany to be angry after their earlier

fight, to follow through on her promise not to be nice. But here she was, with what appeared to be another treat. "Drink this," she said matter-of-factly and shoved a tall glass at her.

Sam relieved some of the tension in her collar, but she couldn't widen it very much. The padlock made that impossible, or she would've slipped it over her head and gotten out of it. "What is it?" Was Tiffany going to kill her? Was she going to do it with poison?

"I don't have time for this," Tiffany replied. "It's better than dog food, okay? That's all you need to know."

Sam took the glass because her stomach was growling too much to refuse it. The drink looked and smelled like a strawberry smoothie. Strawberry was her favorite.

She dipped her tongue into the cool iciness. Delicious. But after dog food, Raid would probably taste good. "Why'd you make me this?" she asked.

"It has nothing to do with being friends. After this morning, we're not friends."

Then there was another reason, and Sam could easily guess what that might be. The smoothie wasn't necessarily poisoned, but there was some type of sleep medication in it. Likely the same stuff Colin had given her before. It was the only other time they'd brought her a drink other than the water in her bowl. It'd made her so tired she couldn't even lift her arms.

If they weren't trying to kill her, they wanted her to sleep. Why?

Her stomach growled as she eyed the glass. "Are you going out tonight?"

"That's none of your freakin' business, okay? I'm not going to forget how you treated me, you know."

Sam wasn't sorry in the least, but she knew it would be smarter to pretend she was. "I should apologize for that. I—I was upset."

Tiffany glanced at the place where Sam's chain was attached to the ring in the floor. "You want me to let you off that chain, that's all. Even when it's not choking you, it's heavy, huh?"

"How would you know?" Sam asked.

Tiffany didn't answer. "You're not getting off it."

"What if I promise to be nice?"

She seemed tempted but ultimately shook her head. "I don't have any choice. Not tonight."

"What's happening tonight?"

"Wouldn't you like to know." She scowled at Sam's lack of progress. "Are you going to stare at that all day or drink it?"

"My stomach's upset. I'm not sure I can get it down." She tried to give the glass back, but Tiffany's scowl deepened.

"No! You have to get it down."

"Why?"

"Don't you want it?"

"I want it. I just…I'm sick."

"So? Do it! You have to."

"But I *can't.*"

"If you don't, Colin will knock you out some other way," she warned.

It was as she'd thought. Someone was coming over, and they didn't want her to make any noise. "Are you having company?"

Tiffany stepped closer, looming over her. "Shut up and drink it."

"I told you, I'm sick." And the reeking kitty-litter box was proof. She wasn't sure how Tiffany could stand it, except that she was more preoccupied than usual.

"Drink it anyway! Or would you rather I choked you again?"

Sam was pushing her luck, but she knew this might be her only chance. "C-can you give me a few minutes?"

Tiffany's sneer wasn't pleasant. At least her perfume improved the smell in the room. "I don't have a few minutes." She snapped her fingers. "Come on!"

"I can drink it if you'll give me some time. Why don't you do whatever you have to do and come back for the glass later?"

Tiffany laughed. "So you can dump it? I'm not that dumb." With a curse, she picked up the chain, obviously determined to force the issue, and Sam began gulping as fast as possible.

"Oh, so now you'll cooperate," she said, her words dripping with sarcasm as she dropped the chain.

The smoothie felt so good going down that she almost couldn't endure the thought of throwing it up.

"There." Wanting to get rid of Tiffany before her stomach could absorb any of the drug, she handed Tiffany the glass.

Fortunately, Tiffany was in a hurry and didn't seem to think twice. She took it and hurried out, and Sam slid over to the kitty-litter box. Although she'd never made herself throw up before, she'd seen a friend do it in the bathroom at school, and it'd seemed pretty easy.

Sticking a finger down her throat, she gagged, almost threw up but then chickened out. She couldn't do it. It was too painful, too gross.

But then the strangest thing happened. She didn't need to try anymore. Just sitting there, leaning over the foul-smelling kitty litter with her stomach so unused to being full was enough. She began to retch and kept vomiting until she was sure there couldn't be anything left inside her.

Afterward she slumped onto the floor and listened. The walls in this room were thicker than usual. She couldn't hear much of what went on outside, at least beyond the hall directly in front of the door. But she'd finally realized that if she was very still and put her ear to the wooden floor, a few sounds drifted up from below. Faint though they were, she was learning to decipher the differences between the opening of the door, the phone, voices.

The house seemed silent, but she knew Tiffany or Colin would eventually come to check on her.

After shaking the box to cover the vomit, she crawled back to the mattress, dragging the chain as she went, hoping the stench that had already filled the room would cover the smell of puke.

She prayed that she'd vomited soon enough and had gotten it all out. She *couldn't* fall asleep. She had to remain aware, had to figure out who was coming over. Colin and Tiffany had to be expecting company. They wouldn't need to drug her if they were only leaving; they left all the time, and she'd never been able to get free.

Forcing herself to sit up, she hugged her knees to her chest and waited for sound or movement. If they came again, she'd pretend to be asleep so they'd stop worrying about her. Then, when it was clear their company had arrived, she'd use what little energy she had to cry out, rattle the chain, stomp—create enough noise to attract the attention of their guests.

But if Colin or Tiffany were the only ones who heard her, she wouldn't have anywhere close to sixty-six marks on the baseboard.

It was Tiffany who answered the door when Zoe got to the house. "Hello." She smiled but seemed so reserved and aloof that Zoe stayed at the door instead of proceeding inside, even though Tiffany stepped back to admit her.

"Is anything wrong?" she asked.

Tiffany's effort to pump more energy into her smile was obvious. "Of course not. What makes you think that?"

"You seem a little…stressed."

"It's nothing. Just a bad day at work. And then your private investigator caught me as I got home to ask a few questions about Sam, so I'm running late." She fanned her face; Zoe assumed she'd been racing frantically to pull the meal together. "I didn't mind, of course," Tiffany went on. "But there's nothing I can do to help. And I already told the police that."

"I'm sorry. He's just…hoping that someone saw or heard something that's been overlooked. Especially since you were home that day."

"I wish I *had* heard something."

"I know. And I really don't mean to cause you extra work." Zoe wanted to either come inside or leave. She didn't want to remain standing on the stoop where Anton might see her. She wasn't sure how she felt toward him and didn't want to deal with any residual resentment or confusion. If not for Sam, she wouldn't have returned to the neighborhood at all. "Would you rather I came over after you and Colin have had a chance to relax and eat? You don't have to feed me—"

"It's no problem," Tiffany cut in. "The food's almost ready." She waved toward the couch. "Have a seat. Colin's not home yet, but he'll be here any minute."

Zoe moved into the living room she'd glimpsed the day Sam went missing. It was as neat today as it had been then, but the furnishings weren't nearly as good a quality as they appeared from a distance. The couch, coffee table, even the pictures, had probably been purchased from a discount store. She'd been with Anton long enough to spot a fake. He held any object that wasn't the most authentic and the very best in the highest contempt. But everything here matched, right down to the pictures of Mediterranean villas on the wall. Only the roses on the dining-room table didn't fall in line with the peach-and-beige decor.

"How lovely," she said, gesturing at the roses.

Tiffany nodded. "Thanks. Colin gave them to me."

"I hope I'm not intruding on your anniversary or some other special event."

"No. He sent them to me just to say he loves me." She smiled brightly, delighted by the flowers.

"How thoughtful." *And reassuring.* Anything that proved Colin's love for his wife made Zoe feel more comfortable about how interested and friendly he was with her. "Can I help with dinner?"

Tiffany's teeth sank into her bottom lip as she considered the offer. "Is it normal to help when you're a guest?" she asked. "I mean, would it be impolite of me to accept?"

"Not at all," Zoe said with laugh. "I'm perfectly happy to pitch in, especially since it was my investigator who made you late. Please tell me what you'd like me to do."

"I was making the salad. If you could finish slicing the carrots and cucumbers and add the beets and candied walnuts, I could go and change before Colin gets home."

"No problem."

Tiffany showed her into the kitchen, then hurried away as if Colin was a highly anticipated guest instead of joint host. But Zoe wasn't offended that he was the person Tiffany most wanted to impress. She found it rather endearing.

Zoe was just adding the beets to the salad when Colin walked in. "Hello? Tiff? Hey, where's Zoe?"

Zoe poked her head around the corner. "I'm here. Your wife's upstairs getting changed."

For a moment, he stared at her with such undisguised

appreciation Zoe had to glance at the roses to remind herself that he and Tiffany must be getting along well. "Hungry?" she said to distract him.

"Definitely," he replied, but she had a funny feeling that he wasn't talking about food.

"Your wife's done a beautiful job with dinner." She ducked back into the kitchen, hoping Tiffany would show up, and wasn't disappointed. Seconds later, she heard the rapid beat of footsteps hurrying down the stairs. "Colin, you're home!"

"Finally," he said. "I swear I don't know what they'd do at that firm without me. I'm the newest one there, but I do eighty percent of the work."

Zoe found that unlikely. She got the impression from his overloud voice that he was hoping to impress her, but tried to give him the benefit of the doubt.

"Because you're so smart," Tiffany said.

Silence ensued, making Zoe hope they were hugging and kissing. Then Colin appeared at the entrance to the kitchen sans briefcase and Tiffany slipped around him to take over the salad.

"How do you like our home?" he asked.

"It's beautiful," she said.

"Has Tiffany given you the grand tour? We have a slightly different floor plan than Anton. We have one less bedroom, but still have the bonus room over the garage."

Would it be different enough that there was any reason to show her? She couldn't imagine it was but didn't want to be impolite.

"Not yet," she said. "I just got here a few minutes ago."

"Let me show you what we're going to do with the backyard." He left and returned with a drawing that included a barbecue pit, a fancy patio, and a pool and hot tub, along with improved landscaping.

"This will be great. When are you planning to start?"

"In a year or so."

"Will you fence off the pool once you have kids?"

This question was met with a blank look. "Why would we do that?"

Zoe had thought it would be obvious. "For safety reasons."

"Colin's never wanted children," Tiffany piped up. "And I'm fine with that. We just want to be together."

Zoe directed her gaze at Colin. Hadn't he told her just the other night that they wanted a family? "I hope what's happened to Sam hasn't changed your mind."

"No, it's not that." He shrugged. "We'll probably have a kid someday. But that's later. *Much* later. I'm only twenty-five. There's a lot to do before we tie ourselves down."

"Children are certainly a commitment," she murmured.

"You got that right." He winked at her. "But pets I can handle. They're a different story entirely."

She'd never heard him talk about animals. "Do you have any pets?"

"Not yet." Tiffany shot her husband a look that indicated this might be a contentious issue between them.

"We're considering a dog," Colin said.

"What kind?" Zoe asked.

He opened a bottle of wine and poured her a glass. "What kind would you guess I'd like?"

She smiled. "I'm not sure."

"One that can be trained to please," he said, but before he could elaborate, Tiffany interrupted again and seemed almost…upset.

"Dinner's ready."

21

"Are you high?" Tiffany whispered to Colin once they were in the kitchen. They'd finished eating dinner—a painful affair for Tiffany with her husband so attentive to Zoe. Now Zoe was using the bathroom.

He scowled at her. "Of course not. What are you talking about?"

"Don't lie to me. You're on drugs. I can tell." Having Zoe over was a bad idea. Tiffany had been worried about it from the beginning, but now she was getting *really* worried. She could tell by the way Zoe kept glancing at her that she'd noticed Colin's altered behavior. She could probably sense his sexual interest, too. He kept leering at her as if he wanted to rip her clothes off. "Is it Ecstasy?" she asked.

"What's it matter to you?" He set the dishes he'd carried in the sink. "We were planning to party later. So what if I got a head start?"

"What'd you do?"

"I had one line of coke before I left the office, okay? No big deal."

"You couldn't have waited, Colin? We need to be careful around Zoe!"

"I haven't given us away."

"But if you keep talking about pets and how smart some of them can be she's going to think it's weird, okay?

Don't mention animals again! You're making her nervous, and me, too."

He shook his head as if he didn't believe it. "You're overreacting."

"No, I'm not. If you want to have James and Tommy over tonight, and you want me to show them a good time, you'd better hurry up and get this route planning over with so she can be on her way."

He grabbed her by the waist. "Now you're threatening me?"

She blinked rapidly, fighting tears. "I won't go to prison like my brother."

"Oh, shit. I told you, no one's going to prison—"

"Be quiet!" Tiffany broke in. "You're talking too loud. Just get rid of her."

He let go and folded his arms. "What if I don't want to get rid of her? What if I want another pet—a mother-daughter combo?"

Tiffany's knees went weak. She'd been afraid of this, afraid of where her husband's mind had been wandering. "We can't keep her!"

"She won't be able to escape any easier than Sam. And she'll be no harder to dispose of when we're through."

"She's not a child. She'll be cunning, more resourceful, stronger. So it *will* be different. And who knows how many people she told that she was coming here for dinner?"

"But imagine how she'd react to finding her daughter again. In a way, we'd be doing her a favor." He laughed, cocking his head as he gazed down at her. "We'd be giving her what she wants."

And what *he* wanted at the same time. He couldn't wait to witness that painful moment when she realized she'd been stabbed in the back by someone she considered a friend.

Tiffany bit her lip. Sometimes he truly frightened her…. "Colin, no—"

"Yes! Then she'll understand that you and I have an open relationship. That she doesn't have to resist her attraction to me," he argued. "You're a big stumbling block for her. I can tell. All she does is talk about you."

Tiffany felt her jaw drop. She was losing Colin, and this was proof. That realization alone was enough to make her feel faint. As much as he frightened her, she was more frightened of living without him. "We don't have an open relationship," she breathed.

"You're going to have sex with my friends tonight. What do you call that?"

"You're the one who begged me to go along with it!"

"But if *I* don't mind, you shouldn't mind. I told you, casual sex is casual sex. It's just for kicks, a new twist to an old party."

"*Kicks?* We'd be slitting our own throats if you kidnapped Zoe. Don't even think about it."

He pressed her up against the counter and started kissing her neck. "Come on, babe. For me?"

She began to waver, as she always did when he pleaded with her. Colin was so much fun—and so loving—when he was happy. But it was getting harder and harder to keep him happy. "She's been in constant touch with the police and that investigator. What if she mentioned her dinner here?" she asked again.

"Why would she? It's dinner at a neighbor's. She doesn't give them a schedule, only a phone number where they can reach her if they find Sam."

Tiffany heard the flush of the toilet, knew they were running out of time. "It's too risky."

"Come on. Even if she told them she was having dinner with us, I can cover."

"How?" she whispered.

"Leave that to me."

"But I don't want to do this!"

"Sure you do. When I'm done using the collar on her, we'll let James and Tommy have her."

Now Tiffany *knew* Colin was going too far. "Then James and Tommy will know she was with us!"

"We'll give her a roofie, tie her up and put a bag over her head. They'll be so high they'll think she's a friend of yours and it's all in fun. Anyone would struggle being choked by that collar. That's the exciting part."

She wouldn't struggle if they mixed the roofie with more alcohol. She'd be completely out of it.

Tiffany curved her nails into her palms. Was that all it would take? Some drugs and a few hours? If Colin got what he wanted, would he be satisfied?

Temptation beckoned. She couldn't tolerate his sudden crush on their former neighbor. Not only was Zoe pretty, she was a few years older and would probably be more of a challenge to Colin's intellect, keep him interested longer.

Tiffany refused to go back to being undesired. Anything but that. Which meant she had to put an end to his infatuation permanently—or she'd have to wonder if her husband was dreaming about another woman. If he continued to pursue Zoe and it turned into a full-fledged affair, Tiffany stood to lose a lot more than if she gave him one night of sexual freedom. Colin knew how to charm people. Tiffany could easily imagine him buying Zoe flowers and jewelry and supporting her in her grief until he'd worked his way into her affections. Better to give him what he wanted now than to pay a higher price later.

"What do you say?" he coaxed, caressing her breasts. "Will you let me do it?"

Her resolve slipped even further. She loved it when he treated her with such tenderness. "How can we manage it?"

The faucet in the bathroom was turned off as he removed a foil-wrapped packet from his pocket. "Put this in her drink. She'll never expect it coming from you."

She stared at the little white pill inside the bubble. She'd seen Rohypnol before, had even taken it for Colin a time or two, because he'd been curious to see how long it took to work and what she'd remember afterward.

"If I do this, you have to kill her. I won't have her living in my house." At least then it would be over; Zoe would never be a threat again.

"You're getting vicious," he teased, pulling her earlobe into his mouth. "I guess it's true what they say about jealousy."

Tiffany imagined her former neighbor drying her hands, oblivious to what they had planned for her. "Is that a yes?"

"I'd rather not have to get rid of her so soon. She'd make a great pet." He gave an exaggerated sigh. "But…one pet's enough, I suppose."

"So you'll do it?" she said. "Tonight's the end?"

"If that's what it'll take to get you to agree."

The door opened down the hall, and Tiffany's heart jumped into overdrive. "Colin, wait. I don't think I can go through with it."

"Sure you can." With a smile and an encouraging nod, he put the pill in her palm and closed her fingers around it. "She's a snooty bitch. She deserves it."

The high he'd achieved just before he left work was already wearing off. A single line never lasted long, only about an hour. Colin wanted to snort some more—he had a baggie of cocaine in his briefcase—but he forced himself to wait.

That'll come later. It's gonna be one hell of a night.

Now that he knew he'd get what he wanted, and soon, he could forget the frustration he'd felt before and focus on the charade, the image he and Tiffany needed to portray in order to make it all happen. *We're just a fine, upstanding young couple eager to help our neighbors and the community. See?* He perfected his expression of concern. *Look at me working hard to organize this search.*

Tiffany was doing the dishes. He could sense her nervousness, caught her glancing at them through the doorway every once in a while. But he knew Zoe was too absorbed in what they were doing to notice. She sat next to him at the dining-room table, her head bent over the maps he'd spread out as they tried to determine how many homes, or how many square feet of land, would be manageable per volunteer.

"We need to cover as much ground as possible while we have them." She frowned over the less densely populated area to the east. "But that gives this volunteer more than he or she could handle on foot."

"We should break it up, then. We want everyone to complete their routes within a reasonable amount of time," Colin said. "That way, if we have to search again, we'll know exactly what's been covered and what hasn't. Better to be methodical than overly aggressive."

"The police were methodical."

"Doesn't matter. I once saw a show where the missing girl was right in the middle of the park they'd been searching for days. It's easy to overlook something."

"I suppose." She seemed more relaxed now that dinner was over. Or maybe it was the sedative taking effect. She'd drunk about half the wine Tiffany had brought her after dinner.

Hurry up and finish, for crying out loud, he thought,

lingering over his own glass. Experience had taught him that Rohypnol took effect in about thirty minutes, but she'd been sipping her wine at least that long. Had she drunk enough of it? If so, he should see a change in her fairly soon….

"I say we go as far as Stanford Ranch," he said.

She nodded, and once again he wished she'd finish her damn drink. He didn't want to wait for Tommy and James to arrive. He preferred to have Zoe to himself first, alone in his bedroom, as if she was his wife instead of Tiffany. Maybe he'd share her later, once he'd had his fill, but he planned on taking hours and didn't want anyone rushing him. If he was going to kill her anyway, he could do whatever he wanted without fear of hurting her so badly she wouldn't recover. And that promised to add a whole new dimension to the experience. He generally tried to keep his slaves alive as long as possible, which meant he had to be somewhat careful or he'd destroy the object that was bringing him pleasure. It wasn't as if slaves were easy to come by. He'd only had four. One was in a coma. And Samantha was passed out upstairs. Four wasn't that many. At times, he feared the consequences of getting caught as much as Tiffany did.

But his cravings were growing more and more powerful and so was the thirst for blood and violence. There had to be pain, excruciating pain, or he could no longer achieve the same kind of climax. That was why Rover had finally rebelled. That was also why Colin couldn't have regular sex with Tiffany anymore. It did nothing for him. Even with the bondage and the hot wax, he couldn't satisfy himself.

He remembered his first slave, a ten-year-old girl named Laurie he'd kidnapped from a park only six months after he and Tiffany were married, back in Virginia when he was in law school. Tiffany still believed he'd let Laurie go, but he'd killed her and hidden her body in the woods—hidden it so well he didn't think it'd ever been found. At the time, he hadn't been sure that Tiffany would go along with such a permanent solution and hadn't wanted to tell her. Since then, he'd acted as though he'd been forced by necessity to take the situation further each time. She didn't need to know he'd been perfectly comfortable with it from the beginning; this image served him better.

Laurie was back when humiliation had been exciting enough. Now he needed a more visceral high.

"Colin?" Zoe's voice, filled with curiosity and confusion, broke into his thoughts.

He blinked, suddenly aware that he'd been staring past her. "Sorry." He faked a yawn. "It was a long day at work, and I'm tired. How're you holding up?"

"Fine. We're almost done, aren't we?" She sat back and drank the last of her wine, and he motioned to the glass as she set it aside. "Would you like some more?"

"No, thanks."

"We've already got routes for the ten volunteers I have confirmed—and one extra. But I say we do one or two more, in case someone brings a friend."

She leaned over the maps again. "It's better to have too many than too few. But the railroad tracks are pretty far away. We should focus on this area over here." She indicated the part of the map that dipped down into Roseville.

"Tough call. Sam could be anywhere." *Like upstairs…*

"When I talked to Detective Thomas about this, he said we should concentrate our efforts within a two-mile radius of the house."

"Detective Thomas knows we're searching?" Colin felt no fear; he'd expected as much.

"I told him when I spoke to him earlier. He'll be

joining us, along with some of the other men and women on the force."

This shattered the fantasy Colin had been building, but he had to deal with reality, had to know exactly what he was up against. "Did you tell him you were coming over?"

She slid her glass toward the center of the table. "No, why?"

"Just wondering if we should've invited him. He's got to be more experienced at organizing a search than we are. And he's already been through there."

"But like you said, we need to look again. You're doing a fine job," she said with a grateful smile.

She was so sincere, so anxious for an escape from the situation *he'd* placed her in. It made him feel incredibly powerful to be the person in control of her happiness.

He couldn't have James and Tommy over tonight, he decided. They'd just get in the way....

"Besides, I don't get the impression he's had to deal with many child abductions," she was saying.

"What about your private-investigator friend?" Colin asked. "Should he be here?"

She glanced at her empty glass as if wondering when she'd finished it—or why she was feeling so light-headed after only one glass with dinner and one afterward. "He couldn't have come, even if we'd invited him," she said.

"Why not?"

"He had some interviews tonight."

"Who's he meeting with?"

"Sam's best friend and her parents."

Perfect. "Jonathan" was preoccupied. "Does he know who you're with?"

She closed her eyes and gave her head a little shake. Sure enough, the Rohypnol was starting to work.

"Zoe?"

She opened her eyes but squinted at him. "Hmm?"

"Does he know you're here?"

"Mmm hmm."

"He does?" he prompted. "You told him, Zoe? You told Jonathan you were coming to our house for dinner?"

She nodded. "He said...to come over to his place...later."

Too bad. It would've been easier if she hadn't told him. Her car was parked across the street, not in Anton's driveway, but it was a familiar enough sight that none of the neighbors would think twice about it. They'd probably assume she was visiting Anton even if they'd heard about the break-up.

But Colin could cover his tracks.

"Where're you going?" she asked, her words slurring.

He hoped one tablet was the right dosage. He didn't want her unconscious. He preferred to witness her reaction to his ministrations. That was the fun of it.

"Just helping Tiffany clean up."

"You have a...really nice wife."

"Except for when she's helping me murder someone."

Tiffany had come to stand behind them. She gasped at this, but he laughed and waved her off. Zoe was too out of it to realize he was serious. She even laughed with him.

"I'm getting cold feet," Tiffany whispered, pulling him close.

"Are you kidding? Look at her! She's helpless!"

Zoe obviously wasn't listening. She was too busy trying to figure out what was wrong. She got to her feet—and staggered back into the chair.

"Watch it," he said. "I think you should sit down in the living room."

"S-s-sorry. I...I don't know...I can't...I must be drunk, but..."

"You'll feel better once you rest," he told her and guided her over to the couch.

"Colin…" Tiffany's voice was a warning. "You heard her. That P.I. guy knows she's here. If she goes missing we'll be the first ones they question. And that could get us in trouble for Sam, too."

But everything else was lined up so perfectly! He couldn't let the opportunity slip past him. "I can take care of that."

"How?"

"Do you have your cell phone in your purse?" he asked Zoe.

"What?" She squinted up at him.

"Your cell phone. Where is it?"

Although her movements were awkward and uncoordinated, she managed to get her phone from her purse. "What are…you doing?" she asked when he took it from her.

"I'm sending a text to Jonathan."

"Oh…good. Have him…pick me up."

"Don't worry." He ran his fingers down the side of her beautiful face. "You're safe with me."

"Colin, this is crazy." Tiffany hovered over his shoulder.

"Shut up. I told you, I've got a plan."

"It's too risky!"

"I said shut up! And take off your clothes."

"What?"

"She's taller than you, but with a pair of heels, you could pass for her from a distance."

"I don't understand…."

"You will." When he took Zoe's purse, Zoe didn't even protest. She lay on the couch staring up at the ceiling as he emptied it out on the floor and sifted through the contents. "These will help," he said and handed Tiffany a pair of sunglasses.

"But it's dark," she argued. "No one wears sunglasses after dark. That'll draw more attention to me."

"You don't know jackshit! She's been wearing them a lot lately, to hide the fact that she's been crying. After what happened to Sam, no one in this neighborhood will question it."

Tiffany gaped at him. He could tell he was pushing her a little too far, but he had no patience left. "Come on." He snapped his fingers to get her moving. "If you do as I say we'll be fine."

Reluctantly, she began to disrobe while he stripped Zoe.

"Wai…what's goin' on?" Zoe fought him when he started to peel off her pants. "Anton?"

Leaning close, Colin whispered lovingly in her ear. "That's right, baby, it's me. I'm just trying to put you to bed. You need some rest."

After that, she didn't balk. Her breathing grew slower, shallower, and her mouth hung open. He would've laughed at how messed up she was, but he was in too much of a hurry to enjoy it.

A moment later, she looked like a life-size rag doll tossed on the couch in her bra and underwear. "Hey, where's the fancy lingerie?" he asked as he eyed her simple white underwire bra and pink polka-dot bikini panties. "I expected more of you."

"Colin!"

He turned to see a pout on his wife's face. "Quit worrying! I love you, and you know it. Now get dressed. Then move her car." He threw Zoe's clothes and keys at her. "Honk and wave if one of our neighbors is out or driving down the street. Try to be seen leaving the neighborhood, if you can do it without being too obvious or getting out of the car."

"Where should I go?" she asked.

He shook Zoe's shoulder. "Hey, where'd you stay last night?"

"Hmm?"

"Where's your room?"

No response.

"Zoe!"

Her eyes rolled back in her head, and she started to giggle.

Somehow her inability to respond enraged him as much as it excited him. He was going to rape her for hours, then kill her. He'd never done anything like that before. He'd always held back. But he wouldn't need to tonight. He could fulfill whatever fantasies he dreamed up, no matter how extreme.

"Where should I move the car, Colin?" Tiffany asked again.

"Drive it to a motel."

"What motel?"

"One at least a half hour's drive away. A chain that deals with lots of people so you can go pretty well unnoticed."

She looked at him, wide-eyed. "Why does it have to be so far away?"

"Because when she disappears, we don't want it to happen anywhere around here." And he wanted some time alone with her, without Tiffany standing jealously by.

"Oh."

"Leave the sunglasses on when you go in to rent the room, and use her credit card and driver's license. Keep your head down in case there's any cameras around."

"How will I get back home?" she asked.

"Take a taxi to any gas station within a mile or two of here. Go into the restroom, change into your own clothes and bury hers in the trash so they won't be found."

"Then what? Do I call you to come and get me?"

"Are you a complete idiot?" he said. "We can't have one of our cars seen leaving the neighborhood. They have to stay in the driveway." Besides, and he knew this was the part that worried Tiffany, he planned to be far too busy enjoying his latest prize.

"So I should walk?"

"It won't kill you."

"But what about James and Tommy?" She glanced at the clock. "They'll be here in an hour."

"I'll cancel with them."

Tiffany looked even more stricken. "But you promised you'd pass her off to them!"

Unwilling to let her ruin the fun, he whirled on her. "I'm going to kill her, okay? That should be good enough for you! One night. I'm only asking for one night! So unless you want me to kill you, too, I suggest you do exactly as I say. Now!"

Her chest rose, then fell in quick succession. "Kill me?" she echoed. "I know you didn't mean that."

He shook his head. "Just get out of here."

She didn't move. A tear rolled down her cheek, so he made himself give her a hug because he knew he'd gain her compliance more quickly that way. "I'm sorry, babe. Work with me here, okay? I'm stressed out. We've gone too far to stop now. We have to prepare for the worst."

She sniffed as he pulled away. "Okay. I'm gone. I'm going right now," she said, but didn't actually leave. "What about the private investigator?"

"I've already taken care of him."

"How?"

"I used her phone to text him, saying she's leaving our place and getting a room for the night, that she'll call him in the morning. Eventually, when she doesn't check out of the motel tomorrow, someone will find her car, and they'll connect it with the room rental. We'll be fine."

"That's smart," she said. "You're so smart, Colin."

"I'm a lawyer, babe. Would you expect any less?"

"No. Nothing less." The door slammed shut as she went out.

"Zoe?" Colin grabbed her chin and jerked her face toward him. He was looking into her eyes, but he wasn't sure she was really seeing him. "Zoe, can you hear me?"

His words didn't seem to register. "Damn. That stuff hit you harder than I thought it would." He shouldn't have used it. He should've just dragged her upstairs and tied her up. But he'd been planning to put on a show for his friends. And he'd never attacked an adult before, hadn't wanted to underestimate what could happen. If she got loose long enough to scream or throw something at a window, it could attract the attention of a neighbor. Maybe even Anton.

Rolling her forward, he unhooked her bra so he could stare at her while he canceled with his friends.

"What do you mean you can't do it tonight?" Tommy cried. "We were all set, man!"

"Sorry, Tiffany has the flu."

There was a slight pause. "Okay, so we'll get together at my place. Leave her at home to recuperate."

"I can't leave her when she's sick."

"Why not?"

"What kind of husband do you think I am?" he said and hung up. Then he scooped Zoe into his arms and carried her upstairs.

22

To stave off his exhaustion, Jonathan took a big gulp of the coffee—now long cold—in the cardboard cup he'd left in his car. He'd just finished visiting Marti Seacrest and her parents. If not for the boy in the hospital, which could turn the situation around, Jonathan would've thought Sam's case was hopeless. There just weren't any leads. He'd never confronted a missing-person situation where he had less to go on. Even his interview with Sam's best friend hadn't yielded any new information. Just as he'd been told before, Marti insisted that Sam hadn't acted any differently in the week leading up to Monday. She hadn't met anyone new, wasn't talking about a particular boy or an Internet pal or an adult who'd befriended her since she'd been off school.

Once he mentioned that Zoe and Anton had split up, she did elaborate on Sam's dislike of her potential stepfather. Marti said Sam called Anton a "control freak." But that didn't come as any shock to Jonathan. He'd already sensed her disdain for Anton from the way she'd hidden his face whenever he was in one of those pictures on her bulletin board.

An image of the Simpson boy appeared in his mind. Would Toby regain consciousness? Would he ever remember?

Jonathan's BlackBerry vibrated. Putting down his cup,

he leaned back so he could retrieve it from his pocket and found a text message waiting for him:

Not feeling well. Getting a motel. Call u tomorrow.

It was from Zoe. Surprised that she'd decided not to come over, and that she hadn't called to hear whether he'd managed to uncover anything new today, he tried to call her back but got her voice mail.

Obviously, she was avoiding him. And even if she wasn't, he was crazy to keep pushing for more contact. He was setting himself up to get burned. Again. But she needed friendship and support; she shouldn't be alone in some motel room in the midst of such a crisis.

Or was that his libido talking?

He tried to reach her again, with the same result.

Sighing, he put his phone on the console and started his car, but a call came in just as he left the neighborhood—and this time the number brought a smile. "Finally," he muttered and pushed the Talk button.

"Now that you're Mrs. Fornier you don't have time for your old friends?" he teased.

Jasmine's laugh made him miss her all the more. "Sorry. Romain and I were out on the bayou."

"The same bayou that has those crocodiles you're so scared of?"

"Boy, you're a real nature buff," she said with another laugh. "They're *alligators*."

"They both have sharp teeth and can make a mess out of you, right?"

"Right. I wouldn't want to come face-to-face with one. But they usually keep their distance. Romain knows what he's doing, so I'm safe as long as I'm with him. What's going on?"

Planning to stop by Zoe's neighbor's house to see if she'd left yet, he got onto Highway 65—and encountered a sea of brake lights. There'd been an accident or a spill or something up ahead. "I need your help, Jaz," he said.

"Your message made it sound as if you're on a tough case."

"I could be dealing with one of the sickest bastards I've ever come across."

There was a pause. "What have you got?"

He explained what they knew about Samantha Duncan's abduction, including the recovery of the Simpson boy.

"He was found in the woods?" she said when he'd finished.

Wondering what was blocking traffic, he tried to see around the cars ahead of him, but there were only more cars, stopped just like he was. "That's right. Near Placerville."

"I'd check to see who owns any houses, cabins, even businesses in the area."

"A lot of the cabins are rentals."

"Then I'd get hold of the rental records."

He'd already been planning to do that. "How far back do you think I should go?" he asked. "One year, two years, more?"

"I'd go two years, at least. You never know—a name might jump out at you. Criminals typically confine their activities to familiar areas, areas where they feel most comfortable and in control. Maybe Master lives in Rocklin now, but he probably had a legitimate reason for being in Placerville at one time or another."

Problem was, sifting through the property and rental information would be a long and painstaking process, and might yield no results. Meanwhile, Samantha could be in the hands of the man who'd brutalized Toby Simpson. For her sake, he'd been hoping for easier, faster answers.

"If this Master wasn't familiar with the area," she said, "I feel he would've turned the boy loose somewhere off Interstate 80, not Highway 50."

"Something had to draw him in that direction instead of toward Auburn, which would be a more natural choice if he was coming from Rocklin," he agreed. "But I don't believe he meant to set the boy free. I think Toby escaped."

"What makes you think that?"

Reluctantly, and only because he needed the caffeine, Jonathan swallowed another gulp of stale coffee. "One look at him would convince you he wasn't meant to survive. You should see the poor kid."

"I'm glad to be spared that." She didn't have to explain why; he knew she'd seen enough in her profiling career.

"So, when they found him they didn't get anything more out of him, other than that comment about Master treating him like a dog, and Rocklin?" she asked.

"That's it. He was pretty out of it. But as hurt as he was, they still had a hell of a time catching him. He wouldn't trust the man who first encountered him, so that guy got his wife, assuming a woman would seem less threatening."

"Did it help?"

"Not much. Toby would let her come closer but dodge away before she could actually touch him, all the while crying for his mother."

"Have any other bodies turned up?" she asked.

He could tell by her brisk tone that she didn't want to dwell on Toby's condition. "Not that I've heard. I spoke with Skye's husband earlier."

"David's with Sacramento PD, not Rocklin."

"But I knew he'd get further with the other departments than I would." Jonathan inched forward, along with the other motorists on Highway 65. "There've been no homicides in the past several months, at least of pubescent or prepubescent children," he told her.

"What about the detective in charge? What's his name?"

"Thomas."

"Does he believe there might be a connection?"

"I talked to him a few hours ago. He's looking into it."

"He might be able to get someone to check the rental records."

That didn't mean Jonathan wouldn't have to do it himself. Only then could he feel confident that nothing had been missed or overlooked. "I hope."

The next few seconds passed in silence as Jonathan gave Jasmine some time to mull it over.

"So what do you think about this guy?" he asked at length. "Anything?"

"Because Master had the boy for so long, I'm tempted to assume he's a recluse, an outcast who hovers on the periphery of the community. He's got to be able to hide his prize, doesn't he?" she said.

"If he's going to hang on to a victim for two months, he does."

"But something isn't right about that theory. I'm not…comfortable with it."

"Could be the neighborhood," he said. "It's too new and affluent for the lonely, blue-collar worker you're picturing."

"True, but…it's more than that. There could be a few outcasts, a derelict son who's living with his parents, or a renter who doesn't fit the normal demographic."

"There aren't rentals in this part of Rocklin. I'd be surprised if there's more than one or two."

"Maybe Master inherited a fortune from his parents. Heck, maybe he even inherited their house and doesn't have anything to do all day but prey on kids."

Jonathan had already talked to all friends, family and neighbors and hadn't come across a situation like the one she described. "What about motivation?" he asked. "You think these are sex crimes?"

"The boy was found without his clothes, wasn't he?"

Several cars in front of him, an Explorer nosed over, trying to change lanes, and almost caused another accident. "Just what we need," Jonathan muttered.

"What?"

"Nothing. Master could've used nudity as a form of control. Or humiliation," he said. "I mean, if he's a sex offender, it's odd that he'd switch genders, isn't it?"

"Not especially. Not if he's more interested in sex as a form of torture than sex for its own sake. Studies have shown that a lot of psychopaths are working to fulfill one particular fantasy, to act it out until they get it 'perfect,' which never really happens because it's more like an itch that comes back even after it's been scratched. The fantasy revolves around their particular fetish."

As interested as Jonathan was in this discussion, he was growing impatient with the traffic jam that kept him idling. At this rate, he'd miss Zoe for sure. But he had no option except to wait it out. The other lanes weren't moving any more quickly, and the next exit was quite a ways off. "Isn't that why so many of them choose similar victims? This guy went from a fourteen-year-old boy to a thirteen-year-old girl."

"These kinds of offenders have to weigh the odds of getting exactly what they want against fulfilling their craving. It could be that Master would rather have had a girl when he took the Simpson boy or would've preferred a boy when he took Samantha, but one or the other became available to him, and he capitalized on the opportunity. Or…"

There was a slight break in traffic and he pulled ahead, hoping the congestion was finally about to ease, but it didn't. He had to brake again to avoid hitting the motorcycle in front of him. "Or what?"

"Or you're grasping at straws. Maybe there's no connection between the Simpson boy and the Duncan case. You could be dealing with two different perpetrators. You know that."

"I admit there's not much to link them—except the Rocklin connection. That has me convinced Master's our scumbag. And Sam was taken on the same day Toby was found. For two crimes against children of a similar age to happen one right after the other in such a small geographic area, an area that sees very little of this kind of thing…it's too much of a coincidence."

"Well, if it is him, he's confident, I'll give you that."

"What makes you say so?"

"Any normal person would be shaking in his shoes if a victim got loose, would decide to lie low for a while."

"Probably."

"Yet he took Samantha immediately after the Simpson boy's escape."

"Maybe he's *over*confident," Jonathan muttered.

"Or his compulsion is growing so strong the usual inhibitors are no longer effective. And there could also be other reasons. That's the problem with profiling. It's not an exact science."

A siren sounded behind him, and Jonathan inched to the side to make room for the ambulance. "The type of area he lives in leads me to believe he's not a disorganized personality," he said.

"That'd be my guess, too. And I'd say he's smart."

"Which means we have to be smarter. But we have no leads." Red and blue lights flashed up ahead. He was almost at the scene of the accident, but still couldn't tell what'd happened.

"Have you checked out the postman, the meter reader, the lawn service, the pool service—anyone who had a reason to go there on a regular basis?"

"The police and I are both working on the same list, so those people are getting checked and rechecked. I've talked to a lot of them. I just need to verify a few alibis."

"Maybe Samantha got bored and walked to the closest convenience store," Jasmine suggested. "Have you spoken to the clerks at any of the nearby stores? Examined their security tapes?"

"The police have checked the tapes, but I haven't. She had mono. I highly doubt she walked anywhere."

"Still…"

"The more I get to know her mother, the more I doubt she'd leave home without permission."

There was a brief pause. "The more you get to know her mother? How close *are* you?"

"Not particularly *close,* but I've spent a few days with her."

"Be careful."

He knew the emotional hazards of the job. Maria, the first woman he'd ever loved, was also an early client of his. He'd had other relationships, but none as intense as the one he'd experienced with her. She'd come to him for help documenting her husband's abusive behavior and many affairs so she could gain sole custody of their son. Jonathan had had no trouble gathering the evidence she needed. Dan Bartolo was a dirty son of a bitch. But love—and all that evidence—wasn't enough to save Maria. One day she suddenly went back to Dan, who shot and killed her two weeks later.

In Jonathan's line of work, it was never smart to mix

business with pleasure. Maria's death had been a painful lesson. "She's not married."

"And you're not getting involved with her."

"No. Ours is a professional relationship," he said and tried to tell himself he could keep it that way.

"Good. The world can get pretty warped when you've just lost a child. Her love life might look completely different to her in a few weeks or months. Chances are she'll go back to her fiancé."

"I don't think so."

"She was with him for a reason, Jon. Once she adjusts to whatever the future holds, that reason might reassert itself."

He had a hard time believing Zoe would reconcile with Anton. But he realized it was possible. She had issues with father figures, and no doubt it was those issues that'd attracted her to Anton. It didn't take a psychologist to figure that out—or to understand that acknowledging the cause didn't eradicate the problem. "I've been around the block a few times, Jaz," he said to get her off the subject.

"I know, but you like to fix people, and she's probably pretty broken right now. Remember that abused woman you took in who ultimately went back to the man who'd been abusing her?"

He rolled his eyes. "Thanks for the reminder, but Maria thought reuniting her family was best for her son."

"I don't care why she did it. Find someone who's whole and healthy, who has something to offer *you,*" she said.

As frustrated by the stalled traffic as he was with Jasmine telling him what he'd already learned—the hard way—he crept forward. "Enough advice."

"Fine. I've done my duty as your pseudo–big sister. So…do you want to send me an article of clothing or a cherished item that belonged to Samantha Duncan?"

This was why he'd been trying to reach her in the first place, what he'd secretly been hoping for all along. He hadn't mentioned Jasmine's special abilities to Zoe. He knew she'd think he was crazy if he admitted that he was planning to turn to a forensic profiler who was also a psychic. But he'd seen Jasmine work, witnessed how many of her predictions came to pass.

He prayed she'd be able to help Samantha. "Would you mind?"

"Not at all. But don't get your hopes too high. You know how it is. Sometimes I get impressions, other times I get nothing at all. And half the time I don't know how to interpret what comes, or even whether to trust it. I'm not sure I'll be much help."

"I know you don't have a crystal ball. Whatever you can give me…it's worth the chance. I'm hitting one dead end after another."

"I'll do what I can," she promised.

After ending the conversation, Jonathan rolled down his window so he could lean out. There was a cop allowing one car to go through at a time, but several lanes fed into that drip system.

Surely Zoe would be gone by now. Despite that, he called her again—to see if he could swing by her motel to pick up an article of Sam's clothing.

Hello, this is Zoe. I'm currently unavailable. Please leave your name and number and I'll get back to you as soon as I can….

With a curse, he sent her a text instead. Call me. I need to talk to you.

Sam was tired. She wasn't sure if it was because she hadn't gotten all the drug out of her system or because of the mono, which made her tired all the time, or the anxiety of the evening, but she was having difficulty fighting the drowsiness. She wanted to close her eyes and drift away, but she knew nothing would change if she did—at least nothing would change for the better. She had to remain alert so she could make out a slam, a voice, a thud. Anything distinctive enough to tell her what was going on. But everything felt so hopeless. It'd been forever and she hadn't heard much of anything yet. Had Tiffany's company even arrived?

She was afraid her plan wouldn't work, but desperation kept her fighting. Lying with her ear pressed tightly to the floor, she could hear a sound now and then. Or she thought she did. Maybe she was imagining it because she *wanted* to hear something so badly.

So when should she act? Was it only Tiffany and Colin moving around the house? Had whatever they'd planned been canceled? Or had their visitors come and gone without her knowledge? Had she missed her opportunity?

Her prison was so quiet, so isolated. It was as if they'd locked her into a different universe.

Finally giving up, she curled into herself, and the crudely made marks on the baseboard near the mattress began to blur as her eyes filled with tears. She couldn't survive sixty-six days like this; she couldn't survive another week.

"Mommy, where are you?" she whispered. She wasn't sure how long it'd been since she'd called her mother Mommy, but she felt so young and frightened. "I want you," she said, pleading with the silence.

And then she heard something that came to her as more of a vibration. At first she couldn't tell what that vibration signified, but when she pressed her ear to the floor again, she could tell that someone was shouting.

"Colin! Hey! Your cars are in the driveway, so where the hell are ya? Tiff?"

"Dad? Stay downstairs! Tiff's not dressed," came the equally loud response and, a moment later, footsteps pounded down the stairs.

"Whatever happened to knocking, for God's sake?" she heard Colin snap before his voice dropped too low for her to make out the words.

Shoving herself into a sitting position, Sam began to shiver. Someone besides Colin and Tiffany was definitely in the house. It was time to draw the attention of their guest.

But if Colin's dad came to see what was going on, would he take her side—or his?

23

Colin couldn't believe it. What was his father doing stopping by unannounced? Paddy knew Colin and Tiffany valued their privacy. Almost every visit occurred at Paddy's smallish tract house in Antelope, and that was how Colin liked it. That was the only way the relationship could work.

At Easter, Paddy's new wife, Sheryl, had said it'd be nice if Colin and Tiffany would host dinner at their place for a change, but Paddy had immediately responded by telling her to shut up and get them all a beer. He'd seen how easily Colin had cut Tina, his real mother, out of his life. He wasn't about to push Colin. He was too busy trying to make up for allowing Tina to get away with what she did when Colin was little. At least he and Colin were still on speaking terms. Colin's sister had sided with their mother and, after the divorce, refused to communicate with him or Paddy.

Colin didn't like his stepmother much more than he liked his own mother. But she was a decent cook and, because she didn't enjoy serving them, he gained some satisfaction in making her do it practically every holiday. Being on friendly terms with his father enabled him to use his father's vacation cabin, too, which had proved to be a great perk. Some of his fondest memories involved torturing his second pet at the cabin. Her remains were even buried up there.

"What're you doing here?" he asked as soon as he reached the living room.

His father stood in front of the fireplace, staring up at the photograph that'd been taken for their wedding announcements. He turned and watched as Colin finished pulling on his shirt. Colin had Zoe tied up, the video camera positioned just right, and had barely removed his clothes when he'd heard his father's voice. Being interrupted at a moment like that was beyond enraging. But at least he'd heard Paddy before the old man surprised him in the bedroom.

His father didn't seem to care that he'd dropped by at an inconvenient time. He shoved a shaking hand through his short gray hair, which was still thick despite his age, and met Colin's impatient eyes. "I need to talk to you."

Colin couldn't help glancing toward the stairs. He had all his toys ready, was eager to see how long Zoe could survive what he had in store for her, how she'd react to the pain and degradation—and now this. "Can't it wait?" he said.

"No."

Son of a bitch! Something was obviously wrong, but Colin didn't want to hear about it right now. It probably had to do with his little sister. Paddy had been trying to reconcile with Courtney for the past two years. He wanted to apologize and make up, but she either avoided his calls or changed her number.

Paddy was getting so damn soft in his old age, Colin thought. Where was the man who used to let Tina beat on him at the drop of a hat? There were times he'd even held Colin down for her. A man like that deserved to reap what he'd sown, didn't he? He couldn't start whining at this late date; it wasn't fair.

"Okay, what's up? Spit it out," he said.

"I'm sorry. I—you'll have to apologize to Tiffany for me. I'm not even sure I should've come here, but…"

Colin realized he'd pulled his shirt on wrong side out and corrected it. "But what?"

"I just saw something on television that has me…concerned," he admitted.

He'd seen something on TV? Who gave a rat's ass about that? "If this is about politics—"

"No. It's about *you,* Colin."

"What does anything on TV have to do with me?"

"I hope nothing."

Colin slouched on the sofa. "You're being really cryptic, you know that?"

His father waved toward the stairs. "Could you get Tiffany to come down for a minute? I think she should be in on this."

"Tiffany's not interested, Dad. She's waiting for me *in bed,* okay? She's not coming down just because you saw something you didn't like on TV. Now, explain what's going on or get the hell out of here, because you just interrupted some of the best sex of my life."

Paddy's chest lifted as he drew breath. "A boy was found wandering in the woods."

Colin hadn't expected his father to connect him to Rover. In his obsession with Zoe and his irritation over being interrupted before he could even touch her, he'd almost forgotten his last pet.

Fear suddenly offset his irritation, but he wasn't stupid enough to show it. "I saw that myself, a couple nights ago. Poor kid. Has he come out of his coma?"

"No. They're not sure he ever will."

"That's tragic. But..." Colin gestured as if Paddy had him at a loss. "I don't understand. You came all the way over here to tell me some sad story about a teenage boy?"

"They showed a map, pinpointing where the boy was found."

"And?"

"It was right by Mike's cabin."

Colin's erection had long since disappeared. He adjusted himself, acting as though he wasn't worried, but he was. He had reason to be. "Who's Mike?"

"My friend from work, remember? He took over management of the lawn-mower shop when your useless stepbrother got mad and walked out on me."

"Oh, right. Mike."

"I set it up for you and Tiffany to rent his cabin a couple years ago because I already had Sheryl's family staying in mine. You wanted to go camping for a week."

Colin maintained a carefully neutral expression. "Wow! The kid was found by *Mike's* cabin? What a small world. I hadn't realized. But then, they didn't get specific in the segment I saw."

"They're appealing to the public for help."

"Good idea."

Paddy peered at him more closely. "That doesn't mean anything to you?"

"Why would it?"

"The boy insisted the person who hurt him lived in Rocklin."

Colin shrugged. "Maybe he does."

His father lowered his voice. "Colin, I'm here because I'm afraid you had something to do with the disappearance of that boy."

The adrenaline pumping through him allowed Colin to react with the proper amount of indignation. "You think I'd beat up a *child?*"

He'd expected Paddy to get defensive in return. As much as his father had changed over the years, he still had a temper when sufficiently provoked. But he didn't react with anger. His voice had a pleading quality to it. "I don't *want* to think that," he said. "To be honest, I can't imagine a worse scenario, but the man who hurt him insisted on being called Master. As soon as I heard that, I felt like I'd been shot."

"Are you serious? God, will you give me a break?" Colin managed a laugh. "Maybe I made Courtney call me Master when we were young, but I was just playing around. That doesn't make me the son of a bitch who hurt this kid."

"Playing around? She didn't think it was any fun."

"It was normal brother-sister stuff."

His father didn't comment.

"Come on!" Colin said. "I'm not the only one who's ever used the word. What about domination freaks? It could be anyone. How would I even have come into contact with this boy?"

He knew before he'd finished speaking that he'd said too much. The answer was obvious, and his father spit it out immediately.

"He went missing from *my* neighborhood."

The regret in his father's body language made Colin's knees go weak. On some level, Paddy knew. He didn't want to face it, probably because he didn't want to shoulder any responsibility for what his son had become. He'd been so proud of Colin, especially since Colin had graduated from law school.

But, in his heart of hearts, Paddy knew. And the truth made him sick.

Colin jutted out his chin. "I didn't do it."

"You have a connection to where he was taken and where he was found. And…"

"And what?" Colin snapped, going on the attack. "You believe Mom, don't you! You believe I have a cruel streak."

"I'm not sure what to believe."

"Even if I *wanted* to kidnap somebody's kid, how would I do it with Tiffany around? Whoever it was kept that kid for what, two months?"

A tear caught in Paddy's eyelashes. Colin had never seen his father cry before. He didn't know what to do, what more he could say, but he couldn't let the encounter end like this or his father would go to the police.

"What?" he snapped.

"They didn't say how long Master had the kid," Paddy replied.

Shit! He'd done another line of coke after Tiffany had left and wasn't thinking clearly, wasn't handling this well. His father was growing more convinced of the truth. How was he going to get out of this?

Sweat soaked the underarms of Colin's T-shirt, made the cotton stick to his back. "They did in the segment I saw."

He'd forced enough calm into his voice and manner that a flicker of hope returned to his father's eyes. "They did?"

"Yes! How would I know that otherwise?"

"But what about the girl who's gone missing? They showed her mother. She looked exactly like your neighbor."

Son of a bitch! How had he recognized Zoe? Paddy and Sheryl hardly *ever* came over. But Colin and Tiffany had lived next door to Lucassi and Zoe for nine months. It was certainly conceivable that they'd bumped into each other at some point.

Should he say the person on TV wasn't his neighbor? That was what he wanted to say. But it would be far too easy to disprove. And then he'd be in the untenable position of being caught in a lie.

Raking his fingers through his hair, he clicked his tongue.

"Right. That happened earlier this week. Can you believe it? Someone snagged the kid from her own backyard. Zoe was just here, by the way, helping me organize a big search for tomorrow. The other lawyers at the firm and some of the support staff are going out with us."

"Why do you need to look for her?" his father asked.

Colin's muscles ached from the tension. "Because she could be in danger. You just told me yourself—someone took her."

"Was that someone *you,* Colin?"

"No!" Colin wasn't willing to give up yet. He could lie his way out of this just as he had out of every scrape in the past. His mother was the only one who could see through him when he made shit up. She'd tried to beat the devil out of him, but that'd just heightened his desire to hurt and maim. "I know it seems like quite a coincidence. But it wasn't me. If I'm not at work, I'm with Tiffany. I could never get enough time alone to snatch one kid, never mind two."

"I thought of that," Paddy said. "The whole ride over here, I told myself I had to be crazy to be feeling such fear. It couldn't be you. Not *my* son. For the sake of holding my marriage together, my *family* together, maybe I let your mother get a bit too harsh when you were little. I feel bad about that. But Tina's been out of the picture for a long time, Colin. You could've gotten some help. I offered, more than once, to pay for a therapist, but you always insisted you were fine. You pointed to your grades in school, your law-school diploma, your happy marriage, your lovely home. And I figured anyone who could achieve all that *had* to be fine. But we both know how Tiffany worships you. She'd slit her own wrists if you told her to."

With anyone else, Tiffany's presence in his daily life would provide a foolproof alibi. But this was his father; Paddy had had a front-row seat to the way they interacted.

"You're underestimating Tiffany," he said. "She'd never go along with kidnapping and…and attempted murder!"

His father wanted to believe him. That was why he'd come over, to convince himself that his suspicions were unfounded. "You're sure it's *her* I've underestimated?"

Colin grabbed his arm. "Are you kidding me? You're just like Mom. Full of false accusations. Always thinking the worst."

His father didn't like being compared to Tina. Rocking back, he searched Colin's face. "You didn't hurt those kids? Tell me the truth, Colin. I can't help you if I don't know the truth."

Paddy's doubt made it possible for Colin to breathe again. He gave a skeptical-sounding laugh. "Relax. I haven't hurt anybody," he said. But then Samantha started kicking and screaming upstairs and, even with the added insulation, Colin could hear her calling, "Help! Help me! Please! They've chained me to the floor. Call my mom! *Please* help me."

Colin's father's ashen complexion made it obvious he'd heard her, too. "Good God," he whispered and broke away, headed for the stairs.

Paddy thought he could save her. He thought Colin would just stand there and let him pass.

"Not so fast," he said and shoved his father so hard he fell, striking his head on the corner of the wall. A gash on his forehead oozed blood and left him dazed. He blinked up at Colin as if he couldn't quite focus, but the sight of him lying there didn't bother Colin in the least. He felt only relief. "You never should've married Mom, you know that? She was a mean bitch, even if she was a helluva lot smarter than you. And you shouldn't have come over here alone," he added. Then he smashed his head with the base of a lamp.

When he was sure his father was dead, Colin leaned back on his knees, winded but wildly exhilarated. Killing an adult wasn't much different from killing a kid. "You're not so big and tough these days, are you, Dad?" he said, then he grimaced at the dent he'd created in the brass lamp. "Now look what you made me do. That lamp was expensive."

Dropping the makeshift weapon onto the carpet, he listened for Sam. He hated her at that moment, hated her more than anyone in the world. He'd kill her in the most painful manner of all, he promised himself. But the house was quiet. As far as he could tell, Zoe hadn't responded to her daughter's calls, which probably meant she was still in a stupor. And Sam had either given up or given out. Either way, he could take care of them later. He had to deal with Paddy first.

Breathe deeply. He shut his eyes in an attempt to overcome the adrenaline rush causing his hands to shake. Everything was okay. He'd had a close call, that was all. But he'd saved the day. All he had to do was dispose of his father's body and he'd be fine.

But how?

Standing, he paced back and forth across the carpet. He'd drag his father into the garage, out of sight, and clean up the blood. As soon as Tiffany returned, he'd have her drive Paddy's car to the pool hall the old man visited almost every weekend. Then, later, when the neighbors were asleep, he'd drive his own car into the garage, put his father's body in the trunk and take it into the mountains to bury. Tomorrow, Paddy Bell would be just another missing person.

He pivoted and made another pass. Would that work? It should. Paddy hadn't told Sheryl what he suspected; Colin was sure of it. He wasn't the type to share information like that until he was absolutely certain. But if his stepmother knew Paddy was coming over here, Colin could face some questions.

It wouldn't matter. She'd never seriously believe he'd hurt his father. It was *her* son she'd blame. A notorious hothead, Glen Hagen had busted up the business partnership he and Paddy had going when he walked out of the lawn-mower shop they owned together.

Yes, Glen would get the blame. If Sheryl or anyone else placed Paddy in the neighborhood, Colin would simply say he stopped by on his way to see Glen about patching up the rift between them. She knew Paddy wanted to make peace with Glen. These days, Paddy didn't like being at odds with anyone.

All Colin had to do was pull himself together, be more careful—be *smart.*

But no sooner had he dragged the corpse into the garage and started to clean up the blood than someone knocked on the door.

As he stood on Colin Bell's stoop, waiting for a response, Jonathan checked his phone again. Nothing. While emergency crews cleared away the three-car pileup that'd kept him sitting in traffic for twenty minutes, he'd sent three texts to Zoe—but she hadn't returned a single one, and she wasn't answering when he tried to call.

What was going on? It didn't make sense that she wouldn't keep her phone handy, just in case he had news.

When Colin finally answered Jonathan's knock, he opened the door a crack. Jonathan could tell he didn't really want to be bothered. But his smile was as friendly as ever. "Sorry for the wait," he said. "I was in the garage."

Jonathan nodded. "No problem. I'm looking for Zoe. Have you seen her?"

"She was here for dinner."

"How long ago did she leave?"

His eyebrows knotted as if he was thinking hard to come up with the correct time. "'Bout an hour ago."

"Did she say where she was going?"

A drop of sweat trickled down from his temple. Jonathan would've thought he'd been working out, but he was dressed in jeans and a T-shirt and he wasn't wearing shoes. Had he just finished exercising, stripped off his clothes to hop in the shower and put them back on at the sound of the doorbell? If so, it was no wonder he didn't want to be interrupted....

"She mentioned she was tired," he said. "But maybe Anton saw her heading to her car and waylaid her. They broke up, you know."

Jonathan peered at Lucassi's empty driveway. "Her car's not there."

"Maybe they left together."

That possibility didn't make Jonathan feel much better. Perhaps he was wrong about her. Perhaps she'd go back to Anton, regardless of all her talk about a "loveless relationship." Maria had returned to Dan, hadn't she? And he was the man who'd broken her nose and her arm—and eventually killed her.

"I guess they could have," Jonathan said. "Thanks." But he managed to contact Lucassi on his cell phone only five minutes later, and Lucassi swore up and down that he hadn't seen Zoe since she'd left his house last night.

24

Tiffany's knees buckled when she saw her father-in-law's body. Covering her mouth in horror, she slid down the inside wall of the garage, staring at the pool of blood fanning out from his head. "He's dead," she said through her fingers. That was obvious. The minute she walked into the house and caught him cleaning up, Colin had said as much, and this was proof. But seeing wasn't necessarily believing. Since they'd married, Colin had been somewhat ambivalent about his father. Sometimes he blamed him for not stopping the abuse he suffered at the hands of his mother. Other times he seemed to forgive and forget. But Tiffany had always had a soft spot for Paddy, who, unlike Colin's mother, had been kind to her from the beginning. If he knew they were coming over, he kept her favorite cookies on hand. "The ones with the M&M's," she thought distantly.

"Get up!" Colin growled. "I need your help." She didn't move, so he gave her a little kick. "Come on. What the hell's wrong with you?"

She blinked, then focused on her husband. "What's wrong with *me?*" She tried to control her voice, but it went shrill anyway. "You just killed your father! You're going to spend the rest of your life in prison, just like my brother!"

"Shut up!" he cried. "Do you want someone to hear

you?" Raising his fist, he loomed over her as if he'd hit her, but she didn't cower. She was too bewildered to be afraid of him.

"Why, Colin?" she murmured, struggling to come to terms with what she saw. "Why would you do such a terrible thing? I—I loved him."

His lips curled back from his teeth. "Oh, give me a freakin' break, will you? You hardly knew him."

As always, she'd taken off her shoes when she entered the house. The air in the shut-up garage retained the heat of an unseasonably warm day, but her bare feet felt like blocks of ice on the cool concrete. "I did too know him."

"Only how he was in later years. He wasn't so nice before. He always took my mom's side. When I was in high school, she tried to have me institutionalized, and he nearly went along with it."

"No, he left her. That was the last straw, he said."

"He almost went along with it *before* he left her."

She reached out to touch her father-in-law, fingered the rough calluses that distinguished his hands from anyone else's. It took actual contact to convince her it was really him. His face was barely recognizable after what Colin had done. "So…that's why you did it? Because…because you're still angry about the past?"

Mindful of the neighbors, Colin kept his voice low, but his harsh whisper revealed his panic. "He walked in on me, Tiffany." He began to roll his father's body in a blanket. "He'd seen Zoe on the news, crying about losing her daughter. And he'd put it all together."

She let go of Paddy's hand as Colin tucked it into the blanket. "But…how? That's not possible."

Breathing hard from the exertion, he straightened. "Are you *stupid?* I explained it before I brought you out here. You know how he figured it out."

"Rover told him about Master." She remembered that much, but the rest, the part where Paddy had connected the name Colin had made his sister use with the fact that Rover had disappeared from his neighborhood and Sam had disappeared from theirs—from the house next door—seemed unfathomable. She couldn't comprehend Paddy being involved in this most secret part of their lives. He'd always been so removed.

Colin bent to cover Paddy's feet. "Rover didn't *tell* him. It was on the news!"

"Rover had to tell *someone*. Does that mean he's come out of the coma?"

Finished, Colin wiped the perspiration at his temple and accidentally smeared blood on his forehead. "I don't know. But we have to act fast."

"Act fast," she repeated, mesmerized by that streak of blood. "What should we do?" Paddy was gone. Their lives would never be the same. Why did Colin have to do this? Why Paddy?

"Listen to me." He pulled her up by the shoulders and shook her. "I need you. Don't flip out on me."

"But…"

"But nothing," he said. "This is *your* fault. If you hadn't let Rover get away, we wouldn't be in this mess."

"I couldn't stop him!"

"Then what about Sam? She wasn't supposed to be conscious. How was she capable of raising such a ruckus?"

Tiffany remembered finding Sam passed out on her mattress. "I don't know. I ground up two pills and put them in a shake, and she drank it. I saw her! And the last time I checked on her, she was out cold."

"She couldn't have drunk it. Two pills would knock out a man my size—for hours. That makes this even *more* your fault."

Her fault Paddy was dead? Tears burned behind Tiffany's eyes, clogged her throat. "But I loved him," she whispered again.

"He didn't love *you.* He didn't even love me."

"That's not true!"

Colin shook her again. "I don't give a rat's ass, do you hear me? If you do as I say, everything will be fine. If you don't, we're going to prison. Understand?"

She told herself to wipe off the blood he'd gotten on his forehead, but she couldn't make herself touch it. "I just…I don't know what to do," she said. "Nothing will bring him back."

He released her and began dragging his lifeless father away from the door. "We're not trying to bring him back. I'm going to bury him where he'll never be found. But right now I need you to help me carry Zoe down here and get her in the trunk."

Zoe's name cut through Tiffany's shock and panic. "So you can bury them together?"

"No, so I can drive her to the motel room you rented and leave her there."

"Alive?"

With a final grunt, he shoved Paddy against the wall. "Yes."

"But then she'll wake up in the morning."

"That's what we need her to do."

"You said you'd kill her, but you killed Paddy instead!"

"What do you want from me?" he said as he came back toward her. "You're the one who let Rover get away! I'm doing the best I can here, trying to save both our asses."

"But you said you were going to kill her." Tiffany couldn't get beyond that because she didn't want Paddy dead; she wanted Zoe dead. Then Colin would be as attentive to her as he'd ever been. She had to get their lives back on track, back to normal. She could do that with a pet. Colin had had pets before. It was Zoe who'd made this situation different, more difficult—frightening.

Once again, he wiped the sweat rolling down from his hair, smearing Paddy's blood even farther. "I can't! Don't you get it? That private investigator of hers came by only thirty minutes ago. He's already looking for her."

"So? He won't think *we* have her."

"He will when he finds out she's not in her motel room." He grabbed one of the towels he used to wash the cars and mopped up the blood. "This is exactly where he'll come because it was the last place he knew her to be."

Tiffany watched him work, watched as each swipe seemed to make a bigger mess. "But how will he find out she's not in her motel room? He doesn't know which motel I chose."

"He can figure it out easily enough."

"How?"

He squirted some cleaner on what remained of the blood. "By calling every motel in Sacramento. He can do that in maybe an hour. And then, when he reaches the one where you registered her, they'll ring her room."

"And she won't pick up."

He got out a garbage bag and put the bloody towel inside it. "So then he'll drive over and go door to door until he finds her. Or he'll use his ID or some cop contact to make the clerk give him her room number. We have to get her where she's supposed to be before that happens."

"But if we let her live, she could tell him you forced her to have sex with you."

He put the cleaner away. "I didn't have sex with her. I didn't get the chance to touch her before my dad arrived."

Despite everything, Tiffany felt a measure of relief at this news. She hated the thought of Colin with Zoe. She didn't care when he made his pets do him sexual favors because he usually made them serve her, too. It was a game. But Zoe was different. "She could remember us taking off her clothes."

"There's no chance of that. She's completely out of it and has been ever since you left."

"But it takes eight hours for a roofie to wear off. At least, it did with me. What if Jonathan Stivers finds her before that and can tell she's been doped up?"

"We'll buy a small bottle of sleeping pills and leave it on the nightstand, so it looks new, as if she bought it herself. He'll assume she took one, and she won't remember what the hell happened, so hopefully she'll go along with it. It's our best shot. If she disappears right now, the whole thing will come crashing down on us."

Tiffany gazed at the inert figure hidden in that blanket. The blood was gone, the rags were gone, the body was neatly put aside so they could carry Zoe through the door and dump her in the car. Maybe there was still hope. "Okay, so we leave her in the motel room and then we bury…him." She couldn't force herself to say 'Paddy.'"

He tossed the garbage bag with the towel on top of his dead father. "That's right."

"Where?" she asked.

"You let me worry about that."

"Okay." Thank God she wouldn't have to deal with the digging.

She took two deeps breaths, then remembered what Colin had said about Sam. "Is it time to kill Sam, too? To get out of it all?"

"No, I'm not done with her yet. But you're going to have to take her to Paddy's cabin. We need her out of the house as soon as possible. I'll stay here and lead the search in the morning like I'm supposed to, then join you tomorrow night."

Tiffany recalled what they'd done to Colin's other pets at that same cabin. Was there such a thing as ghosts? She'd wondered about the possibility before, asked herself if the spirit of the girl Colin had killed there could still be hovering around the place. But the idea had never frightened her as much as it did at this moment. "I don't want to go there by myself, Colin," she said. "Unless you're with me, that place gives me the creeps."

He held the door to the house for her to pass through. "Why? It's just a remote cabin. There isn't a neighbor for miles."

"That's the problem. It's so…isolated. And…what if I get lost? It's tricky driving through those back roads. There aren't many signs."

"Doesn't matter. You've been there often enough to find it."

"I'd rather wait for you."

His fingers bit into the flesh of her arm. "You can't wait for me, damn it! That P.I. is hanging around, looking for Zoe. And when Paddy doesn't show up at home, Sheryl could come over here, too. We can't have Samantha upstairs with all this going on. It's just…too much attention. She might start screaming again. Besides, we need to let people wander through the house at will. How we handle the next twenty-four hours will be very important."

At least this incident had spooked him. At least he wasn't telling her she was worried for nothing. He was worried, too—and finally being cautious. "But what about the boards covering the windows in the bonus room?" she asked. "And the heavy-duty lock on the door?"

"What about them?"

"They could raise questions."

"I'll remove the lock and stick my drums in there to explain the soundproofing." He urged her through the door. "Just help me get Zoe dressed."

Her step faltered. "Oh, no!"

"What?"

"Her clothes are in the trash in the bathroom of a Wendy's!"

With a curse, he shoved her into the house and toward the front door. "Go get them while I put her in the trunk. We can dress her at the motel."

With a nod, she hurried to reclaim her shoes—and stepped in a large wet spot that nearly made her retch. It was *Paddy's* blood…or what was left of it after Colin's attempt to clean up.

"Hurry," he admonished when she froze.

Choking back the bile that rose to her throat, she slipped on her shoes. She didn't want to think, didn't want to acknowledge that Paddy was gone for good. Because if Colin could kill Paddy, he could kill anyone.

She remembered her husband's hands around her throat the night she'd accidentally let Rover escape. Was it possible that he'd someday kill *her?*

No. Never. She was special to him. Wasn't she?

"Colin?" she said, hesitating at the door.

The uncertainty in her voice brought him back to the foot of the stairs. "What?"

"You love me, right?"

"You mean *everything* to me, Tiff. I'm never going to forget this, I swear."

They'd put it behind them. Somehow. Someway. And then they'd be happy like they were before.

Even without Paddy.

She gave him a smile that trembled on her face. "You'd better wipe that blood off your forehead."

Although her vision was blurry, Zoe could tell she wasn't alone. Scooting up in the bed, she squinted to see the man sitting across the room from her. But her head throbbed so badly she could scarcely lift it off the pillow, and she couldn't make out his features. The shadows were too deep in that corner; the only light came from the bathroom.

Who was it? Jonathan? It had to be him, didn't it? Anton wasn't part of her life anymore, and her former fiancé certainly didn't look that lean or muscular, even in shadow.

Where were they?

In a motel room, obviously. But she couldn't remember which motel, which part of town, how she came to be here or why. Last she could recall, she'd changed her mind about getting a motel room and had decided to let Jonathan put her up. Staying at his house was free, it was safe and she needed his friendship. If allowing herself to lean on him was a mistake, she'd have to deal with the consequences. But she'd do it later, when this catastrophe was over. Breakups weren't that painful, not if she was careful from the start. She'd just be sure to handle Jonathan the same way she handled all men these days—she'd enjoy his company as long as it was better than being alone. But she wouldn't allow herself to become too emotionally attached. Maybe withholding the most intimate, sensitive part of herself wasn't playing fair, but it was the only way to survive.

So, if she wasn't worried about getting hurt, why had she rented a motel room? Or was it Jonathan who'd brought her here?

"Jon?" His name came out as more of a scratchy croak, but the sound was enough to rouse him. His head snapped up as if he'd barely drifted off.

"Zoe?" He stood and walked over to sit on the bed. "You okay?"

She wasn't sure. She felt as if she had the world's biggest hangover. But she hadn't drunk more than a couple of glasses of wine last night, had she?

She couldn't say for sure. She could remember sitting at the table with Colin and Tiffany, and planning the search for Sam, but nothing that came afterward. "I don't feel so good," she admitted. "What—what happened? How'd I get here?"

Jonathan smoothed the hair off her forehead. It was a tender touch, the touch one might receive from a lover, and it made her crave more contact with him—the escape he promised just by looking at her, just by being here and being concerned. "Your car's out front. Didn't you drive?" he asked.

"If you didn't bring me, I guess I must have, but…if you weren't with me when I got here, how'd you get in?"

"David."

"Skye's husband?"

"After I tracked you down, you wouldn't answer the door, so I called him and he came over and had the manager open it. We were worried, needed to be sure you were safe."

"So…how *did* I get here?"

"You can't remember?" he prompted.

There seemed to be a big gap that stretched from dinner until now. "Maybe it's this headache." Obviously, the constant turmoil and stress were getting to her, playing tricks on her mind. She'd eaten and slept so little over the past week, and she'd mostly picked at the tri tip, mashed potatoes and green beans Colin and Tiffany had served. The alcohol must've hit her harder than she'd realized. "What time is it?"

The digital alarm clock on the nightstand was turned away. He leaned over to check it. "Nearly 4:00 a.m."

"If you didn't bring me here, how'd you know where to find me?" she asked. "Did I call you?"

"No. That's what had me worried. After your text, I couldn't get hold of you—"

"My text?"

He gave her a strange look. "Don't tell me you don't remember that, either."

She must've had some sort of nervous breakdown. She couldn't remember *any* of it, and that terrified her. Was she losing her mind? Was Samantha's disappearance sending her over the edge?

Frantically searching for some hint of familiarity, she glanced around the room but drew an absolute blank. She was certain she'd never seen this place before. Then she spotted the sleeping pills on the nightstand. She couldn't say where they'd come from, but they had to be the reason she felt so groggy.

Why had she taken a sleeping aid? What if they'd heard some word on Sam? What if Sam had needed her?

Jonathan still sat next to her, but he was preoccupied with his phone. A moment later, he held it up so she could see the screen.

Not feeling well. Getting a motel. Call u tomorrow.

"That came from me?" she asked.

"At 8:06."

Her heart pounded as she read it again. She could no sooner remember sending that text than driving to this unfamiliar motel. But she didn't want to acknowledge it. Jonathan would think she was going crazy. She was wondering herself. "Oh…yeah. I guess…I guess the sleeping pills made me a little loopy."

"How many did you take?" he asked.

She told him she'd taken two, but she really had no idea.

He shifted on the bed. "Why'd you drive so far from Rocklin, Zoe? Especially with the search scheduled for early this morning?"

That was a good question. She wished she knew the answer. "I hate to admit it, but…I'm afraid I might've been tipsy when I left Colin and Tiffany's house. I only drank a couple glasses of wine, but…" She rubbed her face. "I can't believe I drove. That was so irresponsible and dangerous."

"The motel clerk said you were sober when you arrived."

"Maybe it hit me afterward." But then, why couldn't she remember coming here? None of it made sense.

"Maybe," he agreed, but he was watching her closely.

"Is everything okay?" she asked.

"It's fine. Go ahead and get some sleep. Hopefully, you'll feel better in the morning."

He started to stand up, but she caught his hand. "Will you stay?"

He didn't question her. He just lay down beside her, and the next thing she knew, her head was on his shoulder, and her hand was on his chest where she could feel the steady rhythm of his heart.

The warmth of his body, even the smell of his clothes and skin, brought her a measure of comfort. Soon the pain and confusion disappeared as she dropped into a dreamless sleep….

25

Something didn't add up. Jonathan couldn't tell what it was, but Zoe had seemed so disoriented, more disoriented than a couple glasses of wine at dinner would warrant. Maybe she'd had a drink or two besides what she'd counted—or was willing to admit to. Or her behavior was due to the combined effects of the alcohol and the sleeping pills. That was plausible, he supposed. But if she'd had too much to drink, why did Colin and Tiffany allow her to drive? According to Colin, she'd been fine when she left his house, and the desk clerk had confirmed it.

As soon as Zoe seemed to be sleeping deeply enough that his movements wouldn't disturb her, Jonathan carefully extricated himself and got up. She'd looked at the text as if she'd never sent it, at the sleeping pills as if she'd never bought them. And even she didn't seem to know why she'd driven thirty minutes to rent a room downtown. There were half a dozen motels in Rocklin, which was where she had to be early in the morning, and rates weren't any cheaper down here….

But it was the state of her clothes that raised the biggest question. Until he'd talked to her, he'd ignored it as one of those things she'd explain when she woke up. Now that she *couldn't* seem to explain anything, he couldn't stop thinking about how curious it was. He and David had found her with half the buttons on her blouse undone and her jeans unfastened. As far as he could tell, she hadn't even brought in her makeup bag.

Moving as quietly as possible, he took the sleeping pills into the bathroom, where there was more light. They looked brand new, just as she'd said. Which meant he should be able to tell how many she took.

He removed the lid and dumped them into his palm. The label said the bottle contained forty-eight tablets. If she'd taken two, there should be forty-six. But a quick count turned up only forty.

"Did she take eight?" he muttered and counted them again.

There were forty, all right. That could explain why she was so disoriented, but he had a hard time believing she'd overdo it with Samantha still out there somewhere.

He got the garbage can and pulled it into the bathroom, too. Since she'd just bought the pills, there should be a pharmacy sack somewhere. He was hoping to find a receipt, to be able to tell where she'd stopped and at what time. Maybe the person who rang up her purchase would remember more about her condition and behavior.

But there was no trash, no sack, no receipt.

He thought of her phone. Maybe she'd spoken to someone who'd be able to tell him about her frame of mind, someone he could reach. But without her permission, it was too much of an invasion of privacy.

He sat in the chair where he'd fallen asleep earlier, thinking about the way he'd found her and how confused she'd been—and decided he didn't care about invading her privacy if it was for her own good. A lot of women who'd been drugged blamed it on the alcohol they'd drunk. And those same victims typically reported extreme hangover-like symptoms afterward. If something had happened tonight that shouldn't have, he needed to know about it.

Carrying her purse into the bathroom, he pulled out her phone and checked her Sent folder. Besides the one to him, she hadn't sent any text messages. And her recent call history showed no calls originating from that number after 5:33 p.m. As far as incoming calls went—he scrolled through a few more screens—she'd received four from him, one from Detective Thomas and one with a southern California area code. He guessed it was from her father's lady friend, the woman they'd met at his trailer.

Last, he opened her in-box. There he saw the message he'd sent telling her to contact him, and another one from Anton. Her ex-fiancé's had come in after his. But the odd thing was—they both registered as having been read.

If Zoe had received his urgent message, why hadn't she responded? For all she knew, he was trying to tell her that Toby had come out of his coma, or that he'd managed to obtain some information on Sam.

She loved Sam so much and yet tonight it seemed as if she didn't care at all. As if she'd just decided to throw it all to the winds. That wasn't like her, which was why it bothered him.

His finger hovered over the Select button that would show him Anton's text. He told himself he shouldn't read it, but he was confused enough about what had gone on this evening to give himself permission.

You're not easy to get over, Zoe, it said. Seeing you tonight, knowing you no longer welcome my touch, broke my heart.

When Jonathan had talked to him, Anton had said he hadn't seen Zoe. Had he meant that he hadn't spoken to her? Or had he been lying? Had he drugged her and—

Picturing Zoe as he'd found her—lying across the

spread as if she'd been hastily dumped there—Jonathan stepped out of the bathroom and gazed at the bed. When they were in San Diego, Zoe had said she wouldn't take a sleeping pill. Even if she'd changed her mind, he was pretty sure she would've returned the text she'd read from him first, and probably gotten ready for bed, as well.

What the hell had gone on tonight? If she'd been fine when she arrived here, as the desk clerk said, what had happened afterward? Had Anton met her here—or followed her? Had someone else?

Jonathan didn't know, but he thought he should try to ascertain that she hadn't been raped.

She stirred and rolled onto her back when he flipped on the light. "Jonathan?"

"It's me." Leaning over her, he grasped her chin and tilted her face from side to side as he examined her eyes, cheeks, nose, throat.

Frowning, she shaded her eyes. "What're you doing?"

"Checking for injuries."

"Why would I be injured?"

"I'm hoping you're not."

She pulled a pillow over her face to block out the light. "I just need more sleep."

"Can I take off your shirt, Zoe? Can I see if you have any scratches or bruises on your chest?" He'd dealt with enough rape cases to know that if there were marks, he'd probably find them there. He'd worked one case, in which teeth impressions left by a rapist on a woman's breast had actually led to his conviction.

She didn't respond.

He set the pillow aside and gave her shoulder a gentle shake. "Zoe?"

She mumbled something, but it was incoherent; he wasn't going to get a clear answer right now. So he quickly undid the few buttons that were still fastened and took off her blouse.

He found the strap of her bra all twisted in the back and hanging together by a single hook, which added to his suspicion. No woman would put on her bra that way, would she? Not unless she was extremely drunk. But the desk clerk claimed Zoe's clothes had been perfectly straight, and she'd been perfectly sober, when she came in. So why had she subsequently removed her clothes, taken enough sleeping pills to risk a potential overdose, then dressed again, but in a haphazard manner?

Someone else had dressed her. That was what it looked like. And if that was the case, whoever it was had probably *un*dressed her, too—or why bother?

Convinced that *something* had happened, he slid off her jeans and examined the rest of her—what he could see without removing her panties. But besides a red line on one ankle, which *could've* come from a ligature but certainly wasn't conclusive, he saw no evidence of abuse or injury.

While he was studying that mark, she roused again and gazed up at him from beneath heavy eyelids.

"I want to take you to the hospital, have you checked out," he told her as he lowered her leg.

"What for?" she mumbled sleepily.

She'd been through so much. Did he really want to tell her? "It's just…a precaution."

She didn't say anything, but when he started to put on her blouse, she stopped him—and guided his hand to her breast. "I have a better idea."

Every muscle in his body tensed as he allowed himself to cup her. He wanted her. He'd wanted her from the first moment he'd met her. Despite Sheridan. Despite the fact that she was a client.

But now wasn't the time.

Gently freeing her grip on his wrist, he ran a finger over her cheek instead. "You deserve more than you've ever gotten, Zoe."

Her breathing had gone as shallow as his. "Does that mean you're going to give it to me?" Her husky voice and sexy smile indicated she'd interpreted his words in a sexual way. It wasn't what he'd meant, but he didn't correct her. He knew she didn't want a relationship that went any deeper than the physical; she was no longer willing to take the risks associated with it.

"Jon?" she prompted when he hesitated.

His pulse was racing. It wasn't easy to keep his mind where it needed to be. But he didn't have a choice. "No."

Zoe hadn't been raped. As he leaned against his car in the parking lot of Sierra College, listening to Colin organize the searchers, Jonathan wasn't even sure she'd been drugged. With no physical injuries to prove foul play, the emergency-room doctor attributed her behavior and memory lapse to too much stress and too much alcohol. He'd ultimately agreed to run some toxicology tests, but only because Jonathan insisted on it. The results wouldn't come back for a few days.

Jonathan was infinitely relieved by the doctor's findings. But he still didn't have answers to the questions that nagged at him. And after another night with so little sleep, he felt like roadkill as he watched Colin pass out maps to his lawyer friends and several volunteer neighbors. The press and the police were there, too. Detective Thomas had already spoken and was now circulating flyers provided by the police department.

Jonathan hated the fact that Zoe couldn't join them. He knew how much she wanted to, but the doctor had insisted on keeping her in the hospital until she'd fully recovered.

Something last night had made her ill. She'd tried to argue with the doctor's decision, of course, but she'd been too weak to be effective. When Jonathan left, she'd told him she'd never speak to him again because he wasn't taking her with him.

He sort of hoped that was true. Then maybe he could stop replaying those few moments when she'd guided his hand to her breast....

As the searchers got into their cars and started off for their designated areas, Colin approached. "Morning."

"Morning." Jonathan smiled, but he was surprised by Colin's appearance. Although he was as meticulously groomed as always, his eyes were bloodshot enough to suggest that he, too, had passed a hard night. "You okay?"

"Me?" He raised a hand to his chest. "Of course. Why do you ask?"

"You look like I feel."

"I was up late," he said with a sheepish grin. "What's your excuse?"

"Same thing."

He bent to peer inside Jonathan's car. "Where's Zoe? I thought she'd be here."

"She's not feeling well."

He frowned. "That's too bad. What's wrong?"

"I don't know yet. Maybe you can help me figure it out."

"How can *I* help you?"

"How many glasses of wine did she have last night?"

Colin rubbed his clean-shaven chin. "Three, maybe four. I wasn't really counting. Why?"

"Did she seem tipsy when she left?"

"Hell, no. Or I wouldn't have let her drive."

"Did she eat much?"

"Not as much as we would've liked."

Four glasses of wine could do it, especially on an empty stomach.

"We're worried about how she's holding up through all this," Colin went on. "Sounds as if it's beginning to wear her down."

"Maybe. Where's Tiffany?" Jonathan had been hoping to speak with her. She might have a different perspective on Zoe's behavior than Colin did.

"She left for my father's cabin. Until Sam went missing, we were planning to spend the whole weekend there."

"She went without you?"

"I'll join her when this is over. She wanted to lug the groceries up there and do a little cleaning while she had the chance."

It made sense. Everything made sense except Sam's disappearance and Zoe's condition last night.

"Too bad we can't offer the reward Zoe mentioned at dinner," Colin said. "These flyers would be a lot more appealing if they looked like this." He scrawled $10,000 Reward across the top. "That'd motivate the casual observer, eh?"

On their way back from L.A., Zoe had told Jonathan about the reward. She hadn't said plans had changed, but he could understand why they might have. "Anton reneged?"

"He dropped by this morning to tell me I could go ahead and advertise it—he'd come through. But now that they've broken up, I don't know whether to trust that. Could be a ploy to get Zoe back. Once he realizes it won't work, then what? And I couldn't reach her, so…"

Jonathan wondered what Zoe would've said about it. He knew she'd do anything to find Sam. He also knew she probably wouldn't want to feel beholden to Lucassi. "Let's keep Anton out of it."

"Right. Maybe I'll post the reward myself," Colin said.

Jonathan couldn't tell if Colin was just bragging, but he suspected that was the case. "Tiffany wouldn't mind?"

"Are you kidding? She cares as much about Zoe and Sam as I do."

"You two have been good to her."

"We *should* be good to her. We're her neighbors. Well, we *were* her neighbors."

Jonathan's BlackBerry rang before he could respond. Caller ID revealed a southern California area code, but it was a different number than the one he'd seen on Zoe's cell phone.

"Thanks for all your help," he said, and answered, but before he could determine who it was, Colin interrupted.

"You gonna stick around today?"

"I've got an appointment. I just came over to make sure everyone got off okay. I'll stay in touch with Detective Thomas to see how it goes."

"Okay." He handed Jonathan the flyer he'd written on. "Tell Zoe I hope she feels better."

"Will do." Staring down at Sam's picture, Jonathan turned his attention back to the phone. "Hello?" he said again.

"Is this Jonathan Stivers?" It was a male voice. "Yes, it is."

"This is Franky Bates."

The man who'd raped Zoe at fifteen. Jonathan had given him a card but hadn't really expected to hear from him. "What can I do for you, Mr. Bates?"

"Um, I know you probably…well, *Zoe* probably doesn't want to hear from me. But…I've been doing a lot of thinkin' and…I'd like to help. If I can. I mean, if she'll let me."

Jonathan sank into the driver's seat but didn't start his

car. "I appreciate the sentiment behind your offer, but there's nothing you can do, Franky."

"I figured you'd tell me no. But I'm here in Sacramento. I'm willing to do whatever you ask."

Jonathan sat straighter. Did Franky's presence have any connection to last night? "When did you get into town?"

"Couple hours ago. I just grabbed some breakfast. I didn't want to call too early."

"*What* are you doing here? Maybe that's a more relevant question."

"I was hoping you'd believe I'm for real if I came all this way."

"Did you fly or—"

"I drove. I figured, hey, why keep stressing over the situation. I'm gonna go up there and see what I can do."

"Have you had any contact with Zoe?"

"No, no, of course not. But my grandma sent her a few things. I mean, it's just baked goods and a crocheted afghan, and a little gift for her daughter if…if we can find her. Nothing to get excited about. But Gran really wants her to have it."

If Franky had been driving all night, there'd be ways to prove it. "You got gas receipts to show where you were last night, Franky?"

He hesitated for a second, but his voice was strident when he answered. "Yes, sir. Would you like to see them?"

"It's likely. Hang on to them for me."

"Okay."

Jonathan rubbed his eyes. Franky wasn't their problem. Not this time. "I don't think you should bother Zoe," he said. "I think you should go home and stay out of this."

"I'm not plannin' to cause trouble. That's why I called you. I just…I need you both to know that I'm here and

I'm willing to do whatever it takes. If you want me to spend the next two weeks digging through paperwork or tramping through the woods, that's fine. Or I could pass out flyers or knock on doors. Shit, I don't know. *Something.* I mean, I'd even be willing to pay your bill if Zoe needs me to."

Jonathan wasn't under the impression that Franky had much money. "I'm afraid Zoe's financial obligations would be more than you could afford, but…I'll tell her." What else could he say? Franky sounded so damn sincere….

"How much does she need?" he asked.

Jonathan held up the flyer. It certainly couldn't hurt to offer some added incentive. "Ideally?"

"I guess we could start there."

"Ten thousand dollars."

Franky whistled. "That's a lot."

"Yes, it is."

"That's the amount of your bill?"

"No, I'm not charging. We want to put up a reward for information leading to Sam's whereabouts."

"A reward would be a great idea. I shoulda thought of that."

"It's worked in the past."

There was a moment of silence. "Okay."

"Okay what?" Jonathan said in surprise.

"If…if I can come up with the money, how will I get it to you?"

After a glance at his watch, Jonathan started his car. He had an appointment with a woman who worked at the property-management company that rented out quite a few of the cabins near Placerville. Because she'd agreed to come in on a Saturday just to help him, he couldn't be late. "I don't want you out robbing a bank because I said we need ten thousand dollars, Franky."

"I won't break the law. No way. I've changed."

"You have other means of getting the money?"

"Just one. But it should work."

Jonathan was tempted to doubt him, but the conviction in his voice suggested he had every intention of following through. "Fine, if you're that determined, give me a call when you have it and we'll meet up."

26

The cabin was so remote it didn't have running water or electricity. Tiffany had already made one trip to the outhouse and needed to go again, but she kept putting it off. The smell was almost overwhelming, and so were the flies. But that wasn't the main problem. The cramped, dark space, and the eerie creak of the door when she opened it, made her feel as if she was stepping inside an upright coffin. And, in a way, she was. This was where Colin had dumped the pet he'd had before Rover, the one they'd taken from Nevada when they'd gone to Vegas to celebrate Colin's graduation from law school. Colin said the lime and the septic tablets his father used to improve the smell would speed decomposition. Whenever she went in there, she couldn't help wondering what was left of the girl—and if her ghost was wandering around the forest, waiting for them to return. She would've gone in the woods, but she had to go to the outhouse to get the toilet paper anyway.

With a shiver, she tossed her magazine aside. No matter how many times she read that article on star hookups she was too nervous to comprehend it. She kept thinking of Sam out in the shed.

Forget it. She deserves it.

Getting to her feet, she meandered around the cabin,

eventually winding up in the kitchen. She liked this room best, but she didn't stay there because everything reminded her of Paddy, from his favorite seat at the table to the beef jerky in the glass jar on the counter. He'd been with his second wife longer than Tiffany and Colin had been married, but Sheryl refused to rough it. She said she saw no purpose in giving up the comforts of home and never came up here, probably didn't even know exactly where it was.

This was every bit Paddy's domain. But he hadn't visited in over a year. As he got older, he seemed more and more content to simply hang out with Sheryl and let Colin use the cabin.

Maybe Paddy hadn't been here in months, but Tiffany could still smell him. The damp wool of his hunting shirt, combined with cigar smoke, made for a unique scent that lingered forever.

"I hate losing you," she muttered, wringing her hands.

Where was Colin? She needed him to reassure her that all was well. They'd been out of touch ever since very early this morning, when he'd forced some sleeping pills down Samantha and shoved the girl into his huge suitcase. He'd been about to load her into Tiffany's trunk, but after what'd happened with Rover, Tiffany had insisted he put her in the backseat. At least if Sam woke up and started calling for help, she'd be where Tiffany could reach her.

But Sam never woke up. She didn't make a peep the entire trip. Even after they'd arrived at the cabin and Tiffany jerked the heavy suitcase out of the car and rolled it over the bumpy ground to the shed, she didn't come to.

With a sigh, Tiffany went out to check on her again. The hunting shed that had become her temporary home stank almost as badly as the outhouse. But Tiffany wasn't about to allow Samantha inside the cabin, not after what she'd done last night. It was her fault Paddy was dead. If she hadn't started screaming, Colin might've been able to convince Paddy that his concerns were unfounded. Colin had said so himself.

"Sam?" Tiffany pulled open the door and poked her head inside. She'd unzipped the suitcase so she could hammer the end of Sam's collar into the ground with a stake as Colin had told her to, but Sam remained curled up inside the bag. She didn't answer; she didn't even open her eyes. Colin had doped her up good this time.

"You think you're pretty smart barfing up that shake, don't you?" she said to the girl's inert form. "Well, I hope you like sleeping outside. It gets pretty darn cold up here. You were too out of it to notice anything last night, but you'll get a taste of it tonight." The mosquitoes wouldn't be fun, either.

With a taunting smile, she let the door slam shut and finally forced herself to use the outhouse. That was when she heard the approach of Colin's vehicle. Finishing quickly, she ran to greet him.

"There you are!" She threw herself into his arms as soon as he climbed out of the car. "I've been *so* worried about you."

"I'm fine." He kissed her temple as he released her and that small gesture made her inordinately happy—despite everything.

"What happened?" she asked. "Have you heard from Sheryl?"

"She called me while we were searching for Samantha."

Tiffany could feel that moment of acute pleasure slipping away from her. "What'd she say?"

"She said my father never came home last night and asked if I'd seen him."

"So she didn't know he was coming over?"

"No."

"That's a relief." Trying to judge his expression, she shaded her eyes from the dappled sunlight that filtered through the pine trees.

"It sure makes things easier."

"What about the search for Sam? How'd that go?"

"Like clockwork." He grinned. "No one found anything. I even ordered pizza and invited everyone back to the house for lunch. I thought that was a nice touch."

She gasped. "What about the blood? Are you sure we got it all?"

"We got it all. I was very careful about that. And the more people who stomped through the house, the better. If the police ever do search our place for evidence, it'll be that much harder to find."

"Oh. Good."

"I told you I've got it all under control."

Tiffany kicked a pinecone to one side. "Is Sheryl very worried?"

The white lines around his mouth and eyes told her how exhausted he was. "She's getting that way."

This news made Tiffany's spirits plummet. She liked Sheryl almost as much as she'd liked Paddy and didn't want her to suffer. "How'd you leave it with her?"

"I told her I'd go out and look for him." He pulled his cell phone from his pocket, even though they both knew there wasn't any service up here.

"So you can't be out of contact for too long."

"No. It'll seem strange if I am."

Tiffany didn't want to spend another night here alone. "What about Mother's Day?"

"What about it?"

"We had plans."

"Yeah, well, our plans have changed. I'd better go. I just came to make sure you were okay."

Tiffany wanted to take that as further proof of his love, but then he added, "I couldn't risk you letting Sam get away like Rover."

He started to get back into his car, but she hurried over to catch him before he could close the door.

"Wait! I should go back with you. I can't be gone if Paddy's missing. That's a family crisis. It'll seem weird if we're not together, and doing whatever we can."

His sudden scowl told her he was about to refuse her, but then he seemed to reconsider. "You've got a point." He glanced toward the shed. "I guess there's no reason you *have* to stay up here."

"No. Sam's got her collar on. She's not going anywhere." Tiffany preferred to be able to mourn Paddy with Sheryl, to offer as much comfort as possible. It was the least she could do.

"Then we'll leave her some food and a blanket in case it gets really cold and come back when we can."

"Okay." She no longer cared about punishing Sam; she just wanted to go home with Colin. "I'll get her ready," she said and started back, but Colin caught her elbow.

"Wait. Are you sure you got that stake in the ground nice and tight?"

"Positive."

"I'd better check myself. Get in the car." He got a big quilt, some granola bars and a jug of water from the cabin, then stalked off to the shed.

When he came back, he gave her an affirmative nod. "A man twice my size couldn't pull that stake out of the ground, but I drove another one in, just to be sure. Get in."

Tiffany silently wondered if they'd find Sam dead

when they returned, but she refused to let that stop her from leaving. Sam had to die sometime. She'd known that from the beginning.

The way Kino, who'd been sleeping at Jonathan's feet, came to attention alerted Jonathan when Zoe entered the kitchen.

"Do you really think your psychic friend will be able to help us?" she asked.

Wondering if he'd made a mistake by telling her, he glanced up from his computer, where he'd been cross-referencing the electronic files a second property manager had sent him that morning against the list he'd compiled of anyone who'd ever had contact with Sam.

"We'll see. I sent her Sam's sweater, along with the teddy bear she won at Disneyland a few years ago. I hate to give you false hope, especially when today's search proved such a disappointment, but Jasmine's done some amazing things in the past."

"She's that good?"

Realizing he had the opportunity to make a new friend, Kino lumbered over to her. Obliging him with a thorough scratch behind the ears and a warm smile, Zoe perched on the arm of a nearby kitchen chair. She was wearing his sweatpants, her own T-shirt and no shoes. He'd brought her home from the hospital only an hour ago and had carried in her luggage, but most of her stuff was still in her car, in those black bags. Understandably, when she'd left Lucassi's she hadn't taken time to pack with any kind of organization, which was why she'd needed to borrow his sweats. She'd gotten out of the shower to discover she had a shirt in her suitcase but no casual bottoms.

"She's that good," he said. "But her particular gifts don't solve every case. That's the problem."

She pulled her hair into a ponytail and secured it with a rubber band. She wasn't wearing any makeup, but she didn't need it. She had beautiful skin, eyes he could drown in.

Having her so close, smelling like heaven, reminded him of last night and the sight of her without most of her clothes. The resulting charge of testosterone shot his concentration all to hell. "How're you feeling?" he asked.

"Better." She met his gaze with a directness that surprised him, that let him know she wouldn't refuse a sexual advance. Since he'd already revealed his interest, she was probably expecting one. But he also knew he'd be foolish to get involved with her in that way. Zoe was a survivor for a reason. She'd barely blinked at her breakup with Lucassi. She wouldn't invest in a relationship emotionally, and he wasn't sure he wanted to be on the losing end of another affair.

"I'm glad."

She angled her head toward the computer. "Any luck with the rental records?"

"Not yet. But I still have a lot of names to go through, and this is just one of two companies. I've been in touch with others who manage properties in the area."

"But these two are the ones that manage the cabins closest to where Toby was found. Didn't you say that earlier?"

"That's right. He was so badly injured he couldn't have traveled very far, so these are the best places to start."

She moved behind him, put her hands on his shoulders and began to knead away the tension. "I think it's time you got some rest," she said.

He closed his eyes as her fingers worked to soothe his sore muscles. "Do I look that beat?"

"Like the walking dead."

"That's not too flattering," he said with a laugh.

"You look sexy. But then, you always look sexy."

Unless he'd misinterpreted the hunger behind that statement, it was an invitation, not just a compliment. He twisted around to see her expression. "You don't have to offer me an incentive to stay focused on the case, Zoe. I'm going to stick it out."

Her hands stilled. "I'm not trying to manipulate you. This isn't about trading favors."

He guided her around in front of him. "Then what *is* it about?"

She blushed and glanced away, and he got the impression that she wasn't often so direct. "An escape, I guess. A few moments of forgetfulness."

With him. He could easily give her that. She was worried about Sam, in need of a reprieve, if only a short one. But where would it lead? Despite what he'd told Sheridan, he was ready to settle down, get married. Sex simply for the sake of getting off wasn't enough for him anymore. He wanted a family, with the right woman. And he was beginning to realize that finding the right woman was going to take some restraint.

"You remind me of a girlfriend I once had," he said.

"Oh really?" She hesitated as if she could tell that wasn't a good thing, but asked anyway. "What was she like?"

He pictured Maria. "Beautiful. Great to be with." He lowered his voice. "And in love with someone else."

Bending close, she brushed her lips across his. "I'm not in love with anyone else."

He caught her face in his hands and let his gaze fall to her mouth. He wanted much more than the quick taste she'd just given him.

For the briefest of moments, he allowed himself to imagine her on the mattress beneath him. But he knew, no matter how tenderly he made love to her, that he had very little chance of ever *reaching* her or that added dimension of meaning he craved. "No, you're not in love," he said. "Not with Anton. Not with anyone. And my guess is you never will be."

She jerked away. "What's that supposed to mean?"

"It means I've had enough casual encounters, Zoe. I'm nearly thirty, ready to grow up. I'm looking for more."

She bit her lip as she stared at him. "You don't think I'd be willing to give you more?"

"I don't think you *can,*" he said, and then he went to bed.

Alone.

It didn't take long to regret his decision. But Jonathan was stubborn enough to toss and turn for three hours before he was willing to acknowledge that despite all his good intentions, it all came down to one thing: capitulation. He wanted Zoe too badly for it to end any other way. Which meant he hadn't grown up nearly as much as he'd thought.

You're making another mistake, he told himself, but that didn't change anything.

As exhausted by the battle inside him as he was by his hours the past week, he got up and crossed the hall. Kino, who was sleeping in his room, didn't bother to follow him.

Zoe hadn't shut her door all the way.

Jonathan pushed it open with one finger. The hinges whined as it moved, and she rose up on one elbow. Standing there in the doorway, he could see her hair falling over her shoulders, which were bare except for the straps of some nightgown. He hadn't put blinds on this window because it faced away from the neighbors, and the room was mostly for storage, anyway.

"Jon?"

Knowing she couldn't see him as well as he could see her, he spoke. "Yeah, it's just me."

Caution entered her voice. "Is something wrong?"

"No." But obviously there was.

"What do you want?"

He thought about repeating the line she'd used earlier. *An escape…a few moments of forgetfulness.* But for him it was much simpler than that. What he wanted could be summed up in one word. "You."

She pressed her fingers to her eyes, and he realized she'd been crying. He felt guilty about that, wished he could go back to their encounter in the living room—and say less. Do more.

"No," she murmured. "I was stupid to think it would make a difference. We're both better off keeping it impersonal."

Impersonal? There was nothing impersonal about what they'd been through the past week. But she pulled up the covers and turned toward the wall.

Jonathan waited, hoping she'd change her mind. Just the memory of her lips brushing his filled him with need. But when she didn't move or speak again, he went back to his own room.

Zoe listened to the creak of Jonathan's footsteps. *Thank God, he's leaving.* As desperate and alone as she felt, she'd just left one relationship; she shouldn't jump into another. Especially with a man who affected her as deeply as Jonathan. Maybe she'd decided Anton had the qualities she needed in a partner. But rational thought seemed to play a very small role in her attraction to Jonathan. It was all instinctive—a gut-level desire to make love with him despite the consequences.

Submitting to that kind of animal attraction had gotten her in trouble before and always made it more difficult to walk away afterward. She didn't know who she was anymore or where she was going. She only knew she had to find Sam, and that meant remaining strong and focused.

In other words, she had to use her head.

But she was losing hope, grasping at anything good that was left in the world. And the last good thing seemed to be Jonathan.

She stared into the darkness long after the house fell silent, thinking about Toby. Would he ever wake up? She'd been praying, day after day, that he'd regain consciousness. But his condition hadn't changed.

The line between life and death was so thin….

Maybe the biggest mistake she could make wasn't getting involved with the wrong man. Maybe it was not being with him while she could.

27

When Zoe entered his room, Jonathan didn't speak; he simply turned back the blankets.

He'd had a T-shirt on before but must've taken it off as he returned to bed, because it was lying on the floor. She could see the broad outline of his muscular shoulders, his bare chest—and felt her body yearn.

Thoughts of Sam entered her head, but she quickly blocked them out. *No more pain. Not right now.*

She'd pulled off the sweats he'd lent her before bed, they were too hot to sleep in. Now she was wearing a short spaghetti-strap nightie and a pair of panties. But the intensity with which he watched her move toward him made her feel completely naked.

Once she reached his bedside, she hesitated, suddenly a little shy, a little nervous. But he didn't give her time to reconsider. He came to his knees on the bed and slipped both hands under her nightgown to circle her waist, turning her so he could make the most of the moonlight filtering through the gaps in his window blinds.

Kino's tail thumped against the floor as if he approved, but Zoe didn't care about the dog's presence. She cared only about touching Jonathan, about being touched by him.

"Wait." She stopped him. "What about birth control?"

"I've got a condom," he said. "Don't worry about anything."

Slipping her arms around him, she let him kiss her and felt an involuntary shiver as his tongue slid against her own.

"It'll be okay," he said. "Everything will be okay."

She clenched her hand in his thick hair as he took the kiss deeper, and desire spread through her veins, heightening every sensation until the slightest touch made her tremble. "I like the way you kiss," she whispered.

His hands pushed up her nightie until he'd taken it off entirely. "What a sight," he said, his voice low and reverent. Then he leaned forward just enough to graze the tips of her breasts with his bare chest.

Light though the contact was, it felt like an electric jolt. Zoe heard his quick intake of breath before he drew her fully against him.

It wasn't long before they fell back on the bed. Zoe purposely forgot about everything as she lost herself in the sensations he evoked, purposely shoved it all away and felt carefree for the first time in days, weeks, years. When he rolled her beneath him, she was so eager and ready she almost groaned in frustration when he stopped.

"Look at you. I've never seen a more beautiful woman," he said, gently pinning her hands above her head.

"How many have you seen like this?" she asked with a teasing smile.

"Enough to know what I'm talking about." He gave her a sexy grin and lowered his mouth to her breast.

By the time he lifted his head, she could scarcely catch her breath. "This was inevitable," he told her.

As she took in his earnest expression, fear seeped through the pleasure. What if she *could* still fall in love? What if she *did*—and it didn't work out? *Again?* Where would that leave her?

She was tempted to flee to the safety of her own room. When their relationship ran its course, she wouldn't be able to walk away from him the way she had Anton. She knew that as surely as she knew making love with him wouldn't be the same, either. What would that do to her? Or Sam, if—*when*—she ever got her daughter back?

She needed to be more cautious. But she'd come too far to turn back….

Zoe woke naked in a tangle of sheets. Caught between Jonathan on one side and Kino on the other, she could hardly move. She didn't care; she was in no hurry to go anywhere. Warm and content, she closed her eyes and pretended she was someone else and this moment could last a lifetime.

But then her cell phone rang, reminding her that she wasn't someone else and her daughter was still missing.

Nudging Kino out of her way, she got up and hurried into the kitchen to grab the phone. She didn't take time to dress. After such a wonderful night, she couldn't help hoping that maybe this was the call she'd been waiting for.

Maybe the nightmare would end today….

But her phone identified the caller as Colin Bell.

Disappointment slammed into her. It wasn't the good news she so desperately craved. If her daughter had been found, Detective Thomas would be calling to tell her. But Colin had done a lot to help her look for Sam and she hadn't followed up with him after the search yesterday. Once Jonathan had notified her that they hadn't found any trace, she'd decided to give herself some time to deal with the letdown before making the obligatory thank-you call.

Swallowing a sigh, she figured there was no need to put it off any longer and answered as pleasantly as she could, considering he'd just pulled her out of a warm bed and away from the first real comfort she'd known since Sam went missing.

"Hey," he said. "Happy Mother's Day."

Was it Mother's Day? She'd forgotten. Considering the circumstances, she'd rather not have acknowledged it. And she thought most people would understand why, but she supposed he meant well. "Thanks."

"How are you doing?" he asked. "I've been worried about you."

She would've felt more comfortable if he'd said *we*. "I'm fine. Better." She left the kitchen to find a more comfortable spot on the couch.

"What happened to you yesterday? It had to be serious to keep you away from the search."

"I don't know exactly." She didn't want to mention the sleeping pills. "I must've had a touch of the flu."

"The flu's miserable."

She opened her mouth to respond when a strange scene—a flashback? a dream?—played in her mind. She was sitting at Colin's dining-room table, looking at…maps? Tiffany was in the kitchen doing dishes. Colin, who'd been sitting beside her, was getting up.

In her own voice, she heard a question. *Where're you going?*

It was Colin who'd answered. *Just helping Tiffany clean up.*

You have a really nice wife. Her voice again, said with a smile.

Except when she's helping me murder someone came Colin's response, and then he'd laughed.

The memory was out of focus and a bit surreal. Did that mean it was a dream? An hallucination brought on by the alcohol she'd had with dinner?

It must be. No one would make a comment like that to a guest.

"Zoe?" Colin said.

"I'm here."

A noise in the hall told her Jonathan was up. Folding his arms, he leaned against the doorway. He'd put on a pair of boxer briefs, which made her self-conscious about her own nudity. Even though they'd made love last night, it felt awkward facing him in broad daylight—especially naked in his living room. Somehow that was different than being with him in the bedroom. "Who is it?" he asked.

She pulled a throw from the back of the couch to cover herself. "Colin Bell."

"What does he want?"

She tried not to admire Jonathan as he stood there, barely dressed. While she was living with Anton, she'd made an effort to convince herself that physical attraction, or the lack of it, didn't matter. Kindness. Loyalty. Dependability. Those were the traits that mattered.

She still believed those traits mattered *more*, but it was astonishing how powerful physical attraction could be. Especially when Jonathan seemed to possess kindness, loyalty and dependability, as well. "He's just checking in."

"Who're you talking to?" Colin asked. "Is someone staying at the motel with you?"

The jealousy in his voice disturbed Zoe but it wasn't overt enough that she could call him on it. "No, I'm—" She caught herself. She didn't owe him an explanation. Her relationship with Jonathan was none of his business.

"Is it Anton?" he pressed.

"Colin, stop."

"I'm just wondering if you two are back together."

"We're not."

There was a pause. "You didn't pick someone up…."

Filled with fresh irritation, she tightened her grip on the phone. "I really don't feel like talking right now. Maybe I could call you back later."

"Are you mad at me?"

"No, of course not. I'm grateful to you. I've been meaning to thank you for yesterday. I really appreciate all you've done. It's just that…today's going to be hard for me, you know?"

"Right. Of course. I understand."

"Great. I'll talk to you later," she said, but he didn't respond with goodbye. He surprised her with another question.

"It's not Jonathan, is it?"

Zoe glanced up at the man in question, who was now scowling. "Excuse me?"

"The man you're with?"

"Colin, stop. I'm not with anyone."

"You might as well tell me. I'll find out eventually."

"Why are you so interested?"

"Because it's not fair."

"Fair?" she echoed.

"You haven't even given me a chance."

"You're married!"

He burst into laughter. "I'm *kidding.*"

She let go of her breath. "Oh. You had me going for a minute there."

"I know. You think every guy wants you."

She stiffened. "No, I don't."

"Then why couldn't you just answer the fucking question?" he said and hung up.

Too shocked to move, Zoe stared at her phone.

"What's wrong?" Jonathan crossed the room.

She looked up at him. "It's Colin Bell," she said. "He just…screamed at me. It was weird." But no weirder than that snatch of dream. Or was it a dream? With Colin's sense of humor, she wasn't sure what he might consider funny.

"What'd he say?" Jonathan asked.

Shaking her head, she put her phone aside. "Nothing." She couldn't explain her former neighbor's odd behavior. And she certainly didn't want Jonathan to accuse her of what Colin just had: *You think every guy wants you.*

He nudged her knee. "You hungry?"

Did they really have to face the day already? It was Sunday. Mother's Day. They wouldn't be able to get any more rental records, wouldn't be able to talk to people without the risk of interrupting family celebrations. What could they do to find Sam?

Nearly a whole week had passed, and they didn't even know where to look.

She reached over to smooth the hair out of his eyes. "Can we just go back to bed?"

He studied her for a moment. Then he swept her into his arms and carried her into the bedroom.

That was stupid.

Closing his eyes and shaking his head, Colin shoved his phone into the middle of the table so he wouldn't chuck it across the restaurant. He shouldn't have lost his temper with Zoe. He'd worked too hard to become her friend.

And now she wouldn't trust him anymore.

"Shit!"

The old woman in the next booth had been gaping at him since his outburst on the phone. He glared back, but when she wouldn't look away he flipped her off.

Her eyes bugged out and she insisted her husband get up and move to a different table with her. She was complaining to the manager when Tiffany returned from the restroom.

Leaving forty dollars on the table to cover their check, which hadn't come yet, Colin got up and motioned for his wife to go out ahead of him.

"We're leaving?" she said in surprise.

"I'm standing up, aren't I?" He spoke quietly so he wouldn't be overheard. He'd drawn enough attention.

She glanced longingly at her plate. "But I wasn't done."

"You are now." He wasn't about to stick around so some stupid, overweight manager making fifteen bucks an hour could waddle over in a grease-stained tie and reprimand him for his language.

"Why?" Tiffany asked. Then she noticed the tension in the room. "What's going on? This was supposed to be my Mother's Day celebration. I get to eat whatever I want today. You said so."

"I changed my mind." He waved her through the door but she didn't move.

"I only had a couple bites."

"So? You're not a mother," he whispered.

"Because we've chosen not to have children. But I'm a *woman.* I could be a mother if you wanted children."

"Just shut up. You had enough to eat. It's all I can do to keep you from turning into a whale. Now move your ass!"

"Colin—" She eyed the old folks and the manager conferring together, and lowered her voice. "What'd you do?"

He didn't answer. "If you don't come now I'm leaving you," he ground out.

Finally, she walked outside, and he used the button on

his key to unlock the car doors. They were about to get in when the manager poked his head out of the restaurant.

"Next time you come to this establishment, please remember your manners," he said.

Colin wasn't about to put up with any shit. "That's what I think of you and your *establishment,*" he said and flipped him off, too.

The manager came out farther—but not far enough to constitute a real challenge. "Hey, mister, don't *ever* come back!"

"You couldn't pay me to eat here again!" Colin said.

Tiffany, her face bright red, ducked into the car. "What's gotten into you?" she asked as several of the waitresses came to peer out at them, too. "We're in public."

"Yeah, well, I hate this dump."

"It's not a dump. It's a nice restaurant. You're the one who chose it."

"That was before I tried their lousy pancakes."

He started to back out of the parking space, then realized he'd left something behind. "Son of a bitch!"

"What now?" she asked.

He pulled in again. "Go get my phone. It's on the table."

Fortunately, she didn't argue because he wasn't in the mood to tolerate it. But when she returned, he could tell by her expression that she was upset.

"You called Zoe," she said as soon as she got in.

"So what?"

"*So what?* We were lucky last night, to get out of the mess we were in. Why can't you leave her alone? We have her daughter, Colin. Isn't that enough? What is it about her?"

He wished he knew. He wanted Sam, but he wanted Zoe more, especially since he'd had her tied to his bed. He'd been *so* close to becoming a god to her—master of her pleasure, master of her pain, master of her every breath. But then his father had ruined it. And now Zoe was spreading her legs for someone else, or she wouldn't have had a man in her motel room at eight in the morning.

She came across as so circumspect. *You have a wife, Colin.* But she was a whore, just like most women. Why couldn't he get her to respond to him? Wasn't he good enough for her? He was young, attractive, successful. He'd never tried so damn hard or been so ineffective with another woman.

"Are you going to answer me?" Tiffany asked.

"She's…stuck up," he said. "She needs to be taken down a few pegs."

"You've already done that. You stole her daughter—"

"*You* stole her daughter," he broke in.

"For *you!* And I regret it, okay? I was trying to make you happy, but all it's done is make me *un*happy. Do you love Zoe, Colin? Do you love her and not me? Is that what this is about?" She broke into a full-blown sob. "If you're not going to kill her, you might as well kill *me!*"

He was losing control of the situation when he most needed to retain it. He'd gotten through yesterday by the slimmest of margins. He couldn't fall apart, couldn't allow Tiffany to fall apart, either. His stepmother was expecting them in less than an hour. They had to be at their best so they wouldn't make any blunders.

Slipping out of the flow of traffic, he turned onto a residential street and pulled to the curb.

"Why are you stopping?" Tiffany said with a sniff. "What're we doing here?"

"We're talking."

"About what?"

"You have to calm down."

"I *can't* calm down. Every time I think Zoe's out of my life, you drag her back into it!"

"You could change that, if only you'd help me lure her to a secluded spot—"

"No!"

He held up a hand. "Just listen. All I want is to take her up to the cabin and make her watch what I have planned for Sam. Then I'll kill them both."

"We need to quit taking risks. We need to live like normal people. What we've been doing is *wrong*, Colin. And you know it."

"We'll stop. This is it. I promise. I love you enough to do anything."

Struggling to rein in her emotions, Tiffany wiped her eyes. "You do?"

"Of course. How could you not know that?"

"Sometimes it doesn't feel that way."

"That's just the doubt talking, the old insecurities."

"So…if I help you this one last time, you're done with it all?"

"I am."

"No more pets, nothing?"

He leaned over to kiss her, using his tongue, making it convincing. But even then he was thinking of Zoe's lips, Zoe's body. "Of course, babe. It'll be just you and me," he said, gently wiping her tears. "You and me, together forever."

She clung to him, shaking. "That's what I want. That's all I've ever wanted."

"Then bring me Zoe. Give me one weekend with her—and you'll never have to worry about her again."

She stared off into the distance for a moment before meeting his eyes. "This'll be the end? I have your promise?"

"That's what I said, isn't it?"

She nodded. "Okay, I will."

28

The twittering of birds was louder than Sam had ever heard. That meant *something* had changed. But her eyelids were too heavy to lift. She remained where she was, curled up tightly, not quite sure whether she *wanted* to wake up. Where was she? The air was cold, the smell was awful and she was in a box.

Had Colin and Tiffany buried her alive?

With a gasp, she managed to open her eyes. She was in a small space but it was a suitcase, not a box, and it was unzipped. Above her, sunlight peeked through cracks in what appeared to be a ceiling of wooden planks. She was in a shed of some sort; she guessed from the smell that she'd be lying in mud if not for the suitcase.

Had she ever been to this place before? She didn't recognize it—and that frightened her. How would her mother ever find her if she didn't know where she was herself? And where were Colin and Tiffany?

She searched her recent memory, but it was blank. She'd been unconscious; she had no idea for how long. She remembered Colin's footsteps pounding down the hall. Colin unlocking the door and banging it against the wall. Colin whispering his hate in a dark, angry voice. Colin nearly choking her to death for making noise. She'd thought her life was over. His father hadn't come to her rescue; no one had.

I'm going to kill you as soon as I have the time to do it right, Colin had said. *You're a dead girl.* Then he'd held her head back by pulling on her hair and nearly drowned her as he forced her to drink a glass of water that had the bitterest taste.

And now this….

Was she dreaming? Or was she dead? The sound of birds was like something she'd expect from paradise, but surely God had a better place in mind for her than a smelly old shed.

She wasn't dead. She wasn't even dreaming. When she tried to move, the cold, heavy weight of the collar around her neck told her that much. Colin and Tiffany had probably abandoned her here. Which meant she might be able to find her way home—or at least try to find help.

In order to do that, she had to get up, make her move while she could. But her limbs wouldn't cooperate. She was so weak, so cold…

It was no good.

Falling back, she stared at the black lining of the suitcase wondering how much longer it would take to die.

Jonathan had to get out of bed. In February, his parents had gone to their hometown in Iowa, to nurse his mother's dad back to health following a moderate stroke, and they were still there. His sister was spending Mother's Day with her in-laws. So it wasn't as if he had to dedicate much time to the family today. But a call was imperative, especially since he'd only mailed his mother's card yesterday. With the week he'd just had, it was surprising he'd remembered it at all.

Raising his head to see the clock, he yawned. "I gotta get up."

Kino seemed to agree. He nudged Jonathan with his wet nose, no doubt ready to go out.

"Already?" Zoe was sleeping half on top of him. They'd made love twice since he'd carried her back into the bedroom. And now that he was finally sated, he was beginning to feel guilty. What was he doing? Even if she could give him the "more" he was looking for, he wasn't sure he'd be satisfied with it. He was in love with someone else.

As incredible as the sex had been, he was an asshole for touching Zoe, and he knew it.

"I have about fifteen minutes to reach my mom or she's going to burst into tears," he said. "And then my dad will call me to tell me how disappointed he is that I didn't show more consideration. At which point, I'll explain that I've been busy, but neither of them will understand because they haven't seen busy in a long time."

"Oh. Right. You'd better call her, then." She moved off him and buried herself in the blankets, and he knew he needed to get her up and dressed before she slipped into such a deep depression she *couldn't* get up. She was teetering dangerously close. There'd been a fatalistic abandon in her lovemaking this morning that hadn't been there last night, a recklessness that suggested she didn't care as much about her own life as she should.

She had a lot to face, but she needed to face it, or matters would only get worse.

He pulled on his boxers and a pair of jeans. "Ready to grab a shower?"

"Not especially. If you've got stuff to do, go ahead. I'll wait here," came her muttered response.

She needed a purpose, something to do for Sam's sake. "I've got another idea."

Her head popped out of the covers. "What?" she said, but it wasn't a hopeful *what.* It was a "if you're not staying in bed, leave me alone" *what.*

"Let's go over to the hospital to see Toby. I'm sure his parents could use a break. We can sit with him while Mr. Simpson takes his wife out for brunch."

She rubbed the sleep from her eyes but continued to watch him with an uncertain expression. "I'm sure they have other family members."

"Who might also like a break. What do you say?" he prompted.

"What can I say?" she replied.

He smiled. "You'll feel better in a bit. Towels and washcloths are in the hall." He thumped the closet door to show her where as he and Kino passed through to the kitchen.

"Got it," she said, but he barely heard the response and didn't follow up on it.

It was going to be a hot day in Sacramento. At eleven the sun was bearing down on his glass door, heating up the kitchen.

He let Kino out in the backyard, then called his mom, who was fortunately in a great mood. He promised to take her to her favorite crepe place once she got home, then visited with his father for a few minutes and, having fulfilled his familial obligations, felt slightly less guilt-ridden about taking advantage of someone with as little to lose as Zoe. He'd make it up to her somehow, be more restrained in the future. It'd just been too long for him; that was all. And she was such an attractive woman.

He fed Kino and was heading back to the bedroom to see why she wasn't up when his BlackBerry rang. Caller ID indicated it was Sheridan.

He hesitated, wondering if he should pick up. He

hadn't spoken to her since that short encounter at The Last Stand the day he'd found out about Sam. But they couldn't avoid each other forever. It wasn't even fair of him to try. It wasn't as if she'd cheated on him or given him false hope. He hadn't even made his feelings clear. He'd been too busy waiting, expecting it to happen when she was ready.

He supposed he should answer the phone, get this over with.

With a silent curse, he ducked back into the kitchen and hit the Talk button. "Hello?"

"Hi."

"Hi," he said. "What's up?"

"This is a friendly reminder to call your mother."

He chuckled. "Thanks, but I'm ahead of the game. I just hung up with her."

"Good. How is she?"

"Tired of being away from home, but Grandpa's almost back on his feet."

"Will he still be able to live on his own?"

"Looks that way."

"That's a relief."

"He's a stubborn old guy."

"Reminds me of someone else I know."

"Me? Stubborn?" he said.

She laughed softly. "Skye told me that you're helping Zoe Duncan find her daughter."

"I'm trying."

"That doesn't sound too encouraging. It's not going well?"

"Not as well as we'd like."

"If you can't find her, no one can, Jon. You're the best."

"There isn't a lot to go on." He opened the back door to let the dog back in and missed her response.

"You having dinner with your folks today?" he asked, changing the subject.

"Cain and I just took them to breakfast. My sister and her husband are in town, too, so they brought the baby."

He couldn't help feeling he should've been there instead of Cain. "Sounds like a nice family outing."

She paused as if she'd picked up on his sarcasm. "It *was* nice."

"What're you working on these days at The Last Stand?" he asked to cover his gaffe.

"An odd case."

"Tell me about it."

"My client believes he once had a second younger sister."

"What does he think happened to her?"

"He claims his mother might've killed her, but he has only some bizarre memories to support that theory."

"He can't afford a P.I.?"

"No, and it's such a long shot the police won't touch it."

"What does the living sister say?"

"She corroborates part of his story."

"But you don't believe them?"

"I haven't decided. It's not exactly common for a mother to kill her own child. And with the few who do, the crime generally doesn't go undetected for twenty-some years. It's almost too incredible to be true, isn't it?"

"Anything's possible. Just when we think we've seen it all, we're surprised again."

"That's why I'm taking the case, doing what I can to look into the matter. If I can prove it's not true, maybe he can achieve some peace of mind. And if it is true, maybe I can bring him closure. Regardless, I could use help on the investigative end when you're available."

"It might be a while."

"I meant when the Duncan case is over."

"I've got quite a few other cases going." Which was true. His voice mail was full. He had yet to sort through his messages.

There was a short pause. "You've always had time for me before."

"I've never been this busy before."

"You don't want to work with me anymore, do you?"

He muttered a silent curse. "That isn't true."

"Yes, it is."

He didn't deny it again. Silence fell between them, but he could hear Zoe moving around and wanted to get off the phone. "I'd better go," he said.

"Jon?"

He hesitated. "Yes?"

"Why are you being so shitty to me all of a sudden?"

"I'm not. I'm just…working."

"Cain said something to me last night that…that made me wonder if maybe I've misinterpreted our relationship."

Oh, no… "Cain came back into your life a few months ago after being out of it for twelve years, and now he's a specialist on our friendship?"

"That's just it. He says it doesn't sound like friendship. It sounds as if—" her voice dropped, letting him know she was embarrassed to be so bold, but equally determined to forge ahead "—well, he says you must be in love with me."

Jonathan's breath whooshed out as though she'd slugged him. After all the years he'd hidden his feelings, here it was, the moment of truth.

He wanted to deny it. But he was pretty sure she'd see his lie for what it was. Skye knew how he felt and might've mentioned it to her, as well. All of that, together with his recent behavior, meant there was very little chance she'd believe him even if he did lie.

"That isn't true, is it?" she asked tentatively.

"How I feel doesn't matter, Sheridan. You're in love with someone else."

"That's not a denial."

He laughed incredulously. "You were expecting one?"

This time, the pause lasted much longer. "No, I guess not," she said at length.

The shower went on, making him feel more comfortable about speaking freely. "So why are you calling? To hear me say it?"

"To figure out what the hell has suddenly come between us and to find some way to fix it."

"There is no way to fix it." If Cain hadn't come between them, it would've been someone else, he thought. But he didn't really believe it. He knew Cain was the only man who could give him any competition where Sheridan was concerned. She'd been in love with Cain for years, since she was sixteen. He'd remained in Tennessee when she'd moved on. Jonathan had never dreamed they'd get together. He'd always assumed Sheridan would eventually be *his* wife.

"Why didn't you ever tell me?" she asked.

He'd been waiting for her to get over the boy who'd broken her heart at sixteen. But that boy was now a man, and when she returned to Whiterock the encounter had been very different than before. "Would it have made a difference?"

"I don't know."

"Not when it comes to Cain."

"Probably not," she admitted. "I've been in love with him almost my whole life."

"Exactly. I gotta go."

"Will you *talk* to me?" she said.

"About what? This is a waste of time. You're married. There's nowhere to go from here."

"Just because I'm not *in* love with you doesn't mean I don't *love* you, Jon. You're one of my best friends!"

She was crying; he could hear it in her voice. But he couldn't change how he felt or what it meant for their relationship.

"Don't cry, Sher. You've got Cain. Isn't one man enough?"

"Does loving him mean I have to lose you?"

"Don't you get it?" he said. "We can't be friends. We'll be lucky if we can continue to function as work associates. Knowing how I feel about you, Cain won't want us together all day."

"What are you saying?"

"I'm saying that sometimes you can't have it all."

He'd disconnected and was massaging his temples, trying to digest what'd just happened, when a noise caught his attention.

Zoe was standing at the entrance to the kitchen, her long legs bare beneath *his* oversize T-shirt. The fact that she wasn't wearing a bra and her hair was mussed from their lovemaking meant she'd turned the water on but hadn't yet taken her shower. And the look on her face said she'd heard more than enough to understand what was going on. "You don't think *I* can give *you* what you need?" she said, mocking his complaint from last night.

He winced at the disappointment in her eyes. "I'm sorry," he said, but it didn't help. He felt about two inches tall as she turned and walked back to the bathroom. A second later, the door closed behind her—and the lock clicked.

Zoe couldn't get anything right. And, apparently, that wasn't about to change just because she'd lost her daughter—even though that was enough to go wrong in *anyone's* life. Earlier this morning, she'd slept with a man she'd known only a week. And she'd let it mean something to her. How stupid could she be? Hadn't the past taught her *anything?*

At least she'd found out early this time, before she'd wasted the next few weeks or months hoping for a commitment that wasn't going to come.

"You haven't said a word since you got out of the shower." Jonathan sat across from her at a little sidewalk café on L Street, where they'd stopped for breakfast before going to the hospital. "What're you thinking?"

Zoe considered him through the dark lenses of her sunglasses and had to concede that physically he appealed to her as much as any man she'd ever met. Maybe *that* hadn't changed since his telephone conversation with Sheridan, but everything else had. "That I'm an idiot to have fallen for your 'I'm looking for more' speech. Why didn't you just say you needed a quick lay?"

He blanched. "I wasn't using you, Zoe. I'm attracted to you."

"Well, thanks for that," she said with a laugh.

"Listen, I made a mistake last night, and I'm willing to admit it. I shouldn't have touched you. It was insensitive and unprofessional. Besides, neither of us was in the best state of mind. But…that doesn't mean I don't care about you."

"Oh, *please.*" She took a sip of her latte. "You don't have to care about me. Because you were right. I don't care about you or anyone else. Just Sam. All I want is my daughter back safe. I'd sleep with anyone in the world if it would give me that."

When a muscle flexed in his cheek, she knew she'd hit her target. She regretted the harshness of her response. But not enough to lower her guard again. Just when she thought she could be indifferent to any man, Jonathan had managed to hurt her, and she was the stupid one who'd let it happen.

"You're saying it meant nothing to you," he said.

Grateful for her sunglasses, she lifted her chin. "Less than nothing."

His lips, the lips that'd kissed her in so many places last night, formed a hard straight line. "Then we were equally at fault."

"I'll accept that." She tossed her cup in the garbage. "Let's go to the hospital."

"Zoe—" His voice had softened, telling her that what he had to say was probably conciliatory, but she was more afraid of "nice" than she was of "indifferent" or even "mean." *Nice* was harder to defend herself against.

"Don't," she said. "It's over, it won't happen again and I don't want to talk about it." If she was going to do a better job of protecting herself in the future than she'd done in the past, she had to take a firm stand. She'd lost focus, given in to the need to feel loved. But she'd improve.

"I'm sorry if…if I've somehow made your situation more difficult," he said.

He was determined to get that apology in there, but she couldn't let it matter, or she'd be right back where she'd been before—open to letting him comfort her, letting herself need him.

"You have nothing to be sorry for." She threw him a careless smile. "My situation couldn't possibly get any worse."

"I guess not."

She got up and started toward his car, telling herself that if he was anyone special he wouldn't be driving a beat-up Mercedes. Those thoughts should've made it easier to forget that last night had been one of the best nights of her life. But she recognized such criticism as a mere echo of Anton's opinions about being a productive citizen—a flimsy attempt to make Jonathan seem less special. It didn't work because she knew Jonathan's financial situation had nothing to do with a lack of character. It was all about priorities, and she couldn't help admiring the fact that he didn't feel the need to prove himself by acquiring possessions the way Anton did.

She reached the car before realizing he wasn't behind her. Retracing her steps, she found him at the corner of the building, talking on his phone.

"I'm with her right now," he was saying. "Where are you…? That's not far from Sunrise Mall. Why don't we meet there…. Okay, see you in fifteen minutes."

"Who was that?" she asked as he pushed the End button.

He slipped his BlackBerry in his pocket. "Franky Bates."

She'd assumed that encounter in San Diego would be an isolated incident. What was this? "It sounded as if he's *here,* in Sacramento."

"He is."

"Why?"

"He claims he's putting up a ten-thousand-dollar reward for Sam."

That couldn't be true. "There's no way. He just got out of prison and is staying with his grandma. He doesn't have any money."

"He says he does and it's in cash. He's planning to give it to you. Unless you'd rather I met him alone."

Zoe considered her options. What had happened in that trailer had left deep emotional scars. She wasn't eager to have Franky back in her life. But the man she'd met in southern California hadn't been the frightening monster she remembered. And seeing him as he really was, a man like any other, had been cathartic.

"Is this for real?" she asked.

"We won't know until we get there, but it sounds pretty real to me."

She'd never expected to get anything positive from Franky and was hesitant to accept his help, even if he was sincere. But she definitely wanted to offer all the incentive she could to get people looking for Sam.

It couldn't hurt to meet him, could it? Not with Jonathan there.

She hiked her purse higher on her shoulder. "Let's go."

29

Franky looked exhausted. Dressed in a white T-shirt and a pair of baggy jeans that hung low on his hips, he had a dark shadow of beard covering his jaw. And he seemed even more nervous than tired. Zoe saw him wiping his palms on his pants and rocking onto the balls of his feet as they pulled up. A taxi, idling a few feet behind, was waiting for him.

Taxis weren't a common sight in Sacramento, especially in the suburbs.

"Did he fly?" she asked Jonathan as he shifted the transmission into Park.

A frown of confusion made grooves in Jonathan's forehead. "He told me he drove."

They didn't have the chance to say more. Franky was watching them. Zoe figured it was time to see if he was sincere about the reward. With a deep breath, she got out of the Mercedes.

Franky didn't walk toward her. He was standing beside a large brown sack while holding a smaller one and seemed afraid to move for fear he'd scare her off. He kept his focus on Jonathan, as if he found it too difficult to look at her. Every once in a while his gaze would slide her way, but the moment he saw her looking at him, his eyes would dart back to Jonathan, and his face would go red.

Before they could greet him, he pulled a big wad of cash from the smaller sack. "I've got the money," he announced.

He held the bag and the money out to Jonathan, but Jonathan didn't take it. "Where'd you get that?"

"Don't worry. I didn't do nothin' illegal." He fanned through some of the bills. "It was a clean deal. It's all good."

"Then tell me where you got it," Jonathan said.

Franky gestured to the taxi driver, asking him not to leave. "My grandpa had a collection of really old coins. Some of 'em dated back to the Civil War. It was really cool, something we used to look at together. He left it to me when he died. Along with his truck," he added.

"You sold the collection?" Zoe asked.

"I had my grandmother pawn the coins and wire me the money while I took the truck to Cars for Cash." His voice turned apologetic. "I'm still a little shy of the ten thousand you wanted. But this is close. Nine thousand two hundred and forty dollars," he said. "I had to keep a hundred and sixty to fly home."

Zoe couldn't believe it. He'd sold his two most precious possessions, the only things he owned of any value, to provide the reward money?

"Here you go," he said when Jonathan still made no move to take the sack.

Obviously, he wanted to hand over the money and go. Being in her presence was too uncomfortable for him. But Jonathan didn't make it easy. He jerked his head at Zoe. "It's not for me. Give it to her."

It was still quite obvious that Franky didn't even want to meet her eyes. But he was so happy to be able to offer her this gift that he shuffled closer and, staring down at the pavement, held it out to her. "I hope you find your daughter," he mumbled.

Tears blurred Zoe's vision as her hand closed around

the sack. Nine thousand, two hundred and forty dollars. He'd kept only enough to get home. "Thank you," she said.

He nodded, then lifted up the bigger sack. "My grandmother sent you this. If you don't want it, that's okay. It's just…some banana bread and other stuff she made."

Their hands brushed as Zoe accepted it. His skin was dry and rough, a typical blue-collar man's hand, but the contact confirmed what she'd come to believe in San Diego—he was as human as she was. After all the time she'd feared him, that realization put the man who'd hurt her in perspective for good. So did the tears filling his eyes.

"I'm sorry," he said. "I hope someday you can forgive me."

Apparently, he didn't expect her to do it now. Lowering his head, he turned and got into the cab. But before he could drive off, Zoe flagged down the driver, reached into her purse and gave Franky the picture of Sam she'd used to make the flyer.

"This is for *me?*"

"For you and your grandmother. I—" Zoe had to clear her throat twice to speak past the emotion that threatened to choke her. "I appreciate your sacrifice."

His mouth curved in a bittersweet smile as he looked at the picture. "She's beautiful, isn't she?"

"I think so." She extended her hand, and he shook it. Then the taxi drove off.

Tiffany couldn't sit still. Watching her mother-in-law agonize over Paddy's disappearance was absolute torture. How could Colin tolerate it? She had no idea, but he didn't seem to be having any trouble. Sitting at the kitchen table, he'd polished off a big piece of cake and was currently scraping the last of the frosting from his plate.

"Where could he be?" Sheryl stood between them and

directed this question at Colin, a question she'd already asked at least five times. It was a shock to see her, stoic even when her daughter was diagnosed with cancer a year ago, *this* upset.

"He'll show up," Colin said.

Sheryl's puffy face made her look like a caricature of her usual self. With her hair dyed an unlikely shade of red and teased into a stiff globe, and makeup thick enough to be reminiscent of onetime TV personality Tammy Faye Baker, she wasn't particularly attractive in the first place. But she was a fair person and tried hard to please those she loved. "How come you're not worried?" she asked. "He's never done anything like this before."

"To *you*." Colin's fork clinked as he put it down and pushed his plate into the center of the table. "He left my mom all the time. Once he took off for three weeks and went to Vegas. I think he was planning to divorce her, but, in the end, he didn't go through with it."

The pucker of Sheryl's mouth grew more pronounced as she struggled to cope with the hurt. "But we weren't having any problems. Why would he leave me?"

"Maybe he wasn't as fulfilled as you thought." Stretching out, Colin crossed his legs at the ankles. "Maybe he wanted his freedom. Or he met someone else. That happens more often than anyone would like to believe."

"You think he ran off with another woman?"

Tiffany winced at the tremor in Sheryl's voice. She wanted to interrupt, put a stop to Colin's gibes, but didn't dare.

"You said you found his car at the pool hall," he said.

"But the bartender told me he never came in last night."

"Exactly. Doesn't that give you some idea of what happened?"

"What?" she said helplessly.

"He met someone there." He sniffed. But that sniff wasn't due to tears. It was all the coke he snorted. It caused sinus problems and sometimes a bloody nose. "I'm guessing it was a lady friend. They left his car and took hers."

"No, he loved me," Sheryl said with a sob, but Tiffany could tell she was tempted to believe the scenario, simply because there was no plausible explanation. People had affairs much more often than they went missing or got murdered.

"I'm not so sure," Colin went on. "I don't mean to rub salt in the wound, but you sort of asked for it."

Sheryl's eyebrows drew together as she wiped her eyes. "I did?"

"You can be a real nag, Sheryl. If you want him back, you're going to have to work on that."

Covering her face, Sheryl broke into sobs, and Tiffany's restraint snapped. She couldn't take any more. Wasn't what Colin had done bad enough? Sheryl would never see Paddy again, and she'd never know why. Did Colin have to make the situation worse by giving her reason to blame herself?

Maybe Colin didn't like his stepmom, but Tiffany did. Sheryl was a good wife, a good mom. "That's not it," she said.

She'd spoken quietly, but the fact that she'd spoken at all drew their attention.

Sheryl lowered her hands. "What'd you say?"

Tiffany refused to meet Colin's penetrating gaze. She knew he'd make her pay for contradicting him, but just then she hated him almost as much as she loved him. "Whatever happened, it's not your fault."

The hope of obtaining some relief brought Sheryl over to the couch. "You don't think it could be another woman?"

"Absolutely not. Paddy loved you too much. He'd never leave you because no one else could give him more," she said with conviction.

Tiffany wasn't good at demonstrating love to other females. She'd always been shy and awkward, probably because her mother had spurned every advance. But a moment later, her step mother-in-law had sunk down next to her and was crying on her shoulder—and it wasn't stiff or uncomfortable. It felt perfectly natural because Tiffany shared Sheryl's grief. She wanted Paddy to come home, too; she didn't want him to be dead.

When she looked up, she found Colin glaring at her, but she didn't cower as she normally did. She was glad she'd intervened. If he wanted her to lure Zoe to the cabin, he could trade her a little kindness for Sheryl.

"But what else could it be?" Sheryl's words were muffled because she'd spoken into Tiffany's shoulder.

"Tiffany doesn't know," Colin said. "She doesn't know jackshit."

"And you do?" Tiffany wasn't sure what had made her say it. She'd gone too far already. But the relief on Sheryl's face when she pulled back made Tiffany's small defiance worth it. "Some stranger must've tricked him into…into going somewhere with him," she ventured. "You know…out to jump a dead battery or…or over to some house to check out a gun for sale. You know how much Paddy liked to hunt. The promise of a good gun would convince him to go anywhere. Then he was probably hurt and robbed."

Sheryl quickly agreed. "That's possible."

Colin took his own plate to the sink for a change. "Maybe that person was Glen," he said. "Has anyone checked to see where he was last night?"

The mere suggestion that Sheryl's son might've hurt her husband made Sheryl blanch. "Glen would never hurt Paddy. He wouldn't hurt anyone."

"Glen hated Paddy," Colin said. "And you know what his temper is like."

"No. Glen didn't do anything. Paddy will come back. He's probably lying injured somewhere, dazed. Someone will find him and help him come home."

"Right," Colin said. "Well, call us the minute he walks through the door. I have some work to catch up on before I go to the office in the morning."

Colin jerked his head toward the door, letting Tiffany know it was time to leave, and the bravado she'd felt just minutes earlier evaporated. Soon she'd be in the car with him *alone.* And then they'd be inside their upper-middle-class home, in their seemingly peaceful neighborhood, located in the newest part of one of the safest suburbs in Sacramento.

And she already knew that anything could happen behind that perfect facade.

"So now you're Sheryl's best friend?" Colin asked as he drove them home.

Tiffany didn't answer. She stared straight ahead as if she expected a severe punishment. She deserved one—another session with the collar and whip, at least. But there was still a hint of defiance in the lines of her body, and that made Colin less angry than worried. He'd taken for granted that Tiffany would side with him regardless of what he said or did, support him in anything. She had in the past, hadn't she? She'd let him kidnap and torture four kids.

Yet, after going along with that, she'd just taken a stand against him. Because of Paddy. She could forgive him for the pets. She'd never liked that part of their life together, but she was willing to tolerate it because it wasn't personal. She didn't expect Colin to care about kids he didn't know, kids neither of them had any attachment to. But she did expect him to care about Paddy. That he could kill his own father so easily and feel no remorse frightened her.

Deep inside him, it frightened Colin, too. He wasn't sure why he didn't feel what other people felt; it made him wonder if his mother had been right about him. He'd spent his entire life trying to prove to her and the rest of the world that he was as bright as anyone, as capable as anyone, as productive as anyone. And yet he couldn't really *care* if he didn't.

Tiffany understood that lack of caring now. She finally saw what his mother had recognized when he was young, what his father had refused to believe until the very end. And Colin knew where it would lead. She'd begin to doubt his love for *her,* and that was the one bond that kept her with him.

"Are you going to answer me?" he asked.

She adjusted her seat belt. "I just feel sorry for her, that's all."

"And you think I don't?"

She turned toward him. "You didn't act like it."

He could almost read the questions in her mind as she studied him. "Because this isn't easy for me, either." Reaching over, he took her hand.

She jerked in surprise, as if the pleading quality in his voice couldn't be trusted and she expected him to hurt her in some way. But he merely ran his fingers over her soft skin.

"Do you think I really want to face the truth?" he asked. "Paddy was my *father,* Tiff. I'll never get to see him again—and *I'm* responsible for that." He tried to conjure up a few tears, but it was no use. They weren't there. He hoped the tortured expression on his face would be convincing enough. "I mean, I'm not inhuman. Sure it's painful for Sheryl. She'll miss Paddy. So will you. I feel terrible about that. But neither of you will have to live with what *I* have to live with, right?"

She frowned at their entwined hands. "You shouldn't have done it."

"We've been over this. I didn't have any choice. Would you rather have lost him—or me? That's what it came down to. He would've turned us in, Tiff. We would've gone to prison. I did it to protect *you,* to protect us both."

She blinked repeatedly. "This has been such a horrible week."

"I know. I haven't been myself. Especially today. I'm sorry. I just… I don't want to deal with the pain of what happened to Paddy. I don't want to accept it. It's easier to be flip and…and angry that it had to happen at all."

"I can understand that," she said, softening.

"How would *you* feel if you were me?" he asked.

She grimaced.

"Exactly. I'm in hell, so if I seem hard-hearted, please allow me a little denial."

Giving him a sympathetic look, she took his hand and kissed it. "We'll be okay," she said. "Somehow, we'll get through this."

The terrible tightness that'd made it difficult to breathe since they'd gotten in the car began to ease. "I'm so lucky I have you. You can get me through any tragedy."

"That's what a wife's for."

"For better and for worse."

She rubbed his hand against her cheek. "That's right."

He felt *something.* He hoped it was more than relief. "I have a present for you."

"You do?"

"For Mother's Day and to make up for…Zoe and Paddy."

Her mood visibly improved. She even squeezed his hand for reassurance. "What is it?"

"Remember that diamond ring you wanted?"

Her eyes widened. "Yes?"

"I'm going to buy it for you."

"You are?" she breathed.

"Yep. Tonight."

"But it's five thousand dollars, Colin! We can't spend that kind of money."

"Hey, you married a successful attorney, babe. I can afford to buy my wife an expensive present now and then."

"But it'll have to go on credit."

"Don't worry about it. Soon I'll be making a lot more than I'm making now."

Her smile grew wider than he'd seen it in a long time, and the pain in his chest went away altogether. He had her right back where he wanted her; she wasn't going anywhere.

"Everyone at work will be so jealous."

"They should know you're special." He put down the top of his convertible and smiled as the warm afternoon breeze ruffled his hair. It made him feel carefree. And why *not* feel that way? Nothing had significantly changed. Paddy was gone, but they could live without him. They had it all.

But then a call came in on his cell—and because the only person he wanted to hear from was sitting beside him, he felt a strong reluctance to even check it.

"Is that your phone?" Tiffany asked when he made no move to retrieve it from his pocket.

"Yeah." With a sigh, he brought it into the light.

"Who is it?" The tone of her voice suggested she'd already noticed the change in his expression.

"I don't recognize the number, but…"

"What?"

"It's long-distance, with a Los Angeles area code."

"Then it's got to be your mother."

That was his guess, too. The last time Paddy had talked to Colin's sister, Courtney had been living down south. It was a no-brainer that Tina wouldn't be far away. They'd stuck together all along.

Tiffany bit her lip. "Do you think she expected you to call her today?"

"I doubt it. I haven't called her in years."

"Then what does she want?"

He wasn't sure, but he knew, whatever her reason, her call wasn't a good thing. The very last time he'd seen her, he'd been a senior in high school and had still been living with Paddy. She'd come to visit and had blamed him for slashing her tires while she was there. She'd screamed at him, called him the spawn of Satan.

He *had* been the one to ruin her tires, but she shouldn't have been so quick to accuse him. She should've had *some* doubt, or at least some desire to believe him.

"We'll see." He hit the Talk button just before it went to voice mail. "Hello?"

"Colin?"

It was his mother, all right. "What do you want?" he said.

"I want you to tell me where your father is."

The tension was back, clawing at his gut. She'd always known about him. That was why he hated her so much. When he looked into her face, he saw his true self staring back at him. "Who told you about Dad?"

"Sheryl called me. She wanted to know if he went back to me. Can you believe that? After all this time?"

Colin cringed because he'd probably caused that call. "She's jumping to conclusions," he said. "Dad's taken off, but he'll come home. He always came home before, right?"

"He was happy with Sheryl. He wouldn't leave."

"Well, I don't know what to tell you, then. He didn't check in with me. I have no idea where he is."

"I think you might. He tried to call me last night. I wasn't there, but he left a message, said he needed to talk to me about something very important. He said it had to do with you."

Colin tightened his grip on the steering wheel. "You've been out to get me for a long time."

"Only because I've been expecting something like this. Years ago, I promised myself that if anything ever happened to any member of the family, I'd look to you first."

"Would you listen to yourself? You're crazy, you know that? Any normal mother would assume the best of her son."

"Those mothers don't have a son like mine."

"How do you know? How can you be so sure that I'm different?"

"Because you've been different from the day you were born, Colin. The first words out of your mouth were a lie, and you haven't stopped lying since. I tried to remedy that by taking you to church. I thought religion might help you develop the conscience you lacked. But you simply played everybody—church leaders, your schoolteachers, even your father."

"If I'm screwed up, it's your fault! You were abusive!"

Laughter filtered through the phone, as derisive as it was incredulous. "*I* was abusive? Because I tried to discipline you? Because I refused to let you manipulate me? Sure, I spanked you. There had to be some consequences for your behavior, and I didn't know what else to do. I was at my wits' end and was still fighting to save a son I wanted to love. I believed if you could only learn to take responsibility for your actions and to respect the rights and feelings of others, you'd be okay. But it was no use. You were purposely cruel to your little sister. And you turned Paddy and me against each other, broke up what would've been a happy marriage. You even convinced your teachers and coaches, the parents of your friends, that I belonged in an asylum."

It had almost worked, too. He'd nearly had his mother committed, right after her nervous breakdown. They'd tried that on each other. "That is where you belong. What mother could do what you did?"

"Disappear with Courtney? It was my only choice. I had to save the one child worth saving."

"Go to hell," he said and almost hung up, but her next words made him freeze.

"I'm calling the cops, Colin. And I'm telling them that I think you're dangerous."

"If you do that, you might find out how dangerous I can be," he said.

"Is that a threat?" she countered.

He jammed a hand through his hair. He had to be careful, couldn't let his temper get away from him. She could be recording this call. "Of course not. I'd never hurt you or anyone else. You just…get me so angry that I say stupid things. You always knew how to push me to the point of lashing out."

"Tell me what you did to Paddy, Colin."

"I didn't touch him!"

"He loved you, you know. The poor bastard loved you, more than he loved me or Courtney, or he and I would still be together. You owe him a lot for his blind faith. I hope you haven't repaid him the way I think you have," she said and hung up.

Colin's heart and lungs were pumping as fast as if he'd run five miles. "That bitch! God, I hate her!" He threw his phone against the dash. "She's still making my life miserable!"

Tiffany had overheard enough that her face had gone pale. She didn't even pick up his phone, which had ricocheted and hit her before landing at her feet. "How does she *know?*"

"She doesn't know. She can't hurt us. Even if she gets the police involved, they won't be able to prove anything. All I have to do is fight fire with fire."

Tiffany's eyes were as round as silver dollars. "What does that mean?"

"Don't worry." He breathed in through his nose, held the air, then let it go, twice, and soon a steely calm came over him. "I've gone up against my mother in the past, and I've won every time. Bottom line, I'm better at eliciting sympathy than she is. And these days, the poor child is always right." If she gave him any trouble, he'd claim she was out to get him—and he'd be able to show a documented history of it.

30

The Simpsons weren't in the room when Zoe and Jonathan arrived at the hospital. A nurse stopped them at the entrance to the intensive care unit and asked their names. Then she placed a call before giving them clearance to go in.

The blinds were open, admitting the sun, and there was a radio playing, as if Toby's parents didn't want him left in silence. The flowers on the bedside table created a cheerful effect, but from what Zoe could tell, Toby's condition hadn't improved.

It was painful for her to see the boy still lying in the same bed, hooked up to the same machines, because every day he remained in this state made it less likely he'd ever come out of it. But at least the Simpsons knew where their son was. There had to be some small measure of comfort in that, in knowing Master couldn't hurt him anymore.

"You're one hell of a bastard, Master," she muttered under her breath as she took the boy's hand.

Jonathan stood at her elbow. He tried to put his arm around her, to show her some support, she supposed. But she avoided his touch by crowding closer to the bed. She couldn't let herself lean on him again; she knew where it would lead. Memories of last night intruded almost every time she looked at him. Commitment or no commitment, their lovemaking had possessed a spiritual dimension she'd never experienced with anyone else.

But that was the problem. She couldn't allow Jonathan to be the thread that made the rest of her unravel.

"We're going to get you," she promised Toby's attacker.

Hearing a noise at the entrance, Zoe turned. Mr. and Mrs. Simpson were coming in, carrying a bag of takeout. The smell of Chinese food filled the room as they slipped around the foot of the bed to the other side.

Zoe didn't want to intrude on their privacy. She started to apologize for stopping by unannounced, but at Mrs. Simpson's twinkling eyes and wide smile, she stopped in midsentence.

"What?" she asked curiously.

The other woman exchanged a glance with her husband. "Lyle didn't want me to call you, but now that you're here, I'm telling you anyway."

"Theresa—" he began with a note of admonishment, but she ignored him.

"Toby squeezed my hand this morning!"

The breath whooshed out of Zoe's lungs. "He *what?*"

"He squeezed my hand!"

"Honey, you know the doctor told us not to get too excited. It could've been a reflexive action. That's why I asked her not to call you," he added apologetically to both Zoe and Jonathan. "I didn't want you to…get your hopes up if…well, you know."

"I know." Zoe understood completely. But adrenaline, triggered by his wife's excitement, was already pouring into her bloodstream.

"I don't believe it was reflexive," Mrs. Simpson argued. "Our boy's mind is clicking away in that slumbering body. He was trying to tell me not to give up on him. I said, 'It's Mother's Day, baby. Come back to me.'"

Her voice cracked, but she cleared her throat and forged on. "And he gave my hand a squeeze. I swear it happened at that very moment. The timing couldn't be a coincidence, whether the doctors believe that or not."

"Honey, we spent over an hour trying to get him to repeat the action or to respond in some other way, but…nothing," Mr. Simpson said.

Just the possibility made Zoe's heart beat faster. But…did they dare read more into that than the doctors suggested?

Taking the boy's hand between her own, she leaned close. "You're going to be fine, Toby. You have a family who loves you, and they're waiting for you. They're right here," she told him and, unlikely though she knew it was, she couldn't help wishing he'd squeeze *her* hand—or give her some other small token on which to hang all her hope.

He didn't move. It wasn't until hours later, after she and Jonathan had returned from creating a new flyer—one advertising the reward sponsored by Franky Bates—that they received a call from the hospital.

"He just opened his eyes!" Mrs. Simpson screamed into the phone.

"Can he talk?" Zoe asked, but that was all the news she could get because the poor woman was crying too hard to say more.

"I've met Sheridan."

Jonathan glanced over at Zoe, who was walking beside him, and guided Kino away from the neighbor's yard so they could cross the street. Except for a few streetlights, it was dark and colder than it had been for the past week or so. Zoe was wearing one of his sweatshirts to ward off the chill, but she wouldn't let him touch her. He'd tried a few times. He didn't know why.

"At the victim support group?" he said, but only because it seemed like the most innocuous response. He didn't want to talk about Sheridan, especially to Zoe. Considering he'd made love to Zoe last night but admitted his feelings for Sheridan this morning, it wasn't the most comfortable topic.

"Yeah."

He was hoping they could let it go at that. But Zoe spoke again. "She's a nice person, Jon. And very pretty."

She was no prettier than Zoe, but he knew Zoe wouldn't believe him if he said so. He tried to change the subject. "I'm so relieved that Toby's out of his coma."

Turning back the sleeve of her sweatshirt, which hung down to her knuckles, she checked her phone for missed calls. Never mind that she'd been holding it ever since she'd talked to Mrs. Simpson and would've heard it ring if someone had tried to reach her.

"I wonder if he'll be…you know, all there," she said, her voice worried.

They hadn't received a full report. Mr. Simpson had called back to say that Toby recognized his name, and that was the last they'd heard from the family. To avoid bothering them repeatedly, Jon had called Detective Thomas, and Detective Thomas had contacted the doctors at the hospital. But they were being typically cautious. The official word was that it would be a few days before they'd know how well Toby would recover.

That didn't stop him and Zoe from wishing it would be much sooner, however. And Jonathan had an extra reason to be glad of this positive turn of events. Earlier, Zoe had mentioned that they needed to get home in time for her to move into a motel. He'd expected her to leave as soon as she had the chance, but so far she hadn't acted on that comment. She was preoccupied with waiting. It was easier to wait with someone than to wait alone.

"I saw a *Dateline* once that featured a girl who'd been in a coma for five weeks," he said. "It took some time, but she recovered completely."

"I hope Toby can do the same...."

Kino did his business on a tree and sniffed a gopher hole before they headed down the sidewalk on Jonathan's usual circuit. "Even if that happens, it might be touchy getting information from him about what he suffered," he said, concerned that she might be hoping for too much.

Zoe frowned but nodded, and they walked in silence until they came to the corner, where Jonathan held Kino on a tighter leash so another dog and his owner could pass without an overenthusiastic greeting.

"So how long have you known Sheridan?" Zoe asked when they resumed their walk.

Stifling a groan, Jonathan kept his gaze on the sidewalk in front of him. "About four years."

"Did you ever date?"

"For a while."

"What went wrong?"

He blew out a sigh. "She liked me, but I broke it off because I wasn't all that into her. Then I liked her, but she broke it off because she wasn't all that into me."

"Sounds like you've been involved with her for a long time."

He shot her a quick look. "Do we have to talk about this?"

"Aren't we friends?" she asked.

It was tough to think of her as a friend when he kept imagining her soft body pressed up against his, kept replaying that moment last night when she'd moaned his name. But what could he say? "If that's what you want to call it."

"I was hoping that two or three orgasms moved me out of the 'just another client' category, at least."

He grimaced. She was striking out, but he deserved it. "You're not just another client. You never were."

"Thank you." She gave a little bow. "And you're not just another P.I." She laughed, but he didn't think her comment was funny. "Anyway," she went on, "if you're so heart-broken over Sheridan that it hurts to talk about her, I—"

"It doesn't *hurt,*" he interrupted, irritated without really understanding why.

"Then what's the big deal? She knows. I know. We all know how you feel."

But it wasn't Sheridan on his mind. It was Zoe. The longer he went without touching her, the more he wanted to. And he knew his chances of making love to her again were diminishing by the second—if he'd had any to begin with, after this morning. "My relationship with Sheridan isn't important. She's married. We're coworkers. That's it."

"Have you ever made love to her?"

"Zoe—"

"It's okay, you can be honest. I wanted you so badly last night I probably would've done what I did despite Sheridan."

Did that mean she didn't want him anymore? Because repeating the experience was all he could think about.

"I'm equally to blame for what happened," she was saying. "And it's not as if I was expecting any sort of commitment." She raised her hands. "I don't know why I let it bother me."

Although he wasn't willing to speculate on exactly why, he liked it *better* when it bothered her.

"I mean, it's not as if it was anything special," she said. "I'm sure you were thinking about Sheridan the whole time."

Now she'd gone too far. Stopping, he faced her. "If you're trying to let me know I don't have a snowball's chance in hell of getting in your pants again, consider me notified," he said and cut the walk short.

Zoe had made her point. Maybe she'd driven it home a little *too* hard, she thought as she took a hot shower. Still, Jonathan hadn't tried to touch her since their walk. It was safe to stay with him—for a night or two, anyway. She couldn't impose on him any longer than that. She wouldn't be here tonight except that she couldn't deal with pacing the floor of some nondescript motel room, wearing a hole in the carpet as she hoped and prayed that Toby would recover fully—for his sake as well as Sam's.

Grabbing a towel as she stepped out, she dried off and donned the pajama bottoms he'd lent her and her own T-shirt. After she'd brushed her teeth and used a blow-dryer, she left the bathroom, expecting to find Jonathan at his computer. He spent a lot of time at the kitchen table, working. But he was lying on the couch with a remote in one hand, watching TV—and wearing a scowl.

"Anything good on?"

His eyes flicked her way, focused pointedly on her braless chest, then moved to her face. "Nothing better than that."

She covered her breasts with her hands to stop them from tingling. "I'm sorry. Would you rather I wore something else?"

"If you'd rather I looked somewhere else," he said.

She thought about his response but ultimately shrugged. What she was wearing wasn't particularly revealing. Besides, it seemed a bit pointless to become modest after the fact. He'd already seen her breasts, touched them, *kissed* them. "It doesn't bother me if it doesn't bother you."

One eyebrow slid up but he made no further comment.

He turned back to the TV and didn't deign to notice her again. Until the program went to a commercial. Then she spoke up, which drew his attention. "Where did Sheridan meet her husband?"

"We're *not* talking about Sheridan!" he said, his words clipped.

She saw the hard set to his jaw and realized he was angry. She couldn't seem to maneuver them into a place where they could both feel comfortable. Sheridan was the only topic that seemed to diminish, at least to a small degree, the sexual tension between them. There were simply too many erotic memories, too much desire.

Maybe she'd been wrong to think she could stay….

"I should leave," she said, standing.

"That isn't the problem."

"What *is* the problem?"

He got up and came close, his eyes riveted on hers, and the tingle she'd felt in her breasts went through her whole body. She told herself not to back away, although her instincts were screaming for her to do just that. Retreating would only let him know that she was still affected by him.

Slowly, his palm cupped her breast over her shirt, gently teasing her nipple, and his mouth lowered to hers.

His kiss was a slow exploration, achingly sweet. Zoe told herself to pretend indifference, but she was sure he could feel the way her body responded to his touch. "What you do to me. That's the problem," he said and left her standing in the living room.

31

Should she go to her bed? Or his?

Several minutes passed as Zoe deliberated.

He was in love with someone else.

But that person was married. *Happily* married.

She had no business taking this kind of risk. She wasn't herself these days, wasn't in control.

But would it really hurt to be with him while she had the chance? Wouldn't there be plenty of time to be alone later?

Sitting on the edge of an old green ottoman, she waited for her body to settle down. Hormones must be clouding her judgment because earlier she'd had lots of reasons sleeping with Jonathan again wouldn't be a good idea.

Funny, she couldn't seem to think of any that mattered more than feeling his hands on her.

Maybe it would be okay, now that she was better informed. Maybe it could be casual. People had casual sex every day, didn't they?

Yes, *they* did. But *she* didn't. She'd been in a committed relationship with every single boyfriend. This was her first experience with wanting a man who didn't really care about her in return.

She'd just remind herself of that, she decided. During every minute in his bed, she'd silently chant, "He loves

Sheridan…he loves Sheridan…he loves Sheridan." Then there'd be no way she could forget.

Jonathan could tell it was different this time. Mechanically everything went even more smoothly than before. Their bodies seemed to be made for each other. But whenever he said something flattering, something that would've made Zoe smile or hold him closer the first night, she'd either pretend she hadn't heard it, or she'd turn her face away as if she refused to believe it.

The only "improvement" was that she trusted him more in a physical sense. The familiarity they'd established made them both comfortable and confident. He loved that in their most recent encounter she was able to abandon herself to the pleasure he wanted to give her without resisting it. At one point, she'd even awakened him for more….

Jonathan?

Hmm?

I want you.

Her hand had slipped down to caress him and some of the most passionate lovemaking he'd ever enjoyed had followed. And yet…when morning arrived, Jonathan was almost *more* frustrated than he'd been before. He'd made love to Zoe three times since she'd overheard him talking to Sheridan, but it wasn't enough. He wanted to do it again and again—until she finally relented and…what?

Began to care. That was it. He hated that she was holding back. He'd accused her of being closed off, but she'd actually begun to feel a real connection. *He* was the one who'd blown it.

He told himself it was better that she knew about Sheridan, that it was more honest.

But was it really?

He angled his head to watch her sleep. Had he ruined what they'd shared on purpose—because she'd surprised him? Because she hadn't held him at arm's length as he'd expected her to? He'd had to put a stop to what was developing between them, didn't he? He'd felt the potential, the threat. It had been far more powerful than any encounter he'd experienced before, even more powerful than what he'd felt for Maria….

Shifting his attention to the alarm clock, he waited for the second hand to tick its way to seven o'clock. He didn't want to analyze his own feelings, but the questions he'd already asked forced another: Was Sheridan *really* standing between them? Or was it the hurt and disappointment he'd experienced with Maria? The fear of letting himself love again—and allowing those feelings to culminate in a serious relationship, with all the struggles and potential pitfalls that entailed? Had he set his sights on Sheridan simply because he'd known she was safe? That she'd always care about him but not in a way that would ever threaten his freedom? Was that why he'd never declared himself or tried to advance the relationship?

There had to be a reason. He hadn't really *tried* with Sheridan, or she wouldn't have needed Cain or anyone else to tell her how he felt. He'd been happy to remain friends indefinitely. Why?

Zoe stirred beside him. "We've got to get up." She'd mumbled as if trying to convince herself to open her eyes, and he understood why she might be reluctant. She was in bed with a man she'd known only a week. And her daughter was still missing. Daylight put an end to the brief respite.

Scooping her into his arms, he buried his face in her neck. She stiffened slightly, as if having him be so affectionate without sexual intent took her by surprise—even put her on the defensive. He wasn't sure why he'd done it. He'd acted on impulse. But it felt right. Almost as good as making love.

"Maybe today will be the day," he said.

"I hope so." She stopped fighting her natural inclination to curve into him. "I'm going to circulate the new flyers as much as possible, then maybe I'll go over to the hospital this morning. I—I know I should probably give Toby and his parents some space, but…I *have* to be there, rooting for him."

"I understand."

"What about you?"

"I'll be here for part of the morning. I have half a dozen people screaming for my attention, wondering why I've suddenly disappeared from their cases. And I need to make a few more calls to various cabin-rental companies."

"Detective Thomas said he's meeting with you this morning, too."

"And there's that. We plan to compare impressions of our various interviews."

"Thank you," she said.

"You're welcome."

She clasped his face between her two hands. "No, I mean it. I—I don't know how I would've gotten through this so far without you."

As he gazed down at her, something passed between them, something he was hesitant to name or even acknowledge. But on his part it had a possessive quality, along with a strong desire to protect.

"We'd better get up." She moved as if she expected him to let her go that easily, but he caught her before she could go anywhere.

"What?" she said.

Too confused to put what he was feeling into words, he gave up trying to talk and kissed her. It started out as a gentle melding of their mouths. But when she parted her lips, *gentle* quickly turned into *passionate*. He slid his hand down her flat stomach to find the warm, wet softness he already craved. "Make love to me one more time," he murmured.

Then the phone rang.

With a sigh, he rolled onto his side. His heart was hammering too fast to answer immediately, but he knew he'd lost Zoe's interest—and he didn't blame her one bit.

"It could be good news," she said.

It could also be bad. The way she bit her bottom lip told him she knew that as well as he did.

Grabbing his cell phone from the nightstand, he said hello even though he was still a little breathless.

"Jon? Is it too early?"

Jasmine. "No. Did you get my package?"

"It just arrived."

He'd paid to have it delivered before ten, Louisiana time. "And…"

"And the energy around it is so strong I could *feel* Sam the second I took the teddy bear out of the box."

He sat up. "That's good…isn't it?"

"She's alive. I'm sure of it."

Zoe raised herself to lean against the headboard, holding the blankets to her chest. He sensed that she felt completely vulnerable. What little she had in the way of defenses, she'd reserved for him.

"Can you tell me any more?"

"When I close my eyes, I hear birds. Lots of birds. More than you'd notice in a city. I think she's outside somewhere. Maybe in a forest. It's cool, dank, even dark."

"Right now? In the daylight?"

"She's inside something. That's what it feels like. Enclosed."

Listening to Jasmine work was fascinating. She spewed out the impressions as they hit her. But what Jonathan had heard so far didn't tell him much about where to find Sam. Sacramento sprawled at the base of the Sierra Nevada, which meant the foothills weren't far away. There were miles and miles of forest, all within easy driving distance. "Are there more noises? Any scents?"

"Nothing."

"Keep trying, Jas."

"I'm afraid the only other detail I can relate is one you won't want to hear."

He swallowed hard. "What is it?"

"She's extremely weak. This girl needs help, Jon. And she needs it fast or—" She didn't finish. Jasmine's "gift" put her in touch with some very poignant emotions. He knew it was a sacrifice for her to get involved at all, but she was a strong woman who did anything she could to fight for victims of crime. She didn't shy away from her impressions just because they could be painful.

He glanced at Zoe.

"What is it?" Her voice was reedy.

"Jasmine believes that Sam is alive."

Her fingers clenched the blankets. "Thank God. But…where is she? Can Jasmine help us find her?"

"She thinks Sam's in a forest somewhere."

"A forest?" Tears streamed down Zoe's cheeks.

"What about the man who did this to her?" Jonathan asked Jasmine. "Can you give me any details about him? Is it Master? Are we on the right track there?"

"I have no idea. I only know that this guy must seem normal or he would've stood out by now, drawn attention. He has a good job. He has a family. Something. He's no one you'd typically suspect."

"How can he have a family and get away with this kind of thing for days, weeks, months?" He knew it happened, but it still surprised him.

"It's easier than you might think. You heard about the man in Austria who kidnapped his own eighteen-year-old daughter and imprisoned her in a cellar for twenty-four years, didn't you?"

"Yes." That was a highly publicized case, one with a very sick twist. That same man had fathered seven children with the daughter.

"His wife had no idea. She believed him when he said their daughter had gone missing."

"That would be much less likely to happen in Rocklin, where we've got new houses built on small lots with no cellars."

"But it would be possible if the perpetrator hid his victims somewhere else," Jasmine suggested.

"Like out in the woods," he said grimly.

Had anyone he'd spoken to during the investigation been out of town recently? No. Except—

Suddenly, Jonathan remembered Colin telling him that Tiffany was at some cabin. She hadn't participated in the search on Saturday because she was gone.

His hand tightened on the phone. What was he thinking? He had to be jumping at shadows. Colin couldn't be Master because he and Tiffany were together whenever they weren't working. And they both had regular jobs that kept them tied to the city, except for a brief weekend getaway here and there. They couldn't keep someone hidden out in the forest. Besides, Colin was at work when Sam went missing.

But then a snippet of conversation he'd had with the deputy about Toby rose to his consciousness:

He wouldn't trust the man who first came upon him,

so the guy got his wife, thinking a woman would be less threatening.

Did it help?

Not much. Toby would let her come closer, but dodge away before she could actually touch him, all the while crying for his mother.

Toby was equally frightened of the woman. Was that significant? "You don't think it could be a…*couple?*" he said to Jasmine.

"That wouldn't be unheard of, either," she said. "Remember that husband and wife in Canada who victimized the wife's sister in addition to murdering two other girls?"

The odd circumstances surrounding the way Jonathan had found Zoe in that motel room made the idea seem more feasible. She'd just had dinner with Colin and Tiffany Bell….

But couples like the one in Canada or England's Hindley and Brady, who'd committed the Moors murders, were a rare exception in the criminal world. And if Colin and Tiffany were guilty of harming children, why wouldn't they maintain a lower profile? Why would they invite Zoe into their house? Help organize a search for Sam? Call Zoe on Mother's Day?

Because they thought it would make an effective cover? Possibly.

Jonathan thanked Jasmine, told her to call if she came up with anything else and disconnected. Colin and Tiffany were a long shot, but he couldn't get them out of his mind. Partly because of Colin's involvement in the case since Sam's disappearance. A lot of criminals tried to insert themselves in the investigation of their own crimes….

He pictured Zoe's neighbor standing in the parking lot at Sierra College talking about how desperately they needed to find Sam. Was it all a charade? "How well do you know Colin and Tiffany Bell?" Jonathan asked Zoe.

"Not well," she said. "Hardly at all, actually, until Sam went missing."

Until Sam went missing. Those four words sent chills down his spine. "You don't think they could've taken Sam…."

Shoving the hair away from her face, she scowled. "You're kidding, aren't you?"

"No."

She shook her head. "In the nine months we lived next to them, they paid very little attention to her. Colin has always acted more interested in me. And, like you said, he was at work the day Sam disappeared. I can't see Tiffany hurting anyone."

Zoe was probably right. There were other things that didn't add up, either. If Colin and Tiffany had Sam, why would they drug Zoe and remove her clothes only to dump her, unharmed, in a motel room? If the person who'd hurt Toby had another incapacitated victim, he would've taken advantage of it.

"I can't imagine Tiffany going along with the brutality of what happened to Toby," she added.

"Neither can I." He didn't want Zoe to feel she'd been betrayed by her neighbors if she hadn't. But Sam's kidnapper had to be close. And Colin and Tiffany lived right next door.

32

The receptionist at Scovil, Potter & Clay was on the phone when Jonathan arrived, but she gave him a broad smile and held up a finger to indicate she'd be with him in a moment.

"You bet I'll tell him," she said into the phone. "Yes, sir, I always do. Why…thank you. Maybe I'll let you hire me away." She laughed. "Okay, you, too."

Her smile lingered as she made a quick note on the telephone pad. Then she removed her headset and glanced up. "Can I help you?"

"Yes, I—"

"Wait! I recognize you!" She managed to get out of her chair, but for someone her age—twenty-six or twenty-seven—it shouldn't have required so much effort. Those extra hundred pounds obviously weren't easy to lug around. "You were at the search on Saturday. For a minute, anyway. I have a good memory for faces. Not that a girl would be likely to forget yours," she added with a nervous chuckle.

He grinned, hoping to put her at ease. "I'm a private investigator. I—"

"I thought maybe you were a detective. With the police, I mean."

"No, I've been retained by The Last Stand, a victims' charity here in town, to find Samantha Duncan."

She sighed. "That is *such* a sad situation. I've been

hoping and praying she'd be found safe. Have there been any breaks in the case?"

"None."

"Phooey!" She smoothed her hair, self-consciously fighting the static electricity caused by the headset. "So…you're here to see Colin?"

"Yes. Is he in?"

She nearly knocked a small stuffed dog off the file cabinet with her elbow but caught it before it could fall. "I'm afraid not."

"His car's in the underground parking," Jonathan pointed out.

"Oh, right." With obvious chagrin, she checked the hallway leading to the offices, then lowered her voice. "Actually he's here. It's just that he's in a meeting with the senior partner, and I've been told to hold all calls."

"I see. Must be an important meeting."

"It is. I think he might be in trouble." She winced, even friendlier now that she felt the need to make up for lying to him.

He lowered his voice to match hers. "Has he done something wrong?"

"Not *wrong,* exactly. It's just that—" She caught herself. "Listen to me. I'm *so* bad." The giddy edge to her laugh would've made it clear, even if she hadn't already told him, that she thought he was handsome. "I shouldn't be telling you this."

"Why not?" He raised two fingers in the traditional Scout's honor salute. "I won't tell a soul. I promise."

She mouthed the next words. "He might be getting fired."

"Really?"

Her eyes widened innocently. "His productivity has fallen *way* off. And they don't put up with a lot around here. Each attorney has to perform, or that's it."

He took one of her cards from a holder on the desk. "Any idea why Colin's productivity might've fallen?"

"None."

"Problems at home?"

She nibbled on her bottom lip. "I doubt it. He and Tiffany seem happy together. She came to the company Christmas party in this low-cut slinky dress that showed his name tattooed on…well…" She blushed. "Tattooed on her *chest,* if you know what I mean. Before the night was over, they were both smashed, and he had her prancing around like a show pony."

"If it's not his marriage, maybe he hasn't been feeling well." Jonathan doubted Colin had health issues, but it was an easy way to keep the receptionist talking.

"He's not sick." She leaned toward him. "Actually, Mr. Scovil thinks he might not be mentally capable of handling the job."

"Why does he think that?"

She turned and gave the hall another cautious glance. "You'll never hear Colin talk about it, of course. All he says is Georgetown this and Georgetown that. But he didn't start at Georgetown. He started at a *third-tier* law school in Maryland. It's all in his employment file."

"But he graduated from Georgetown?"

She shrugged. "Somehow he managed to get the grades he needed to transfer."

Colin was plenty smart. Jonathan was sure that wasn't the problem. "I see. So…you don't like him?"

A guilty expression appeared on her round, soft features. "I like him, I guess. I like everybody. But…I don't know. He has a mean streak."

Jonathan refused to draw any conclusions from that statement. For all he knew, a few cross words could be interpreted as "mean" to this Pollyanna. "What's he done to make you believe he's mean?"

Her mouth twisted as if she was fighting tears.

Surprised by this sudden show of emotion, Jonathan reached out to touch her elbow. "Are you okay?"

"It hurts to think about it."

"About what?"

"Several months ago someone left me a nasty note." She adjusted her purple, clingy blouse to get it to hang more smoothly over the bulge of her middle.

"What'd it say?"

"'I'd love to…'" Her face beamed scarlet. "Never mind. I shouldn't have mentioned it."

Jonathan caught her eye. "Tell me."

"No, you two might be…friends, or whatever."

"I'm just the P.I. investigating Samantha Duncan's disappearance. I know Colin only in relation to my work during the past week."

"So why are you here?" she asked.

"This is just a courtesy visit to let him know I'm doing a background check on him and several other neighbors. I wanted to get permission to talk to his boss and some of the other lawyers and people who work here." Actually, Jonathan was more interested in his *reaction* than his *permission,* but that didn't sound as benign.

"You don't think he had anything to do with the girl's disappearance, do you?"

"Would that surprise you?"

"Yeah! I mean, he can be a jerk, but he'd never kidnap a child."

"This is just a precautionary measure."

Coupled with the devilish gleam in her eye, her smile made her appear almost childlike herself. "I bet it's gonna make Colin mad. He doesn't like people snooping around. He screamed at me once for being in his office when he came to work, and I was only delivering his messages."

"Doesn't take much to get him riled up, huh?"

"For me, *breathing* is enough."

"So…what happened with that note you referred to a minute ago?"

"Oh, I'm sure he's the one who left it. He did it because he didn't have some copies he needed for a meeting and he had to go in unprepared. But it wasn't my fault."

"What'd the note say?" Jonathan asked.

"It said—" she cleared her throat "—'I'd love to make you squeal.'"

She'd muttered the last part in a voice so low he could barely make it out. "That kind of talk has other connotations," he said. "Are you sure whoever wrote it meant it in a bad way?"

"It had a picture of a pig and was stuck to my seat with a pair of scissors."

Jonathan shoved his hands in his pockets. "I see how that might concern you. When was this?"

"Just after Colin came on last summer."

"Was it handwritten?"

"No, typed. In a really big font."

"It couldn't have been someone else?"

"No one else would do such a thing. I've worked with the rest of these attorneys for years. They all treat me great."

"Except Colin."

She seemed to wrestle with her answer. "He treats me okay part of the time. But his jokes can be…insensitive. You know, a snicker here or there about my weight. Or a subtle comment in the break room about leaving enough food for everybody else. A plastic padlock on the fridge." Her expression grew contemplative. "And there's something missing in his eyes. There are times when he looks at me as if he *hates* me. Just because I'm fat, I guess, since I've never done anything to hurt him. That day he asked me to make those copies?"

"Yeah?"

"I was in meetings all morning. How could I make copies if I wasn't even here? When he saw I was gone he should've made them himself instead of leaving me a message."

Okay, so Colin wasn't the kindest boss. But was he capable of nearly beating a boy to death? "I take it you won't be sorry if he gets handed his walking papers," Jonathan said.

"I can't say I'd miss him." She adjusted her blouse again. "You won't tell him I said that, though, will you?"

"Of course not."

A door opened down the hall, and a gentleman in his mid-fifties stepped out. Colin exited immediately afterward, looking so angry Jonathan suspected the meeting hadn't gone well for him.

"Misty, has FedEx come by this morning?" the older man asked.

"That's the boss," Misty whispered, pointing a finger she shielded from the man's sight with her body. "Not yet, Mr. Scovil," she replied, her smile bright and professional once she turned to face him. "Are you expecting a package?"

"I am. And I need it right away."

"I'll make sure you get it as soon as it arrives."

"Thanks." The man nodded in Jonathan's direction. "You waiting for me?"

"Actually, I was hoping for a word with Colin."

Mr. Scovil waved one hand in a manner that suggested he'd rather not even hear the name. "There you go," he grumbled and went back into his office. The bang of his door made Misty jump, but Colin seemed to ignore it.

"What are you doing here?" he asked.

"I was hoping to speak with you," Jonathan said.

"And you couldn't wait until I got home?"

"If it's a problem, I can meet you at your place later."

He hesitated, glanced at the closed door of his boss and motioned for Jonathan to follow him. "No, you're here now. Come on back."

"Thank you."

"What are *you* looking at," Colin barked at the receptionist.

She sank into her seat and avoided eye contact with him, but after they started down the hall, Jonathan could feel her gaze trailing after them.

"I have no idea what Misty was telling you, but that fat bitch doesn't know squat," Colin said as they entered his office.

Jonathan was grateful they were out of the poor woman's earshot. "So I shouldn't believe her when she says you'd never harm a child?"

"Wait a second." His step faltered, but Jonathan noticed that he wasted no time in closing the door. "You don't think—" his voice shifted up an octave "—you don't think *I* took Sam."

"I'm not sure who took her. But something happened the night Zoe had dinner with you. I want to know what it was."

Colin rounded his desk, loosened his tie and undid the top button of his shirt, but he didn't sit down. "My God, are you for real? First, I get some crap from my boss about being put on 'probation'—" he used his fingers to make quotation marks in the air "—and now you're accusing me of harming someone I care about? Am I having some sort of nightmare?"

"When you state it like that, it sounds more like a persecution complex to me."

"Screw you!"

Jonathan took a chair and stretched out his legs. "Zoe said she and Sam didn't really know you before this happened."

"So Zoe's behind this? She's pointing a finger at *me?* How could she do that? Who was it stayed up with her all night making those flyers, huh? Who took the heat from her sugar daddy when he was waiting for us the next morning? Who's been considering putting up the reward money? *Me,* that's who!"

Jonathan refrained from pointing out that he hadn't actually put any money on the line. What did *thinking* about it prove? "You didn't answer the question," he said calmly.

"Shit!" He slammed the chair into the desk, then threw up his hands. "I've got enough going wrong in my life. I don't need this. Zoe and I were neighbors, okay? Neighbors come together in the face of tragedy. But you're making me regret I ever tried to help. It just goes to show that no good deed goes unpunished."

"Are you doing good deeds, Colin?" Jonathan asked.

A vein stood out on his forehead. "Where is this coming from?"

"Zoe's clothes were askew when I found her in that motel room."

"So?"

"She was passed out on the bed. I can't imagine she'd undress herself, then put her clothes back on so haphazardly."

"I didn't even know she passed out."

"It was right after she'd been with you."

Incredulous, Colin shook his head. "*And* Tiffany. You're forgetting that part. How could I rape someone with my wife in the room?"

"Maybe she's not unfriendly to the idea. Or maybe she's afraid to stop you. Or maybe she just lets you get away with too much."

"You think you're so smart, don't you?" He kicked a small metal file cabinet, causing another resounding bang. "What's the matter, Mr. Stivers? You can't solve the mystery so you…you make some pathetic attempt to blame the closest bystander?"

Jonathan felt a muscle twitch in his cheek. Colin's volatility made it difficult to tell whether or not he was lying. But now that the conversation had gone in such a negative direction, Jonathan could only hope that if Colin knew anything about Sam, he'd get flustered enough to trip himself up. "What did you say to Zoe on the phone yesterday?" he asked, trying a different tack.

"When?"

"When you called her on her cell."

"I don't know what you're talking about."

He couldn't have forgotten already. "Yes, you do. You made a strange comment, yelled at her. I could tell from her reaction."

He pressed his lips together so tightly they turned white.

"Colin?"

"It was you, wasn't it." His voice and eyes were now deadpan, but instead of giving the impression that he'd regained control of his emotions, his behaviour suggested deeper feelings. Jonathan had just crossed a line that angered Colin even more.

"It was me what?"

"You were with her at barely eight in the morning. You've been sleeping with her! Her daughter's missing and you're offering her a shoulder to cry on just so you can get in her pants. That's rich, isn't it? And you're worried about *my* deeds!"

Jonathan battled the impulse to let his hands curl into fists. "Watch it…" he warned.

Colin's face jutted forward. "Oh, *you* can sling accusations, but I can't? Is that it?"

"Whether or not I'm sexually involved with Zoe has nothing to do with Sam's abduction."

Spittle shot from his mouth as he spoke. "Well, I don't have anything to do with it, either. So I suggest you get the hell out of here and do your fucking job!"

Jonathan knew if he stayed any longer he'd climb over Colin's desk and break his nose. But he wasn't done quite yet. Studying him, he got slowly to his feet. "If you've hurt Sam, I'll make you very, very sorry," he said and left.

Colin barely refrained from throwing his paperweight at Jonathan. How *dare* Zoe's investigator—her *lover*—show up at the firm! No doubt Misty was already gossiping about his visit to all the other attorneys, speculating on Colin's involvement. And this, after he'd organized that big search.

There was gratitude for you. It was almost as embarrassing as it was enraging.

Pacing behind his desk, Colin ground his teeth. Zoe's private eye thought he was so tough, didn't he? He didn't know anything, had no idea what Colin was capable of. But he was about to find out. Colin would never allow anyone to get the best of him. He'd turn on his own mother, if necessary—and had done exactly that, many times.

So how could he teach Jonathan a similar lesson? Mr. Scovil had just told him he had to finish the real estate contracts for Joseph Garundy before lunch or he'd be fired, but Colin wasn't about to let that crotchety old bastard dictate what he could and couldn't do. If he'd gotten a job here, he could get a job anywhere. He always landed on his feet.

His phone rang, but he didn't answer it. The jingle on his cell phone went off next, and he ignored that, too. He needed some time to think....

Pivoting, he started back across the room. Jonathan had complained about the state of Zoe's clothes. He'd acted as if he thought that detail might be related to Sam's disappearance. But what suggested there might be a connection? Nothing. He was just jealous, afraid Colin might've enjoyed a little pussy himself.

That it was the other way around grated on Colin. Jonathan had taken Zoe away from him when he'd been making some inroads. They'd been getting along fine before that trip to Los Angeles. It was Jonathan's fault she'd changed. But Jonathan would pay, and so would she. No woman led him on only to shut him down. He'd show them both just who they were messing with.

A light rap at the door brought his head up. Irritated by the interruption, he snapped, "What is it?"

Easily cowed, as always, Misty called through the door instead of opening it. "Your wife's on line one. She says it's an emergency."

The calls he'd missed. He should've taken them. "Got it." He pumped some cheer into his voice, but the receptionist didn't respond. She was on Jonathan's side, that fat bitch.

Sinking into his seat, he picked up the phone and hit the flashing button. "Hello?"

"Colin?"

Tiffany wasn't whispering, as she normally did when she called him from the nursing home.

"Hey, why aren't you at work?" he asked.

"I am at work. Well, actually, I'm sitting in my car. I'm on break, thank God."

Misty had said it was an emergency. "Why *thank God?* What's wrong?"

"Jonathan Stivers called me a second ago, that's what's wrong. He was asking some upsetting questions."

"I know. He came by here. Don't worry. I'll take care of it."

"How?"

Colin drummed his fingers on the desk. That was the question he'd been asking himself since Jonathan stalked out. But the answer was suddenly very clear. He needed to take the offensive, strike back. And he needed to do it fast, before Zoe's P.I. could get the better of him. "Call Zoe."

"Me?" Tiffany cried.

"Yes, you."

"And tell her what?"

"Tell her my father went missing. Tell her he drove his truck to the pool hall on Saturday night, then disappeared."

"Why would I say that?" Her voice rose. "That'd let her know there are two people who've disappeared from our lives in one week. Isn't that a little obvious?"

"No, it's ideal. Paddy had the opportunity to come into contact with Sam the same way we did. We'll simply hand them the connection they're looking for."

"I don't understand."

"You'll tell Zoe you first thought Paddy had gone on a binge. But when he didn't come back you began to wonder if he could be to blame for Sam's disappearance."

"Colin, no! I don't want to say that about Paddy."

He lowered his voice because he could hear two of the other attorneys talking in the hall outside his door. "Listen to me, damn it. I know what I'm doing. She's missing. He's missing. We can sell the fact that he took her and ran off."

"She disappeared before he did."

"Doesn't matter." Colin started the perpetual motion skier on his desktop as he quickly worked out the best way to spin the details to his benefit. "He was hiding her, but then I grew suspicious and began questioning him, and he took off."

"What would make you suspicious of your own father?"

"The way he talked about Sam the last time he came over."

"He never mentioned the neighbors...."

Colin rolled his eyes. Sometimes it took a while for Tiffany to catch on. "We'll say he did, stupid! We'll claim he often talked about how pretty Sam was."

"I'm not stupid, Colin. I hate it when you call me stupid."

To keep things simple, he tried to backtrack. "You're right. I'm sorry. I didn't mean it. I'm only trying to figure this out."

"That's what I'm doing, too. And I can't see why anyone would believe that about Paddy."

"They'll believe it because we'll insist he molested me while I was growing up. I'll say it happened to my sister, too."

"That's sick!"

He watched the skier move back and forth with such ease, as easy as the lie he was creating. "Exactly. The accusation alone will be enough to cast suspicion on him. We'll be providing the answer to both mysteries at once, and explaining why we seem to be involved."

"But your mom and sister will deny it, Colin. It's not as if the cops won't ask them."

He held the phone with his shoulder while buttoning his shirt and fixing his tie. "That's okay. Let them. The fact that my mother took my sister and moved away without a forwarding address will seem to support it."

"Tina and Courtney will blame *you* for that, not Paddy."

It might've bothered him to have Tiffany point that out—nothing angered him more than the fact that his mother and sister had abandoned him—but he was too excited about outsmarting Jonathan Stivers. Colin would be able to indulge his darkest fantasies and walk away without a hint of suspicion. Even better, Jonathan would lose Zoe, and he wouldn't be able to do a damn thing about it. "So? It'll be their word against mine. It's been that way all my life."

Tiffany didn't respond.

"What do you say?" he asked.

"Colin—"

"What?" He found a breath mint in his top drawer and popped it in his mouth. "Have I ever been wrong before?"

"No, but—" she huffed into the phone "—you don't think straight when it comes to Zoe."

"I'm willing to fulfill the promise I made you in the car yesterday. I'm asking if you'll do the same."

"I would, but…if we let Zoe know your father's missing, it could make her take a closer look at *us*. And no matter what you think it's not stupid to worry about that," she added, still peeved.

He grappled for patience. "Except that they're already taking a look at us, Tiff. We need to distract them with a likely scenario, deflect the attention. If Zoe hears about my dad from someone else she'll wonder why we never mentioned it and won't believe a damn thing we say ever again. This is the only way to retain some credibility."

She groaned. *"Really?"*

The resignation in her response made him feel as if the world was no longer off kilter. "Really. Then life can return to what we've always enjoyed. They'll never find Sam or Paddy, so it's not as if they'll be able to prove we're lying. And the damage to Paddy's reputation can't hurt him at this point."

"It'll hurt Sheryl," she said in a sulky voice.

He stifled the impulse to complain about her sudden loyalty to Sheryl. It drove him crazy, but they didn't have time for an argument. Tiffany had to call Zoe before Jonathan checked in with her. If they hurried, they could whisk her away, right out from under his nose. Otherwise, he'd insist on going to the cabin with her, and Colin preferred to avoid a direct confrontation.

"It can't hurt Sheryl," he insisted. "She won't believe it."

"She'll hate us."

"We don't need her!"

"What happens when Zoe tells the police what I said about Paddy?" she asked.

"It'll send them on a wild-goose chase."

"Except that wild-goose chase might lead right back to us! It'll lead to the cabin, at any rate, because that's the most obvious place to look."

"Tiff, Sam will be long gone by then. As soon as Misty goes to lunch, I'll slip out and head up that way. Tell Zoe that Paddy owns a cabin and you think that might be where he's keeping Sam. Then take her up there. I'll be waiting."

"I can't leave work in the middle of the day."

"Sure you can. Tell Hargraves that you're sick."

"What about you? You won't be able to get back before Misty returns from lunch."

"I'll tape a Do Not Disturb sign on the door. She won't even know I left."

"What if she comes in to deliver a message? The moment she sees you're gone she'll run straight to Mr. Scovil."

"I've made it clear to her that she's not to come in when I don't want her to. I'll say I'm going to be working all afternoon and don't want to be interrupted for any reason." When he didn't have the work done, he'd be in trouble. But that would happen later. After the meeting he'd just had with his boss, he doubted he could save his job, anyway. Although Scovil had been one of his biggest supporters, he'd become disenchanted over the past few months. Drawing out the end, forcing the firm to fire him instead of walking out, was the most Colin could hope for.

"They could still catch you…somehow."

"I'm not worried about my job. I'm sick of working here. I can find something better."

"I thought you loved it!"

He loved the image it gave him, but he could maintain that without them, if necessary. "This firm isn't my style. It's too restrictive. Maybe I'll open my own practice."

This met with stunned silence. Then she said, "You're changing, Colin."

"No, I'm not."

"It's the drugs, isn't it?"

"It's not the drugs. I haven't taken anything today. Will you calm down?"

"How will we get by without your paycheck?"

"We'll manage."

"But you just bought me this diamond ring!"

"Didn't you hear what I said? I'm sick of having my every move monitored. I hate it here. Do you care more about that than me?"

No response.

Pulling a hand mirror out of his desk drawer, he checked his hair and smoothed it down. He'd let Scovil and Stivers upset him, but he shouldn't have. He could get away with anything. His mother had always hated that about him. "Tiffany?"

"What?"

"Will you help me or not?"

"I don't think we should kidnap Zoe."

"Why not?"

"It's too…bold."

"We can pin it on Paddy. It'll be easy. You wait and see."

"Colin, please… I want to solve our problems, not make them worse."

He stopped the skier and sprang to his feet. "We had a deal, Tiffany. After this, it'll all be over, like we agreed. But you have to trust me. I can't get us out of this if you won't work with me."

"We can't go to the cabin. Zoe will call the police and they'll head right up there."

"Doesn't matter. Giving them one wrong turn will get them lost for at least an hour. You know what it's like. By the time they reach the cabin, I'll have Sam and Zoe and be outta there."

"Where will you go?"

"I'll talk Tommy into getting me his cousin's rental house in Chester."

"And where will *I* be?" she asked.

There was that jealousy again. He was getting tired of it. How many times did he have to reassure her? "You'll be waiting to relate the terrible tale of how you arrived at the cabin to find my father with Sam. You'll say he pulled a rifle on you, forced Sam and Zoe into a car you didn't recognize and took off."

"No! We can't get away with it!"

"Sure we can. We'll muss your hair, scratch you up a bit, make it look like you fought to save them. You'll be a hero. And I'll have what I want, too."

"What *you* want," she said.

He ignored the bitterness he heard in that comment. "It's perfect. So, will you call her?"

"Now?"

"Of course."

"Tell me again why I'm doing this?" she said.

He smiled. "Because you love me."

33

Jonathan stood inside Colin Bell's living room and turned off his cell phone so it couldn't surprise him when he least expected it. He knew Colin and Tiffany were at work—he'd spoken to each of them—but there was no guarantee they wouldn't come home for lunch. Or that Colin wouldn't get himself fired from Scovil, Potter & Clay and be asked to pack up his desk and leave.

Slipping the tool he'd used to break in via the back door into his pocket, he donned a pair of latex gloves and looked around. He was taking a risk by being here. If he got caught, he could be charged with breaking and entering. But he had little hope that going the legal route would work at this particular moment. There wasn't enough evidence to justify a search warrant. He had nothing—except a very bad feeling about the Bells and a sense of urgency—probably because he'd heard from Jasmine again, right after he'd spoken to Tiffany, and she'd been frantic.

She said he needed to find Sam *now.*

That gave him no time to go through other channels. A warrant could take days, if it happened at all.

A quick look around was the quickest, most efficient way to achieve his goal. And he didn't feel too guilty about it. If he was right about the Bells, this could save

Sam's life. If he was wrong, there'd be no harm done, especially if he was careful.

Vacuum strokes scored the carpet, and the place smelled mildly of lemon furniture polish and other cleaning supplies. That meshed with what he'd seen from the front door when he'd spoken to Colin on previous occasions, so it didn't seem unusual. But he knew this level of cleanliness wouldn't bode well for finding any residue of Sam's presence—if she'd ever been here. Jasmine insisted she was in a forest somewhere, but if Tiffany had kidnapped her—which had to be the case since Colin hadn't been home at the time—Sam would've been in this house at some point.

An extensive search provided no proof of it, however. Except for the master bedroom, the rooms upstairs were mostly devoid of furniture, which made them easy to check. One had a desk and scrapbooking materials in plastic organizer drawers—obviously a crafts room for Tiffany. Another, heavily soundproofed, had a set of drums and nothing else. But that wasn't surprising, either. Young couples often furnished only the main rooms of the house until they had children or some other reason to spend the extra money.

The mirror affixed to the ceiling of the master bedroom might be a tacky addition, but certainly wasn't proof of wrongdoing. And he saw nothing kinkier than that, nothing he would've expected to find in the home of a man who could torture a child for months.

Thirty minutes later, after going through every nook and cranny including the attic and garage, Jonathan returned to the living room. He'd discovered some sleeping pills in the cupboard over the refrigerator. They were the same brand as the ones Zoe had supposedly bought the night he found her in the motel room. But it was a very common brand, so that wasn't incriminating in itself.

He'd also noticed a mattress leaning against the wall in the garage—probably a hand-me-down—and some dog food. A large sack that was open and partially used, it called to mind Toby's claim that he'd been treated like a dog, especially because the Bells didn't seem to have any animals. But for all Jonathan knew, Colin and Tiffany occasionally agreed to dog-sit for a friend.

Regardless, Sam wasn't here. There wasn't a single solid indication that she ever had been. And he'd seen nothing to make him believe Colin and Tiffany were anything other than what they appeared to be.

Shit. He was going to lose this one, was going to lose *Sam.* Zoe's child….

Every heartbeat pounded like a fist as he closed his eyes. He'd never felt so frustrated, so helpless or so inadequate. Apparently, he'd been wasting his time today, chasing a very unlikely culprit, just when Sam needed him most.

Maybe it was the discouragement, or the fact that he was preoccupied hashing over every detail of the past week, wondering where he'd gone wrong and what he could've done better, but he didn't realize someone was home until he heard the jingle of keys.

And by then, there was no time to get out.

Where was Jonathan? After what she'd learned from Tiffany Bell, Zoe desperately wanted to reach him. But she'd tried his cell at least a dozen times, and her calls kept going to voice mail.

She'd just left him another message and was leaving one for Detective Thomas, as well, when Tiffany's call—the call she'd been waiting for—came in. "Hello?"

"I have the directions," Tiffany announced, more somber than strident.

The adrenaline pouring through Zoe's system

brought a quaver to her voice. "So you think you can find it?"

"The cabin's pretty remote, but…" Her sigh seemed nervous. But Zoe could understand why she might feel out of her element. It was a serious accusation she'd launched against Colin's father. "…I've been there before and can probably manage. I just worry that I could be wrong. In a way, I hope I am. But, God, it would be terrible to make this kind of mistake."

"I appreciate your willingness to come forward. I know it couldn't have been an easy decision."

"It feels *really* disloyal. I hate it. But Colin wanted me to call you just in case."

"How many times did Paddy mention Sam?"

"Over the months? A few. He said…well, you know, that she was pretty."

Zoe couldn't help wincing at the way he must've meant that compliment.

"Still, I never would've thought anything of it, even after he went missing," Tiffany explained, "if Colin hadn't reminded me of…of his own childhood. It's really Colin you have to thank. He's the one who remembered the cabin, too."

Guilt made Zoe repent the negative thoughts she'd entertained about her neighbor. He'd had a horribly abusive childhood. It was astonishing that he'd turned out as normal as he had.

"And the cabin's surrounded by pine trees? It's in the mountains?" She knew it was, but she had to hear it again.

"Yes."

Jasmine had told Jonathan that Sam was in a forest. It all fit. The second Zoe had received Tiffany's initial call, her intuition had told her this was it. She'd found her daughter—or would, soon.

Now it was just a matter of getting to Sam as soon as possible.

"It's the best lead we've had so far, definitely worth a shot," Zoe said. Maybe her gut was wrong, but after spending all morning with Toby, who could barely recall his own name, let alone the name of the man who'd beaten him, Zoe was willing to take almost any risk if it might bring her daughter home.

"I don't know," Tiffany mused. "I'm sort of having second thoughts."

"About what?"

"About taking you with me. Maybe you should stay here and let me go by myself. I could call you."

"There's cell reception?"

"Not at the cabin, but…I'd just drive partway back."

That could take forever. What if Sam needed her mother? "No, I want to be there. You shouldn't go alone, anyway."

"Oh, Paddy would never hurt me. He's not like that."

He was if he was the man who'd nearly killed Toby. "I hope you're right."

"I could ask Colin to come with me instead," Tiffany suggested.

Zoe dug at her cuticles. It might be good if he joined them, in case Paddy got violent. Tiffany said Paddy wasn't like that, but Zoe wasn't convinced. "Is he available?"

"Not yet, but we could wait until he gets off work."

"No, we can't put it off." Zoe had too much riding on this. Sam was at the cabin, in the forest. She had to be. Everything Tiffany said made sense. Zoe had talked to someone at the police station who'd confirmed that a missing person's report had been filed for a Paddy Bell. Even the questions Jonathan had asked her this morning lent credibility to Tiffany's words. The Bells *were* involved—just not the way he'd suspected.

She couldn't wait to tell him it wasn't Colin and Tiffany but *Paddy* Bell who was at fault.

If Paddy was the one at fault.

"You're *sure* you want to come?" Tiffany asked.

Zoe could tell she wasn't very excited about the idea. She was probably as afraid of what they'd find, and what it would mean, as Zoe. "I'm sure."

"Okay, then. I'm turning in to the hospital to pick you up. Do you see me?"

Zoe stepped away from the building and shaded her eyes. Sure enough, Tiffany's blue BMW was at the main entrance. "Yes, I see you. I'm standing right in front."

"There you are." Coming to a stop, she hung up without saying goodbye but offered Zoe a tentative smile when she opened the door.

"I can't tell you much I appreciate this," Zoe said.

Tiffany wiped the sweat beading on her upper lip and adjusted the air-conditioning vents while Zoe got in and fumbled with her seat belt. "No problem."

"Colin knows we're going without him?"

Tiffany nodded. "He called the police about Paddy, too."

"Good. At least there are people who know where we're heading, and Colin will be around to give them directions."

Tiffany adjusted the vents again. "Did you get hold of your P.I.?"

Zoe finally managed to fasten her seat belt. "Not yet."

"That's too bad."

The doors locked automatically as Tiffany gave the car some gas.

Just get her out of town... Just get her out of town... Just get her out of town. Then Colin will be there, and he can take over.

Tiffany tried to remain calm, but she was sweating so

much she was nearly soaked, and the anxiety made her stomach ache. Maybe Colin had killed a previous pet up at the cabin, but only because he'd gotten carried away. It was the drugs, pushing him into an act he hadn't really meant to carry out. He'd let his first pet go along the highway in Utah, and he wouldn't have harmed Rover if Rover had obeyed.

This was different. It was the first time she'd purposely lured someone off to be killed, knowing in advance exactly what would happen.

But she wanted this. Somehow, she hated Zoe as she'd never hated anyone. Zoe had stolen Colin. Maybe she hadn't done it intentionally, but ever since he'd become infatuated with her he hadn't been the same. Zoe threatened everything Tiffany loved, everything Tiffany had. Zoe needed to go. And Tiffany wanted Colin to do it, to prove he cared more for her than he did their former neighbor.

That did little to ease the fear, however. There were so many things that could go wrong. She kept imagining Jonathan Stivers calling Zoe on the cell phone Zoe held on her lap. He could insist they stop and wait for him. Or that detective who'd been involved could do the same. Tiffany had been lying when she said she'd notified the police. She'd only been hoping to learn if Zoe had already contacted them herself—and to stop her if she planned to.

Just get her out of town. If they could reach the mountains, they'd lose reception and Tiffany could relax. A little bit, anyway.

Eyeing her own cell phone, which rested on the console, she finally broke down and called Colin. She had to have some idea of where he was, some assurance that he'd be able to escape the office when he thought he could.

"Hi, how's work this afternoon?" she asked when he

answered. She made sure her voice sounded casual, but she hoped he'd clue in to what she was really asking, and he didn't disappoint her.

"I'm not at the cabin yet," he said. "I ran home to get the credit card on my desk. I'll need some way to pay for groceries and gas. And that put me behind."

He must've left it when he'd ordered those bondage implements over the Internet for their party with his friends. The package had arrived the following day—express courier—but she hadn't seen it since Paddy died and Colin had scrubbed the house from top to bottom. All the toys they owned were gone. Colin had cleaned out everything, including the bonus room. "Where—where did you put the things in that box that was delivered last week?"

"What things?"

"You know, the party favors for Friday night that you ordered over the Internet."

"Oh, they're safe, in my trunk."

He was bringing them with him. Tiffany's stomach gave another painful lurch as she imagined the night ahead. She wanted Zoe dead, but she didn't want to watch Colin have sex with her first. If he acted too kind or loving, it'd break her heart. And, even if he wasn't loving, even if he only wanted to hurt her, Tiffany had no desire to watch. She didn't have the appetite for torture that he did. He found it funny, exhilarating, stimulating. He achieved some sort of sexual gratification from making others scream and cry. But it just made her sick.

She wondered if he'd let her leave or if he'd demand she watch.

Or participate…

Or help bury the bodies…

She stifled a shudder.

"Tiff?" Colin said.

"What?"

"Zoe's with you, right?"

"Yes. She's here. We're on our way."

Zoe glanced over and smiled. She was nervous, too, Tiffany realized. She seemed intensely focused and hardly talked at all, which was fine. Tiffany couldn't manage much of a conversation at the moment. She was too afraid she'd sound strange or make a revealing comment, accidentally alerting Zoe that the situation was not what she'd represented it to be. Tiffany knew how quickly an errand such as this could go bad. Take Rover, for instance.

"How close are you to the cabin?" Colin asked.

"Another hour or so."

"Then you need to slow down. Misty was late going to lunch today. The first freakin' day she isn't dying to feed her fat face at exactly noon. Can you believe it? Anyway, I think I'm behind you."

No! Not behind. She wanted to get this over with, turn Zoe over to her husband as soon as possible.

Tiffany checked her speed but didn't dare ease off the gas. She could always pretend to get lost once they exited the freeway and were out of range of any cell towers. "I hope he didn't do it, either," she said randomly, for Zoe's benefit.

"Tell Colin I'm so grateful for his support," Zoe murmured.

Tiffany gritted her teeth against the jealousy that welled up. "She says to tell you she's grateful for your support."

"Tell her I'd do anything for her," he said with a satisfied chuckle.

"He hopes it helps," she said instead and hung up.

Her eyebrows furrowed in an expression of concern, Zoe nodded and stared straight ahead.

Then Zoe's cell phone rang. It was a wrong number,

but it still put Tiffany on edge. Because she knew Jonathan Stivers or Detective Thomas could call at any moment….

Whoever had come home and nearly surprised Jonathan hadn't stayed long. Just as the door opened, he'd dashed into the garage, where he'd only had to wait a minute before a car that'd been left running in the drive pulled away. He wasn't sure if it was Tiffany or Colin. He hadn't been willing to risk detection in order to look. He'd provoked Colin after the man had nearly been fired; he wasn't about to hand him a big stick.

It didn't matter who'd come home, anyway. It only mattered that he hadn't been seen. That gave him the chance to get out, and he immediately did just that.

But he wasn't happy about the wasted time. Colin and Tiffany were young, attractive, successful. Not your average pedophiles. What had he been thinking following up on such a long shot?

He unlocked his car, which he'd parked around the block so it wouldn't be seen on Colin's street.

He'd been thinking he'd solved the mystery, of course. But now he just felt foolish. If Colin was as twisted as the man who'd attacked Toby, there would've been some sign of it in his house—videotapes, pictures, pornography, sex toys, *something*—especially if his wife was aware of his perversion and he didn't have to hide.

"What a waste," he grumbled and turned on his phone. He had an appointment with Detective Thomas at 1:30 p.m. and wanted to check the time. Fortunately, he still had an hour, but he'd missed a slew of calls, most of which had come from Zoe.

Eager to find out what was so urgent, he called her right away. And she answered on the first ring.

"What's going on?" he asked. He hoped Toby had revealed some specific information about the man who'd hurt him, enough that they could catch the bastard. He heard Jasmine's voice echoing in his head—*You need to find her, Jon. You need to find her now*—but he was no closer to saving Sam than he'd been the day she disappeared.

"Didn't you get my messages?" she asked.

"Not yet." Deciding to call her instead, he hadn't listened to his voice mail messages.

"Where are you?"

"On my way to Truckee. We've got a lead on Sam." The words came in a breathless rush.

"What?" His hand froze halfway to the ignition. That was exactly what he'd been hoping. "Because of Toby?"

"No. Toby still has a lot of healing to do. He's not completely coherent yet, and the doctors don't want us bothering him, anyway. His condition is too fragile."

"So where did this lead come from?"

"Right next door."

"You're *kidding!*"

"It's not what you think, though," she hurried on. "Colin's father, a man named Paddy Bell, has a history of pedophilia. He molested Colin while he was growing up. His sister, too."

"No…"

"Yes, but Colin and Tiffany thought that was old news. A terrible period that ended when Colin's mother found out and left him." She paused. "Until he went missing on Friday night."

Jonathan let his head fall back. "Colin's *father* went missing?"

"Yes."

"What happened to him?"

"We're not completely sure. We think he's on the run.

Colin saw a news report on Toby, noticed that the boy was kidnapped from his father's neighborhood and mentioned it to him."

Jonathan watched a middle-aged man drive by in a car that needed a muffler. "And then?"

"A day or so later, Colin realized that his father also knew Sam, or knew of her. Paddy had even mentioned her a few times."

Jonathan's blood ran cold. No wonder he hadn't been able to solve the case. There was nothing to give Paddy Bell away. He was too distantly connected.

"When he started asking Paddy about Sam, it must've made Paddy nervous, because he took off not long after," she said.

"Why didn't Colin tell me this when I saw him a couple hours ago?"

"I've got Tiffany here. Let me see what she says."

Zoe asked her the question, and Jonathan could hear Colin's wife's response.

"He wasn't sure," Tiffany was saying. "We were both hoping that…that we were wrong and he'd show up. No one wants to accuse a family member of something like that. If he's just off with another woman, he'll never forgive Colin, or me, for bringing up the past and ruining his reputation. But when Mr. Stivers came by the firm and then called me, we both realized we had to take that chance."

Jonathan felt bad for the way he'd behaved in Colin's office. The guy had already been having a bad day. And, happily married or not, Colin had a crush on Zoe, which complicated matters. Not surprising that he hadn't wanted to reveal what he suspected of his father.

At least he'd done the right thing in the end. "So we know who might've taken her and we think she might be in Truckee?" he asked Zoe.

"Jasmine mentioned a forest, remember?"

How could he forget? It had been on his mind all day. "I remember."

"Paddy owns a cabin in the mountains outside Truckee."

"Holy shit." Spurred into action, he jammed his key into the ignition. "I'm coming. Where are you?"

"We just passed Auburn."

"Who's *we?* You and Tiffany?"

"Yes. We're in her car."

He pulled into the street, heading for Interstate 80. "And Colin?"

"He's still at work."

Of course. Jonathan had seen the way Scovil had treated him, knew he'd probably lose his job if he left. "Where should we meet?"

"We can't stop, Jonathan. We can't even slow down. I'm too frantic."

"Zoe, I know what you're feeling. But I'd rather be with you. We have no idea what you might find."

"Can't you just meet us there?"

He knew no amount of warning would convince her to stop now that she thought Sam was so close. She'd walk through fire if she had to. And he wasn't that far behind. He could catch up or arrive shortly afterward. "Okay. Where is it?"

"Here, I'll let Tiffany give you directions."

"Have you notified the police?" he asked before Zoe could pass the phone.

"I've left a message for Detective Thomas. I think we're covered. Colin reported it, too."

"Great. Let me talk to Tiffany, then."

"I'll see you there."

"Whatever happens, Zoe..." He wasn't quite sure what he wanted to say. He hated the thought of her finding Sam in Toby's condition—or worse. He wished she'd let him shield her. But every minute mattered; he understood that. "…I'll be there as soon as I can."

"Okay." She sniffed and he knew she was crying. "Thanks."

He reached the freeway while he was talking to Tiffany and nearly floored the gas pedal—only to be slowed by traffic through Lincoln a few minutes later. After he hung up, he continued to drive as fast as traffic would allow. But he didn't see Tiffany's BMW anywhere along the interstate.

And although he followed the directions Tiffany had given him very carefully, he couldn't find the cabin.

34

The only thing wrong with his plan was that he didn't have the time to implement it properly, Colin thought. He had to rush, and he was running late.

He'd sent a text to Tiffany telling her to waste half an hour and she'd responded with "HURRY!!!" But there was nothing he could do to get there any faster. He'd had to stop by Tommy's cousin's house before he left Sacramento to pick up keys to the rental he'd asked to use. The house, little more than a shack, was in Chester, not Tahoe or Truckee, which meant he had a long drive ahead of him after he grabbed Zoe and Sam. But it would be worth it. Using someone else's place meant there'd be no records of any kind, and Tommy's cousin was a distant enough contact that he probably didn't even know Colin's full name. Bill Bristol was lending it out for the whole week on the promise that Tommy would make it up to him by letting him use his sandrail for a summer trip. And Colin was making it up to Tommy by letting him use Tiffany for two nights this week while he was gone. He'd tried to whittle his side of the trade down to one night, but Tommy had driven a hard bargain and Colin had been too desperate not to agree.

Now he just needed to convince Tiffany to do whatever Tommy wanted. He'd promised she'd be open and completely flexible. He'd even drawn some graphic images to encourage Tommy to jump on the deal. Hopefully, that diamond he'd bought his wife yesterday would help make her amenable. He'd get her another present, if necessary. Maybe a new car. And he'd remind her that once this week was over, Zoe would be gone for good and so would Sam.

Because he'd been speeding, Colin checked his rearview mirror for cops, breathed easier when he didn't see any and eased over toward the next exit. He was almost at the cabin. Once he took care of business in Tahoe and reached Chester, he'd be safe. He'd have to drive back to Sacramento and put in an appearance here and there over the next few days, just to let everyone know he hadn't gone missing along with his father, Zoe and Sam. But he could blame the long hours he spent away from home on the fact that he was so busy searching for his father.

God, he couldn't have set it up any better.

Sam heard her name as if from a great distance. She was swimming deep beneath the water, enjoying its shimmer and smoothness, and ignored the voice that was calling her. Somehow she could breathe, stay under as long as she wanted, which should've told her it wasn't real. But she didn't care about real. She just wanted to be comfortable.

She would've stayed right where she was, but her mother stood at the water's edge, telling her she needed to talk to her immediately.

Fighting hard to obey, she struggled to lift her heavy eyelids and gazed up at the blurry image looming over her. "Mom?" she said, her voice a mere croak.

"Oh, good. I thought you were dead."

That was Colin's voice. And he didn't sound as if he

really cared one way or another. Maybe that was why he'd abandoned her. She'd eaten the granola bars he'd left and drunk the water, then used whatever energy she had to dig at the spike that held her in place. But it had been no use. She was too weak to free herself.

For the past—she didn't know how many hours—she'd slipped in and out of consciousness, listening to the flies buzz. They landed on her all the time, tickling her cheek, her forehead, her arms and legs, but she couldn't even swat them away. "You're…evil," she said.

"Sticks and stones," he responded with a laugh. "Anyway, I've got some good news."

"You're dying of…cancer?" Her eyelids closed again—it was too much trouble to keep them open—but she managed a smile at her own joke. She had to be delirious to provoke him, but she was too numb to care, too numb to feel fear.

"Ha. You're funny, you know that?"

"And you're…a…a dumb fathead."

Shoot. Couldn't she come up with a better insult? Not in her current state. Her mouth was so dry she could hardly speak.

"Oh, yeah? If I'm such a fathead, how come I'm the one in control? You're in a suitcase, where you've been peeing on yourself."

She curled up. "I'd still…rather be me."

He laughed again. "Deathly sick? Wearing a *collar?* Staked to the ground? And smelling like shit?"

"At least—" she licked her cracked lips "—I'm worth loving."

"What a little bitch you are!" The tenor of his voice told her that her words had stung. It was a small victory, but with Colin a victory was a victory.

"You'd rather I was…stupid…like Tiffany?"

"What do you mean by that?"

"…thinking you're…some…something special?"

"If you don't shut up, I'll kill you before your mother even gets here," he snapped.

At this, she dragged in her first sharp breath. "What'd you say?"

"I said you stink like a pig."

"What about my mother?"

He didn't repeat it. He left and returned with a container of water, which he poured over her to rinse away the urine. Then he carried her to his car, put her in the passenger seat and handcuffed the end of her chain to the steering wheel.

Zoe was frantic by the time Tiffany found the cabin. It'd taken them more than two hours to reach a place they should've been able to get to in an hour and a half. But as they drove through the trees and the wooden A-frame appeared in front of her, fear overtook frustration.

"There's no car," she said.

"I don't see one," Tiffany agreed.

"Then Paddy can't be here. No one could reach this place without transportation. It's too remote."

Tiffany didn't respond.

"So…what now?" She was asking herself more than Tiffany, asking herself if she could deal with the disappointment.

"We should look around, don't you think?" Tiffany said. "See if anyone's been here?"

Zoe nodded. *Please, God, help me find my child. And let her be okay.*

Tiffany opened her door. "Maybe…maybe you should stay here for a minute. You know, just in case."

Zoe's heart lodged in her throat. Just in case…what? Just in case they found her daughter dead?

The macabre image that rose in her mind nearly made her throw up. "No, I'll come. G-give me a minute." She put her head between her knees to reestablish her equilibrium.

"You don't look so good. Stay here." Tiffany hopped out before Zoe could conquer the sudden nausea. Now that the cabin seemed to be empty she'd lost the sense of urgency that'd propelled her this far. Fear and dread acted like fifty-pound weights on each limb, making it difficult to move. Why not let Tiffany tell her if it was safe to look? Zoe didn't want her last memory of Sam to be the sight that might very well greet her if she walked through that door….

So she watched Colin's wife hurry to the cabin and disappear inside. Then she coaxed herself to lean back and draw deep breaths while she waited. She had to be prepared for the worst, had to be ready to bear up under…whatever.

Fortunately, Jonathan would be coming soon. Knowing that made the situation just a little easier.

But no car pulled in behind the BMW. And, a moment later, Tiffany emerged from the cabin and crossed over to a ramshackle outbuilding without even glancing up.

What was going on? Tiffany knew how anxious Zoe was….

Impatient, she opened her car door and got out. Her knees felt less than steady as she stumbled toward the shed, but determination kept her moving. "Sam, be alive. Be alive, baby," she whispered.

Before Zoe could make it halfway across the clearing, Tiffany came out and let the spring-loaded door slam behind her.

"Anything?" Zoe asked hopefully.

"She was in there, all right." Tiffany gestured behind her.

Zoe's eyes zeroed in on the shed and her vision narrowed until it was all she could see. "How do you know?"

"There's some granola wrappers and an old blanket inside."

That was it? How did that tell Tiffany anything? Anyone could've left some trash. "But no—" she swallowed hard, made her mouth form the word "*—body?*"

"No." She beckoned Zoe toward her. "Come see for yourself."

Something was wrong. Tiffany had stepped out of the car as one person—solicitous, worried, sweet—and returned as another. Her eyes glittered with some emotion Zoe hadn't seen earlier, and her nostrils flared as if she was extremely agitated or excited.

Zoe managed a smile that felt too tight on her face. "That's okay. We'd better get the police."

Tiffany's eyes widened, and her nostrils flared again. "You don't want to see what I found?"

"I wouldn't want to destroy any forensic evidence." She took a step back. "If Sam's not here, the police will be better equipped to deal with any leads your father-in-law might've left."

Tiffany glanced behind her. "But…but you drove all this way."

To find Sam. To save her, if possible. But Tiffany had just said Sam wasn't here. "I'll go over every detail with the police."

"But there's—" she frowned, glanced behind her again "—something you should see."

"What is it?"

"Take a look." Hoping Jonathan would arrive, Zoe twisted around to check the road again. But the dust kicked up by their tires had long since settled and there was no sound—nothing but the drone of insects.

"I don't want to."

"You don't have to go all the way *inside,*" Tiffany

said. "Just poke your head in. Maybe you'll recognize the swimsuit top I saw in there."

If she'd spotted a girl's swimsuit top, why didn't she grab it and bring it out?

You have a...really nice wife.

Except when she's helping me murder someone.

Considering the way Tiffany was looking at her, that snatch of conversation no longer felt like a dream. And there were other gut-level reactions rushing in on Zoe, like the revulsion, fear and dizziness she suddenly associated with her time at the Bells' house.

Jonathan... She should've waited for him.

"Don't be difficult," Tiffany said. "It'll just make this tougher."

"Make what tougher?" Zoe calculated the distance to the driver's side of the car. Had Tiffany taken the keys out of the ignition? She didn't think so.

"The...surprise."

"The only surprise I want is my daughter."

Tiffany lowered her voice. "I promise you'll see her again if you come with me."

Even if that was true, Zoe wouldn't be able to save Sam, not if Tiffany's *surprise* was anything like she now suspected. Zoe had begun to sense a strange malevolence in her former neighbor.

She needed to get help, or she'd cost Sam any chance she had. "Jonathan will be here soon," she said as if his name served as some sort of talisman.

Tiffany smiled triumphantly. "Of course he will. *If he doesn't get lost.*"

Oh God! It was Tiffany who'd given Jonathan directions. Zoe hadn't even listened to what she'd told him. She'd been too preoccupied, too sure they had it all figured out.

Her eyes darted to the shed, and she saw the door move an inch or so. Someone was peeking out at her. It had to be Colin. He wasn't at work. That was an alibi. He was there, waiting for them….

Was her daughter in that shed, too? The mere possibility made Zoe want to rush over, regardless of Colin. But she couldn't walk right into his grasp. She could be the only hope her daughter had left.

Turning on her heel, Zoe dashed for the car. She'd nearly wrenched open the door when Tiffany caught her, but then they both fell, wrestling, to the dusty earth. The slam of the same door she'd heard earlier told Zoe that Tiffany had reinforcements coming, but she hoped to inflict some damage before she was outnumbered.

Kicking and clawing, she distilled all her pent up rage and anguish into hurting the person who'd kidnapped her daughter—and knew she'd hit her target when Tiffany screamed.

"Colin, help me! She's gone crazy!"

"I won't let you get away with it," Zoe growled. Then she sank her teeth into Tiffany's shoulder, drawing blood before Colin could drag her off.

Where could the cabin be? Jonathan had followed Tiffany's directions to the letter, but he found himself deep in the Sierra Nevadas, where there was no cell service and no landline, either.

"Shit!" He slugged the dashboard and the radio came on, pumping out static since he couldn't pick up a clear signal. What the hell should he do now? He had no idea where Sam was, where Zoe was, or how to find them. He hated to backtrack, since he was sure they had to be close. But, in the end, he had to do just that. After returning to the freeway, he drove down the mountain a few miles, where he could place a call.

“Scovil, Potter & Clay.”

He pulled out the card he’d taken from the receptionist’s desk earlier. “Misty?”

“Yes?”

“This is Jonathan Stivers.”

“Oh, hello Mr. Stivers.”

He ignored the added warmth in her voice. “Is Colin still around?”

“Yes, but…he’s in his office working and told me not to disturb him.”

“This is an emergency.”

“Wow, another one?”

“He’s had others?”

“His wife had one earlier today, and she called with another emergency last week.”

He was so intent on getting hold of Colin that he almost skimmed over that comment. But two emergencies in such a short time did seem a little odd. “What kind of emergencies?”

“This morning Tiffany said she’d been in a car accident.”

Oh God. Jonathan pulled off at the next exit and sat on the shoulder of the road. “Is everyone okay?”

“Everyone? I’m pretty sure she was alone.”

“When was this?”

“Not too long after you left the office.”

He let his breath go. That must’ve been before Zoe got in with her. And she’d been fine at that point, so…the accident was probably just a fender bender. “What about the other emergency?”

“Last week? Colin’s mother fell and hurt herself.”

Jonathan hadn’t heard anything about Colin’s mother—only his father. “What day did this call come in?”

“Let’s see…I can tell if I flip back through my calendar,” she said. “Here it is. Monday. I’d just gotten my hair trimmed and Colin walked in and gave me a dirty look."

Monday. Zoe had lost her daughter on the same day. Was that a coincidence? It could be. But wouldn't most people have mentioned it if their mother had been hurt? Zoe had said Colin's mother had left her husband once she'd learned of his abuse.... Maybe she and her son weren't close. Or maybe she hadn't been too badly hurt in that fall.

"Thanks," he said. "Can you ring Colin?"

"He won't like it," she complained.

"I'll tell him I made you do it. He'll understand. I promise. This is really important."

She sighed into the phone. "Okay, I'll do it for you. But you owe me, and that might mean lunch."

Jonathan opened his mouth to tell her he wasn't in the market. He had no objection to taking her out. She was a nice enough girl. But he was already committed. And this time it wasn't Sheridan who came to mind. "I'm happy to buy you a meal, but...just so you know, Misty, I have a girlfriend."

"The good ones are always taken," she grumbled. "Hang on."

He waited so long he thought she'd gotten on another line and forgotten about him.

Finally, Misty picked up again. "Jonathan?"

"Yes?"

"He must've left. But I don't know when. He didn't come past me."

"Can you do me one more favor and check the parking lot?"

"I already did," she said. "His car's gone."

That was where she'd been. What a sweetheart. "So, you have no idea when he left."

"None. But I can tell you this. Chances are good he won't be coming back. Mr. Scovil heard me asking about him and went through the roof."

Had Colin decided to go to the cabin after all? "Can you give me his cell-phone number?"

"I'm not supposed to share that information, not without permission."

"Come on, Misty. This is about that little girl we're trying to find."

"But if Colin doesn't like it, he'll get some sort of revenge."

"He's not coming back, remember? And I won't tell him how I came by the number. I could probably get it some other way. I just don't have time."

"All right, give me a sec…."

He imagined her thumbing through her Rolodex.

"Here it is."

He entered it in his BlackBerry as she rattled it off. "Perfect. Thanks, Misty."

"Too bad you've got a girlfriend," she said and disconnected.

He chuckled to himself as he dialed the number, but the worry he'd felt before returned when Colin didn't pick up. Every call went directly to voice mail. Had Colin been the one who'd come home while Jonathan was in the garage? If so, he must not have gone back to work.

Trying to figure out what to do next, he tapped the steering wheel. He had to get to that cabin. But how?

Maybe Paddy had remarried….

As it turned out, directory assistance had a Paddy Bell in Antelope, where Toby had been kidnapped. A woman answered almost as soon as the phone rang.

"Hello?" She sounded anxious. Hopeful.

"Is this Mrs. Bell?"

"Yes, it is."

"You're married to Paddy Bell, Colin Bell's father?"

"That's right."

"This is Jonathan Stivers. I'm a private detective investigating the kidnapping of—"

"My husband?" she cut in. "Has my husband been kidnapped? Is that where he is?"

He released his seat belt.

"Not that I know of, ma'am. A young girl, who was living next door to your stepson, went missing last Monday, and I've been searching for her ever since."

"Next door to Colin?" She seemed puzzled. "Curious he didn't mention it. Maybe there's a connection between her and my Paddy," she said with tears in her voice. "Where are all these people going, anyway? The Simpson boy was taken from the school just down the street. I don't understand."

"Colin believes your husband might've kidnapped Samantha Duncan."

"*What?* He doesn't even know the girl. What would he want with her?"

Hoping for a cool breeze, Jonathan lowered the window. "Colin claims your husband is a—"

"No!" she cried before he could finish.

"Yes."

"That's a lie! I know Paddy better than anyone else does. He's not a predator. He's a good man!"

That wind he'd been hoping for stirred his hair. "You've never heard of him abusing his children while they were growing up?"

"Of course not! That's crazy. You can ask his first wife. She'll tell you Paddy was a keeper. She says it to me all the time. She says their marriage would've worked if not for Colin."

"What did Colin do?"

"He was a difficult kid, a troubled kid."

"How troubled?"

"It depends on who you ask. Tina—his mother—thinks he's the equivalent of Damien. Paddy thinks Colin's issues come from the fact that they were too hard on him."

"Do you happen to have Tina's number, Mrs. Bell?"

"I do. I've called her myself since Paddy disappeared. I consider her a friend. Just a minute." He heard her rummage around before coming back on the line.

"Here you go."

When she'd given him the number, he thanked her, but she stopped him before he could disconnect.

"Mr. Stivers?"

"Yes."

"I can tell you what Tina's going to say before you call her. She moved away to escape Colin, not Paddy. Courtney, her daughter, will confirm it."

Jonathan dropped his head in his hand. Colin, the man he'd angered at the firm today. Colin, the man who had a connection to Paddy *and* Sam. And even to Toby, who lived very close to Paddy… Colin, the man who had sleeping pills in his house and dog food in his garage and who'd been with Zoe right before he'd found her dumped on a motel bed with her clothes askew. Jonathan was willing to bet that if he'd had time to finish with all those rental records, he would've found Colin's name in there somewhere—or the name of someone who knew Colin.

Maybe suspecting him hadn't been so crazy, after all.

"I've got a bad feeling about this," he told her.

"You don't think he'd hurt his father, do you?"

A beat-up truck rumbled past and vanished as the road veered out of sight. "How would his ex-wife answer that question?"

"When I called her, she wanted to know where Colin was when Paddy went missing. That's an odd question to ask about your own son, don't you think? I've always agreed with Paddy and thought Colin's problems stemmed from Tina's inability to love him. But now, if it wasn't for Tiffany, I might be tempted to believe Tina."

"You like Tiffany, then?"

"She's a real sweetheart, so eager to please."

More eager to please her husband than anyone else… "I'm guessing she was with him when Paddy went missing."

"That's right. She told me so herself."

Because Tiffany knew. She protected Colin. "Can you tell me how to get to Paddy's cabin, Mrs. Bell?"

"No, sir. It's been too long since I've been there. And Paddy always drove."

He refastened his seat belt. "I need to find it. Immediately."

"Colin and Tiffany already checked the cabin, just yesterday," she said. "No one's there."

"We need to check again. Where can we get an address?"

"Gee, I don't know…." There was a pause. "I suppose it would be on the deed. But there's no telling how long it would take me to find that. It's probably out in the garage in one of those—wait," she said. "What about Glen?"

"Glen?"

"My son used to go up there with Paddy quite a bit. He'll know how to find it."

"Is he available?"

"What is it—three o'clock? I should be able to catch him at work."

"Call him right away," Jonathan said and prayed that right away would be soon enough….

35

"You're a little hellcat, aren't you!" Colin seemed more excited than upset to see Zoe and Tiffany fighting. "I never dreamed you had it in you."

"You're *glad* she hurt me?" Tiffany sat on the ground, covered in dust, her hand over her injury.

Grimacing at the metallic taste of blood, Zoe wiped her mouth and shoved her tangled hair out of her eyes so she could glare up at him. "That was for Sam and Toby!"

"You mean Rover?" He chuckled. "You're feeling protective of him, too?"

"How could *anyone* hurt him like that? How could *you,* someone I *know,* someone I've touched and spoken to and lived beside? You're a monster, not a man!"

He made a show of waving her words away. "Give me a break. You're just as capable of hurting people as I am. Look at poor Tiff."

Zoe didn't care about Tiffany. It was Colin she had to defeat if she wanted to get out of this alive—if she wanted to get Sam out alive.

She climbed to her feet and dusted off her clothes. "Tiffany's an adult. Besides, she attacked me."

"I've never been one for subtle distinctions," he said with a shrug. "Life is about grabbing what you want and taking all you can."

"What have you done with my daughter?" she asked.

His lips curved in a taunting smile. "It's what I'm about to do that matters."

Zoe's fingernails curved into her palms. Sam was alive. "Why'd you lure me up here? To tell me it was you? To kill us both?"

He leaned close, smelled her hair, then licked her cheek. She suppressed a shudder of revulsion, trying to pretend it didn't bother her. "What is it you want from us?"

"I want *you.* I've wanted you since the first moment—"

"Colin!" Tiffany found her feet and pulled him away. "Not while I'm here. I can't watch this. Take her with you and go to Chester. Just make sure I never see her again."

"Ooh," he jeered. "Did you hear what she said? She wants to be rid of you. She's tired of the way you've teased me with that tight little ass of yours."

"I haven't teased you," Zoe said.

"Just seeing you teases me."

"Colin!" Tiffany again.

"Okay, okay, I get it," he told his wife. "You and Zoe have some unfinished business. I'll let you take care of it." He glanced between them. "Go ahead and fight it out, ladies. It'll be like…like a cockfight." He grinned. "You're going to do more cockfighting later, if you know what I mean."

Memories of Franky, of the stifling hot trailer in the dead of summer, washed over Zoe and panic set in.

"No." She shook her head but her denial meant nothing to him. He winked, seemingly happier than she'd ever seen him, and all his odd statements and come-ons filtered through her mind. She'd been so busy playing the polite neighbor and giving him the benefit of every doubt that she hadn't read them as the warning signs they were. She'd trusted what he appeared to be instead of what her instincts told her. Anyone could've been misled, but she was especially vulnerable because she was so determined not to suspect danger around every corner. After what Franky had done, it was the only way she could live a normal life.

"You ready for this?" he asked his wife.

"For what?"

"To fight her!"

"Colin, no!" Tiffany pointed to her wounded shoulder. "Look at me!"

"You're okay, babe. You've had worse."

"Quit it, Colin. You've got to get out of here. Stivers will find this place eventually. It's not as if it's invisible."

"It's so remote it might as well be invisible," he said.

"Why won't you listen?" she shouted. "Are you on something again? He'll be here any minute, Colin!"

"No, he won't. Come on, babe." He grabbed her ass and gave it a lascivious squeeze, letting his tongue dangle out as he did. "You're not willing to duke it out for your man? I thought you hated Zoe. I thought you wanted me to kill her."

Tiffany staggered back a few steps. "Shut up! God, I hate you!"

He stiffened as if she'd slapped him. "What'd you say?"

She covered her mouth. Obviously, she regretted those words, but that didn't seem to matter. Tiffany was right. Colin had to be on something. He was acting bizarre.

The Bells stared at each other for several seconds. Then Colin strode over and yanked Tiffany by the hair. "You want her?" he said to Zoe. "Here she is."

Zoe had to think of some way to prevail. Her daughter was alive. Colin had spoken of her in the present tense. But where was she? Zoe hoped she was in the shed or the cabin. If she was anywhere else, she might never find her.

"Let's go to Sam," she said.

"In a minute."

Tiffany winced but didn't cry out as Colin forced her arms behind her back. "My wife deserves to be taught a lesson." He licked Tiffany's cheek this time. "What do you say, babe? You hate me, huh? Is that it?"

"I didn't mean it," she whined. "You know I love you, Colin. I'd do anything for you. I brought *her* here, didn't I?"

"You brought her here so I could kill her. That's hardly a sacrifice." He returned his attention to Zoe. "If you'll kick her ass, I'll kill Sam quick."

Sam was indeed alive—but how was Zoe going to keep her that way?

"That's really the best offer I can make you," he explained as glibly as if they were discussing an innocuous business transaction. "I can't let either of you go. I won't insult your intelligence by pretending otherwise. But I'll do you the favor of getting rid of her in as painless a fashion as possible. Then it'll be just me and you, all week."

"Colin, you're making me regret this!" Tiffany said. "Let go of me."

"No."

"Let go of me!"

Colin pushed Tiffany closer to Zoe. "Come on, hit her." He used his chin to indicate Tiffany's face. "Right here."

"And what will *you* do?" Zoe asked.

"I'll stay out of it. This is pure entertainment for me. I'll give you three punches. Then you're on your own and whoever wins, wins. If that happens to be you, I'll show you some mercy."

"Colin, stop!" Tiffany squirmed, but he held her fast.

Colin waved at his wife again. "Here you go, Zoe. You wanted to fight her a minute ago."

Zoe hadn't wanted to fight anybody. She only wanted to get away. His perception of everything was all screwed up.

"Hit her," he taunted. "Give her a black eye. Think of how she's treated your little girl. Feeding her nothing but dog food. Making her wear a choke chain. Chaining her to the ground. She's a cruel bitch."

Anger at the thought of Sam being treated in such a fashion made Zoe feel powerful enough to attack anyone.

"She's the one who took her, you know," he went on. "She coaxed her over to the house and locked her up while you were at work. You sure have a gullible child, but I guess most kids would think they could trust a face as pretty as Tiffany's."

"*You* did that?" Zoe spoke to Tiffany. Somehow, it was even more of a betrayal coming from another woman. "You're just as bad as he is."

Tiffany couldn't meet her eyes. "I did it for him!"

Colin jerked on his wife's arms, still twisted behind her back, and caused a grunt of pain. "Oh, and now you turn on me again."

Evidently, Colin could say anything he wanted about Tiffany but couldn't tolerate her slightest offense.

"Let me loose." Tiffany struggled some more, but he laughed and continued to restrain her.

"Maybe I should take you both to Chester, force you to torture each other. That would be interesting. Forget Sam. She's useless, as good as dead."

Terror clutched at Zoe's heart. What had he done to her?

"I'm not going to Chester," Tiffany said. "Not now."

"You're a real downer, Tiff. You should be glad that adding Zoe to the mix makes you exciting again. Without her, you can't even get me hard anymore."

Tears streamed down Tiffany's cheeks. "You don't love me. I should've seen it before."

"You *asked* for this," he said. "Now shut up and you'll get what you want in the end. I'm just having a little fun."

"You've been snorting coke again! I *hate* what it does to you!"

"And you hate me. Yeah, we heard." He dragged her toward Zoe. "Hit her."

"As hard as I want?" Zoe asked.

"As hard as you want." He held his wife to the left of his body in anticipation of a right-handed punch. But Zoe wasn't right-handed. And it wasn't Tiffany she wanted.

Making a fist with both hands so she wouldn't telegraph her intentions, she punched Colin as hard as she could.

"It's about time someone realized that son of a bitch is crazy." Glen Hagen propped one massive, tattoo-covered arm on the car window and continued to chew on the toothpick he'd kept in his mouth ever since Jonathan had met him at the gas station in Nyack. Glen felt confident he could find the cabin, but he couldn't give verbal directions beyond the general vicinity. "It'll only get you lost if I try," he'd said when Jonathan had pushed him on it. "You think you'll know where to go if I say to turn right at the granite outcropping and left at the crooked tree?"

It was a good point, so Jonathan had waited for him, but the hour he lost hadn't been easy to give up. Every minute that ticked away heightened his anxiety. His terror at the thought of what Zoe might be going through told him he cared more about her than he'd wanted to, more than he'd ever intended. Which wasn't a pleasant realization, considering what had happened with Maria.

It didn't help that Detective Thomas had been so late getting into the game. He'd been out on another case most of the day, a grisly murder-suicide, but returned

Jonathan's many calls a few minutes ago. He'd said that Paddy Bell's ex had contacted the Sacramento police to demand they investigate Colin in connection with his father's disappearance.

If only Jonathan had received that information earlier…

"How'd you know he was crazy?" Jonathan weaved through traffic. Their exit was coming up.

"Shit, can you slow down?" Glen said. "I'd like to live another day."

Jonathan ignored him. He'd lost too much time. "How'd you know?" he asked again.

"We met after Colin was an adult, but I've seen him often enough to know he's a sneaky little bastard. Puts on a front, tries to be something he ain't. If he doesn't feel he needs you, you'll see more of the real Colin." He paused. "He pretty much steers clear of me. I don't have anything he wants, being blue-collar and all." He shook his head. "And the way he treats his wife…"

"That badly?"

"Not so much in front of people—although if you watch closely you'll see it. All he has to do is shoot her a look, you know? And she'll shut up or leave or do whatever it is he wants. I can imagine what goes on behind closed doors. I once heard him talkin' to Tiffany in the back bedroom at my mother's place, and I tell ya, I'd stab the prick, if it were me." He patted the pocket of his T-shirt. "Jesus, why'd I have to choose this week to quit smoking?"

Jonathan navigated his way through a handful of slow-moving campers.

Frowning over the absence of cigarettes, Glen braced himself against the dashboard as Jonathan whipped around another semi. He opened his mouth to complain about the near miss, but Jonathan interrupted before he could. "Why didn't Colin's father see what he was?"

"Because Paddy was too busy blaming himself. No parent wants to acknowledge that their kid's a bad seed. They have to trace everything that's wrong with junior back to what they did to cause it, or what they didn't do to fix it. And then the guilt sets in. My mother still blames herself for me not finishing high school. But like I told her yesterday, it was my choice." He chewed on the tooth pick. "Man, I've done some shit I'm not proud of, but nothin' like this. Nothin' that makes me a freakin' pervert."

Jonathan flipped on his blinker just in time to slip between a sports car and a Lexus sedan. "Where do you think Paddy is?"

"I don't have a clue. Colin tried telling my mom *I* must've done something to him. Can you believe it? He knew Paddy and I weren't gettin' along, so he pointed the finger at me. He uses stuff like that, works it to his advantage."

"Why was there bad blood between you and Paddy?"

"We owned a lawn-mower shop together and it just…didn't work. We're too different."

There it was. The Truckee exit. As Jonathan shot through the gap between a trucker and a Prius, Glen let loose with a fresh string of curses. "You're gonna kill us both."

"I go left here?" Jonathan said.

"Yeah, left."

"How were you and Paddy too different?" he asked as he made the turn.

Glen swayed into the door until Jonathan straightened the car. "He was way too controlling for me, man. I couldn't miss a day, couldn't ever expect him to lock up. He had a comment for every damn thing I said and did, watched every move I made. So we exchanged a few words, and I walked out." He shrugged. "I haven't seen him since." He pointed at the next street. "You want this one."

"What happened to your real dad?"

He braced himself again as they veered around another corner. "Died of a heart attack ten years ago."

"If Colin's done what I suspect, your mother might've lost another husband."

"You'd think she could catch a break," he muttered.

They didn't talk any more after that. Jonathan was too focused on reaching the cabin, and Glen was too intent on navigating. They wound into the mountains on one narrow road after another. Jonathan recognized the first two turns as ones he'd taken before, but the third was different and the fourth road was barely visible.

"This thing all but disappears in spring," Glen said.

"Who maintains it?"

"No one. That's the problem."

"Are there other cabins in the area?"

"Not for miles."

"Does Colin come up here very often?"

Glen glanced over at him. "All the time."

Jonathan swerved to avoid a deep rut and entered a small clearing with a rough-hewn log cabin, a stone firepit, an outhouse and a shed. Fresh tire tracks testified to the fact that someone had recently been here. There were granola-bar wrappers and an old blanket in the shed.

But that was all.

Zoe woke in the trunk of a car, her head pounding in rhythm with the thrumming of the tires. She'd tried to use those few seconds of surprise after she'd coldcocked Colin to get into Tiffany's car, but he'd recovered too quickly. He'd pulled her out by the hair and punched her repeatedly.

After the first blow, she'd been too dazed to feel much. Fortunately, he'd been in a hurry, or she'd probably be dead. She must've passed out, and then he must've dumped her in his trunk and driven off, because she didn't remember the middle part.

If only his trunk was a little bigger….

With a groan, she attempted to take stock of her injuries despite the cramped conditions. It wasn't just her head that hurt. She was pretty sure she'd broken her hand when she hit him. And she was pretty sure he'd broken her jaw when he hit her. Not a good showing for her first fight.

So what was she going to do? Even if Jonathan managed to find the cabin, she was no longer there. Would she ever see him again? Would she ever see *anyone* again? And what about her poor daughter?

Tears of helplessness, frustration and fear ran into her hair. She couldn't let Colin win, couldn't end up as another sad statistic.

The car slowed and stopped. Zoe held her breath, expecting the trunk to open, but it didn't. From what she could hear, they were at a gas station. Someone unscrewed the gas cap, inserted the nozzle and began the fueling process.

Zoe smelled gas fumes. Then footsteps echoed on pavement as whoever it was—Colin, most likely—went to the cashier or the minimart or the bathroom…somewhere. And that was when she heard it. *Sam's* voice. Her daughter was calling to her from inside the car.

"Mom? Mommy, are you okay?" She broke into a sob. "Did he *kill* you?"

Such relief overwhelmed Zoe she could hardly speak. Not only was Sam alive, she was close. "Sammie, I'm okay."

"Mom? Are you there? Answer me!"

She hadn't spoken loudly enough. Steeling herself

against the pain of moving her jaw, Zoe tried again. "Don't cry, baby. I'm fine. Everything's going to be okay."

"You're alive? Oh, thank God!"

What kind of condition was Sam in? "How are you, honey?"

"Sick."

Zoe drew a deep, steadying breath. "I'm sorry. I'm so sorry."

"I wanna go home."

"We'll go home, baby. We just…we need to get help."

"He's crazy," she said on a sob. "He's going to kill us!"

"Not if we don't give up. Can you get out of the car?"

Nothing.

"Sam?"

"No."

"Can you roll down the window? Push the button that'll release the lid of the trunk? Anything?"

"My hands are—" she hiccuped "—tied."

"Can you scream, baby? Draw some attention? We'll both scream together. You ready?"

"It won't do…any good, Mom. No one…else is here, except…except the clerk in the minimart, and…he'll never hear us."

Of course he wouldn't. Colin wouldn't have stopped here if there was any risk of being caught.

"Where's he taking us?" Zoe asked.

"I don't know. Someplace called by a—a man's name."

"You've never heard of it before?"

Another hiccup. "No."

"What about his cell phone? Did he leave it behind?"

"Yes, but…I—I can't reach it. And it's a—a BlackBerry. I don't…know how to work it."

"You gotta try, baby. Use your feet, your mouth, anything."

There was a long silence.
"Sam?"
"He's coming!"

36

Sam stared out the window as Colin got into the car. She'd nearly had to choke herself in order to do it, but she'd managed to reach his BlackBerry with her mouth. She'd even pressed some random buttons using her chin. Apparently, it'd been enough to call somebody because she could hear a tinny voice saying, "Hello?… Hello?"

Lucky for her, Colin was too preoccupied to hear it above the crackling of the sack he dropped at her feet. He put his soda in the cup holder and started the car without even glancing at the phone on the console.

Sam wanted to cry out for help, but she couldn't explain where they were, and as soon as she spoke, Colin would disconnect the call. If whoever it was called back, he'd say it was a joke or cover in some other way. He was too good a liar for one crazy call to give him any problems.

So how could she get the person on the other end of the line to help them?

Now that her mother was so close, she felt a huge surge of energy, of hope, despite the situation. They'd been through tough times before. They'd get out of this. Somehow.

"Colin?" She prayed whoever it was wouldn't hang up.

"What?"

"Where…are we?"

He was in a particularly foul mood this afternoon. Probably because of his nose. It was swollen and kept bleeding. And it made him talk funny. "In the mountains."

That wouldn't tell the person on the phone anything. "Where are we…going?"

He scowled at his reflection in the rearview mirror and gingerly touched his nose. "What is this, Twenty Questions? I thought you were sick."

Samantha had never felt worse in her life, even that time she stayed home from school with the flu and barfed for three days straight. But she had her mother back now. That was worth fighting for. "Are you going to…to kill us?"

"What do *you* think?"

She purposely avoided glancing at the phone. "I think you are."

"Someone has to pay for this." He motioned toward his injured face.

She wished he was more badly hurt. "You…already… killed Rover, right?"

"Shut up," he groused. "I don't want to talk about Rover. I don't want to talk at all. I can barely breathe."

Struggling to bear up under the weakness and fatigue, Sam closed her eyes. "Why do you…why do you do it?"

"Because I like it, that's why."

She couldn't hear that voice on the phone anymore. Had whoever it was hung up? *Please, no…* "I thought…I thought a lawyer who worked for…what's the name of that place?"

"Scovil, Potter & Clay. They're one of the most powerful firms in Sacramento."

"Right, I remember." How could she forget? He talked

about it all the time. You'd think he'd won the freakin' lottery the day they hired him. "…Aren't you…afraid of going to prison?"

"Nope."

"Why not?"

"Because that'll never happen."

Keep talking. She had no idea if it was helping, but it was her only chance. She had to get him to divulge as many details as possible. Maybe the person on the phone would call the police. "How do you know…they won't… catch you?"

"Because they're not smart enough to put it all together."

"You told me…you said you killed your…" She was *so* dizzy. What had she been saying?

His father. That was it. "…your father."

"So what if I did?"

"I guess…that means…you'd kill anyone."

He didn't respond.

What else could she talk about? "Where's Tiffany?" she asked.

"She'd better be at the cabin, telling the police what I told her to say."

"Does she always do…exactly what you tell her?"

"Of course."

"Why?"

He laughed. "Because she doesn't have the self-confidence to do anything but follow my lead."

Sam felt herself slipping toward unconsciousness. She'd already given everything she had. "What…what would happen if…if she didn't obey?"

His answer didn't surprise Sam. "I'd kill her."

"Don't you…love her?"

"She's just a piece of ass," he said and turned on the radio.

* * *

What she'd overheard a minute ago hurt so badly Tiffany couldn't breathe. Dropping her cell phone, she clutched at her chest and must've swerved into the next lane, because a car coming up on the right side honked and nearly ran her off the road. She'd almost crashed, but she didn't care. She *wanted* to die. Without Colin, she had no one. Not her mother, who hadn't wanted her anyway. Not her brother, who'd cared more about revenge than sticking around for her. Not the lousy kids who'd made fun of her in high school.

...I'd kill her....

...Don't you love her...?

...She's just a piece of ass....

Surely Colin hadn't meant those words. He was putting on a show. He did that sometimes, liked to shock people.

But deep down, Tiffany knew she was just making more excuses, the same kinds of excuses she made for him whenever he disappointed her. It was easier to do that than face the truth, but right now the truth was staring her right in the eyes and she could no longer deny it. He was self-destructing and taking her down with him, and he didn't even care.

She held out her hand to look at the ring he'd bought her yesterday. She wanted to believe it was proof of his love. But his other actions proved the opposite. Before driving off with Zoe, he'd told her Tommy would be calling, that she was to "spend some time with him and be open-minded and cooperative."

How could he be so unconcerned with how she'd feel about being with Tommy? When Colin was planning to participate it was different. At least she'd convinced herself it was different. But this...this signaled a change in their relationship, and not for the better. He used to be possessive, angry if any other man even looked at her.

She thought of the remains in the outhouse and Rover and Sam. And what he'd done to them…

Look where she'd let him lead her. All in the hope of making him happy, of being everything he could ever want her to be, of securing his love.

She was crying too hard to see the road, so she took the next off-ramp and pulled to the side. Then she called Sheryl.

Her stepmother-in-law answered on the third ring. "Hello?"

"Sheryl?"

"Tiffany? You sound strange. Are you okay, honey?"

Self-loathing threatened to choke her. "No, no, I'm not okay," she said. "I'm not okay at all."

"Why not? Where are you?"

"It doesn't matter. I just…called to—to tell you…" She pictured the man she loved more than she'd ever loved anyone or anything, wearing the smile that dazzled her every time she saw it—and almost lost her nerve.

"What is it?" Sheryl prompted.

Grabbing the steering wheel, she hung on. "Colin killed Paddy, Sheryl."

"What?"

Now that she'd begun, the rest came easily. She blurted it out as if she'd been carrying it for so long she couldn't carry it another second, gulping for breath amidst her tears. "He—he buried him somewhere out in the woods. I don't know where. I didn't go with him. But I saw Paddy. I saw the blood. I saw him clean it up. Then I—"

A soft, heartbroken wail interrupted. "No!"

"I'm sorry," Tiffany whispered.

"Tell me it isn't true," Sheryl begged.

Tiffany wished she could. What had she allowed herself to become? What had she allowed Colin to become? Or had he possessed the soul of a killer all along? "It's true," she said. "And there are others." She did her best to describe Colin's other pets, but Sheryl didn't seem to care about that.

"Why?" she asked, but she was pleading for an explanation no one could give her, least of all Tiffany. She had no idea why Colin found joy in the things he did. As much as she loved him, as much as she admired him in so many ways, she'd never really understood him.

"Why does anyone do what he's done? Because…something's missing." Realizing that she'd parked near a steep precipice, Tiffany got out and peered over the edge.

"Oh God," Sheryl wailed. "Oh God."

Tiffany moved closer to the drop-off, watching as some of the dirt beneath her toes crumbled and fell away. Maybe she hadn't loved Colin as much as she'd always thought. Maybe she was in love with the idea of being loved. She'd done everything she'd done to make someone finally care about her. But it hadn't worked because Colin was incapable of caring about anyone.

Suddenly, she started to laugh.

"What is it?" Sheryl said.

"He was right about me."

"What do you mean?"

"I am stupid."

The tenor of Sheryl's voice changed. "Tiffany, what about the missing girl?"

"Samantha Duncan?" The wind, cooler now that evening approached, ruffled her hair. It was beautiful here. One of the most beautiful places on earth.

"Where is she?"

"Colin has her and her mother. He's taking them to a cabin in Chester."

"Where in Chester?"

"I don't know, but his friend Tommy Tuttle does."

"Colin's not going to…to *kill* them, is he? He killed Paddy because…because they had some sort of argument, right? It wasn't a cold-blooded, calculated murder."

"He killed Paddy because Paddy figured it out, because Paddy guessed the truth. And he killed that other kid, like I told you. He's going to kill again unless you stop him."

"This can't be real," Sheryl muttered. "This can't be happening."

Tiffany understood. The world had taken on a surreal quality for her, too. It'd just been surreal for so long she'd stopped noticing.

But she was noticing now. She wouldn't be going back to her nice home in Rocklin, wouldn't be telling anyone she was married to a successful lawyer, wouldn't be flaunting her new diamond ring or hoping and praying that going without the next candy bar would finally make her perfect enough to satisfy her husband.

She wouldn't have any of those things. But neither would she die a slow death in prison.

"Call the police," she said and snapped her phone shut. Then she got back in her car, floored the gas pedal while it was still in Park and popped the transmission into Drive.

Crazy thing was…she wanted Colin even as the car plummeted into the ravine.

Sheryl Bell's call came while Jonathan was driving back to Sacramento. He hadn't wanted to leave Paddy's cabin—it was where Zoe's trail had gone cold—but he'd given Glen a ride back to Nyack. Now he wasn't sure what else to do. He had no clue where Colin might've taken Sam and Zoe, no clue where to go next. Ever since he'd gotten back into an area that had cell-phone coverage, he'd been calling Colin and Tiffany's home phone as well as Colin's cell phone—incessantly—but neither of them picked up.

He'd tried Jasmine, too, but she couldn't tell him any more. He needed to find them fast, she said. But he'd already known that.

"I can tell you where Colin is," Sheryl announced the minute he said hello.

Jonathan slammed on his brakes. "Where?"

"Chester, up near Lake Almanor."

That had to be two hours away, at least. Probably three, what with the winding roads. Jonathan tried to work out the best way to get there. Up through Reno? Had to be. It'd take forever to go around the other way…. "Why Chester?" he asked.

"He's planning to stay in a friend's rental house. It's such a dump it's been empty for months."

"Who told you this?"

"Tiffany."

"Tiffany?" he repeated in surprise. "I assumed she'd be with him." He was positive she'd been in on everything up to this point. She'd given Colin an alibi for Paddy's murder, hadn't she?

"No."

Jonathan turned around at the next exit. He had GPS on his phone, but he could drive as far as Reno before he had to use it. "Where is she, then?" Had they split up for a reason? Did she have Sam, and Colin had Zoe?

"I'm afraid something's happened to her."

"What?"

Sheryl had been holding up pretty well, but at this she began to cry. "She—she wasn't herself when she called me. She told me everything. Then she hung up and that was it. I've called her number at least twenty times but I get no answer."

"Have you reported what she told you to the police?"

"Yes, of course. But…I knew you were looking for that girl and I thought you'd be interested, too."

Forced to slow as he approached one semi trying to pass another on the two-lane highway, he took the shoulder. "I am. Thank you."

She sniffed. "Tiffany told me Paddy's dead."

Jonathan had suspected as much. "I'm sorry."

A long silence ensued during which she struggled to come to grips with her emotions. "It's over. I'll have to live with what Colin's done. Just—" her voice broke "—just make sure you catch him, okay? Make sure you catch him and put him away before he can hurt anyone else."

"I'll do that," Jonathan promised. But whether or not he could accomplish it before Colin killed Zoe and Sam remained to be seen.

Feeling the same terrible dread he'd experienced the night he'd received that panicked call from Maria, when she'd whispered that she needed him to come and get her, he punched the gas pedal. He'd arrived too late to save Maria.

He would *not* be too late for Zoe and Sam….

His injured nose and the fight he'd had with Tiffany over her refusal to stay behind and wait for the police had taken the fun out of what he'd planned for this evening. Colin got to Chester just as it was turning dark—he'd made good time—but the anticipation he'd felt was gone. He could no longer breathe through his nose, swallowed blood every time he tried. And his head was aching like a son of a bitch.

"I can't believe what that whore did to me," he muttered as he parked beneath some trees. He'd probably have to get a nose job, and nose jobs weren't cheap. How could he afford surgery? He had to assume he was unemployed. He hadn't heard the words *You're fired* yet, but it was only a matter of time. Besides, about a hundred calls from Jonathan Stivers, Misty or someone else at the firm had been trying to reach him on his cell for the past couple of hours. No doubt, Scovil knew he'd left early.

He'd finally silenced the ringer.

His headlights illuminated a dark, poorly built house, but he scarcely looked at it. Jamming the gearshift into Park, he sat in the car, thinking about losing his job and possibly his nice house. Did he know what he was doing? Was he as impervious to reversals as he'd thought?

No. He'd made a terrible mistake. Because of Zoe. Without her, he would've stayed at work, finished the contracts and somehow won Mr. Scovil's confidence. If not for Zoe, he'd still be able to say he was part of a prestigious law firm. Even if he got another job, it wouldn't be the same. He'd lose the instant respect he received when he mentioned the names of his senior partners. And if Scovil fired him, he might not get on anywhere else. Most of the attorneys downtown knew each other. Word would get around. That meant he'd *have* to open his own practice. But he couldn't be successful without clients.

How would he win clients away from the big boys if his reputation was trashed?

Sam was asleep on the seat beside him, but he spoke to her anyway. "You just wait," he said, turning off the engine. He'd offered to kill her quickly. Zoe should've taken him up on that. Instead she'd broken his nose, and now he'd make sure Sam died a slow death—right in front of her mother.

First, however, he had to take more painkillers. He'd gone into the bathroom at the gas station and tried to do a line of coke. He knew he wouldn't need painkillers if he could get high. But attempting to snort caused more bleeding.

By the time he'd carried Sam into the cabin and was on his way back for Zoe, Colin was so depressed he didn't feel like torturing either one of them. He wished he'd brought Tiffany along. She always knew what to do when he didn't feel well. She'd rub his neck tirelessly, put him to sleep.

Maybe he'd leave Zoe and Sam here and head home to his wife….

No, that would require more driving. He'd call Tiffany and have her come to him. That was it. She could skip work tomorrow, call in sick again. He needed her. He'd feel better after he apologized for being such a jerk. She'd said she hated him, and he'd made her pay for it, but he regretted that now. Tiffany hadn't meant it. She was the only person in the world who truly loved him.

What'd gotten into him lately?

Too much coke…

Taking his BlackBerry from his pocket, he stood by the trunk of the car and checked for service. Pleasantly surprised to find he could make a call, he dialed his wife.

"Hello, this is Tiffany Bell. I can't get to the phone right now but leave me a message and I'll call you back."

He waited for the beep. "Hey, why aren't you picking up? I miss you, Tiff. I was an asshole at the cabin today, and I'm sorry. I shouldn't have done what I did. It wasn't me—it was the drugs. I wish you were here. Can you come up?"

He expected her to call him right back. She never let it go more than a few minutes before she returned his calls. But he'd dragged Zoe in from the car, tied her up in the back room with Sam, then watched TV for an hour, and Tiffany still hadn't called.

At that point, he began to call her again and again. Once, twice, three times. Where the hell was she? Four, five, six times. Did she think this was some sort of game? That she could punish *him* for mistreating her? She'd caused *everything* when she let Rover get away. That was the first domino to fall.

"It's your own fault!" he screamed into the phone. "Don't you dare think you can stonewall me, Tiff." Was she with Tommy? Was she enjoying herself too much to care that he was trying to get hold of her? Maybe Tommy was treating her more kindly, showing her what it was like to be with someone gentle.

He could see her falling for a guy like that, and it made him sick. "You'll be sorry," he told her. "I'll drive down there and—"

The phone beeped, letting him know he'd run out of time for his message. He couldn't even bitch her out right now.

Exhausted and truly worried, he sank onto the couch. He'd taken some extra pain-reliever tablets, but it wasn't enough. He needed more. And then he needed to drive home. Forget Zoe and Sam. He'd kill them both so he could go find his wife.

Standing, he went to the kitchen to get a knife.

Zoe huddled close to her daughter, trying to give her as much warmth and comfort as possible. Sam still wore the swimsuit she'd had on when she was kidnapped, and it was far too cold in a house with no heat.

"Everything's going to be okay," she murmured, to keep her as calm as possible. But Zoe wasn't at all sure everything *would* be okay. Sammie was ill. She needed help and she needed it fast.

What could she do? Zoe struggled against the rope that bound her, as she had since Colin had dragged her in here, but the slightest movement caused excruciating pain in her injured hand, which had swollen to a monstrous size. The rope cut off the flow of blood and the swelling had grown worse, but it was her jaw that hurt the most. Colin had kicked her in the face. She remembered that now.

No wonder she'd lost consciousness….

"Sammie? You okay, baby?" she murmured.

Her daughter's breathing was shallow.

"I'm…okay, Mommy," she whispered.

Zoe had to concentrate so she wouldn't pass out again. Using the less damaged side of her face, she nuzzled her child's forehead. It was a blessing just to be able to touch her. "I'm so grateful to be with you."

"Even…here? Like this?" came the soft reply.

"Even here."

"I love you, Mommy."

Zoe breathed deeply, willing herself to remain lucid

for Sam's sake. *Ignore the pain. Hang on....* She had to come up with a plan, do something, before it was too late.

"I love you…too," she said and then the door swung wide and slammed against the inside wall.

37

"What the hell is taking so long?" Jonathan shouted into the phone. He'd been traveling for nearly three hours—this was his sixth call to the Chester Police Department—and they *still* hadn't visited the rental house.

"What do you think, buddy?" came the police chief's irritated response. "That I can pull the address out of my ass?"

"Nothing quite so spectacular. You've got Tommy Tuttle's name, address, employer and phone number. Maybe it's just me, but I'd probably call and ask him how the hell to get to his cousin's place. Did that bright idea occur to anyone in the past three hours?"

"I don't want to talk to some smartass private detective," he said.

Jonathan could tell the man was about to hang up and hurried to stop him. "Look, I'm sorry, okay? It's just… I know what this guy's capable of."

There was a moment of silence, during which Jonathan sensed the police chief wavering. Ultimately, he didn't hang up, but his tone was pretty damn defensive. "We've been working in conjunction with Sac PD ever since the call came in, okay? And they've been doing all they can to get the information we need. They just found Tommy Tuttle five minutes ago. He wasn't at work, where he was supposed to be. He was at some triple-X movie house in Del Paso Heights. That's not the type of place you announce you're spending the afternoon. And it's definitely not the type of place where a man cares whether or not he's getting a call, even if he has his hands free to answer it."

Jonathan rubbed his face. "I get it. I didn't mean to offend you. I'm just…freaked out. This guy has no conscience."

"I understand that. A woman and child are in danger. I sent three squad cars the second I got the location, and I'm heading over in a fourth. We should be there any minute."

"Where's *there?* Can you give me the address?" Jonathan asked. "I'm just pulling in to town. I'll be right behind you."

The chief hesitated. "Maybe you should let us handle this one."

"Now that Tommy's available, I can get hold of him, too, Chief."

"Fine," he said with a sigh and recited the address. "But you'd better stay out of our way or I'll have your ass thrown in jail right along with his."

Colin had a knife in his hand. The shadow of it loomed large against the wall. Zoe was afraid Sam would see it, wanted to shield her from the terror. But she didn't need to. Her daughter was no longer responding.

"Colin, don't do this." Zoe kept her voice low as she watched him advance. "Sam needs a doctor. Do the right thing for a change and get her some help."

"Now you want a favor?" he said. "After you busted my nose?" He kicked her in the leg. It wasn't a full-force blow; it was more to make his point. But the damage he'd already done to her jaw made any jolt so painful spots began to dance before her eyes.

"Would you rather I'd hit your wife?" she gasped.

He didn't answer.

"Come on, Colin." Zoe licked her lips, drew enough breath to speak again. "You can have me, do what you want with me. But first you have to let her go."

"She can't leave even if I do let her go. And I don't want you anymore. You've always thought you were too good for me. But you're no better than my sister or my mother. I don't know why it took me so long to realize that. I want my wife. I want to go home."

"Then go home, Colin. Leave us here to die and go." Zoe didn't much like that option, but at least it would buy her some time—time to continue working at the ropes, time for Jonathan and the police to find them.

"Shut up," he snapped. "My head hurts too much to listen to you."

"But—"

"Shut up!" Squatting next to them, he grabbed Sam by the hair and put his knife to her throat.

Sam came to long enough to open her eyes, but she didn't fight him or cry out. She didn't look like she had the energy.

Her gaze settled on Zoe in a silent good-bye, and Zoe's heart began to pound harder. "Not her, Colin. Kill me instead. Please!"

"I'm not letting you off that easy," he said. "She's what you love. So she's what I'm going to take from you."

With an agonized scream, Zoe fought the ropes, struggling to stop what she had no power to stop. Then she squeezed her eyes closed because she couldn't bear to watch. She thought it would all be over, that Sam would be dead in an instant. But then a gun went off somewhere near the doorway, and it was Colin who dropped.

The deafening blast seemed to echo for several seconds as Colin lay writhing on the floor. "What the hell?" he cried.

Zoe blinked, once, twice, three times. She expected a man in a uniform, or maybe Jonathan, to be standing in the doorway. But it was neither. A middle-aged woman with an attractive haircut and dark, tortured eyes slumped against the wall.

"God, that hurts!" His breath coming in short gasps, Colin rolled over to see who'd shot him and started to laugh. "It's you," he said, the words as bitter as any Zoe had ever heard. "My own mother. Who would've thought you'd trouble yourself to come all the way from L.A.?"

Petite and well-groomed, Tina Bell could've walked out of a Nordstrom ad, except that she wasn't carrying a fashionable purse to match her shoes. She was holding a pistol. "I came as soon as Sheryl called me."

"I guess I owe her one." His breath rattled in his chest. "How'd she know where to send you?"

Tina put down the gun. "She told me Tiffany said you were on your way to Tommy's cousin's house."

Tiffany had betrayed him? He couldn't believe it, wouldn't believe it until he'd had a chance to talk to her. "And you remembered our families having Thanksgiving here."

"Yes. For my own peace of mind, I tried to stay away, but I couldn't do it. I'm your mother, Colin. I will always be your mother."

"So you came to kill the monster you created?" He attempted another laugh but couldn't quite manage it.

Tears filled Tina's eyes as she sank to her knees. "I didn't come to kill you, Colin. I came to save you from yourself. I've been trying to save you all along. But now—" her gaze shifted to Zoe and Sam "—now I can see I'm too late."

Using the wall for support, she pulled a cell phone out of her jacket pocket and called 9-1-1, but it didn't take more than two minutes for the police to arrive. And, to Zoe's relief, Jonathan was with them.

Zoe's daughter was in the same hospital bed she was in. After what they'd been through, she couldn't let Sam out of her sight, even though she was safe and would be fine.

Smoothing her daughter's hair, she managed to kiss her temple despite a broken jaw. The morphine she'd been given numbed the pain. The doctors were planning to wire her mouth shut in the morning so it could heal properly; they'd already set her hand in a cast.

It would be a while before she was back to normal, but she was alive. She had Sam. And Jonathan sat sleeping in the chair by her bed. She had no idea what would happen, but there was something between them—something that hadn't been there with anyone else.

"Mommy?" Sam murmured.

"What, baby?"

"Where's Colin?"

"He's in a different hospital."

"Will he live?"

Zoe hoped not. Colin didn't deserve to breathe the same air as other people. Not after what he'd done to Toby and Sam and those other children—and to his own father.

Fortunately, Toby was doing better. The doctors expected a full recovery. The same was true for Sam. But the other two children…

"Probably. You were in treatment earlier, when Detective Thomas came in, but he said the bullet missed Colin's heart."

"Because he doesn't have one," Sam grumbled.

Zoe chuckled softly. "That's true."

"So…will he go to prison?"

"For the rest of his life, baby." She didn't mention the death penalty, although she believed it would be a possibility. "You don't have to be afraid of him anymore."

"What about Tiffany?"

"Tiffany's dead. She drove her car over an embankment. They found her maybe an hour ago."

"I don't know how to feel about her," Sam said.

Zoe stared up at the ceiling. "Neither do I."

"Do you think Colin will be sad?"

"Detective Thomas said he cried like a baby when he heard."

"So maybe he loved her after all."

"As much as he was capable of loving."

Sam snuggled closer. "I thought I'd never see you again."

"I couldn't have settled for that."

"Where's Anton?" she asked as if she'd only just noticed he wasn't around.

Zoe considered her answer. A lot had changed in the past ten days. She'd seen Sam's real father, spoken to him, accepted money from him and thought she might tell Sam about him someday. She no longer needed his money for a reward but she had a feeling he'd want her to keep it. She planned to talk to him about it. Besides everything that had changed with Franky, she'd also broken off her engagement to Anton, moved out… "I guess he's at home."

"He's not going to come see us? He doesn't care that we're here?"

"Unless it's already been reported on the news, he doesn't know. We—we're not together anymore."

Sam lifted her head. "You broke up?"

Zoe nodded. "After what happened to you, I realized that we weren't…what we should've been."

Sam didn't react right away. "Does that make you feel sad?" she asked tentatively.

Zoe shifted her gaze to Jonathan and saw that he was no longer sleeping. His eyes were heavy lidded, but he was watching them, listening. "No, that doesn't make me feel sad."

"Good. So it's just us again?"

"For now," she said.

She laid her head back down. "Does that mean I can have another dog?"

Zoe hugged her tighter. "Yes. And I'll never take him away from you again."

"I'm sorry about Anton. I—I know you wanted to marry him. I tried not to screw it up for you, but—"

"You didn't screw it up. It's better like this. But we should probably have someone call and tell him you're okay. Or maybe we'll do it ourselves, in the morning. Make sure he's heard."

When Sam fell silent, Zoe thought she'd drifted off to sleep. But then she spoke again, in a whisper this time. "Your P.I. friend seems nice."

Zoe met Jonathan's steady gaze—and his smile. He was sitting near the window, had Sam's back to him. "He is nice."

"I love the way he looks at you," she said.

Zoe loved the way he touched her, too. Just seeing him there made her crave physical contact, if only the brush of their hands. "How does he look at me?" she asked.

Sam's voice sounded dreamy. "Like he thinks you're beautiful…"

* * * * *

In Brenda Novak's next exciting installment of THE LAST STAND stories, new investigator Ava Bixby gets caught up in a rape case that's not as straightforward as it initially seems.

At first, Kalyna Harter, who works at the local air force base, comes to Ava with her story, claiming that Captain Luke Trussell raped her.

But Luke claims he *didn't* rape Kalyna. He says she's a liar—a perfect liar—and despite the evidence, Ava begins to believe him….

New York Times *bestselling author Brenda Novak is known for her thrilling novels of romantic suspense.*

Don't miss THE PERFECT LIAR, out next month from MIRA Books.